ZERO OPTION

for Janet

ZERO OPTION

by

Chris Ryan

Colour
Library
Direct

First published by Century in 1997

CLD 20658

This edition published in 1998 for Colour Library Direct
Godalming Business Centre
Woolsack Way
Godalming
Surrey GU7 1XW

Printed in Great Britain by
Mackays of Chatham PLC, Chatham, Kent

So, for the second time [the Pharisees],
summoned the man who had been blind and said
'Speak the truth before God.
We know this fellow is a sinner.'
'Whether or not he is a sinner, I do not know,'
the man replied.
'All I know is this:
once I was blind and now I can see.'

John IX 24–26
The New English Bible

GLOSSARY

ASU	IRA Active Service Unit
Bergen	Rucksack
BG	Bodyguard (noun or verb)
Blue-on-blue	Accidental strike on own forces
Box	General name for intelligence services
Camp	Stirling Lines, SAS headquarters in Hereford
Casevac	Casualty evacuation
CAT	Counter-attack team/Civil Administration Team: IRA disciplinary unit
Chuckies	Provisional IRA
COBR	Cabinet Office Briefing Room, Whitehall
Comms	Communications
CT	Counter-terrorist
CTR	Close target reconnaissance
Det	Intelligence gathering organisation
DF	Direction finding
Dicker	IRA scout
Director, The	Brigadier commanding Special Forces
DOP	Drop-off point
DPMs	Disruptive pattern material camouflage garments
DZ	Drop zone
EMOE	Explosive method of entry
ERV	Emergency rendezvous
FMB	Forward mounting base
FOB	Forward operating base
GPS	Global positioning system (hand-held navigation aid)
Head-shed	Headquarters
Incoming	Incoming fire
Int	Intelligence
IO	Intelligence officer
Kremlin, The	SAS headquarters

LUP	Lying-up point
LZ	Landing zone
Magellan	Brand-name of GPS
MPI	Mean point of impact
MSR	Main supply route
OP	Observation post
Phys	Physical exercise
PIRA	Provisional IRA
Player	Terrorist
PNGs	Passive night goggles
PUP	Pick-up point
QRF	Quick reaction force
R & R	Rest and recreation
RTU	Return to unit: noun or verb
RUC	Royal Ulster Constabulary
Rupert	Officer
Satcom	Telephone using satellite transmission
SAW	Subversive Action Wing
SB	Special Branch
SEAL	Sea, Air and Land – American Special Forces unit
Shreddies	Army-issue underpants
SOCO	Scene of Crimes Officer
SP	Special Projects
SSM	Squadron Sergeant Major
Stag	Shift/Watch
Tacbe	Emergency radio beacon
Tout	Informer
UCBT	Under-car booby trap
U/S	Unserviceable
VCP	Vehicle control point

WEAPONS

AK-47	Soviet or Chinese made 7.62mm automatic rifle
Barrett	.50 inch American sniper rifle
Browning	9mm pistol
Claymore	Anti-personnel mine throwing ball bearings
Dragunov	Soviet-made 7.62mm sniper rifle
Haskins	.50 inch American sniper rifle
Long	Any rifle
MP 5	9mm sub-machine gun
RPG 7	Soviet-made rocket launcher
Short	Any pistol
Sig 226	Sigsauer 9mm pistol

ONE

It took me a few moments to get myself together. I sat on the arm of the easy chair, practically paralysed, staring at the polaroid photo, unable to believe that my son and girlfriend – my whole family – had gone. My hand began to tremble so badly that the outline of Tim's little face blurred; I could hardly see Tracy at all. Then a shudder pulsed through my body. It seemed to start at my feet, then rose quickly through my knees, hips and trunk. When it reached my head I suddenly regained power of thought and movement.

I studied the picture again. It had been taken with a flash from a few feet away. Tracy was standing in front of the fireplace holding Tim on her right hip. Her face was twisted into a smile of sorts, but I could see the fear behind it. That grin was one of bravado, defiance. Close on either side of her stood two men in black balaclava ski-masks, brandishing pistols like in those crappy, mock-heroic wall-paintings you see on the walls of buildings in West Belfast. Both were wearing dark sweatshirts. They weren't actually holding her, but you could see that if she'd moved an inch either way they'd have grabbed her.

The picture had been taken horizontally, so that it cut off the grown-ups at waist-level. There must have been three intruders at least: these two, and the guy who held the camera.

Fingerprints, I thought. Don't destroy any. I realised I shouldn't have touched the photo at all. Without changing my finger-and-thumb grip I stood up, crossed to the bureau, fished out a brown envelope with my left hand and slipped the photo into it. Then I spread a handkerchief over my palm and fingers before picking up the phone and dialling the emergency number in camp.

'Hello,' said the switchboard girl. 'Stirling Lines.'

'Guardroom, please.'

'One moment.'

I waited, glancing at my watch. It was less than half an hour since I'd checked out of camp and said goodnight. Then I heard, 'Guardroom. Sergeant Howard.'

'Chris,' I said. 'It's Geordie.'

'What's up?'

'Listen, they've lifted the pair of them.'

'Who? What are you saying?'

'They've taken Tim and Tracy.'

'*Who*, for Christ's sake? Who are you talking about?'

'It's the PIRA.'

'Don't be daft. How d'you know? Where are you?'

'At home. I found a photo on the floor. Two guys in ski-masks, either side of Tracy and the kid. Nothing else. Chris, what the fuck can I do?'

'Jesus! You'd better head back into camp.'

'OK. But can you get someone out here to keep an eye on the house?'

'Of course. I'll put a guy on his way. Sit tight until he arrives. Then head right in.'

'OK. And listen: get the police to activate their plan to close every main road out of town.'

'Operation Cougar. I'll tell them right away.'

I switched on the outside security lights and stood in the hall, trying to think. How in hell had the IRA found out where I lived? How had they known that I was abroad?

Waiting was tough. I started pacing up and down like a lion in a cage, frantic to get some action going. Yet there was nothing positive I could do. Every minute that passed gave the snatch party a better chance to make their getaway. Deep down I knew it was already too late to intercept them anywhere nearby: they'd have had far too long to get clear.

I walked out into the dark and made myself take a few deep breaths, inhaling the soft, damp, earthy smells of England in late April. For a few moments I enjoyed the night, but to somebody fresh from the jungle the air felt cool and I was soon back indoors. I tried thinking back, to see where there could have been a leak.

2

What about the man I'd chatted to in the pub on the coast of County Antrim? The one who'd called at the cottage Tracy and I were staying in while I was out?

My other immediate inclination was to blame Farrell – Declan Farrell, the big PIRA player with whom I'd been feuding for months. But now . . . it could hardly have been him. I and my mates in an SAS hit team had captured him in Colombia only a couple of days before, and the last I'd seen of him he was being hauled off to the nick in Bogotá.

Unless, of course, he'd ordered this operation before he went out to Colombia . . .

Less than forty-eight hours earlier we'd blown the shit out of a cocaine processing laboratory beside a tributary of the Amazon. We'd taken one casualty – Sparky Springer, killed by shrapnel from a rocket – but after a dawn shoot-out we'd wounded Farrell and caught him. So now it was a real kick in the bollocks to find that his pernicious influence had struck on my home territory.

Fighting to keep calm I took another look round, keeping a handkerchief draped over my fingers so that I left no prints. As far as I could see nothing was missing; I owned very little of any value, but the obvious targets for a gang of thieves – the hi-fi, the TV, the microwave – were all still in place.

Then, in the dishwasher, I made a small find: two plates smeared with tomato sauce, two glasses, and knives and forks in the basket. In the waste-bin was an empty packet that had held two cod steaks. So they'd had tea, probably at about six o'clock.

I went upstairs. Tim's bed was still made up, his pyjamas neatly folded under the pillow; he'd never gone to bed or had his evening read. The idea of the boy being grabbed made me feel sick, but I forced myself to think. The snatch must have taken place between six and eight – seven or eight hours ago. The hostages could be anywhere by now.

I went to the answerphone. The blinking red light was indicating two messages. I ran back the tape and listened, but the calls were the two I'd made myself – one from the airport, one from Camp on my way home.

The scrunch of wheels on gravel whipped me to the front door. Two of the Regiment's duty Range Rovers had pulled up outside, their sidelights still on. I went to the driver's door of the first and saw that the guy at the wheel was Nobby Clarke.

'Thanks for coming,' I said.

'No sweat. I'm to run you back in. We'll leave Les Abbott here.'

'OK.' I nipped across to the second car and said, 'Hi, Les. Back off till you're level with that bush there. You'll be out of sight of anyone approaching, and you can sit in the vehicle to watch the house.'

'Fine. No one's to enter the house until the police arrive. But I'm not to walk around either. There may be footprints, and they don't want them spoilt.'

'Fair enough. Good luck, then.'

'Have you locked up?' Nobby asked.

'Just going to.'

I pulled the front door to, then at the last minute I realised I probably wouldn't be back before morning, so I dived inside again and grabbed my day-sack, which contained washing kit. Finally I closed the door and turned the key.

Nobby slung the Range Rover through the lanes, making the tyres scrabble, and we were back at the gates of Stirling Lines in eleven minutes flat. In the guardroom the four guys on fire-picket were watching a porn video with that glazed look that comes over everyone on duty in the small hours.

Chris stood up, slim and trim in his DPM shirt and trousers and blue stable belt with its silver buckle. 'Ah, Geordie,' he said. 'I buzzed up the ops officer and he's come in already. The CID are on their way. You'd better get your arse up to the ops room.'

I never looked forward to meeting the ops officer, Major Alex Macpherson (generally known as 'Mac'). He was efficient enough at his job, but he had a sarcastic manner that pissed the guys off. Having been a troop commander in the eighties, he'd returned to his regiment (the Black Watch) for a spell, and then wanted to come back to the SAS as a squadron commander; but the fact that at the age of thirty-six or thirty-seven he'd only made it to ops officer seemed to sour him. Even at the impromptu party which greeted our return he'd been low-key.

I ran up the stairs of the head-shed building, known to all and sundry as the Kremlin. The door of the ops room stood open and I found Mac, dressed in a dark blue polo shirt and jeans, rubbing the sleep out of his eyes. Serve the bugger right, I thought: normally it was he who routed us out of bed in the middle of the night, and took some pleasure in doing so. His short black hair was standing upright, as if he'd forgotten to brush it when he staggered up. His DPM uniform was thrown over a chair, and his kit – bergen and a pair of boots – stood in a corner.

'Christ, Geordie,' he said. 'That didn't take long.'

'What d'you mean?'

'You've only been back in the UK about five minutes and already you've stirred the shit something wicked.'

'For fuck's sake, Boss. It's nothing *I've* done.'

'No – well . . .' He stopped, looking at me. The edge in my voice must have made him realise what a state I was in.

'This is the picture they left.' I held out the envelope. 'I've touched it once, in the corner, but otherwise it's clean.'

He went to a shelf and brought down a new file-holder with a flap of cellophane over the front. I decanted the photo carefully into it so that the picture was protected but visible, and laid it on a desk.

'Bastards!' he muttered as he looked at it. 'Let's get a brew on, anyway.' His tone had softened. 'We're going to have to do some talking. Sugar in your tea?'

'No, thanks.'

He moved off into the little annexe where there was a kettle and stuff for making hot drinks. I glanced round at the room: desks with computer terminals on them, filing cabinets with combination locks, shelves full of books . . . this could have been an ordinary office but for the fact that on the walls drab grey curtains were drawn over boards which carried details of the Regiment's current secret operations.

I heard the kettle coming to the boil, and after a couple of minutes' fiddling about Mac handed me a mug. As I drank it I could feel my head clearing. The ops room started filling up with people. First came the Intelligence Officer, a thin, bespectacled guy called Jimmy Wells, carrying a hefty, buff-coloured file of papers; then his clerk (or gofer), who'd also been dragged out of bed, and brought a laptop computer with him. Then came Detective Sergeant Ken Bates of the local CID – prematurely grey-haired, sporting a spiky grey moustache – together with a dumpy, fair-haired detective constable called Mary.

When everyone was seated round a table the int officer led off, telling his gofer to record everything I said on the laptop. The police girl was also to take down my statement in shorthand, to save me saying everything twice.

'The trouble is, I know so little about it,' I began. 'I just got home, and they were gone.'

'Wait a minute,' said Bates. 'I need to take your full name.' He had a blunt Northern accent – Manchester, perhaps.

'Sharp,' I told him. 'Geordie Sharp.'

'Army number?'

'24369207.'

'Rank?'

'Sergeant.'

'Age?'

'Thirty-one.'

'Where's home?'

'It's called Keeper's Cottage. Out in the country, quite isolated – six miles from town.'

'What's the village?'

'It's not in any village. It's just off the Leominster road.'

'What time did you get there?'

'Just about two.'

'And where'd you been?'

Jesus! I thought. This guy knows nothing. But then, how *could* he know anything about me? I've got to explain everything from scratch.

So I took a deep breath and said, 'We've been on an operation overseas. I've been away six weeks. We landed back at RAF Brize Norton at ten – that's near Oxford – then we came on here and had a bit of a piss-up to celebrate our success. We must have got into camp about midnight.'

'But you'd tried to phone home earlier,' Mac put in. 'You mentioned that at the party.'

'That's right. I called first about half-ten, from Brize, while we

6

were waiting for our baggage. Then again about half-one when we reached camp. The answerphone was on both times. And listen . . .'

I told them about the plates with tomato sauce on them, the packet in the waste-bin, and Tim's unused bed.

'But your wife could have used the plates at lunchtime,' said Bates.

I tried not to glare at him. 'It's not my wife,' I said evenly. 'My wife was killed by a bomb in Belfast.'

'I'm sorry . . .'

'It's all right. We're talking about my girlfriend, Tracy Jordan. She came to live with me and look after my kid after Kath had been murdered.'

'What about Susan?' asked the int officer. 'Where was she?'

'Susan?'

'Susan Jones, the woman who's been sharing the house with Tracy.'

'God – I'd forgotten all about her. She's away a lot of the time, travelling for a cosmetics firm. She's probably on one of her tours.'

The detective sergeant cleared his throat. 'Can you describe Tim, please?'

'Well, you can see him in the photo.' I swivelled the file cover so that the picture faced the sergeant. 'He's four and a bit. Very fair, fine straight hair, and blue eyes.'

'How tall?'

'Jesus! I don't know. Two foot six? But he's normal for his age.'

'What about his clothes?'

'Like here: green polo shirt, grey jogging pants and trainers. That's his regular gear.'

'And can you describe Tracy?'

'She's tall and slim, with red hair.'

'How tall?'

'Five ten . . . Here, look.' I pointed at the photo. 'She's level with both the PIRA guys, at least.'

'And is her hair the colour it looks here?'

'No, it's not as dark or chestnutty really. It's quite a fiery red. I've got better pictures of her at home.'

'We'll need to see them, then. What else can you say about her?'

7

'She's got freckles on her face and arms.'

'Anywhere else?'

I looked up sharply. Was Bates trying to take the piss? He read my reaction correctly and said in a flat voice, 'It may be a body we're dealing with.'

I swallowed. 'All right, then. On her shoulders as well.'

'D'you recognise the clothes she's wearing?'

'Yes. That turquoise top is a loose cotton sweater that comes down nearly to her knees. She was probably wearing dark blue jeans and white Reebok trainers. Those big earrings are regular fixtures too. And she always has that gold chain round her neck.'

'Tracy's how old?'

'Twenty-eight.'

'When did you last have contact with her?'

'Oh Christ, I don't know.' My mind spun as I tried to unscramble events in Bogotá and the jungle. 'Several days ago. A week, maybe. But a mate of mine phoned her from Colombia the day we left. That was yesterday – no, two days ago. She was fine then.'

The questions fired on, one after another. What security systems did I have on the house? Only lights outside. Had I ever been followed back from camp? Not that I knew of. Had I or Tracy ever hung out military uniform on the washing line? No, I washed all my kit at the launderette in camp. Did I ever travel home in uniform or a military vehicle? No. Had we ever seen strangers hanging about near the house? No. Had there been any strange phone calls?

'Yes,' I said. 'There was one. When I phoned her from Colombia she told me a man had rung and asked if I was enjoying myself in the sun.'

'When was this?'

'About a week ago. I spoke to her from Bogotá.'

There was a pause as my inquisitors thought things over, and I began to feel desperately tired. Our flight home had stretched out over more than twenty-four hours, with demoralising periods of waiting in between, and we'd gone through several time zones. That would have been an ordeal on its own . . . and now I had all this.

The ops officer knew almost everything about my background, and the int officer knew some of it; but the detective sergeant, because he was starting from scratch, needed filling in on possible motives for the kidnap. Again, I had to make a big mental effort to go back to the start of the trouble.

'Kath was a Belfast girl,' I explained. 'She'd gone home to look after her mum, who'd had an operation. She was killed by an IRA bomb that went off prematurely outside a supermarket.'

Bates nodded and gave a sympathetic grunt.

'Some weeks later I got posted to Northern Ireland, and I found out from the RUC who'd been responsible for the explosion. It was one of the leading players in Belfast, a guy called Declan Farrell. Of course I wanted to top him, and I got a chance one night when he came to a weapons hide at a farm. But one of the group was the RUC's best informer, so the head-shed wouldn't let us fire.'

I stopped because I could see Mac's eyeballs rotating. The things I was saying shouldn't have been heard by anyone outside the Regiment; not even the police should know what had gone on across the water.

'Where were you stationed?' Bates asked.

'Classified information!' snapped the ops officer. 'He can't tell you that.'

I looked from one to the other before going on. 'Anyway, that was when I decided to go after Farrell on my own. I thought I could take him out single-handed. I was going to shoot him at the place where he was living. Highly irregular, of course, but it seemed the only way. It turned out that some other security organisation already had him under surveillance, and they picked me up . . .'

'So?' the sergeant prompted.

'I came back to Hereford, never finished my tour. But the Regiment were very good: they could have RTU'd me but they let me off with a caution. I tried to call it a day and forget the whole thing. But then it started again.'

I finished my tea and paused before continuing. 'In November a team of our lads went out from here to train the President of Colombia's bodyguard. I was in command. We were half-way through the course at a military camp down country, everything going well, when we travelled up to the capital one weekend for a bit of R and R. And suddenly there the bastard was: Farrell, can you believe it, in a Colombian restaurant, with a couple of other Paddies and some natives.

'Obviously the PIRA was into drug-running and arms-dealing, big time. Anyway, two of the embassy staff were stupid enough to go down to the restaurant to get a look at them. The next thing was, the pair was lifted, along with one of our ruperts who'd been doing liaison.'

'Ruperts?' Bates frowned.

'Officers. Well, that caused a big panic. We got clearance from DAS – the Colombian secret police – to bust the operation. We followed the kidnappers down into the Amazon jungle, and things ended up with a fire-fight at a coke-manufacturing plant miles from anywhere. Farrell got wounded and captured.'

'So you think this kidnap is a vendetta by Farrell?' Bates asked.

'Not directly. It can't be, because he never knew who it was that had come after him. Before that last moment, when we picked him up, he'd never seen me, hadn't a clue who I was. For all he knew I might have been Colombian. He couldn't have equated me with any problem he'd had in Ulster, and in the jungle he was just shot by some strange soldier and taken into custody. Someone else in the PIRA must have ordered the lift – somebody at this end, when news came back that Farrell had been nicked.'

'Unless he's already escaped,' the sergeant suggested.

Jimmy, the int officer, suddenly came to. 'No. No, he's still inside.' Blinking through his spectacles, he turned back to the most recent sheet of paper in his file and said, 'At least, he was yesterday evening. The British and Colombian governments are negotiating about his extradition.'

'In that case,' the sergeant persisted, 'how did the IRA know who to come after?'

'My fault,' I admitted. 'I blew it. After Christmas I took local leave in Ulster. I told my people in the Regiment I'd gone back to the mainland, but in fact I stayed put. I got Tracy across and we took a holiday cottage on the north coast. I'd been told it was a safe area, used by tourists, so one night I went to the pub in the village

10

and got talking to a local about fishing. That was all, but it was enough to give them a line on me.'

'This guy Farrell,' said the ops officer. 'What is he in the PIRA?'

Jimmy flicked through his file. 'At the time of the supermarket bomb incident he was adjutant of the Belfast Brigade. But since then we believe he's taken charge of what they call "international liaison". That means drug-running, arms-dealing – anything that raises funds and weapons from abroad.'

The detective sergeant rubbed his chin, his fingers scratching on the early-morning bristles. 'What sort of a person is he?'

'If that man fell into a pit of shit,' I said bitterly, 'he'd come out smelling like roses. He's got a charmed life. I mean, I ought to have topped him two or three times already, and look what's happened now. He may be in the nick, but that hasn't stopped him.'

Suddenly I remembered the presence of the female constable, scribbling in the background, and felt the colour rise in my cheeks as I turned to her and said, 'Sorry . . .'

Still writing, she gave a quick grin and raised her left hand, and I felt myself warming to her.

'The thing is, he's a well-educated guy,' I blundered on. 'He's got a university degree. He's big, dark, good-looking, he's a bit of a wine buff . . . I don't know what it is that makes him tick.'

A telephone rang. The ops officer swung round, picked up the receiver and listened. After a few seconds he said, 'That's fine. We'll expect you then,' and hung up. Turning back to us he said, 'That was Special Branch. Because of the nature of the incident there's a standby team coming down from London. They'll be here in three hours' time. Geordie, you're looking knackered – you'd better get your head down. Is there anything else, Sergeant?'

'Nothing immediate. We'll want to look at the house first thing in the morning. And Geordie, you'll come with us.'

'Fair enough.'

'I'll take that photo with me. Once Forensic have been over it I'll have it copied, so that we can circulate prints. Then no doubt SB'll want it. By the way . . .' He looked back at Mac. 'No press release of any kind. The last thing we want is for this to get into the papers.'

'Don't worry,' Mac assured him. 'I will personally throttle

anyone who talks.'

'All right, then.' Bates turned back to me. 'Seven o'clock at the guardroom?'

'I'll be there.'

TWO

I spent the rest of that night in the sergeants' mess, in the room I shared with a mate, Pat Newman. He, being married, lived at home, and normally neither of us slept there, using the place as a store for some of our kit. It was a small, bare room, with little more than a bed, a wardrobe and a washbasin as furnishings. The bed was piled with our gear – bergens, para bags and webbing – so I heaved the lot off into a corner. There was a sheet in the cupboard, I knew, but I couldn't be bothered to make the bed at that stage, so I just kicked off my shoes and got under the top blanket. I felt jaded and filthy. Normally I would at least have washed my face and cleaned my teeth, but such a wave of exhaustion had swamped me that all I wanted was to lie down and pass out.

The next thing I knew I was wide awake. For a few seconds I couldn't think where the hell I was: strange room, narrow bed, unfamiliar window already allowing in the grey dawn light, birds singing outside. Then back it all came with a bang.

My watch said 5.35. Jesus! Special Branch would be here any moment. I jumped up, dug out my sponge-bag and went along to the washroom, where a shave and a shower brought me back to reality. My biological time-clock might have been all to blazes, but the combination of hot water over my face and alarm at my family's predicament soon cleared my brain.

By six o'clock I was back at the guardroom, and the Special Branch Rover rolled down to the barrier a few minutes later. The guard commander had been told to take the party to the ops room, so I volunteered to show them the way. The boss figure was Commander John Fraser, a slender, lightly-built guy in his forties with a thin face, sandy hair and a slightly harassed expression: not physically impressive, but with a reassuring manner that quickly

13

inspired confidence. I noticed he had taken trouble over his appearance. He had a slight Cockney accent, but his voice, like his presence, was unobtrusive and comfortable.

With him came a sidekick in the form of a burly detective sergeant called Denis Haynes, wearing a hairy tweed jacket, and a blonde, pale-faced young woman detective constable with looks reminiscent of Barbara Streisand. At the first introduction I missed her name, but it turned out to be Karen Terraine.

In the ops room Mac gave the newcomers a short brief. Fraser's most urgent request was for a room that could act as a control centre for the duration of the incident: somewhere with secure comms in which his own staff and the CID could work alongside each other, with immediate recourse to the military if they needed it. The request presented no problem, because up there, on the first floor of the Kremlin, one room was kept ready for just such an emergency. After a quick look, the commander pronounced it ideal.

Mac realised that the visitors' next most pressing need was to get some food and drink down their necks, so he handed Fraser a print-out of the statement I'd given earlier in the night and despatched us all to the sergeants' mess for breakfast.

As the others started down the stairs I hung back with Mac and asked, 'How much can I tell him, Boss?'

'Anything he wants to know,' he replied. 'With Special Branch, no problem.'

Until that moment I hadn't felt hungry, but as I led the party through the dining room towards the kitchen counter, the smell of bacon brought my appetite alive, and I got myself a big fry-up: two eggs, bacon, sausages, potatoes, tomatoes – the lot. So did Fraser and his sergeant, but I noticed that the woman DC, who had a cracking figure, stuck to tea and a piece of toast.

For privacy we took over a separate table, and as we sat down I saw Fraser look at me in an appraising but sympathetic way. 'Just in from South America, are you?'

'That's right.'

'Not a very nice homecoming, I'm afraid.'

I suddenly felt choked, so I simply shook my head.

'Not to worry – we'll get the villains sorted. You may not know,

14

but there's a major incident plan permanently in place for just this kind of emergency. Within that framework there are three planned responses – one for airport hijack, one for siege and one for hostage-rescue. In your case, the hostage recovery plan, Operation Beehive, is already under way.'

'Sounds OK. But what does it involve?'

'In this case, surveillance on all flights to Ireland, north and south. Increased surveillance on suspected IRA players resident in this country, and increased surveillance on safe houses used by them. Numerous other checks. We'll be looking to see if certain characters are going about their business as normal, or whether they appear to have taken a sudden holiday. We'll put word out through our touts that special payments are in prospect for the right information. Of course, I can't promise anything – but what I can tell you is that our responses are frequently tested on major exercises, and we're confident they work. Now – wait while I read these notes.'

Nobody spoke while Fraser went through the print-out, eating as he read. Then he brought out a mobile phone, dialled, turned away from us, and had a short conversation, his voice too low for me to hear.

Turning back, he said, 'I just threw three or four names into the frame. What about this fellow Farrell? What was he doing in Colombia?'

I gave him an outline of what had happened: how, after Farrell and his colleagues had lifted our rupert and two diplomats from a restaurant near the British Embassy in Bogotá, our follow-up attempt to rescue them had taken us to a brand-new laboratory built deep in the jungle. Fraser listened carefully as I explained how the woman had been killed and the two men saved, but I sensed that his real interest lay in Ulster.

'When your wife was killed . . . how did you find out who was behind the bomb?'

'Through contacts in the RUC.'

'Who d'you know there?'

'A man called Morrison, mainly – a chief superintendent. He came over to lecture us when we were on the Northern Ireland course.'

'Morrison, Morrison . . . I know him. A good man, that; he'll help us. Are there any of your colleagues I can talk to?'

'About Farrell? Not really. None of our guys saw him in Northern Ireland. The people who do know all about him are the Det – the int boys in Belfast. They've got a big file on him.'

'All right. We'll get anything relevant sent over by secure fax.'

'Can *I* ask *you* something?'

'Of course.'

'What's this kidnap in aid of? I mean, what do they hope to get out of it?'

The reply was what I'd been expecting. 'Simple: they want Farrell back.'

'But what can *I* do about that? The man's in the nick in Bogotá. At least, that's where I last heard of him. The Colombians could have topped him by now. They could have moved him somewhere else. I can't get anywhere near him.'

'I know, I know.' Fraser gave a flicker of a smile, quick but friendly. 'But now that these guys have managed to grab a bargaining counter they'll exploit it to the hilt.'

'What d'you expect them to do?'

'They'll wait for a few days. Then they'll come up with a demand for a swap.'

'By phone?'

'Yep. They may call your home or the barracks here. We'll get a tap on your own line – in fact, it's being done already.'

'What if they do come on?'

'Keep them talking as long as possible. The longer they're on, the better the chances we have of tracing the call. They'll try to keep things short, to cut down that possibility, so it's up to you to prevaricate.'

'So I pretend to negotiate – say that we're getting some action over Farrell or whatever . . .?'

'We'll come to that later – but basically, yes, make it sound as though things are moving at your end.'

'They won't ring from an ordinary number, though. If they did, we could get straight on to it.'

'No. They'll use a mobile or a phone fitted with a chip that blocks any attempt to back-track calls.'

'Any idea where they'll be?'

'London, most likely. West London.'

'Why there?'

'Safety in numbers. It's such a vast conurbation, swallows people up. They've got safe houses there in places like Ealing, Acton. One problem is, the players keep shifting their ground. Here today, gone tomorrow.'

'Would they move the hostages too?'

'Less likely. There's always a risk someone will see them. Once they've got them somewhere secure, they'll probably keep them there.'

'Are these the people who've been planting the London bombs?'

'Could be.' He gave an enigmatic smile, as if he knew more than he wanted to say. 'The London Active Service Unit's pretty strong. By the way, where's that photograph?'

'The CID guy has it. Why?'

'I'll take possession of it presently. There are various techniques we can use on it – computer enhancement, for instance. I gather the two men are holding weapons?'

'That's right.'

'Well, if we blow the picture up and enhance areas of it with the computer, we may be able to make out numbers or other distinguishing marks on the pistols. It may turn out that one of the weapons has been used in a known crime elsewhere. Equally, there may be a small area of tattoo or a scar showing on a wrist or neck – something that may give us a clue to the identity of the men. You'd be surprised how much information an infinitesimally small piece of evidence can produce. Now . . .' He glanced at his watch. 'I think the CID will be needing you at the scene of the crime.'

The CID Vectra was parked outside the guardroom. Fraser introduced himself and his team, and after a quick discussion it was agreed that while the bosses carried out the site inspection their number twos would stay in camp and get their incident room set up. For a few minutes the whole crowd disappeared into the Kremlin to discuss the layout, then we were off in the Special Branch Rover, with the Streisand lookalike driving and myself calling the turns.

The sun was just up, setting the brick-red soil on fire and illuminating the hedges, now fully out, their new leaves glowing the freshest green. Except for the black cloud looming over my head, it was a perfect Herefordshire spring day.

'This is it,' I announced as the car turned into our lane, and there stood the little brick cottage, snug among its trees, with the peaceful woods and fields rising gently into the distance all round.

'Stop here, please, Karen,' said Fraser. 'We'll walk the last bit. What a place!'

He and Bates spent a minute changing out of their city shoes and into rubber boots. As I waited, I was hit by a blast of remorse. I should never have brought Tracy here, I thought bitterly. I'd imagined that the cottage would be the perfect home for my family, and yet it seemed to have a deadly effect on any woman connected with it: Kath killed, and now Tracy kidnapped. Even on that fine morning the house had lost a good deal of its charm.

It's not the place that's doing it, I told myself. It's you and your problems.

The two coppers set out slowly, side by side, down the last hundred yards of track, scanning every inch. I followed close behind them.

'What vehicles have been down here since last night?' Bates asked.

'The Cavalier that dropped me,' I said, 'and the two Range Rovers that came out when I phoned. Otherwise, there shouldn't have been any.'

'I see.'

The policemen's manner had altered. Both had suddenly become sharper, more concentrated.

'What's this?' Bates stooped and picked up a piece of paper from the grass at the edge of the track. The scrap was blank, but he put it carefully into the folder he was carrying. In one muddy patch he bent down to examine some tyre tracks, but several had been superimposed on each other so that no clear pattern was discernible.

As we reached the gravel sweep in front of the cottage, a figure in DPMs popped out from behind the bushes to our right and advanced aggressively to challenge us. Although Les wasn't actually holding a weapon, his right hand was in the pocket of his smock. His face was pale from lack of sleep, his expression tense, but as soon as he saw me he relaxed.

I walked towards him. 'Hi, Les. Everything OK?'

'Fine. Your only caller's been a bloody great fox – came past the back of the house about an hour ago and left his calling card by that gatepost.'

'I know him,' I said. 'He's always around. Listen, these guys are CID and Special Branch.'

Fraser stuck out a hand and introduced himself briefly. Then he said to me, 'Right. I want you to tell me exactly what you did when you came home.'

'Got out of the car about here.' I pointed to a spot on the gravel in front of us. 'The whole house was dark. Then I went to the front door and in.'

'It wasn't locked?'

'No. I assumed Tracy had left it open for me.'

'Wouldn't she have had it locked earlier?'

'Probably not. We don't bother much out here until we go to bed.'

'So you didn't walk round outside at all?'

'Not a step.'

'Let's have a look, then. Hang on here, please.'

The two set off clockwise round the house: Fraser slim, sandy, lithe, like the fox reported by Les; Bates greyer, heavier, a badger. Foxy Fraser and Badger Bates, hunting in partnership. Until that moment I hadn't been particularly impressed with either of them, but now that I saw how much time they took, how carefully they moved, what attention they paid to every little detail, it was another matter.

They kept a yard or two from the building and advanced a few feet at a time, constantly glancing from ground to house and back. While they disappeared round the back I looked about me and saw that Tracy had cut the grass during the last day or two: the tracks of the mower were still showing clearly. She'd also weeded the flowerbeds against the front wall, the earth now freshly turned over.

'No sign of any attempted break-in,' Bates announced as the two came back into view.

19

No need for one, I thought. They just walked in.

Fraser looked back up the lane and waved at Karen to drive down. 'We got this,' he said, holding up a spent match. 'Any of your lot smoke?'

I shook my head.

'One footprint, too.' Then he turned to Bates. 'You'll need to take a cast of that. Looks like a trainer.' To me he added, 'It was on a bare patch in the grass, which makes me think they were here in the dark. Nobody would have put a foot down there in daylight.'

I led them inside, trying to remember my every movement. In the hall I said, 'I put my kit down here,' and indicated a spot on the carpet.

Bates took up the questioning. 'What was it?'

'A bergen and a holdall.'

'Made of?'

'Something synthetic − nylon, I suppose. That's the stuff there.' I pointed at the drab olive bundle on a chair at the side of the room.

'OK. And what did you do then?'

'I switched on a light − there − and went upstairs. I tried our bedroom first, then Tim's.'

'You had to open the doors?'

'No − ours was open.'

'Then what?'

'I ran back down and into the kitchen, put the lights on in there. Nothing. So I went into the living room, switched on the light, and then I saw the photo on the floor in front of the stove.'

'Yes?'

'I picked it up, finger and thumb, and sat down on that chair.'

'*In* that chair?'

'No, on the arm nearest to us.'

'What were you wearing?'

'Same as now − these jeans and sweater. But a different T-shirt . . .' I broke off, hearing a vehicle draw up outside the open door.

Bates stuck his head out and said, 'Good. The forensic lads. A squad from Birmingham.'

As men began unloading gear from their van, Fraser said he'd seen enough and was heading back to the incident room. That left me and Bates with the forensic boys.

There were four of them, and they kitted themselves up in white overalls, white hoods, white gloves and white overshoes. I knew that the job was going to take some time. All the same, it was a shock to hear their boss announce that it would last all day at least.

To give us somewhere to base ourselves, they cleared the kitchen first. The care they took was amazing. Having carried in lamps and stands, they lit up each room in a blaze dazzling enough for a film production; then they crept and crawled and peered and prodded, dusting for fingerprints and examining every square inch of every surface through magnifying glasses.

As they worked, I looked for a recent photograph of Tracy. The best likeness was a framed photo of her and Tim which stood on the kitchen window-sill. It had been taken just before I'd gone to Colombia, and she must have had it mounted while I was away. It showed her standing behind Tim at the top of one of the big slides at Alton Towers, about to give him a push off. She'd been laughing and joking as I took it, and her coppery hair was cascading down the back of her neck, shown off by a white windcheater. It was a good shot of Tim, too; you could see his fair hair, broad forehead and blue eyes, all picked up from his mother.

'There's your photo,' I said to Bates. 'That's them to a T.'

'Mind if I borrow it?'

'Help yourself – but I'd like to have it back.'

'Of course. I'll get it copied right away.'

'I can dig out some more negatives of the kid as well.'

'That would be grand.'

After little more than an hour the forensic team declared the kitchen clean – it had yielded no evidence, and the indications were that the intruders had never gone in there – and the search moved to the hall and sitting room, allowing us at least to get a brew on in the kitchen.

The CID boss spent much of the time with the specialists, and every now and then I was needed to answer a question; but for the most part there was nothing I could do except sit around and feel anxiety eating into me. Where had Tracy and Tim been taken? Were they being fed properly? Had they got enough clothes? My mind was filled by a horrible image of them stuck in a blacked-out cellar with only a bucket for a toilet, food being thrown down to

21

them, and rats running about the floor. Anger boiled up inside. I'd just love to get my hands on the bastards who'd taken them.

I'd never had any direct evidence that telepathy can work, but at that moment I exerted my will-power in an all-out attempt to send reassuring messages. Hang in there, I was telling them. Don't despair. We're on our way.

It was six o'clock when the team called it a day. Their leader promised a full report in the morning, but for the moment he let on that they had found signs of a struggle on the landing. Fibres from Tracy's pullover suggested that someone had grabbed her there and sat on her to hold her down before hustling her down the stairs. Again I felt anger taking me over; the idea of other men getting their hands on her, bruising her fair skin, made me see red. I imagined Tim trying to scuttle away from the masked intruders but not getting far on his short legs, maybe yelling out as they seized him.

Different fibres they'd found told a more important story. One of the raiders had sat down and leant back in the chair that I'd perched on, resting his elbows on the arms. As soon as this fact reached Bates he lit up, and said that he knew of one well-known IRA player, Danny Aherne, who had a habit of sitting back in chairs to gloat over victims. Immediately the name went back over a secure phone to London.

With the search completed there was no reason why I shouldn't move back into the cottage. But did I want to? For a while I hesitated. It would make sense, obviously – if I was there I'd be able to take any message that came from the PIRA – but the idea of being there alone, with Tim and Tracy gone, seemed too depressing. On the other hand, the thought of spending another night in the mess pissed me off even more. I had to drive back into camp in any case, because I'd left my bergen there, so I decided to have supper in the mess, then head back out.

In the dining-room my luck took a turn for the better. There, eating on his own, sat Tony Lopez, the American SEAL who'd joined D Squadron for a two-year tour. There was nobody I'd rather have fallen in with. Tony and I had been close ever since we'd been captured by the Iraqis during the Gulf War and spent six weeks together as guests of Saddam Hussein. We hadn't been treated as badly as some other allied prisoners, but our spell in gaol had been tough enough, and it had forged a lasting friendship. On the operation in Colombia Tony had acted as our liaison officer and anchor-man. Being Puerto Rican by birth, and having Spanish as his first language, he'd proved an invaluable link with the natives.

'Hi there, Geordie!' He raised a knife in greeting. 'Any news?'

I shook my head. 'Nothing yet. All right if I come and join you?'

'Go right ahead.'

Thinking of Tony and his penchant for Mexican food, I chose chilli con carne, with a green salad on a separate plate.

'They've searched the house from top to bottom,' I told him as I sat down. 'A couple of small clues, but no fingerprints. They reckon the sods all wore gloves.'

'How many of them?'

'They think there were four. One to grab Tim, one for Tracy, one to take the picture, one to stand guard outside. Very brave of them – the twats.'

'Anything on their vehicle?'

'Nothing. Too many other tyre marks. One print of a trainer in a mud patch behind the house. Otherwise, blank.'

'Geordie, I'm sorry. I wish to hell there was something I could do.'

'Thanks. Listen, why not come back and have a beer? What I need most is company.'

'OK. I'd like that.'

As soon as I'd eaten I checked in at the incident room to see if anything was moving, and found a depressing lack of progress. The place was full of computer terminals, fax machines and newly-installed telephones, but activity had died down for a day and, like me, everybody was waiting – waiting for the word from the other side, waiting for a tip-off from an SB tout.

Tony picked up his car, an ancient red BMW that he had found going cheap in Ross-on-Wye, and followed me out to the cottage. Driving down the lane, seeing the cottage's windows dark, I was hit by a wave of despair. All through our time in the jungle and during the marathon journey back, my expectations had built up:

home, bed with Tracy, decent food, family life, picking up my relationship with Tim . . . now all this had turned to ashes.

Once inside the house, we gravitated to the kitchen. For one thing, the Aga was ticking over and making the room warm; but somehow I didn't fancy being in the sitting room where the photo had been taken.

I got a couple of cans of lager out of the fridge and we sat, one either side of the pine table. 'Cheers!' I said. 'And God rot the PIRA.'

'Amen to that.' Tony's dark chestnut eyes were watching me steadily. 'Geordie,' he said, 'you look pretty much washed up.'

'I am. I didn't get my head down till after three. Then I was up at five-thirty. I'll try and get a proper kip tonight.'

When the telephone rang, I jumped a mile. 'Jesus!' I exclaimed. 'This could be them.' I snatched the receiver up and snapped, 'Yes?'

Silence. I was on the point of saying something more when I realised what was happening. I listened a moment longer. Nothing. Then the line clicked and went dead.

'It *was* them,' I said. 'They just wanted to know if I was here. Nuisance calls – that's going to be their game.'

I dialled the incident room in camp. 'I had a call,' I reported. 'I'm sure it was them.'

'If it happens again, take the phone off the hook,' advised the SB officer on duty. 'In the morning we'll get the lines re-routed so that any calls they make come in here.'

'OK, then.'

I sat down again and swallowed a mouthful of beer.

'Couldn't they trace it back?' Tony asked.

'Too brief. The line's tapped anyway, but what we need to do is keep them talking, to give the Special Branch a chance of DF-ing them. The trouble is, the fuckers are probably using a mobile and cruising around in a car.'

We sat in silence for a while. Then Tony said, 'Know what? This reminds me of the first time I came here. Remember? That was a low spot, too.'

Tony knew better than anyone how, in the aftermath of the Gulf War, Kath and I had become estranged, how I'd hit the booze, and how, when she had gone back to her parents in Belfast for a trial separation, I was really bumping along on the bottom. For a few weeks he'd moved into the cottage, partly because it suited him, but also because he knew he could help me just by being around. Apart from anything else he was an excellent cook, and with him in residence I'd started eating sensibly again. One way or another, I owed Tony a good deal.

Now he said, 'You just gotta take it easy. I know it sounds stupid if I say "C'mon, relax", but there's nothing else for it. Sooner or later they'll come back on the air with a demand. Or the SB guys will get a lead.'

'Yeah, but what if they're maltreating Tim? He must be shit-scared, Tony. Poor little bugger – he's not even four and a half.'

'I know.'

'And what if somebody's molesting Tracy? Christ, I'd rip his bloody bollocks off with my bare hands.'

'It's tough,' Tony agreed. 'But you can't do anything about it.'

'Why the fuck didn't I drop Farrell while I had the chance? There's something about that guy, Tony. It's as if there's a superior force protecting him. I'm getting to think he's invincible.'

'Aw, you're imagining things.'

But Tony had never seen Farrell. He'd flown out to Colombia with our training team, but when everything had gone tits-up he'd had to stay behind in Bogotá as our anchor-man, liaising with the British Embassy and the Americans. The result was that, to his great chagrin, he'd missed the fire-fight in the jungle. I'd already described the final showdown to him half a dozen times – how we'd blown up a pile of ether drums in the laboratory with a mega bang and fought our way back to the air-strip; how I'd slashed the tyres of the narcos' Twin Otter so that it couldn't take off; and how, as Farrell had tried to slip away into the forest, I'd wounded him with an MP 5 before running out of ammunition. I'd told Tony about that moment, when I had Farrell on the deck in front of me, when a mate had run up and handed me another sub-machine gun with a full mag on it, shouting, 'Go on, finish him off!' But somehow the hatred had drained out of me, and I'd let my victim get captured . . .

'All we needed to do was throw him in the river,' I said now. 'The crocodiles would have had him in a flash. The water was

25

heaving with them. I didn't even have to kill him; the crocs would have done the job for me. He'd just have disappeared off the face of the earth.'

'Too bad,' Tony agreed. 'But don't let the guy bug you. You'll get even with him in the end.'

Neither of us wanted to make a night of it, so Tony went back to camp soon after ten-thirty, and I locked up all round.

Foxy Fraser and his SB team didn't seem to think that I was under any threat myself; on the contrary, he'd said I was the fulcrum over which the PIRA would try to exert pressure with their lever. In other words, they positively needed me where I was, so I could initiate moves to have Farrell released. All the same, I didn't feel like taking any chances. That was why I'd badgered the storeman in the armoury in camp into letting me take a Sig 226 pistol home overnight.

So, after a soak in a hot bath, I took a few precautions before I went to bed. Ever since my bad experiences in Iraq I'd had a thing about the bedroom door, finding it impossible to sleep unless I locked it. I turned the key and stood a chair against the inside with two saucepans balanced on it, so that even if somebody did get through he couldn't come in without making a hell of a clatter. I put the phone on the floor beside the bed, laid the pistol on the bedside cabinet, and finally turned in.

I must have laid awake for some time, because afterwards I remembered how our resident owl had tuned up in the oak tree outside the window, but in spite of all my anxieties I eventually dropped off. Some time later I became aware of a scratching noise. I rolled over on my back and listened. There it was again: a scrape, followed by a click. I knew the sounds exactly because I'd made them myself, dozens of times – sounds of someone picking a lock.

The noise was coming up from the front of the house and in through the open window. Without being able to see anything, I somehow knew that the men at the door were wearing black balaclavas.

Jesus Christ! The PIRA were back. And this time they'd come for me! Moving my hand carefully I reached down, brought phone and receiver under the bedclothes, and dialled the incident room.

All I got was Mac's recorded voice saying, 'Sorry, old boy, we can't deal with your call at the moment, we're rather busy. Call back in half an hour.'

'Twats!' I muttered. 'Fucking useless!' Then I thought: the Sig. Of course, the Sig. What was best? Fire out the window at the intruders, maybe drop one and scare the rest off? Or let them come in and hope to drop the lot?

But it was too late to wonder; they were inside already. I heard a sound on the stairs, a low voice. The door handle of the room turned, and at the same moment there was a different noise outside, the faint clank of my aluminium ladder being stealthily placed in position. Then I became aware of movement at the window and saw a black figure loom up, blotting out the starlight. I was trapped.

I lay dead still on my back, holding my breath. The window was to my left, the door straight ahead. The door began to open. Faint light showed through the crack – a torch. The chair I'd propped against the door fell over and dropped its load with a crash. At that instant I sensed movement in the opposite corner of the room, over my right shoulder. Someone else had got in already, and was coming from that direction. There were men all round me.

I reached for the Sig, felt, groped, snatched in the dark – but the pistol wasn't there. It had gone from the top of the cabinet. Panic. I went to roll out of bed, only to find I couldn't move. A tremendous weight was holding my legs down. I glanced to my left: the black figure was half-way in through the window. I looked straight ahead and saw the man with the torch coming at me from the doorway. Looming bigger and bigger, he was almost on top of me. In spite of the dark I could make out the shape of a pistol in his hand. Within seconds I could see the faint sheen on the muzzle, the ring of death. I was looking straight down the barrel at point-blank range.

BANG! Instantly I was wide awake, shaking and soaked with sweat. The sheets were knotted up around me. Struggling free of them, I felt for the bedside lamp and switched it on. The Sig was still on the cabinet, the phone on the floor where I'd left it. The chair and saucepans stood unmoved against the door. The corner to my right was empty.

I lay back on the pillow, gasping. My watch said 2.45. For a few seconds I glared round the room in disbelief, blinking; then I turned the lamp off again, got up and went to look out of the window, standing well back. By now the moon had risen and the garden was brightly illuminated. I watched for a minute or two and saw that all was peaceful.

I started shuddering. After the Gulf I'd been plagued by terrifying dreams very much like this one. It was those bad nights that started the trouble between me and Kath. My answer to this terror had been alcohol; I'd gone on the booze, and that had made everything far worse. Was all that crap about to start again? And would a Scotch or two be a good idea now?

'No, for Christ's sake,' I told myself. 'The one thing you do *not* need is a drink.' So I went back to bed, sickened by the knowledge that a long, lonely war of nerves lay ahead. I'd just come through one nightmare, but another was beginning, and this one was going to be far worse.

THREE

Even though I was dog-tired I couldn't sleep. I'd got over my fear of an immediate attack, but there was no way I could stop thinking about Tim and Tracy. After a while I went to lie on Tim's bed, imagining the look of his head on the pillow when we came in to check him last thing at night, the way his flaxen hair lay softly on the back of his neck. Even at four and a bit he was still wedded to Billy, his teddy bear, and usually dropped off sucking one of the damn thing's ears. Now Billy sat forlornly on the window-sill, and I knew that Tim, wherever he was, would be all the more miserable because he hadn't got the little bugger with him. What heartless bastards the PIRA were, to lift a kid as young as that.

In time I began to feel cold, and forced myself to accept that lying in his room wouldn't bring him back. So I returned to my own bed and tried to shut my mind down. I heard the clock in the hall strike three, then four – but that was all. I must eventually have nodded off, and the next time I came to it was seven o'clock.

Since I was officially on leave I had no need to hurry into camp. So instead I called the incident room to make sure there had been no developments, then made myself breakfast and spent an hour going through Tracy's things. As usual, her desk was in perfect order: there were a couple of unpaid bills, but otherwise she had everything beautifully squared away. A school exercise book contained a record of her expenses, in her neat writing, and she'd collected the drawings Tim had done at school into a folder. Most of them seemed to have violent subjects – tanks exploding, planes being shot down – and it wouldn't have taken a psychologist long to work out where all that came from. But the tidy way in which Tracy operated nearly choked me, because it made me realise how much she'd done for me.

At the time of Kath's death she'd been working as receptionist in the Camp Medical Centre. A week or two before I got posted to Northern Ireland she and her friend Susan had been thrown out of their lodgings in Hereford, so I had suggested they should occupy Keeper's Cottage while I was abroad. Events then speeded up in a direction I hadn't anticipated: Tracy and I fell for each other, and she had moved into the cottage for good, taking over Tim as though he were her own son. In a few months she had grown up with incredible speed and developed from a lively, knockabout girl into a responsible foster mother. She'd kept on her job for a while, but then, when I went to Colombia, she'd given it up.

Driving away from the cottage wrenched me back to the present. In camp again, I was heading for the Kremlin when I spotted Jimmy Wells, the int officer, coming towards me on a converging path. A scrawny fellow with a narrow face and lank, dark hair brushed sideways over the top of his head, he usually went about with a hunted look, as though he were permanently worried; but his harassed appearance belied him, because he was at heart a cheerful character, always inclined to make the best of things.

'Hi, Geordie,' he called. 'No news yet?'

'Nothing so far.'

'Got time for a natter?'

'Well . . . sure.'

At the top of the stairs I followed him into his office and sat down in front of his desk. As I quickly found out, he was bang up to speed on the kidnap situation, and I realised that he'd invited me in purely to give some friendly support. He was like that; not being a badged officer – not a member of the SAS, but on attachment to us from Intelligence Corps – he had no hang-ups about regimental priorities or feuds and could afford to be himself with everyone, high or low.

'By the way,' he said in a conspiratorial voice after a pause in the conversation, as though letting fall some tit-bit of local scandal, 'Farrell's on his way back to the UK.'

'What?' I was taken aback. 'Already?'

'Well, more or less – I'm jumping the gun a bit. But the Colombian authorities have agreed to extradite him.' He picked up a sheet of fax paper and scanned it briefly. 'It seems they don't want anything to do with him. Don't blame 'em. He'll be flown out by military transport later today. Apparently he's suffering from gunshot wounds in the right arm and flank. Flesh only – nothing serious. Who shot him? I wonder . . .'

'No idea.'

I saw Jim smiling. He knew what had happened, of course, because he'd covered the Colombian operation from this end.

'If only I'd aimed a bit bloody straighter,' I said. 'But it was still only half light, and the bastard was running like the clappers.'

I stopped, suddenly remembering something I'd read about a British weightlifter at the opening of the Berlin Olympics in 1936. 'I read once about this bloke who found himself standing right next to Hitler in some parade,' I told Jim. 'He realised he could have topped the bugger there and then. And afterwards he said, "What a hell of a lot of time and trouble I would have saved." I feel like that about Farrell. I could have saved the country millions. What'll they do with him here?'

'Put him in the nick on remand while they sort out a case against him, I imagine.'

'There's any amount of things they can get him for: drugs, kidnapping the rupert, murder . . .'

We'd been chatting for several more minutes when my eye strayed to a photograph in the in-tray: a blown-up black-and-white mug-shot of a man with a moustache wearing a dark beret. Although the picture was upside-down I felt the hair on my neck crawling, because I was certain I recognised the subject.

It wasn't long before Jim noticed my attention was distracted. 'What's the matter?' he asked, following the direction of my eyes. Then he shot out a hand to cover the photo and said, 'Ah. That's strictly need-to-know . . .'

'I know it's none of my business,' I said, 'but could I have a proper shufti?'

'You're not supposed to. Why?'

'I think I know the guy.'

'You can't possibly . . .'

'Let's have a look anyway.'

'Well . . . I'm not showing it you. You haven't seen it.' Watching

31

me curiously, Jim picked up the photo and flicked it across the desk. The moment I saw it straight, all doubt vanished.

'It's him.'

'Who?'

'Shitface. I don't know his name. But this is the bastard that gave us a hard time in Baghdad. An Iraqi, isn't he?'

'That's right.' Now Jim was looking at me in a yet more peculiar way, as if he was seeing a ghost. 'Geordie, are you certain?'

'Absolutely. He came to the gaol three or four times to interrogate us. There was always a big palaver when he arrived – the guards shouting and saluting as though he was some high-ranking officer. It was this fucker who used to hit the plaster cast on my broken arm with his swagger-stick. That was bloody agonising. But it wasn't the pain that got to me, so much as his attitude. He started saying that if I didn't give him the information he wanted, he'd open up the plaster, infect my wounds with bugs, and plaster it over again, so that I'd get gangrene and lose my arm. Sadistic bugger! I'll not forget him in a hurry. Luckily for me, the war ended before he could carry out his threat.'

'He sounds a sweetie,' said Jim.

'He is.' I shuddered as I remembered the screams that came from other parts of the gaol. 'He likes to see prisoners jump. To be more specific, he likes to see them convulsed. He's a specialist at administering electric shocks, and favours giving them through wet sponges, so that the prisoner gets a high charge but isn't left with tell-tale burns. We called him Shitface because he was always frowning, like here. What's his real name?'

'I can't tell you that.'

'So what's his picture doing on your desk?'

'Classified, I'm afraid. But look: this identification's very important. Can you be absolutely sure you know the man?'

'One hundred per cent.' I saw doubt in the int officer's face. 'You don't believe me?'

'Well, a lot may depend on it.'

'I tell you what. There's another guy here in camp who was in that gaol with me: Tony Lopez, the American. He'll remember the sod as well as I do.'

Suddenly Jim was all lit up. 'Where is he now?'

32

'He's on leave, after Colombia. But he'll be around the Lines somewhere. I saw him last evening. If you like I'll go find him . . .'

'No. I'll ring round and see where he is.'

A flurry of telephone calls ran Tony to earth in the gym, and he said he'd come right up. As we waited, I saw that Jim was in a state of excitement. I realised why he hadn't let me go looking for the Yank myself: he wanted to confront him with the photograph before I'd had time to give any briefing.

In came Tony, looking big and brawny in his ash-grey tracksuit, sweat still trickling down his temples. 'Apologies for showing up like this,' he began. 'I was half-way through my weights, but this sounded urgent.'

'No sweat,' said the int officer – and then, grinning at the unfortunate pun, 'I'd just like you to answer a simple question.' He flipped over the mug-shot, which he had turned face-down. 'D'you recognise this man?'

'Goddamn it!' Tony cried. 'It's Shitface, the sonofabitch who gave us third degree in Iraq.'

'There you are!' I said. 'What did I tell you?'

'Yeah!' Tony went on, his voice loud with indignation, jabbing a forefinger at the portrait. 'We used to think he looked like Saddam Hussein, with the moustache and the beret. But then, all Iraqi officers do. This one always seemed to be scowling. A big guy, shambling, a bit like a bear. Boy, what wouldn't I do to get my hands on that bastard!'

Jim nodded. 'OK,' he conceded. 'That does it. Now you'd better forget I asked you.'

'Wait a minute,' said Tony. 'What's he got to do with us now?'

'Nothing.' Jim stared straight at me. 'As I say, forget it. And don't mention it outside this office. You never saw the picture, and I never asked you anything.'

Of course we couldn't forget it. Tony and I obeyed orders and didn't mention the matter to anyone else, but we talked to each other about it at lunch that day, then again in the evening. Obviously the Iraqi was up to something that involved the SAS, but we couldn't figure out what it might be. We guessed Saddam Hussein might be using him to suppress the Kurds in the north of

33

the country; but at that time the Regiment had no presence in Iraq – at least, none that we knew of – and a couple of veiled enquiries drew blank. On the other hand, secret operations were our bread and butter, and when guys got involved in something really hot they were generally tight as gnats' arseholes about it. So it seemed quite possible that some operation was brewing and nobody was talking.

Nor did the day produce any information about Tim and Tracy. Telephone engineers had re-routed the lines so that anyone calling my old number in the cottage went straight through to the incident room, where the phones were manned twenty-four hours a day, and the line was bugged, so any conversation on it would be automatically recorded. Foxy Fraser of Special Branch, who was there in person for much of the time, decreed that the phone must be answered by men only, with instructions to be as non-committal as possible. That way, if the PIRA did come through, they might think it was me on the other end.

For several hours I sat in on the control room, listening to the check calls that came through from Special Branch in London, Birmingham, Holyhead and other places, fervently hoping that one of them would bring news of a positive lead. At first I was on edge, jumping around whenever a phone rang; but after a while boredom began to kill hope and I settled into a resigned torpor, crushed by the realisation that we were probably in for a grinding marathon of a wait.

Hanging around, flicking through old magazines, I couldn't help being aware of the Streisand lookalike, Karen Terraine, with her swept-back blonde hair and big nose. There she sat, all neat and tidy in a pale blue blouse and grey skirt, taking the odd call, making notes, checking things, going through to the SB central computer for specialised information, and bringing up one list of names after another on her screen. Most of the time she looked totally demure, but twice I caught her giving me the eyeball, and I began to get irritated by her presence.

Fraser saw I was less than chuffed, but he naturally attributed my unease to the general situation and tried to cheer me up by saying, 'Don't worry, Geordie, the touts are out there. The touts are about. They're all hungry, and they're all listening. Our eyes and ears are

34

open.' A search was on in Ulster as well, in case the party had somehow managed to cross the water undetected; but the presumption still was that the hostages had been taken to London.

In the afternoon I went out for an eight-mile run through the lanes, but although I kept pushing myself I couldn't settle into any rhythm. I just had too much on my mind. My anxiety about Tim and Tracy prevented me from concentrating on the exercise. The result was I wasn't looking at the ground properly and I kept stumbling and jarring myself, so that running, instead of being a pleasure, became hard, uncomfortable work.

It was the same when I went to the gym and got on the weights. Nothing would go right. From my own experience – and from watching other guys who were into big lifts – I knew how essential full concentration is; without it, you're at only half strength, and liable to do yourself damage. Now I just couldn't get my timing. After half an hour I thought, Ah, fuck it! and gave up.

As I came into camp next morning – the second day after the kidnap – I went up to the Squadron Interest Room and found a note in my pigeon-hole. I was on the point of reading it when the clerk forestalled me by saying, 'Hey, Geordie. You're to report to the ops officer, soonest.' I went upstairs wondering what this could be about.

Mac Macpherson was in his usual gracious mood. 'Lucky sod, Geordie,' he said. 'Looks like you're in for more action already.'

'What d'you mean, Boss?'

'You're to report to the OC, SAW – immediately.'

'What's on, then?'

'Don't ask me. Ask him.'

'Christ! This isn't a great moment for me to go away anywhere.'

'See what he says before you start worrying.'

Before I'd even reached the bottom of the stairs I had made the connection: this had to do with the int officer's photo.

The Subversive Action Wing was the most secret part of our organisation, the unit that took on the most sensitive jobs, often working in cahoots with MI5 or MI6. Just as the two Government agencies were known as the 'Firm', so the SAW was known simply as the 'Wing', and its operations were the most highly classified of any the SAS undertook. People trying to be clever described it as the cutting edge of the organisation – and in fact that wasn't a bad description. Because of its connections outside the Regiment, it was almost a national force.

To gain entry to the SAW's area, one had to punch a series of numbers into the pad beside the door. Not knowing the combination, I had to bang on the steel door and wait for someone to let me in.

I found the OC sitting at his desk. In his day Major Yorky Rose had been a fearsome boxer and front-row forward. On his way up through the ranks he'd never bothered to shed his Yorkshire accent or drop his native expressions like 'ee bah gum' and 'you'll not get owt for nowt', and similarly he'd never given a bugger what people thought about his ferocious training regimes. Whenever strange noises were heard emanating from his office, it was said that Yorky was practising walking on all fours: toes and knuckles.

Now in his late thirties, he'd lost most of his dark hair, and kept what was left shaved so short that at first glance you might miss the fuzz on his scalp and think he was totally bald. He had a high, domed forehead that made his head egg-shaped, and his thick, arching eyebrows seemed to accentuate the length of his face. Guys in the Regiment tend to age prematurely, due to the amount of effort they put into life; by the time they're thirty-five, they look like they're pushing fifty. Yorky was no exception: he already had deep lines across his forehead and down his cheeks.

'Well, Geordie,' he began, 'I'm sorry to hear about your kid and Tracy. Any news of them?'

'Not a whisper, Yorky.'

'That's tough. I hope you get sorted soon. Meanwhile, I need your help. Take a seat there a minute.'

I perched on the chair at one side of his desk, pretty certain what his next step would be – and sure enough, he opened a folder, brought out a photograph, and turned it round for me to look at.

'You know this gent, I gather.'

I nodded. 'You're telling me.'

'How would you like to top him?'

'*Top* him?' For a second I was taken aback. But a moment later I said, 'Try and stop me.'

36

Yorky smiled briefly. 'As I thought.'

'Where is the bastard?'

'Last seen in Piccadilly Circus . . . No, you'll know soon enough. You've been selected to lead an operation to take him out. We want you to command one of the SAW patrols.'

'Jesus!'

'The timing of it, you mean?'

'Exactly. This isn't a good moment for me to piss off abroad.'

'I know that.' Yorky pushed back his chair and went walkabout, throwing a pencil in the air and catching it as he spoke. 'All the same, it could work out all right. I've talked it through with the CO and the ops officer. Also I had a word with the SB guy, Fraser, about the way he thinks things may go here. I've come to the conclusion that it's on for you.'

Missing a catch, he had to crawl under the desk to retrieve the pencil from the floor. 'The point is,' he continued as he stood again, 'this is going to be a quick job: in and out. You'll not be abroad for more than six days. Two weeks' training here, then less than a week away. To get the hostages back may take a couple of months.'

He saw me grimace, and went on, 'If anything breaks on the hostage front during the training phase you'll be here to deal with it. Your personal problem may well be cracked before the operation goes down. But even if it ain't, we can hold the fort for you while you're out of the country. Besides, you'll have Satcoms as usual, so that you won't ever be out of touch.'

I sat holding my forehead in my hands. My head felt as if it were bursting. Already, with this new deployment barely announced, the stress was piling on. This was going to be a high-risk operation, fraught with danger – could I stand the strain of another episode likely to be as traumatic as the one in the Gulf? Could I handle it on top of my acute personal troubles?

My instinct was to stay home at all costs, to be there when the PIRA called. I couldn't take the thought of somebody else making a cock-up that might lead to the hostages' death. But I knew perfectly well I had no option but to go; if I refused I'd be kicked out – not only from the Regiment, but out of the Army.

At moments of this kind it's easy to let resentment build up. The

37

Regiment is notorious for pushing its members to the limit, putting them under intense pressure without regard to their mental state. The head-shed simply assumes that all the guys are fit, physically and mentally, all the time, and ready to go.

Now, for a few seconds, I thought, Ah, sod them. Why can't they make a few allowances? Why can't they send someone else to do their dirty work? I looked up at Yorky and said, 'Does it have to be me?'

He stopped pacing and stood beside my chair. 'You know what the Regiment's like, Geordie. They'll talk sympathetically about your family, blah, blah, blah. But in fact they couldn't give a flying monkey's, especially when a job like this comes down from Whitehall. If the Government's ordered it, it's got to happen. It doesn't matter what you do – you can go in and spout Army regulations at the adjutant if you like – but I can tell you, it won't wash. Sorry, old mate, but it's got to be you.' His tone wasn't unkind, just matter of fact.

I took a deep breath and said, 'Fair enough. I suppose it might even take my mind off my home problems, having a fastball job to do.'

'Gradely, lad. And you're not just our number-one choice for the job; you're the *only* choice.'

'Why's that?'

'Because you alone will recognise the target without fail.'

'You could show other guys the mug-shot.' I pointed at the photo. 'They could memorise what he looks like.'

'It's not the same thing. You've seen him several times. You know him.'

'The thing is, this mug-shot's well out of date. Even when I saw him two years ago he'd aged a good bit over what you can see here. His face had got a lot heavier and more lined.'

'All the more reason for you to be in command.'

'OK. But Tony Lopez saw him just as much.'

'I realise that. I'm hoping I can get Tony on the operation with you for that very reason. But the whole thing's so sensitive that we're waiting on clearance from the Pentagon before we can include him in the team.'

'For Christ's sake!' I exclaimed. 'Is the target in fucking Moscow or somewhere?'

'Yer daft bat! Listen, Geordie. This is a black operation. You know what that means. Nobody has heard about it – *nobody*. It's not to be discussed with anyone – not even your closest mates. Outside these walls, it doesn't exist. And when it does go down, it will be completely unattributable: nothing you do must leave any trace to show that the Regiment was involved.'

'Yeah, yeah. OK.' I'd been given all this shit many times before. I knew Yorky had to bring it out, but even so I didn't like having it rammed down my throat.

'There's to be a team briefing here at 1600 hours,' he was saying. 'All will be revealed then.'

In the afternoon, on my way across, I checked into the incident room again. Fraser and Bates were both intent on a computer monitor, which I saw was carrying details of the player called Danny Aherne who liked sitting down to eyeball his victims. He was thirty-two, fair-haired, unemployed, and had a weakness for the drink. He was known to have been active in London earlier in the year, but had recently gone AWOL from his last known place of residence, a bed-and-breakfast room in Acton.

'He's involved,' said Fraser with some conviction. 'I'm damn sure of that. But I don't know why he's shifted. That may mean something or it may not. But those fibres . . . I'll bet my boots he was there.'

In Yorky's den I found five other guys assembled. They'd been on the Wing for some time already, and constituted one of its two standing teams. The only one I knew well was Pat Newman, a big, dark, ruddy-faced lad with snow-white teeth, one of the heaviest eaters in the business, but very quick on his feet and a useful fellow to have around if things got physical. There was an obvious reason for him being on this new job: he'd done a course in Arabic, and spoke enough of the language to communicate about everyday matters.

A lesser acquaintance was Billy Walker, a little Londoner known as 'Whinger' on account of the fact that he was always moaning or making snide remarks in his own debased form of Cockney rhyming slang. He had peculiarly coloured hair – very light brown, like tow – which looked so artificial that strangers suspected him of dyeing it or wearing a wig; but anyone who lived and worked with him knew that it was his own, and never changed. He also had a horrible habit of rolling his own gaspers, which stank out any room he was in. But he was a good operator nevertheless: small, skinny and tough.

Of the other three, the tallest was Fred Parry, a fair-haired beanpole from A Squadron who'd had a great time blowing up fibre-optic comms towers in Iraq during the Gulf War. Then there was Stew Stewart, a gingery fellow from Merseyside who'd come into the Regiment from the Cheshires. Stew, sometimes known as 'Turnip', wasn't exactly a figure of fun, because he was a good, willing lad, but he did take a lot of stick because of the trouble he had keeping girlfriends. With his broad, ruddy face, he looked exactly what he was – a farmer's boy – and he was perpetually worried that his head was the wrong shape, a deficiency which he tried to remedy by resorting to fancy haircuts. That left only Norman Paxford, a stocky, dark Glaswegian whose aim in life seemed to be to talk as little as possible. He might easily have been nicknamed 'Jock' because of his hellish accent, but – maybe because he spoke so rarely – he was known simply as 'Norm'. People said that it was his Mexican-style moustache, neatly clipped into an upside-down U, that clamped his mouth shut and made it difficult for him to utter. But he was never rude, and if you asked him something he'd always answer, only in the fewest possible words. If you said, 'Everything all right, then, Norm?' he'd just go, 'Aye, thanks,' and leave it at that. In spite of his taciturnity he was a terrific worker, and utterly dependable.

We had a couple of minutes' chit-chat, and I noticed that the mug-shot of our Iraqi friend was up on one of the wall-boards, with several lines of writing beneath it. Then the ops officer and Jimmy Wells came in towing a middle-aged guy in a shiny grey suit.

'I know this feller,' said Pat under his breath. 'He's been here before. We all know him – from the Firm. Gilbert the Filbert.'

Before we sat down on the chairs facing Yorky's desk, Mac introduced me briefly to the man from London: 'Geordie, meet Gilbert Dauncey. Gilbert – Geordie Sharp, commander of the team.' Then he led off, cautioning us yet again about the need for total security.

'Operation Ostrich,' he began. 'As you know, this is a black operation. That means there's to be absolutely no word of it outside your own team. If anyone drops the slightest hint about it, he'll be RTU'd immediately. OK?'

I saw Whinger bend his head to the left and flip the fingers of his right hand upwards past the back of his ear. He could have been scratching at an itch or knocking away a fly; he could also have been saying 'Fucking roll on!' in sign language.

The gesture wasn't lost on Mac, who said sharply, 'Don't piss about, anybody. Just listen. The aim of the operation is to take out this man.' He indicated the mug-shot. 'You'll all have a chance to memorise the face. The guy in question is General Mohammed al-Khadduri, a top-ranking Iraqi who's defected to Libya. Our colleague here' – he indicated Gilbert – 'will brief you on his background in a moment.

'First, though, the location. Al-Khadduri is now working from a military camp on the outskirts of Ajdabiya. That's a town about a hundred and fifty kilometres south of Benghazi, the Libyan capital.'

Mac turned to face a map of north-eastern Africa, with the Mediterranean spread across the upper half and the Bay of Sirte taking a shallow scoop out of the Libyan coastline top-centre. 'Here's Benghazi,' he pointed with a broken-off billiard cue, 'at two o'clock on the coast of the bay, and here's Ajdabiya thirty ks inland, at five-thirty on the bay. The military complex is about here, ten ks beyond the southern outskirts of the town on the edge of the desert. All this ground immediately to the east is a training area.

'Cross-border insertion will be by heli from the military airfield at Siwa, just inside Egypt.'

He placed the tip of his pointer to the right of a thick purple line running north to south, which marked the frontier between Egypt and Libya. 'A Chinook will put you down as close as possible to the target, but to avoid any chance of your being compromised the LZ will have to be at least fifty ks short of the camp. The run-in will be by quad bike.

'Now . . . timing. We have a strict time-frame, imposed on us

41

by external constraints. The operation has to go down under cover of Exercise Bright Star, which is scheduled for May seventeenth to twenty-second. Bright Star is a major international deployment involving US and NATO forces. The aim is to establish and reinforce a simulated front line at a location in the Egyptian desert, against a threat from baddies to the south. If you like, it's a re-enactment of the start of the Gulf build-up of 1990. The exercise will involve all the NATO airforces as well as the USAF, and a considerable number of army units. That means there'll be a large number of air-movements, many of them from Cyprus, in the middle of which ours will get nicely lost.

'You'll stage through Akrotiri dressed as pathfinders – desert cam clothes, maroon Para berets and belts. As far as Cyprus, anybody who sees you will think you're umpires taking part in the exercise. Then, during the last phase of the flight, you'll change into rough civilian gear. Any questions so far?'

I glanced round the semicircle of faces. Everyone was looking hard at the map, thinking things over, but at that stage nobody had anything to say.

'All right, then. I'll ask for a few words about the target from our colleague from the Firm. Most of you know him anyway: Gilbert Dauncey.'

Gilbert stood up and began talking in a crisp, educated voice, public school but not lah-di-dah. 'General Mohammed al-Khadduri. You've seen his photo, and one of you I know has seen *him*. A big, burly fellow, we guess six feet, and powerfully built. A bit like a bear, but he's going to seed a bit now: we think he's put on a good deal of weight lately.

'His record wouldn't stand him in very good stead at the Court of Human Rights. For several years he was responsible for eliminating the political factions that threatened Saddam Hussein's government – and when I say "eliminating", I mean "eliminating". He didn't disband the dissident parties; he rubbed them out with wholesale executions, families and all. Another feather in his cap: it was he who directed the campaign of extermination against the Kurds in the north during the late eighties. The use of chemical weapons is his speciality, particularly against his own people.

'By the time of the Gulf War, Khadduri had risen to become

Saddam's chief of military intelligence. At that time he enjoyed the President's full confidence, and spent much of the run-up to war with him in Baghdad. In the first days of the air-war he had a narrow escape from an incoming Cruise missile, which hit a building when he was in the basement, but he came through the conflict unscathed.

'Afterwards, however, he and his boss fell out. We're not clear what caused the rift, but subsequent events suggest it was a basic disagreement over policy. Saddam wanted to soft-pedal things while he rebuilt his army and kept the Western powers in play, but Khadduri developed more and more extreme right-wing views. It seems that he took Iraq's defeat by the Coalition as a personal insult, and as time went on he became ever more eager to avenge it. Things reached the point at which he was going behind Saddam's back and privately inciting other Arab states to prepare for a joint assault on Israel, as a kind of reprisal. He was for an all-out attack using chemical and biological weapons.

'In the end, of course, word reached Saddam – and that was too much. Early last year, in February, Khadduri was arrested. It looked like he was for the chop, but then he was let out of prison on parole. He did a runner and pitched up with his friend Moammer Gadaffi, President of Libya. There, he's continued to promote the idea of an attack on Israel. In particular, he's tried to win support from Mubarak, President of Egypt, luckily without success. Worse, from our point of view, he's become a red-hot champion of the IRA. He seems to think that by promoting revolution in Northern Ireland he can get his own back for the humiliation the Arabs suffered in the Gulf. Also, the CIA are worried that he's started supporting the fundamentalists behind the bombs on the mainland in the States.'

'Fuckin' 'ell,' muttered Whinger, maybe a bit louder than he meant. 'What an arsehole!'

Gilbert heard him and went on without a flicker: 'Precisely. Indications are that during the past year the amount of money reaching the IRA from Libya has more than doubled. Arms the same. Remember the merchant vessel that ran aground off Cork back in October? The *Sirius*? She was carrying containers that held more than a thousand AK-47s and several million rounds of

43

ammunition. The manifest listed the containers as having been loaded in Amsterdam, but we believe they came all the way from Tripoli, with Khadduri's signature on the docket.

'In other words, this man has become a severe threat to the stability of the Province. He's also a menace in the Middle East as a whole. Now that he has the ear of Gadaffi, there's no telling what he may touch off. Our friends in the CIA agree his time is up.

'Fortunately we have excellent relations with Egypt, and we can use Egyptian territory as a covert staging-post for an operation. Still more fortunate . . .' Gilbert's face softened into the ghost of a smile. 'As of yesterday we discovered that one of you has the big advantage of being personally acquainted with General al-Khadduri.'

I nodded, aware that the other guys were giving me the eyeball. I glanced along the line and thought I'd better explain. 'When I was in the nick in Baghdad, after the patrol got compromised, this bastard used to come along once a week and give us the third degree. I'd recognise him a mile off in thick fog.'

'He's your man, then, Geordie,' chirped Whinger. 'Nice little solo venture. Piece of cake.'

'Fuck off, mate,' I replied equably. Then I asked Gilbert, 'What's he doing, exactly? I mean, has Gadaffi given him a job?'

'Officially he's in charge of officer training. That's why he's based at Ajdabiya, which is Libya's answer to Sandhurst. But signal intercepts show he's using the place for every kind of political and revolutionary activity. I repeat: he's regarded as the most dangerous single operator in the Middle East, Saddam Hussein not excepted.'

There was a short silence. 'Gadaffi!' exclaimed Pat contemptuously. 'That guy's mad as twenty fucking hatters.'

'That's the trouble,' Gilbert agreed.

'Can you give us any personal gen on the target?' Pat went on. 'Any clue about his movements or habits?'

'Not much, I'm afraid. He's married, with a family, and he tends to join them at a house on the coast whenever he has days off. But while he's working he lives in the commandant's quarters on the base. One point that may prove relevant: we know he's a night owl, and sits up all hours working, when everyone else has gone to bed and things have quietened down.'

'How do we know that?' I asked.

Gilbert hesitated, then said, 'You'll find out shortly. Now, for details of the camp layout we're awaiting satellite intelligence from the CIA. A courier should be in London by tomorrow. I'm afraid some or all of you will have to come to London to see what he brings. The office have judged the material too sensitive for it to go outside, even here. Any more questions? No?'

He sat down, and Mac took over. 'Thanks, Gilbert,' he said. Then he turned to us. 'I don't have to emphasise that your hit team will have to be absolutely clean. You'll wear Arab or some sort of civilian clothes, use Soviet or Chinese weapons and ammunition. None of you must carry any trace of any Western organisation. Webbing, bergens, boots – everything's got to be checked for names or labels. If the team suffers a fatality, it will be absolutely imperative to bring the body out with you. If that proves impossible, you'll vaporise the body with a bar mine.'

'You mean we're going to take nice British bar mines with us?' Whinger said.

'No, no,' Mac assured him, 'we've got a few Chinese ones that'll come in handy.'

'How alarming,' went Whinger. 'Bloody charming.'

Mac ignored him and continued. 'Back to timing. As I said, Bright Star runs for six days. That means you've got to be in and out within this time bracket, while the cover lasts. And it commences on the seventeenth, which means you've got less than two weeks in which to get prepped up. OK? Any questions?'

'What about weapons?' Pat asked.

'You'll draw non-attributable AK-47s from the SAW section of the main armoury. They're being delivered from London in the morning. Once you've got them you'll store them here.' He gestured to the lockers at the sides of the room. 'Anything else?'

'Why isn't Tony Lopez in on this?' asked Fred Parry. 'He was in the nick with you, Geordie, wasn't he? He must know the guy.'

'That's right, he does.' Mac answered for me. 'Tony's an obvious candidate with his special knowledge. But because of American political sensitivities we haven't yet got clearance for him to join the team. We're still hoping he'll be able to come in.'

For a final word, Mac turned to me and said, 'If there's anything you want to know, Geordie, these guys will fill you in. They're all genned up on the way the Wing works. And if there's anything you need, don't worry about asking for it. What you may not realise is that the SAW has its own budget: within reason, money's no object, and there are no restrictions on equipment. If you need civilian clothes, for instance, go and buy them. Any bits and pieces of extra kit – the same. You're in a different game now.'

With the ruperts gone, I got the lads to gather round for a minute. 'Right,' I said, 'we start training proper tomorrow morning. But we can begin sorting out our priorities now. First things first: wills. Have you all made out a will?' I glanced round the team. Pat, who was married, gave a nod, but the other four looked blank.

'Well, even if you don't think you've got anything to leave, I suggest you get organised. There's no guarantee that all of us will come back. Correction: there's no guarantee that *any* of us will come back. Jabs the same. Get your arses up to the doc's office: see the clerk in there, and make sure you're up to date. It's no big deal.

'Now – individual responsibilities. I'll be team medic; I've got the training. Fred, you're in charge of explosives. You'll need to check out these Chinese bar mines, make sure you read the instructions. Right?'

Fred nodded.

'Whinger, signals, OK? We're getting in some special non-attributable kit, and there's a rep coming up from the Firm to run you through it.'

'Yeah. I know most of that stuff, but a refresher wouldn't do any harm.'

'Good. Pat, how's your Arabic?'

'Shit hot!'

'Say something.'

'*Aaaarrgh!*' he went, and then gave a kind of hiccup.

'What did that mean?'

'Fuck off.'

'Don't piss about.'

'Honest, that's what I said.'

'You did the Arabic course?'

'Yonks ago.'

'It'll come back to you. Get on the tapes in the language lab and you'll make it.'

'*Allah karim.*'

I turned to Stew Stewart and said, 'You're from Mobility Troop, Stew. Go down and speak to the MTO about the quads. Get a mechanic to take you through anything we might need to know.'

'Fair enough.'

Because Norm Paxford was already a competent signaller, I told him to work with Whinger as his back-up on the radios. 'Take all the sets along to the signals technician and make sure the frequencies are in line,' I said. 'The other thing is, we'll use throat-mikes rather than booms, because booms would pick up the noise of the wind and the engines.

'And wait a minute,' I went on. 'A bell's ringing. Covert Method of Entry. Weren't you posted to the CMOE wing, Norm? Didn't you do the specialist lock-picking course?'

'That's right,' he said. 'All two years of it.'

'Great. You're our CMOE expert, then.'

In a moment of black humour I saw all the members of our team in terms of what they didn't have – the areas where, in military jargon, they'd gone deficient. I'd gone deficient in terms of family; Norm couldn't be bothered to talk; Stew was definitely deficient in the legover stakes; Pat couldn't control his appetite; Fred wasn't overburdened with brains; and Whinger didn't know when to stop cracking jokes. Still, I thought, we've all got our own strengths, and even if we're not fucking perfect we'll make out.

Back in the incident room I found Fraser still in occupation. 'Hey, Geordie,' he said. 'I've got news for you.'

'What's that?'

'Farrell's back.'

'Christ, that was quick!'

'Yep. He landed at Lyneham after lunch. Maximum security all the way.'

'Where's he been taken?'

'Winson Green, Birmingham.'

He picked up a sheet of fax paper and studied it. 'The prisoner's wounds are infected, and he's suffering from septicaemia. He's running quite a high fever, by the look of it.'

'I'm not surprised,' I said, 'the amount of shit there was in that jungle. Some of it's bound to have been sucked into him with the bullets. Does that mean he's in hospital?'

Again Fraser consulted his notes. 'Yep, he's in a single cell in the hospital wing. He's on fifteen-minute watch. That means one of the screws takes a look at him every quarter of an hour.'

'What about visitors?'

'He hasn't had any yet. One guy tried to see him, and a search revealed that he was carrying an escape kit inside a transistor radio. So that was the end of that. Now the Home Secretary's imposed a ban on visitors until further notice.'

'How long can that be maintained?'

'Only a few days. You can bet that a fellow like Farrell will know his rights down to the last letter.'

'And if the ban's lifted?'

'He'll be able to have one fifteen-minute visit a day, but only in a closed environment with prison officers present. That is, if he's graded Category A – which I've no doubt he will be.'

'And who was the guy who tried to visit?'

Fraser checked his notes and said, 'He identified himself with a driving licence in the name of Peter Smithies – but of course it turned out the licence had been stolen.'

'So the PIRA know where Farrell is anyway?'

'Oh yes. They know.'

That evening, for a change, I ran home. It was a good distance – about my usual eight miles – and I'd sussed out a route through the lanes that was almost entirely free of traffic. But again I had trouble with my rhythm. Even more now I was feeling the pressure, and I was so needled by the contradictory thoughts chasing through my head that I couldn't settle to a steady pace.

I was pleased now that Operation Ostrich was going down, as it promised genuine action to distract me, and the chance of doing a hard job well. Besides, I positively looked forward to topping al-Khadduri. At the same time, I was apprehensive about leaving the UK with my own affairs in such a mess. On the one hand it seemed there was nothing to be gained by hanging around at Hereford. If or when the PIRA came on the air there would be plenty of trained negotiators on hand to deal with them; in any case, I was fairly sure that if I did demur about going, the Regiment would order me to. Yorky Rose had admitted as much. On the other hand, Hereford was the last place I'd seen Tim and Tracy, and my natural inclination was to cling to any trace of them that I had. If I went overseas and someone made a cock-up in my absence, I might never see them again; my whole life would go to ratshit. Similarly, if I went under in a foreign country, Tim would never remember his father, we would never get to know each other properly. What sort of a person would he grow up to be without me to guide him? What would Tracy do, left without support?

Trying to think everything through, I realised that although I'd already made a will I might need to make some adjustments. As things stood I'd arranged to leave a small amount of money for Tim, who'd get it when he was eighteen, and the house to Tracy. She and I had talked all this through before, and she'd agreed that if I died she would adopt the boy. But now — to face the worst — there was a chance that she might not outlive me. I decided that in the morning I'd better go into town to visit my solicitor, the owlish Mr Higgins.

As for Farrell — I couldn't help feeling nervous about the situation. At least the bastard hadn't escaped. I'd half expected the Colombians to let him out, through corruption or sheer incompetence. Now he was behind bars in Birmingham, and it sounded as if he was too ill to cause trouble for the time being.

But sooner or later he'd start to agitate, and when he did he'd stir more trouble than all the turds in China.

FOUR

I was at the solicitor's office by nine o'clock. 'Thos C. Higgins & Partners' said the highly-polished brass plate beside the door. I had no appointment, but I knew Higgins kept the first half-hour of the morning free and was confident he'd see me. In fact he walked up to the front door at the same moment as I did, and greeted me like an old pal, spectacles flashing.

His office smelt of lavender furniture polish, and the handsome grandfather clock was ticking away as steadily as ever in a corner. Since he knew my affairs well, there wasn't much explaining to do, and I soon put him in the picture.

'I don't know if it makes any difference,' I said, 'but Tracy's pregnant.'

'*Is* she?' he exclaimed. 'Congratulations!'

'Well, it's only two months so far.'

'You mean you would like to make the child a beneficiary of your will?'

'That's what I was wondering.'

'I think it's hardly possible. I mean, if she were, God forbid, to be killed during the next few weeks, the child could not survive.' He paused for a moment, then said, 'Is there no one else you could name as a residuary legatee?'

I shook my head. 'As you know, I'm an orphan. I don't have anybody.' Then suddenly an idea came to me, and I said, 'I know. Yes. I'd like to nominate a colleague: Tony Lopez.'

'Is that his full name? Tony?'

'No, it's Antonio. He's American, Puerto Rican by origin. If Tracy and I are both written off, I'd like him to get everything. But the most important thing is that I'd like him to be the guardian for Tim.'

'Very well,' replied Mr Higgins cautiously. 'I'm sure that can be arranged. I shall need Mr Lopez to complete certain documents, of course.'

'*Sergeant* Lopez,' I said.

'Sergeant. I'm sorry.'

Mr Lopez! Just thinking about it creased me up. Tony was so much the professional soldier that the very idea of him being a civilian seemed ridiculous; I knew he'd bust his butt (as he would put it) laughing about it.

The morning's highlight was the arrival of the quads. Seven brand-new Honda Big Reds – one for each member of the team, one spare – were decanted from a truck into the tender loving care of the MT section, which at once set about destroying their glamour and making them look as nondescript as possible. By the time our lads went down to take delivery of the bikes their appearance had changed completely. Not only had every trace of scarlet paint been scraped, rubbed or grit-blasted off and replaced by a drab sand-colour, but the engine numbers had also been ground off the crank cases with emery wheels and the serial numbers scraped off the frames. The ignition keys had been stripped of their numbers so that no identification remained, and the engineers had cut different numbers of notches in their rims, one to seven, so that they could still be matched to the right bikes.

As Whinger remarked, such treatment didn't exactly enhance the value of the machines – but then, after the operation had gone down, we weren't planning to auction them off in the main souk in Tripoli.

We'd all ridden quads before, but we got a quick run-down on this latest model from Mike Molloy, the MT officer, a grizzled little terrier of a captain. 'They're fully automatic,' he said, sitting on one to demonstrate. 'No clutch. The gear pedal's this one, by your left foot. As you move off, just keep coming up with your toe – Super Low, One, Two, Three, Four. For reverse, push this red button on the panel between the handlebars, then down with the gear lever. Nothing to it.'

'Watch your starts, though. The motor's quite poky, and if you give it too much throttle it can put you on your back. As you'll see from the manual, wheelies are *not* recommended.' To demonstrate his point he started the engine, kicked into gear and revved up sharply. For a second I thought he'd overdone it. The bike seemed to leap into the air. It shot forward, but at the same time the front wheels came high off the ground so that it was almost vertical, and Mike was clinging on like a jockey on the back of a rearing horse. A tiny bit more power and he'd have gone right over backwards, but in fact he came down safely and switched off. 'See what I mean?' he said.

'Another thing to look out for is the tyres. As you realise, they're designed to operate at very low pressures – two point nine p.s.i. – cross-country. If you find you've got to run on tarmac, blow 'em up to at least double that or you'll knacker them.'

We were given basic instruction in maintenance – changing wheels, mending punctures, adjusting brakes, fiddling carburettor jets and so on – but Stew Stewart arranged to come back another day and go through the drills for things like ignition faults and fuel blockages.

Most of the guys ignored the manuals that came with the bikes, but a couple of them gave short, satirical readings from the printed instructions. Whinger started honking off in a pseudo-Japanese voice: '"Always check for obstacles before operating in a new area."' He gave a short, sardonic laugh. 'Thanks, mate. Just send us a load of large-scale maps of eastern Libya, all five thousands sheets! "Always obey local off-road riding laws and regulations." Phone the Libyan Embassy, Geordie, and ask for a copy of the desert off-highway code. "Never go fast over the top of a hill." For fuck's sake! If Gadaffi's nasties come after us I'll be going like shit off a shovel, I can tell you, even if I'm right on the summit of the biggest bloody mountain in North Africa.'

That afternoon we loaded into a four-tonner and drove away to the Brecon Beacons for practice over rough terrain – through mud and water, up, down and across steep grass slopes. For me, this was another psychological hang-up to be overcome. It was a motor-bike accident which had led to my getting captured in Iraq: as the squadron had been moving up to a new location in the desert I'd dropped into a hole and smashed my left arm – and then, as an

American casevac team was lifting me out along with other wounded, the chopper had been shot down. Now, once again, I was going to be riding a bike behind the lines in enemy territory. Admittedly I'd now have four wheels instead of two, and there wasn't a war on, but all the same the idea was a bit of a hurdle. To be nicked by the Libyans wouldn't be much less unpleasant than being nicked by the Iraqis – especially as our presence in the country would probably be denied by the British authorities and we could easily be left to rot in one of Gadaffi's penitentiaries.

Was it imagination, or did my arm produce a couple of twinges as I powered off up a rough grass track into the hills? For months it hadn't given the slightest trouble, even when I was on the weights in the gym, but now it seemed to be aching.

I set myself to concentrate on balance, and getting the feel of the quad. With two front wheels the steering seemed much firmer than with one, but it was OK once I'd got used to it. The trick was to sit forward on the long saddle when climbing, back on the way down, and lean uphill on the cross-slopes.

Pretty soon I had got the hang of it and started enjoying myself – and in fact everybody came back well chuffed with the machines, which were comfortable, fast, sure-footed and ideal for the job. Of course, we had been riding them with front and rear racks empty, and we realised they'd be a different proposition when loaded with all the kit and stores we were going to need.

While we were out in the hills, a message had reached camp to say that our American contact had flown in from Langley, Virginia, and would brief us on the camp at Ajdabiya in the morning. With this in mind we stopped work and went home early.

First light next day saw us piling into a Puma and whipping up to RAF Northolt on the western outskirts of London. It frustrated me to think that we were heading into the very area where Tim and Tracy might be held, and during the flight I was seized by the fantastic idea that I'd simply look down and see them being taken along a street – whereupon we'd bin our meeting with the Firm, fast-rope down on top of the prisoners' escorts, overpower them, and recover the captives.

The rest of the journey into town – by road – took so long that we reckoned we could have tabbed it faster, and it was nearly ten o'clock by the time our wagon crossed Vauxhall Bridge, slipped in through twin security gates and pulled up in the basement of the Firm's forbidding new head-shed building on the south bank of the Thames. Our friend Gilbert met us in the basement and escorted us up into the heart of the block, punching in combination numbers to open one locked door after another. Security here was so tight that it felt as if we were in a submarine, passing through a series of watertight compartments. We'd been told that this building got swept electronically at least once a day to make sure no listening bugs had been infiltrated, and we had no difficulty believing it.

We were never told the full name of the CIA agent who briefed us; Gilbert brought him into the lecture-room and introduced him merely as Gus. He was a short, stocky fellow in a navy blazer, with a pointed face, heavy suntan, close-cropped grey hair and shiny brown eyes – a combination that reminded me of a squirrel. Before he spoke, Gilbert gave us another dose of warnings about the need for total security – but here, in this alien environment, our guys were on their best behaviour, and Whinger didn't even scratch his ear.

When the American began to talk we were riveted, because the depth of his information was amazing. It took a couple of minutes to get used to his broad southern accent, but soon we were hooked. Not even his habit of saying 'OK?' after every few words could put us off.

Satellite data had been down-loaded into his laptop, some of it enhanced into three-dimensional computer images, which he fired on to a screen, so that what we got was a series of snapshots taken from a variety of overhead angles. As we sat there watching, all the guys were impressed by the lecturer's high-tech apparatus and approach, but at the same time I couldn't help thinking how typical it was that, although the Yanks could see a fly twiddling its legs on the far side of the world, when they wanted guys to go in and shoot somebody unpleasant, it was the Brits whom they got to do the job.

First Gus showed us the extent of the military camp. It was roughly rectangular, with the sides extending about two kilometres and the main approach road coming down to it from the north. Using a propelling pencil as a pointer, he picked out points of interest. 'The perimeter fence is weldmesh,' he told us. 'OK? Ten feet high, with a two-foot extension tilted outwards on top. Four strands of barbed wire – dannart, you call it? – on angle irons. I don't know whether you'll want to go through that or over it – through it, I guess. On the whole, we believe that security on the base is fairly primitive. The locals reckon the camp's protected by its location, with nothing but desert to the south. We can't tell from the satellite imagery whether or not the watch-towers are manned, but we think not.'

'Excuse me,' I broke in. 'Is it all right to make notes?'

'Go right ahead – so long as you don't write down names, or anything that would identify the place to outsiders. OK?'

'Sure.'

'So far as we can see, the fence isn't alarmed. No electric current in it, either – no sensors. Now, I'll just quickly show you the main areas of the camp. These are the accommodation blocks. Cookhouse, here. Mosque here – very important. Parade ground. Headquarter building, with a communications tower above it. Transport compound – you can see all the trucks lined up – and a few armoured vehicles here. Gasoline tanks in circular bunds. Gas filling point here. Two fifty-yard ranges; the main ranges are out in the training areas to the east. Ammunition bunkers way out on their own . . . here. Armoury here. That's one thing about the Arabs: they can't stand having weapons around the camp. Everything has to be locked away – that is, except for the guns carried by the guards. This is the recreational area: football fields, volleyball court. OK?'

'What are all those round things?' Pat asked.

'These?' Gus pointed to two or three small dark blobs. 'Palm trees. Remember, you're looking at them from right overhead. Now, the building you're interested in is this one. Bottom left-hand corner, as God and our satellites see it. On your left if you approach out of the desert from the south.'

The tip of the pencil-shadow trembled slightly as it hovered over an L-shaped structure set a little inside the angle of the perimeter fence. 'This seems to be a combination of office and residential accommodation. OK? It's on two floors, ground and upper, possibly also a basement. Concrete block construction, painted some light colour, buff or cream. Flat roof, double skinned to give some insulation from the sun. Metal window frames. This is where the target lives during his working week.'

'How wide's that gap between the building and the fence?' I asked.

'Maybe a hundred yards, maybe a little more. I'll take you in closer for more detail.'

In the next image the building occupied most of the picture. Two vehicles were parked in front of it, and part of a swimming pool was visible on the left-hand side. 'OK. The main entrance is here, on the southern side. There's another door on the right-hand end, here, and a rear door at the left, here. See this curving row of trees? It looks as though there's some sort of garden been planted in back. The private accommodation is here, around the west end. The room in which the target works nights is this one, on the corner of the upper floor. Two windows, one facing south, one west. Look at this.'

The speaker put up a night-time shot, taken from an oblique angle. Everything was dim and hazy, and needed explanation. 'You're still looking down, but from a little way out front – a slightly different orbit. These are the lights on the perimeter fence . . . and this is the south face of the accommodation building. The main doorway I mentioned is about there.' He pointed at the middle of the south front. 'Now. See the bright spot in this top corner? That's been there on several satellite passes made between one and two a.m. Rest of the building dark, this window lit, OK? That's where we think he'll be.'

'But how do we know it's him?' I asked.

Gus hesitated and turned towards Gilbert, as if uncertain who should answer the question.

'Inside information,' Gilbert quickly explained. 'We have a sleeper who works in the building – a computer maintenance technician. The guy files us reports on a regular basis. The only thing is, he has one hell of a time because the power supply keeps going down. There are back-up generators, but they don't work too well either.'

56

I was rather impressed. I hadn't realised that the Firm had such a far-flung web of contacts. 'How late does the target stay there?' I asked.

'Typically until two or three in the morning,' Gus replied.

'And where does he sleep?'

'In back of the building, on that same floor.'

'What about guards?'

'Two or three sleep on the premises. There are normally two on duty nights, but that doesn't mean they're going to be awake. You know what Arabs are like.'

Gus paused, thinking. Then he added, 'If you're going in close, one thing in your favour will be the primitive air conditioning. There's no central system. Each room has its own unit set into an outside wall, and the fans are pretty noisy. Whenever the AC's on, there'll be a solid background roar. That'll help mask any sound you make.'

'How far away is the nearest building?'

The CIA man switched to another photo, half-way between the first and second in scale, and measured the space from the house to a neighbouring structure, off to the north. 'Also about a hundred yards, we think. This other thing's some kind of a store, probably uninhabited at night. I don't think it'll worry you.'

For a minute or two we all sat staring, memorising details, and I made a few notes in my book. Then Whinger forgot himself and declared, 'All we need do is take a couple of Uzis with us and accidentally scatter them about the place. That'd put the finger on fucking Israel, all right.'

I saw Gilbert looking rather pained, so I said, 'Not on, mate. We need to keep ourselves clean.'

'Was that a joke?' asked Gus. 'I hope so. Oh, I nearly forgot. I don't want to overburden you guys, but there's a secondary target that would merit your attention.'

He projected yet another image from his laptop and showed us a picture of a satellite receiving station – a thirty-foot steerable dish aerial with a couple of ancillary buildings – in a small compound of its own. 'This is one of the nerve centres of their military communications network,' he said. 'Knock that out and you'd do everyone a good turn. It was built by the Soviets, and with things being as they are now it might not be too easy to replace.'

'Where is it in relation to the accommodation block?' I asked.

'On the other side of camp. The east side. I think you'd see it OK from the perimeter wire.'

'And how far from that gate you showed us?'

'Maybe three hundred yards.'

'RPG,' said Whinger judiciously. 'Slip a rocket up it as we're moving off. No problem.'

'Like I said,' Gus emphasised, 'it's very much a secondary target. Only to be engaged if you've hit Number One. And certainly I wouldn't want you to prejudice the main operation.'

'Got that,' I said. 'Can you fill us in on the surrounding terrain?'

'Sure.'

A wide-angle shot (or maybe one taken from a higher orbit) showed an expanse of desert south of the camp. To our untrained eyes the picture didn't mean much. Apart from a single dirt road coming out from the fence to the south-east and ending at a range, there were a few wadis and stream-beds winding about, but we couldn't identify anything else specific. Yet Gus, armed with notes, gave a useful general description.

During the chopper flight in we would overfly one MSR (main supply route), a metalled road running north-east to south-west, he told us. Once on the ground we'd have to cross another road, a smaller one, and a single large wadi. Down to the south the desert was flat, but as we approached the area of the camp we would come into a belt of dunes a couple of miles across from south to north, the range as a whole lying east and west, the northern edge of which was less than a quarter of a mile from the camp fence. Gus reckoned the dunes were 150 feet high, and should give us an excellent site for an observation post. The elevation was ideal: we'd be looking down slightly. Another picture, taken soon after sunrise, proved his point: strong light coming low from the east caught on the sweeping, curved rims of the dunes, casting pools of shadow hundreds or maybe thousands of yards long.

As I stared at the picture my mind flew back to the Gulf, and the crappy gen we'd been fed in the run-up to the war. For months we had trained in the sand of the United Arab Emirates, firmly believing that the desert plateau in the west of Iraq – where our patrols would be inserted – also consisted of sand. The basis of our belief was US satellite imagery, from which our own int boys had deduced that Iraq was covered with sand from top to bottom. Then, when our patrols had gone in, what did we find? The entire environment was rock and shale, with not a grain of sand in sight. All the kit we'd brought for building OPs was useless, and we were caught with our pants down: you can't build anything out of solid rock.

Were we being given another load of crap now? I didn't want to seem aggressive, but I had to ask – so I put the point as politely as possible. 'Excuse me,' I said, 'but in Iraq we got stuffed because everyone misread the terrain.'

'I know, I know!' Gus grinned in a friendly enough fashion. 'That was real tough. But the fault didn't lie in the imagery. The trouble was, your intelligence guys didn't know how to interpret the data they were getting. Nobody had time to brief them properly and pass information on down the line.'

'So you're confident this environment *is* sand?' I gestured at the screen.

'One hundred per cent. Look at the soft curves on these dunes. They couldn't be made of rock. Apart from anything else, they change shape with the seasons as the winds shift their surface. There's another thing, too: it's the loose texture of the ground that stops the Libyans using this sector for manoeuvres. As I said, they've got enormous infantry training areas, but those are all further north where the desert's harder and more stable.'

He paused and added, 'You're going in on ATVs, I think?'

'That's right.'

'They'll be fine. Roll over the sand no problem.'

That reassured me. At least this info was coming straight from a guy who knew what he was talking about, rather than through a range of filters and competing intelligence agencies hundreds of miles apart.

Gus moved on to show us more detail of the terrain on our run-in. The large wadi was almost two miles wide. 'In winter that can be some river,' he told us. 'But right now it's dry, and likely to remain so. Could be the odd pool still lying in the bed, but my bet is you'll cross dry-shod.'

He then gave us a run-down of temperatures at first and last light. Here again I was on my guard, because in Iraq we'd been totally misinformed. Nobody had warned us that on the plateau in winter we would encounter snow, ice and vicious winds, with daytime temperatures barely above freezing, and night-times well below. The result was that we went in with nothing like enough clothes, and two of our guys died from hypothermia. Now in Libya we were promised a night-time minimum of eighteen Celsius and a daytime maximum of thirty-six. From the magic laptop came three-day weather charts giving temperatures, humidity, moon state, and first and last light. When I challenged the temperatures, mentioning our Iraq experience, the answer was, 'Yeah – but that was winter, and on the plateau you were a thousand feet above sea level. This time it's early summer, and even on those goddamn dunes you'll be at sea-level or maybe even below it.'

Again I relaxed.

Gus continued with an analysis of vehicle movements up and down the approach road to the camp, but these were of less interest to us. I couldn't see us getting up round that side of the establishment at all. We'd come in from the south or south-east, find a lying-up point a kilometre or so short of the fence, and build an OP on one of the dunes. Mine's a steak, as Whinger would say: piece of cake.

Having made sketches and taken some notes, I felt reasonably confident. But one point that still worried me was the sheer number of *jundis* likely to be on site. Gus reckoned that there might be two or three hundred troops on the camp at night. If the alarm went up and that lot got deployed into the desert, they could form a hell of a cordon, through which we'd just have to blast our way.

All the more reason for us to operate discreetly: we'd need to be in and out before anyone became aware of our presence.

Back in Hereford, the knowledge we'd gained focused our training effort. Now we knew that we needed practice at building OPs in a sandy environment, so we loaded the quads into another four-tonner and made away to the dunes near Borth on the Welsh coast. There we had a couple of good days riding the bikes on the loose, steep slopes and making OPs by digging into banks, building walls

60

with bags of sand, and roofing over the hollows we'd made with extending aluminium rods covered with scrim netting and marram grass. The second day turned out fine and warm, so when we'd finished work two of the guys stripped off and rushed into the sea; but the water was so cold that they were out again in short order, cursing wildly and covered in purple-red patches.

After a few hours riding the quads I'd thought of a couple of modifications that might prove useful. One was a bracket mounted above the handlebar panel to hold a Magellan GPS kit, so that we could keep an eye on our little displays while driving with both hands on; the other was a speedometer (as delivered, the bikes had nothing to tell you how fast they were going). So I got the MT Section to give us all Magellan-holders, and to cobble up two of the quads with speedos.

Weapons and weapon-training were another major pre-occupation. From the SAW's own closed-off section of the armoury we drew brand-new AK-47s, silenced Browning 9mm pistols, and one Soviet-made Dragunov 7.62 sniper rifle – a semi-automatic, bolt-action weapon fitted with a telescopic sight. The AK-47s were Chinese-made Type 5611s, with skeleton stocks that folded under for easier transportation, and Chinese characters stamped into the metal. It was obvious they'd never been fired because the working parts were still coated in their original grease; they could well have been part of the shipment seized off the Irish coast which Gilbert had mentioned.

After stripping the rifles and giving them a good clean-up, we took them out to an isolated range and began getting to know them. The AK-47 is a primitive beast, coarsely made and finished, but it's a robust enough weapon, and at normal distances reasonably accurate. The safety-catch, on the right-hand side above the pistol-grip, is dead simple – one click down for fully automatic, two down for semi-automatic – and provided rounds don't jam in the magazine you're laughing.

To free up the working parts we loaded magazines fully with thirty rounds apiece, and fired a few initial bursts, four or five rounds at a time. Three of the mags proved sticky, if not downright defective, so we binned them on the spot. Then we got down to zero the rifles, and found that at a hundred yards we could achieve three-inch groups, firing at plain white aiming marks on a buff background. At two hundred the rounds were falling four or five inches, but an adjustment of the battle-sight, half-way up the barrel, soon put the point of impact back in the bull. Nevertheless we decided that our best policy would be to keep the sight in its normal position and, if necessary, aim a bit high.

I never saw the AK-47 as our assassination weapon. It would be our main armament if we got involved in a contact, but it was too crude and cumbersome for the close-quarter job which I envisaged. Our aim was to take Khadduri out with maximum precision and minimum disturbance: a surgical strike at point-blank range, for which a silenced pistol would be ideal. I therefore paid close attention to my 9 mm Browning.

Like the rifles, the Browning is a basic weapon, but this customised version had a thick cylinder of sound-baffle wrapped round the barrel. Another silencing device is the button which locks the top slide of the pistol forward after a shot, keeping most of the noise inside – the penalty being that you have to knock the lever off to re-cock the mechanism. After a few warm-up shots I fired at a Hun's-head target from close range – between ten and twenty feet. Although the pistol was accurate enough I didn't like the trigger-pull, which was too heavy, and I wasn't happy with the sluggish action. So in the afternoon I took the weapon back to the armourer and got him to polish up all its working surfaces, and next time out on the range I found a big improvement. At twelve feet I could put every round not just into the Hun's head but into a two-inch circle in the middle of the forehead.

I knew that, if I could get close enough to the target, I would nail him.

Our joker weapon was the sniper rifle, which proved deadly accurate. We set the telescopic sight at 300 yards, and worked out how much to aim up or down at other ranges without altering the zero. Already a plan of campaign was forming in my mind: when the assault party of two or three went in to penetrate the building and engage the target, the rest of the guys would be on the perimeter fence, ready to put down rounds if anyone came after us. In this last role the Dragunov could prove a big asset; if it dropped a sentry, for example, three or four hundred yards from the real scene of activity, it would create a useful diversion.

As for the secondary target – that would have to take its chance.

Explosives I left mainly to Fred Parry. After some discussion we decided to bin the idea of taking bar mines, Chinese or otherwise, as they weighed about forty pounds each and we already had too much kit to carry. Instead we indented for a supply of Semtex, with which we could blow the fence, a door or a window, or make diversionary booby-traps that would delay any attempt at follow-up. We could also use it to destroy a quad, if one was disabled, or – *in extremis* – to vapourise a body. A further joker in our pack was a clutch of Claymore anti-personnel mines, which are easy to transport. These curious-looking things – like little green bars in the shape of crescents, only an inch and a half thick, with a leg at each end – pack a nasty punch in the form of ball bearings, which fly out like grape-shot when the mine is detonated. American-made Claymores have TOWARDS ENEMY stamped on the business side. Ours, which were Soviet-made, bore no such legend; but as we were all familiar with the weapon, we knew well enough that the outside of the crescent was the face to show the Libyans.

A trickier subject was rations. We were going in on hard routine – no cooking, no fires, no heating of brews, even – and this meant that for three days at least all our food would be cold. That didn't worry the guys, especially as we would be in a hot climate; all the same, it was a drag having to transfer every boil-in-a-bag meal from its silver pack, which had writing on it, into an anonymous, clear plastic bag with a zipper-lock fastener. By the time we'd cut off one end of each pack and squeezed sausage and beans or steak and kidney into another container, the meal was even more featureless and gunged-up than before. Yet nobody cared much: on an operation, people accept that they're not at the Ritz; they eat only to shove the necessary amount of calories down their necks, and look forward to proper meals when they get home. Besides, the plastic bags would have a useful secondary role: after we'd eaten their contents we could crap into them.

You'd be surprised how dangerous body wastes can be. Not only do piss and shit stink, and attract flies and wandering dogs, but one turd may give away a mountain of secrets. Laboratory analysis can show not only what type of food the guy who laid it has been eating, but also his age and the physical state he's in. Whether or not the Libyans had the techniques for that sort of work we couldn't tell, but it was perfectly possible that undisciplined crapping might reveal that we were a bunch of fit young westerners.

We also devoted time to working out our loads. The maximum weights given in the manual were 60lb. for the rear rack on each quad, and 50lb. for the front; but it was clear that such puny limits were no good to us. We decided, for a start, that each of us must take one jerrican of spare petrol and one of water – these two alone would add up to nearly 100lb. – and on top of that we had weapons, ammunition, explosives, cam-nets and poles for OPs, shovels, other tools, food, spare clothes and other personal kit. I told the guys to cut down to the absolute minimum compatible with safety, and everybody kept packing and repacking to see what they could leave out. Another necessity was to ensure that the kit was properly secured to the bikes. I wasn't happy with the straps I already had, so I went down to Meg, the camp seamstress, who ran me up some webbing straps with ratcheted buckles to my own design.

After discussing what we needed and what we didn't in various Chinese parliaments, with all the team sitting round for a general discussion, we decided to take a single trailer, in which a good load of the heavier, bulkier items like jerricans, spare tyres and cam-nets could travel. One of the quads would have to pull it, but we could take turns – and, as somebody pointed out, if we did get a casualty, the wounded man or dead body could be transported in it. So the MT section obtained a trailer, and put it through the same process of removing all its identification marks.

As always in the Regiment, physical fitness was left to individuals. All the guys knew that they had to be in really good nick; if we hit trouble, our lives might depend on our ability to cover big distances at speed in alien conditions, possibly with little food or water. So there was no need for organised runs or training sessions; people just went on with their own fitness routines whenever they had time. It was the same with inoculations. Right at the start I had told everyone to make sure his jabs were up to date, and, if any were missing, to get his arse down to the Med Centre pronto.

The two RAF crews who would be flying us came down to give us briefings and discuss our requirements. Both were dedicated to special forces support, so that they were old friends, and I recognised Pineapple Pete, the Herc captain, from several earlier missions. (Why he was called that history did not relate; I suppose some Petes just *are* pineapples.)

'Off for a nice little drive in the desert, are you Geordie?' he asked. 'Just the job for the time of year.'

'Yeah,' I agreed. 'Spot of sightseeing. Nothing dramatic.'

The Herc crew were on a need-to-know basis. All that mattered was that they took us to Cyprus, and on to Siwa, according to the schedule that the Kremlin had devised. What we were doing was another matter and something about which they didn't even ask. The crew of the Chinook had to have more information: they knew that we were on a non–attributable operation, and they knew to within a few miles the area in which it would take place. But they, too, were in the dark about our target, and Steve Tanner, the skipper, was no more inquisitive than Pete. Of far greater importance to him was the state of the moon on the night we went in, and he was glad to find that it would be three-quarters full.

Together with him, his co-pilot and his head loadie, we worked out distances, timings, weights and so on. But we never breathed a word about our target. At the back of my mind I kept thinking: there's always a chance that the heli will go down in the desert, and if it does, the less the crew know about us, the better – the less they can give away. All the same we had to plan emergency drills with them, in case the chopper's navigation systems went u/s, or it was shot down or forced down by engine failure. There were emergency rendezvous points to be memorised and procedures to be worked out. In the last resort, we might have to destroy the aircraft with explosives to make sure that no Libyans got their hands on it.

The crew also needed a cover story, to account for why they were in Libya at all. We decided they would say that they'd been taking part in Exercise Bright Star, that their navigation systems had gone down, and that they'd flown into Libyan air space by mistake. That might not sound very convincing but it was the best that could be devised.

FIVE

My own trouble was that I couldn't seem to shake off the tension which still built steadily. Normally I find the best answer to mental stress is hard physical exercise, but this time the remedy wasn't working. I was forcing myself to run and work out every day, yet still I was unable to relax, and sometimes I thought my head was going to burst with the pressure.

My days were packed with activity; not so the nights. Back at the cottage I had far too much time to brood. Several times I had asked the SB guys if there was any future in making some initiative on the hostage situation ourselves, trying to put out feelers, but the answer was always, 'No. The PIRA have got to move first. Unless, one of these days, a tout picks something up, or we get an intercept that gives us a line.'

Tired as I was, I found it hard to sleep – and the nightmares started again, similar to the one I'd had after the Gulf. Usually I was travelling fast through the dark, on a strange kind of roller-coaster or maybe a bike, until suddenly something grabbed me by the left arm, so that terrific forces threatened to tear me in half, setting up the most horrendous pain, and I'd wake up in a muck sweat, yelling with fright.

Soon there were only five days left before take-off. So far, everything had gone well. Then we had a set-back which caused aggravation and distress at the time but almost immediately bounced back to our advantage.

We'd gone out into one of our nearby training areas to try the quads fully loaded on rough terrain at night; our aim was to run through the main moves of the operation, using a range-hut as the target building. Having ridden to within walking distance we all tabbed forward to a wire fence. Pat and I then cut our way through,

66

leaving the rest of the guys on the barrier, two to guard the opening we'd made, two to lay diversionary charges four hundred metres to the east, in roughly the position occupied by the south gates of the Libyan camp.

The first stages all went according to plan. Pat and I made a covert approach to the building, broke in through a window, fired a couple of rounds through a Hun's-head target in one of the rooms, and then let off a stun grenade outside to indicate that things had gone noisy. As we were moving back to the fence, a big bang went off down the line, simulating the diversionary explosion, and we all legged it to the spot designated as our ERV.

So far, so good. But by then heavy rain had come on, and as we rode away in the dark the bikes began to slither around like snakes on the greasy grass. We were only using bags of sand as weights, but we'd measured them out and made sure that we had eighty pounds on the front rack and a hundred on the back, well strapped on. The loads certainly pushed the quads down on their suspension and made the steering heavier.

Coming downhill close to the lip of a ravine, Fred Parry, our lanky explosives star, hit a rock and skidded towards the edge. The crust of heathery peat broke away beneath his left-hand rear wheel, and a second later he and the bike were rolling over and over down the steep bank towards the stream.

He might have got away with it if it weren't for the lumps of rock sticking out from the sandy bank. By sheer bad luck the quad came down on him and pinned him against a rock that had no give in it, dealing his left leg a fearsome smack. He finished up face-down in some grass with the machine on top of him and the engine still running, wheels turning.

I'd been riding next in line, and there was just enough light for me to see him go arse over tip down the bank. In a flash I was off my own bike and running down towards the casualty.

Fred was pinned down by a handlebar in the small of his back. His right leg was straight, but my torch-beam showed that his left leg was bent out at a diabolical angle.

I yelled, 'Don't move!' and reached under the handlebar panel to switch off his ignition. The smell of petrol was everywhere. I had visions of a sudden *woof!* and the pair of us on fire.

Fred was just moaning, 'Shit! Shit! Shit! My fucking leg!'

'Keep still,' I told him again. With a big heave I rolled the bike off him, back on to its wheels. At that moment heads appeared against the sky on the rim of the ravine above, and somebody shouted, 'Get up, wanker!'

'Bollocks!' I yelled at them. 'He got a bad break. Get on the mobile for the chopper. Tell them the casualty's got a broken leg, high up. Femur or hip.'

I knelt down beside Fred. His eyes were screwed tightly shut. 'How is it?'

'Fucking horrible.' He tried to move and gave a groan.

'Stay how you are. It'll be better if we don't try to move you. The doc's on his way. He'll be here in twenty minutes.'

The other guys came down and gathered round, making sympathetic noises now. Since we were only training, we had only a limited medical pack to hand, and so couldn't give Fred anything to ease the pain. But we wrapped him in our sweaters to keep him warm and covered him with ponchos to throw the rain off. I stayed with him while the others recced round for a place at which the chopper could put down. The ravine was too narrow for the pilot to hover, and it was obvious we'd have to carry the casualty up on to more level ground; but I reckoned it was better to wait until the doc had put a shot of morphine into him and got the leg splinted.

As I chit-chatted to keep up his morale, the rest tied ropes on to the stranded quad. With one guy steering it and two bikes pulling from above, they heaved it up on to the open hillside. The fuel tank had been punctured on the top, presumably by impact with a rock, but apart from a few dents and scratches the machine still seemed in remarkably good nick. The rest of the guys then got their bikes deployed in a big circle, with their headlamps shining inwards, to make a pool of light on which the chopper could put down.

The recovery went without a hitch. In twenty-two minutes from call-out the standby Puma was overhead and settling towards the lighted patch. In a few more seconds Doc Palmer and his medic were beside the injured man with their bags of tricks. Within five minutes they had him hot to trot, well doped with morphine, his left leg secured in a pneumatic splint blown up like a giant condom, which held the broken limb snugly alongside the good one in the stretcher. While they were working we loaded the bent quad into the Puma and lashed it down. Then four of us carried Fred up out of the ravine and slid him on to the floor of the chopper. The last we saw of him, he was giving a cheerful wave as the helicopter lifted away.

On our way back to camp I felt depressed. With four days to go, we were a man down and urgently in need of a replacement. But then, as if Pat had intoned *Allah karim* ('God is good') a few hundred times, I found we had one: that afternoon, clearance had at last come through from Washington for Tony Lopez to join the team.

For me this was a big breakthrough, and it gave my morale a boost. Tony was the guy I wanted more than anyone else – partly because he too would recognise the target and remove any possibility of identification error, and partly because I knew he was a ferociously effective operator, veteran of many hairy operations in Panama and elsewhere. Having spent five weeks in gaol with him, I was absolutely confident that we could rub along together. Besides, he knew more about the Arab world than the rest of us put together, because, a couple of years before the Gulf, he'd run a SEAL team job in Abu Dhabi, instructing the local forces in weapon training and close-quarter battle techniques. Like Pat, he'd done a course in Arabic, and had a smattering of the language.

Until then I'd observed the letter of the law and hadn't given him (or anybody else) the slightest hint about what I was doing. I'd had to tell Fraser that I'd be abroad at the end of the week for six or seven days, but I hadn't said what the operation was or where it would take place.

Now, with the agreement of the ops officer, I was able to put Tony in the picture.

When he heard what the deal was, he leapt up and punched the air with loud whoops of 'Great fuckin' snakes!'

'You're going to have to do the explosives,' I warned him. 'That was poor old Fred's job.'

'No sweat!' he cried. 'I've blown the shit out of more goddamn automobiles, trucks, houses, trashcans, bridges and railway lines than you could ever imagine.'

For a more thorough briefing, we decided that he should come out to the cottage and cook a celebration dinner.

The enemy, however, had other plans. At six-thirty that evening I'd just reached home when the incident room rang to say that the PIRA had called what they thought was my own number. I was to return immediately.

Having scorched back, I listened with a mixture of rage and fascination to the brief tape recording.

'I'll speak to Geordie Sharp,' said a man with a strong Belfast accent.

'I'm sorry,' replied Karen, the Streisand girl, who was on duty, 'he's working at the moment.'

'Can I call him somewhere else?'

'Afraid not,' she said. 'He's out and about.'

'Who are you, then?'

'I'm looking after the house for him. Shall I get him to call you? Who's speaking, please?'

'Nobody he's heard of. What time will he be back?'

'What time is it now? I haven't got a watch.'

'Now? It's twenty-five past six.'

'Well . . . he said seven o'clock.'

'Half an hour, then?'

'That should be fine. Can I give him any message?'

'No. I'll call.'

'What name shall I tell him?'

'No name.'

'No name?'

'You can say Kevin.' And with that the man had switched off.

The call had been made from a mobile. From the way the signal came and went we were pretty sure he'd been in a car, driving around. He'd been on the air only a few seconds; Special Branch would have needed four or five minutes to DF him accurately. But at least there was now a chance of another call coming through for them to work on.

I listened to the tape three times. The twang of the accent – 'nay', almost 'nayee', for 'now' – took me straight back to Northern Ireland and the slimy, sleazy methods of the PIRA. In

70

particular I thought of the night when, lying in a ditch a few yards from an isolated farmhouse, I could have topped Farrell as he stood there bollocking some underlings for failing to go through with a shoot. I remembered how he'd roared 'Cunts!' at them, addressing them as though they were shit. The guy had been barely thirty yards from me. My companion and I could have dropped the whole group of players – but the head-shed had forbidden us to open fire because one of them was then the most valuable tout in business.

This guy on the tape had the same sort of peremptory, domineering manner. The way he'd started in – 'I'll speak to Geordie Sharp' – immediately put a stamp on him. There was no question of 'can I . . .?' or 'please', just arrogance and bluster.

'Christ!' I muttered. 'Just wait till the bastard comes through again. I'll sort him.'

'Take it easy, Geordie,' said Fraser, who'd come flying back into the incident room from the digs he'd taken in town. 'Whatever your feelings, it's no good getting stroppy with these people. They're always hoping to make you lose your rag, and if you do you play into their hands.'

I settled in to wait. The girl had said I'd be back in half an hour. Kevin, whoever he was, should call again around seven. I rang Tony and told him I'd been delayed. 'Why not go on out to the cottage and make yourself at home?' I suggested. 'You know where the key is – on the hook.'

'OK,' he agreed. 'I've been to the supermarket and got the stuff to cook something real good. I'll see you later.'

As I hung around, the SB girl, Karen, began to get on my tits again. I had to admit that she'd handled the call as well as anyone could have – she'd tried to keep the guy on the line, and given nothing away – yet there was something about her that annoyed me, an air of complacency that came over more in the way she looked and acted than in anything she said. She was wearing a track suit of dark-blue velvety material, and she seemed unable to keep still. She was forever looking at her nails, filing one of them for a second or two, bringing a mirror out of her handbag, tweaking at her eyebrows, patting her fair hair into place, all as if she was trying to attract attention. The trouble with her, I decided, is that she's too damned pleased with her looks. I also caught her staring at me a couple of times in a way that was strictly unoperational. I realised that she must have been bored to tears, sitting around day after day on her fanny with nothing happening, living in some dreary bed-and-breakfast dump away from her home, wherever that was. I knew I should have made an effort to chat her up and be friendly, but I just had too much on my mind.

Seven o'clock came and went. Seven-thirty, eight, eight-thirty.

Fraser could see I was getting more and more steamed up. 'Relax, Geordie,' he said. 'This is standard practice. They do it to wind you up. Don't fall for it. Stay cool.'

'It's OK for you,' I said. 'It isn't your kid they've got.'

'I know. But I do have a little girl about Tim's age. I can imagine what you're feeling.'

I'd been so wrapped up in my own problems that I'd never paused to think about Foxy's domestic circumstances. The news that he had a family made him seem suddenly more human. Looking at the lines on his forehead I thought, You must have started late, to have a daughter of four. And he, as if reading my mind, added, 'I didn't get married till I was thirty-seven.'

'Sorry,' I mumbled. 'I didn't mean anything personal.'

He smiled, and as he came past where I was sitting he gave me a bump on the arm with the heel of his hand.

At nine o'clock I rang Tony. 'Listen,' I said. 'The bastards haven't called. They're stringing us along.'

'Aw, shit. I've made a hell of a Mexican bean stew.'

'Go ahead and eat it, then. I don't know when I'll get back.'

'I'll keep some warm for you anyhow.'

'Thanks, Tony.'

It was nearly eleven when the call at last came through. I was sitting by the phone, but not wanting to appear too eager I let it ring five times before I picked up the receiver. Then I just said, 'Yes?'

'Geordie Sharp?'

'Yep.'

'I'm calling about your family.'

Was this the same voice as on the tape? I didn't think so. A Belfast accent, all right, but somehow different. The connection was brilliantly clear, as if the call was short-distance. I looked across at Fraser and raised a thumb.

'Kevin, is it?' I said.

'It is not. A friend of Kevin's.'

'Oh – right.'

'You're wanting them back.'

'Where are they?'

'I said, you're wanting them back. Are you not?'

'Of course.'

'You know what to do, then.'

'What?'

'Get our man out.'

'What man?'

'Declan Farrell.'

'Farrell?' I said. 'Who's he?'

'Look, if you want to see your little boy again, or your girlfriend, you'll not mess about.'

'Wait a minute. I don't know who you're talking about. Who is Farrell?'

'It's the man you were after murdering at Ballyconvil. You know him.'

'Bally-what? I never heard the name before. Where's this guy supposed to be?'

'The Brits have him.'

'What, in Belfast?'

'No, on the mainland.'

'What's happened? Is he in the nick or something?'

'In gaol, so he is.'

'What am I supposed to do about that?'

'Ask around. Find out where he's been put, and spring him.'

'But I'm army, not police. I don't have the contacts. Besides, I'm working. I don't have the time.'

'I said – ask around.'

'All right. Listen, I'll do what I can. Give me a couple of days. Then I'll get back to you.'

'You will not. I'll call you in two days' time. That's Thursday. Seven o'clock.'

'Hello?'

73

I was going to try and glean some scrap of information about how the hostages were, but the line had gone dead.

'Well done!' said Fraser keenly. 'That was great, the way you kept him on the air. Let's see what the boys have managed.'

A couple of minutes later we learnt that the call had been traced to a phone box in West Belfast. Of course, by the time the RUC arrived there the caller would have gone, but there was a chance of getting some fingerprints. The fact that the PIRA had rung from Northern Ireland alarmed me, as it seemed to work against Special Branch's theory that London was the most likely place for the hostages to be held. But Fraser remained unruffled, saying that, naturally, their spokesman would phone from Belfast wherever the prisoners were.

The exchange left me screwed up with a seething mixture of anger and frustration. The arrogance of the guy's manner had really pissed me off. That was bad enough, but almost worse was my own helplessness. What the hell could I do? If I'd lost my rag and called him a scumbag he'd merely have laughed. If I'd admitted I knew where Farrell was he'd have gone on saying, 'Get him out, then.'

Did the PIRA realise I'd been in Colombia and had been responsible for Farrell's capture? The caller had given no sign of knowing that, but it made little difference. Somehow the terrorists had established the connection between me and their big player, and little details – like the fact he was in a high-security prison – were not going to worry them.

Screw the nut, I told myself. Like Foxy says: stay cool.

It was midnight by the time I got home. I found Tony asleep on the settee in the sitting room with the TV burbling some crap about fitted wardrobes. Going in quietly I switched it off, got down behind the armchair and let out a loud yell – whereupon he leapt eight feet in the air and came down facing the door in an exaggerated crouch, as if to take on all comers.

'Great sentry you'd make,' I told him, rising into view.

'Boy!' he gasped. 'Did you give me a fright!'

'Have a drink. How about a Scotch?'

'You having one?'

'Sure. I need something after that.' While I poured two drinks I told him about the telephone contact. He brought out the remains of the bean stew he'd cooked with such care, and I ate it at the kitchen table – gratefully enough, though gasping a bit at the chillies – while I filled him in between mouthfuls on what had happened.

'This is driving me crazy,' I told him. 'There's no way we can get at them.'

'What are Special Branch doing?'

'Looking around and listening. Checking the movements of known players, going through their own records on the central computer. That's about all they can do. Tony – d'you think I'm crazy to go on this operation?'

'Not at all. You wouldn't achieve anything if you *didn't* go – except making yourself feel real bad.'

'That's true. But what if I get written off?'

'Might be the best way of getting the hostages released.'

I stared at him. 'You're joking.'

'Nope. I mean it. If you disappeared from the scene the terrorists' emotional blackmail would be at an end. They couldn't exert anywhere near the same pressure through anyone else. They'd probably just turn Tracy and Tim loose somewhere and call it a day.'

'You think so? Do the IRA ever release hostages?'

'Sure, if they've nothing to gain by holding them any longer. I was talking to Fraser about it this morning.'

'But Tracy's seen their people. She knows several faces by now.'

'Nobody important.'

'In that case,' I said, 'next time they come through, maybe the word should be that I'm dead and they've missed the boat. Anyway . . . sod that. Let's talk about the operation.'

I opened out a large-scale map of north-east Africa and spread it on the table. The area for which we were heading was an extension of Egypt's Western Desert, birthplace of the Regiment during the Second World War. It was there that David Stirling had formed his Long-Range Desert Group, from which the SAS had emerged, and created havoc by blowing up aircraft far behind enemy lines. It was there also that Jack Sillito had made the most famous escape in SAS history, tabbing more than a hundred miles through the desert after he had been cut off behind the German forces.

'What the hell did he do for water?' Tony asked.

'Good question. Some people reckon he drank his own piss. Others say he managed on condensation that formed at night in old jerricans. Either way, it was some feat.'

Talk of this and other exploits carried us into the small hours. We also pored over the map to discuss our route to the target. From the Egyptian airfield at Siwa, a Chinook was due to lift us over the border and then due west across 300 kilometres of empty desert. The map showed the single MSR running from Ajdabiya in the north-west to a place called Al Jawf, 800 kilometres out in the Sahara to the south-east. Once we crossed over that we'd be within striking distance of our drop-off point, and the chopper would land us only sixty kilometres short of our objective.

'Funny, having another Al Jawf just there,' I said. 'That was the name of the place where we had our FMB in Saudi.'

'It means "interior",' said Tony. 'It can also mean a hole or depression, but down there I guess it's the interior. I expect there's dozens of Al Jawfs, if you look around. Hell of a place we're going.' He jabbed a forefinger at the map, indicating the vast empty spaces, unmarked by roads, towns or any other sign of civilisation. 'Nothing for hundreds of miles.'

'I know. But you know as well as I do: the biggest hazard's going to be wandering goatherds. If Iraq's anything to go by, the Libyan desert'll be full of the bastards too. They arrive out of nowhere, just when you least want them. And then, if they see you, you're faced with a bad decision. If you let them go they tell someone else there are nasties about; if you top them their friends come looking.'

In the incident room next morning the idea of my disappearing from the scene went down like a lead balloon. Fraser reckoned that if I vanished, the PIRA's response might easily be to knock the hostages off and make the bodies disappear.

'Forget that,' he said. 'What we need is a controlled release of information to keep them in play. Next time they come on the line, tell them a little bit about Farrell. Tell then you've found out that they're right: he *is* in gaol, and you're trying to discover where.'

'I see the point,' I agreed. 'But look, as I told you, I'm off abroad on Sunday for a week. What happens while I'm away?'

76

'I've been thinking about that. I'd like to find someone with a similar accent, and have him stand in for you. We can brief him up on what to say.'

I didn't like the sound of that. Again, it would increase the chances of a cock-up. But I couldn't really hold out against it. 'Well,' I said, 'there's no shortage of Geordies in the Regiment. I can think of two others straight away.'

Then I had an inspiration. 'Listen – I know the man you want: Billy Bracewell, a staff sergeant on G Squadron. He was in command of the QRF that got us out of the jungle in Colombia. He saw Farrell when we captured him – flew back with him to the forward base, in fact. He can talk about him better than anyone.'

So Billy was roped in to impersonate me if the occasion arose.

But for the whole of Thursday and Friday my mind was in turmoil with a new idea. In the Wing, on the range, in the laundry, in the gym, in town, at the cottage . . . no matter where I was or what I was doing, I could think of nothing else. The first time I'd run up against Farrell, in Ulster, it had proved impossible to top him in legitimate operations, and in the end I had reached the conclusion that the only way to get him was to go after him on my own – which was what I did. Now I'd begun to think that my only hope of recovering Tim and Tracy might lie in another extra-mural effort. I knew Farrell was in Winson Green. If I could discover the routine there – or, better still, find out when the prisoner was going to be moved somewhere, possibly for a court hearing – I and a few of the lads might be able to ambush the police convoy, spring him, and hand him back to the PIRA. We could buy an old banger for a couple of hundred quid cash, or even steal one, and ram the police van with it, then use one of our own cars with phoney licence plates for the getaway. The activity would be criminal, I realised – but when you're growing desperate, as I was, you think up desperate measures.

I didn't want to involve Tony in such a wild scheme, because if anything went wrong it would bring his service with the SAS to an abrupt end. Pat Newman, though, was a different matter. He was eighteen months older than me, and already talking of leaving the Regiment when he'd completed ten years (in a few months' time), so he had less to lose.

77

That Wednesday evening I waylaid him and suggested we went for a pint at the Crooked Billet, a pub out in the country not much frequented by our lads. There we got stuck into a corner of the public bar, which contained nobody else but one typical old Herefordshire cider-head, with a face as purple as a beetroot and greasy hair half-way down his back.

I started in talking about details of our imminent operation. I noticed Pat giving me the eyeball in a peculiar way, and after a while I stopped. 'What's the matter?' I asked. 'Don't you want to hear all this?'

'Yeah, yeah,' he went. 'It's just that Yorky asked me to keep a close eye on you, make sure you didn't try to run out.'

'For fuck's sake! Who said I was going to run out?'

'Nobody, but he wasn't sure you were really on for Libya. He told me to chat you up about it, keep you on side.'

'Thanks, mate.'

'I didn't, though. Did I?'

'Not a word. Good on yer, Pat. But, Christ, what bastards they are! Always trying to get round your back and put pressure on from behind.'

'Forget it, anyway.'

'All right.' So I switched to talk about my new plan.

Pat's reaction was forthright. He put down his mug, stared at me incredulously, and said, 'Geordie, you're fucking *mad*! The strain of this thing is getting to you. That's the craziest idea I've ever heard. Even if we managed to spring the guy from the convoy we'd all be nicked. There'd only be a few of us against hundreds of coppers. What are we supposed to do? Shoot our way out and leave a trail of corpses? It's not as if we're in bloody Ulster. It might be different if we could mobilise a whole army – but Christ! No: think of it. The thing would end in a pitched fucking battle, a civil war.'

'Well, if we did it at night we'd have a better chance of getting away with it.'

Pat shook his head and said, 'They don't take star prisoners to court at dead of night. Forget it, mate. I know they've got you over a barrel, and I'm sorry for you, but this is *not* the way out.'

'For "barrel" read "Farrell",' I said savagely. 'I just hope the bastard's rotting in gaol. I hope his wounds have turned gangrenous. By the sound of it, they have: I hear he's quite sick. He's got a ban on visitors too.'

'Oh? How's that?'

'Foxy Fraser told me. The first guy who went to see him got searched on the way in, like all visitors are, and they found something on him – an escape kit he was trying to smuggle in. That was the end of that.'

'So the feller never made it?'

I shook my head. But for all the cold water that Pat had poured, I couldn't abandon my idea. Maybe if I got together a few guys who'd left the Regiment recently, a few old hands . . . What I needed first was inside information about Winson Green – and as I thought about this problem I had a brainwave. A former member of the SAS, Jim Roberts, whom I'd known, had joined the prison service as some kind of welfare officer. Maybe if I found out where he was, he would give me some leads.

One certain fact was that I didn't have time to get anything going before Operation Ostrich went down. There were only two days left before take-off, and both were hectic with last-minute preparations. I therefore said no more to Pat, except that I told him not to mention my madcap scheme to anyone.

For me, the next hurdle that needed clearing was the second PIRA call, due on Thursday evening. Together with Foxy Fraser I'd worked out more or less what I was going to say. As far as he knew, the ideas I suggested were not an action plan but pure fantasy, designed to keep the PIRA interested; there was no way Foxy could tell that I was seriously considering putting my scheme into practice.

'Excellent!' he said several times when I proposed intercepting a police convoy. 'Capital. I like it.'

It seemed highly unlikely that the PIRA would meet the deadline of seven o'clock, but I got down to the incident room on time, just in case. Once again Karen was on the desk, wearing the same slinky tracksuit, and she gave me one of her flirtatious sideways looks as I came in. Also present was Billy Bracewell, fair-haired and beefy, my alter ego, who'd come to listen in to what was said and tune in to my reactions.

To everyone's amazement, my home line rang at seven-fifteen, barely quarter of an hour late. This time I waited for the caller to speak. There was a pause of several seconds before a man said, 'Hello?'

'Yep,' I went, very curt.

'Is that Geordie Sharp?'

'Yep.'

'What news?'

'You're right. Farrell's in this country.'

'Where?'

'Winson Green.'

'Where's that?'

'Birmingham.'

'Jaysus! What have they put him there for?'

'Don't ask me.'

The way the man had hesitated before asking 'Where's that?' made me certain he already knew where Farrell was. That was why I gave him the true answer: otherwise he might never have trusted me again.

Presently he went, 'Well?'

'Well what?'

'What are you doing about getting him out?'

'Listen, Kevin. Kevin, is it?'

'It is. Go on, now.'

'I've been thinking. To spring him from gaol would need a fucking army. I've got a few lads lined up, but we can't muster that strength.'

'So?'

'The way to do it is to wait till he's being moved. Wait till he's outside the gaol, on his way to court or something. He's on remand at the moment, but soon they'll have to take him to court to charge him. Then we may be able to hit the convoy and do a snatch.'

'Good. That sounds better. So when's he going to court?'

'I'm trying to find out. The preliminary hearing's bound to be soon. I can get a question to one of the screws who works in the prison through the father of one of my mates. He's retired, but he used to be a screw as well. He's abroad at the moment, back at the weekend. I'll get news then.'

'Fair enough. Is your contact on the hospital wing?'

80

'I don't think so. But even if he isn't he'll know the guys who are.'

'All right. But you need to get a move on. Your family's deteriorating.'

'What d'you mean?'

'They're missing you. Listen to this.'

I heard a couple of clicks, then a hissing noise. I realised the guy had turned on a small tape recorder and was holding the mouthpiece to the loudspeaker. Suddenly I heard Tracy's voice, shaky and peculiar: 'Geordie,' she said, 'for God's sake do something to get us out. For God's sake . . .' Then came more hissing, and suddenly Tim's voice: 'Daddy, I don't like it here. I want to come home.'

That was all he said, but it nearly cracked me up. 'Hello!' I called loudly. 'Tim! Hello!'

'Seven o'clock on Monday, then,' said the Belfast voice.

Suddenly everything was too much. '*Hey, cunt!*' I shouted. '*Give me my kid back!*'

The line had gone dead. 'FUCKING ARSEHOLES!' I yelled. I crashed the receiver down so hard that it split the cradle of the phone clean in half. The whole instrument disintegrated in an explosion of grey plastic. In a surge of frustration I hurled over the table and sent a shower of files cascading to the floor.

Fraser and Bates were standing back against one wall, both looking shocked by the violence of my outburst. Fraser was speaking into another phone, and I heard him saying urgently, 'Mobile, moving around in the Ealing area of West London.'

Bates came forward and laid a hand on my shoulder, muttering, 'Take it easy, Geordie.'

I fought down a wild instinct to belt him one, so furious did I feel. I shook off his hand and said, 'Ah, get away!' Then I took a grip of myself and apologised.

'That's all right,' Bates said gently. 'I know how you feel.'

When I recovered I found SB much encouraged, as though they'd got a breakthrough. The fact that the call had come from the area they'd been predicting raised everyone's hopes.

People filtered away into the room next door, and as I sat there on a kind of bar-stool in front of a counter, still feeling stunned, I became aware that Karen had come up close and was standing right behind me.

'You look creased,' she said quietly. 'Would you like me to come out and cook supper for you? Or you could come to my place . . .'

I tensed myself, unwilling to believe my ears. The woman was making a proposition. I nearly spun round and belted her away with the back of my hand, but I held myself in check and grunted, 'Thanks, but I'm all right.'

'Sure? I'd really like to. You could stay the night if you wanted. There's a spare room. Or, as I said, I could cook supper at the cottage.' As she spoke she leant forward to pick up the telephone, deliberately brushing her breasts against my shoulder blades.

I should have stood up and walked away; I knew what she was after, and wanted nothing to do with her. But I was in such a low state that I sat tight and said, 'All right, then. Maybe I *would* be glad of company. Let's go to the cottage. There's plenty of food in the freezer.'

'I'll get something fresh on the way out of town,' she said. 'Half an hour?'

Everything went fine at first. Karen drove her Fiesta back to her digs and changed into a white frock with blue polka dots on it, which made her look very feminine. Then she dived into the supermarket and came out with a couple of steaks and some stir-fry vegetables. Having showered and changed while she was on the way, I dug out a bottle of red wine from the cupboard under the stairs and sat at the kitchen table chatting while she cooked.

We ate, and it was all harmless enough. She seemed genuinely sympathetic, and when she asked about my family background I found it a relief to describe how, after getting wounded and captured in Iraq, I'd found it impossible to settle back in with Kath, how I'd hit the bottle, and become so difficult to live with that a trial separation seemed the only answer.

'The worst thing of all was that she'd agreed to come back,' I said. 'I was on the up again. When I rang and suggested we got back together it was all she wanted to do. Another week, and she'd have come . . . Then that bastard Farrell sent his young feller with the bomb.'

'Tough,' Karen agreed. 'Really tough. But what's so special about Tracy?'

At that point I should have scented danger. But the words weren't said in an aggressive tone, and I took them at face value.

'Well, she was fantastic. She just took over the house and became a foster-mother to Tim.'

'Right away?'

'No . . . after a decent interval.'

'How did you meet her?'

'She'd been around for ages. She was working as one of the receptionists in the Med Centre.'

'Obviously you fancied her.'

'What d'you mean? Everyone fancied her. Guys positively looked forward to reporting sick with some minor ailment, just so they could chat her up.'

'But what *is* it about her?'

I wasn't going to say that her gloriously long legs turned me on, or that she did wild things in bed. I just told her, 'She's a gassy person. Always full of jokes. She's great at making stupid remarks that crack me up.'

'So you're planning to get married?'

'That's on the cards.' I wasn't going to mention the baby to this inquisitive cow.

'You must have made advances,' she said abruptly.

That *did* jar, and I retorted, 'What's that got to do with you?'

Karen didn't answer but stood up, walked across to her handbag and brought out a cigarette, which she lit. That pissed me off as well. I don't like people smoking in my house, especially without asking.

'Is there any more wine?' she asked.

'Sorry, that's it. I just had the one bottle.'

'How about a Scotch, then?'

'You oughtn't to; you've got to drive back.'

'Oh, one won't hurt. Not after all that food.'

'Help yourself, then.'

'What about you?'

'No, thanks.'

She moved across to the dresser, took down a glass and the bottle of Haig, and poured herself a measure. I wasn't chuffed with that, either. She did it with her back to me, trying to conceal the amount she was taking, but I sneaked a glimpse and saw that it was three fingers at least. Then she ran some water into the glass and came back to the table.

Instead of livening her up, the spirit made her morose. I tried to draw her out about her own background, but she seemed reluctant to discuss it and, beyond the facts that she was twenty-six and came from Norwich, I learnt practically nothing. It sounded as though she had no steady boyfriend, and never kept one for long. 'My career,' she kept saying. 'It's all down to my career.'

By eleven o'clock she wasn't making much sense, but still she needled away about my relationship with Tracy. I kept my cool and fended her off with non-committal remarks, until suddenly I'd had enough. At that point I stood up and said, 'Look, Karen, thanks for coming. I'm grateful to you for keeping me company, but it's time to break up the party. You can't drive back in that state. You'd better get your head down in Susan's room and go back to town in the morning.'

'Shushan?' she said. 'Who's that?'

'The friend who's been sharing the house with Tracy.'

'Another of these smashing red-heads, I suppose.'

'Don't be stupid. Come on, now.'

'Washing up,' she slurred.

'It can wait. Leave it. I'll find you a towel.'

I ran up the stairs three at a time, and saw her clawing at the banisters as she came up behind me. On the landing I switched on the light in the spare room and said, 'Here you are. The bed's made up. The bathroom's next door – there. It's all yours.'

I half expected her to make a grab at me because she'd previously shown such obvious signs of sexual frustration. But she simply said, 'Good night then, and thanks,' and went into the room, closing the door behind her.

Five minutes later I locked my own bedroom door and crashed out, so exhausted that I went straight to sleep. The next thing I knew, somebody was knocking on the door. For a moment I couldn't think who the hell it was. Then I struggled up on one elbow and called, 'What's the matter?'

'It's me – Karen.'

'What's the problem?'

'There's water dripping.'

'For Christ's sake! Forget it. I expect the roof tank's filling up.'

'No, this is coming through the ceiling somewhere.'

Ah, hell, I thought. But I said, 'OK. Wait one, I'll have a look.'

I pulled on a bath-robe and opened the door. As I went to step out on to the landing I walked straight into Karen. She was standing in the doorway stark naked. In an instant one arm was round my neck and the other hand going for my crotch. Instinctively I brought up a knee and bumped her in the groin, whereupon she gave a scream and threw herself at me like a lunatic. I don't know if you've ever been attacked in the dark by a naked, sex-starved female – but it's quite an experience, I can tell you. Half the time I was trying not to get myself ripped and scratched, and the rest I was trying not to hurt her; but inevitably, as we wrestled, I kept getting a handful of this and that, with the result that she became still more desperate.

On me, the effect was anything but arousing. All I could think of were those terrible women brought into escape and evasion exercises to humiliate students who get captured, stripped and interrogated. When a guy's naked and at his lowest ebb, one of these old slappers comes in and starts insulting him with remarks like, 'Is that an acorn you've got stuck between your legs? I can hardly see it.' That was how I felt when I was pushing Karen around. She had a firm, meaty body, and in easier circumstances might have been a great lay – I could feel that all right – but she turned me on about as much as did the idea of Farrell and the IRA.

Things finished up with me getting her in a double half-Nelson and giving her a couple of slaps on the rump, whereupon she burst into tears.

'For Christ's sake!' I said. 'Go back to bed or go home, I don't care which. If the cops get you on the way, that's your lookout. But just stop bothering me.'

Those were the last words we had. I re-locked my door and eventually fell asleep again, and at about half-past six I heard her car start up outside. When I went to shave and looked at myself in the mirror, I saw I had a couple of scratches down one temple, and straight away I began to think of a way of explaining them to the lads.

SIX

As at the start of any operation, the guys were tense and quiet, exchanging the odd bit of chit-chat while we waited for the off, but thinking all the time of what lay ahead and wondering what they might have failed to pack.

Whinger was dragging on one of his filthy, home-rolled fags. He'd had an amazing haircut that left his head covered with short, tow-coloured fuzz and made him look like a coconut. To everyone's amazement Norm had shaved off his moustache, on the grounds that a Mexican appearance might not do him much good if the Libyans caught him. ('You never know,' said Tony, who'd picked up the vibes of the team very quickly, 'it may loosen his tongue. By the time we make it into the desert he'll be talking his head off.') Stew, also, had had a fancy haircut – a flat-top job, in imitation of Tony – and was taking stick from everyone about his girlfriend.

'Managed to slip her a length, did you?' sneered Whinger.

'Bollocks, mate.'

'You mean she wouldn't have it? Must be your technique that's at fault. Puts the wind up her something chronic.'

'Take her by surprise,' said Norm – and I thought, By God, Tony's right!

'Belay her to the bed-head,' I suggested. 'Then she wouldn't have much option.'

Poor Stew had gone red as a beetroot, and I lifted my chin at Whinger to say, 'Hey, leave him alone.' As for me, I kept thinking uneasily of my best-of-three-falls with Karen, and hoping she wouldn't try to take it out on me while I was away. But to have mentioned that episode to the lads would have made my life not worth living, so I kept mum.

Now it was operational details that mattered. I'd already made one last check to ensure that everyone was properly sterilised – that is, not carrying anything, however insignificant, which might betray our origins if any of us was killed or captured. One box of matches, a chocolate-bar wrapper, a bank note or coin, an envelope, a label on a shirt-collar or the tongue of a boot – any of these would be enough to give us away. In keeping with Regimental practice, preparation had been left to individuals, and nobody had done anything so old-fashioned as line the team up for inspection: I'd just asked everyone to make doubly sure he was clean.

As for me, I made yet another mental check of my possessions: AK-47, spare magazines, Browning, spare mags, Semtex, detonators, det cord, clackers, Magellan, covert radio, torch, spare batteries, camera, binos, Commando knife, PNGs, ski goggles, medical kit, water-bottles, food, extra fuel, cam-net, poles, shovel, sand-bags, shamag. My only personal item was a tiny silver St Christopher, given me by Tracy, which I wore on a chain round my neck. Seeing it one evening in the shower, Tony had suggested I'd do well to leave it behind; but I pointed out that no Arab would know what it was, except some kind of good-luck charm, and therefore it wasn't a risk. By then I was really attached to the little figure, which seemed to have protected me in Colombia, and with things being how they were I wanted to preserve any possible connection with Tracy and Tim.

Our departure from Hereford was by no means routine. Except for a few small items in day-sacks, all our kit, including weapons and ammunition, was packed and strapped down on to the quads or in the trailer, and we didn't intend to touch it again until we were over Libya, about to come out of the chopper and start driving towards our target. We were wearing desert DPM fatigues with Parachute Regiment berets, so that as we staged through Cyprus we could pass as umpires taking part in Exercise Bright Star; but we carried no money, no passports, and no means of identification. Our desert clothes had been packed up in one large bundle, and we planned to change into them once we'd taken off from Akrotiri on the last leg of the flight. We all had shamags to wrap around our heads, and our shirts and trousers were the kind of cheap cotton, drab olive or grey or brown, that low-grade Arabs wear to work.

An intelligence update during the past few hours had reduced our window of opportunity to a dangerously narrow span. Some bright int guy had belatedly realised that the Arab weekend consists of Thursday and Friday, rather than Friday and Saturday as our briefing had laid down. This meant that our target might well leave the camp on Wednesday afternoon or evening. Since we weren't going to reach our location until very late on Monday night we'd have only Tuesday night on which to get him.

We'd just taken this news aboard when yet another update came in, emanating from the sleeper-agent within Ajdabiya itself. This last message said that al-Khadduri had a very important visitor coming to see him for secret discussions on Thursday morning, so that he'd definitely be around on the Wednesday night. That evened the score a bit – it gave us two possible chances – but the tightening of our schedule naturally made my adrenalin flow all the faster. And of course, the sooner we got through our business in the desert, the sooner I'd be back to sort out the mess at home.

The quads went on ahead by four-tonner, and a minibus collected us at 1530. For me, leaving camp seemed like an echo of the recurrent dream in which my left arm kept getting caught and dragged backwards; although I was departing in the general direction of North Africa, part of my mind was stuck fast in Hereford, anchored there by the fact that Tim and Tracy were in enemy hands. As we drove off eastwards, I felt as if the knowledge was tearing me apart.

At RAF Lyneham, Hercs were lumbering off the runway every few minutes, and a whole line of them was drawn up on the pan, but one aircraft stood apart from the rest in a distant corner of the field. We drove straight out to it, and found that our bikes had already been loaded. The trailer had been backed in first, and the quads had been strapped down to rings in the steel deck, facing the tail-gate in a zig-zag line so that we could ride them straight out when the time came.

The flight crew greeted us like old pals. Pineapple Pete was his imperturbable self, and Alf the head loadie – a huge guy with arms covered in tattoos – gave me a run-down of all the units taking part in the exercise.

'You lot are never part of it,' he said teasingly.

'Of course we are. Can't miss out on the chance of getting ourselves some decent suntans.'

Although Alf didn't say any more he winked, and I saw that he knew we were up to some special villainy.

In spite of the high level of activity everyone seemed relaxed and happy. Our take-off was scheduled for 1830, and at 1810, as Pete and his co-pilot walked out, I fell in with them.

'Once we're airborne you're welcome up front any time,' Pete said. 'Make yourself at home.'

I thanked him and climbed into the back, where the lads hadn't waited for any invitation but had been busy slinging para-silk hammocks from the cargo nets on the sides of the fuselage.

Soon the engines were turning and burning, but we could tell at once that something was wrong: one of the motors kept back-firing, and ran so rough that after a while the crew shut all four down. A few minutes later they tried again, but the result was the same: one explosion after another shook the aircraft. Eventually, after a second shut-down, word came over the intercom that we were to abandon ship.

'This fucker's no better than a heap of scrap metal,' said Pete contemptuously as he stood on the tarmac and kicked one of the aircraft's tyres. 'I'm not flying the bastard anywhere, least of all to the middle of bloody Egypt.'

To the consternation of the movements officer he demanded another Herc immediately – and so forcefully did he state the importance of our deployment that after only half an hour he got one taken off the main exercise rota and seconded to us. Naturally that left someone else in the shit, but it was no business of ours.

Then, of course, all the paperwork had to be re-done and the load transferred. Among our own guys there was a good deal of honking as they dismantled their sleeping accommodation and bundled it away – but after a delay of two hours we were at last airborne and on our way.

The noise in the back of a Herc – a high, ringing scream – is so punishing that talking requires a major effort. The result was that nobody bothered to make conversation. Anyone who wanted could pull on one of the head-sets dangling from the sides of the fuselage and listen in to the crew, but that soon palled and we generally preferred to get our heads down, aiming to doze or sleep the seven-hour flight away.

A couple of hours out I started worrying about our late take-off, because our timings on the following night were going to be critical. I suspected that after the long haul to Cyprus the crew would have to have a regulation break. Then there'd be a three-hour flight to Siwa, the Egyptian military base – and we needed to be there by early evening, so that we could do a quick transfer to the chopper and be on the ground within reach of our objective while there were still several hours of darkness ahead.

Sweating about it, I headed for the flight deck to ask the skipper what the drill was. Up there, everything seemed pleasantly relaxed; the atmosphere was less claustrophobic than in the back, the noise level much lower. With the plane on autopilot, Pete and his co-pilot sat chatting over their head-sets, and through the windshield a vast array of stars was visible above us, with the lights of some German town twinkling far below.

'Fear not,' said the skipper when I put my question to him. 'We can fly, and remain on duty, for up to sixteen hours at a stretch. If you want we could take you straight on to your destination with only an hour to refuel. It's up to you.'

'No, no,' I said. 'We're not that pushed. Let's stick to the schedule. I'd rather come into Siwa just on dark, in case there are eyes around the airfield. Christ knows what the security's like on Egyptian bases. As long as we're there by 2100, we'll be fine.'

'OK, then. Our ETA in Akrotiri is now 0330 Zulu. That's 0630 local. Siwa's an hour behind that. If you don't want to be there before dusk we won't need to take off until 2000 local. That'll put us into Siwa at about 2200, by which time it should be good and dark. That suit you?'

'Perfect.'

'In that case, I'll put in for a departure slot at 2000.' He scribbled a note on his knee-pad.

Reassured, I went back, pulled on some ear-defenders and got my head down like everyone else. The next thing I knew, I heard the engine-note dropping as we began our descent into Akrotiri. After a landing smooth as silk, Pete taxied off to a secure area at one corner of the airfield and we stumbled out into a beautiful dawn.

The sky was clear, the air warm but still fresh, with sharp, lemony scents all around.

'Who's for a peach?' said Whinger, giving an almighty yawn.

'Peach?' said Pat. 'What the fuck are you on about?'

'The beach, cunt.'

'To hell with the beach,' Tony told him. 'What about a shower and breakfast?'

Taking our day-sacks, we bussed across to the sergeants' mess, showered, and got ourselves big fry-ups. Then, and all day, we kept close together in a group, discouraging approaches and questions from outsiders. We were given basic accommodation – bare rooms with two bunks in each – and so spent most of the time in or around the mess. Everybody was eager to spruce up their tans, which the English spring had hardly got going, but by mid-morning the sun was seriously hot and I cautioned the guys about getting burnt. Not that they really needed any warning; because they'd all served abroad in hot countries, they knew that if they did go down with sunburn it would be their own fault and they could be put on a charge, just as if they'd got drunk or caught a dose of clap.

Even if we'd wanted to, we couldn't have left the base – partly for security reasons, but mainly because there was always a chance our departure time might be brought forward. So the lads screwed the nut on any idea of looking for amusement, and accepted that this was just a steady day.

We spent much of the morning going through our plans in an informal O-group, sitting on the concrete floor of an unfinished building which had a roof but no walls, so that plenty of air drifted across it. In particular we confirmed the six away-points, or emergency rendezvous – the points in the desert south of Ajdabiya we'd head for if we were forced to split up – which we'd already punched into our Magellan GPS sets. These were designated 'ERV One, ERV Two' and so on. They existed only in our minds, and there were no marks on any of our 1:50,000 maps, but those sets of figures could easily prove life-savers.

We also concentrated on correlating the latitude and longitude readings punched into the Magellans with the old-fashioned grid-system on the maps. The lat–long figures were more accurate, and there was always a chance that the batteries in the GPS sets would fail or that there'd be a shortage of satellites overhead at some critical moment. If either of those things happened, we'd be forced back on to the more primitive navigational system of grid-references and compasses.

Our Herc remained under guard where it had come to rest, and it attracted no attention because the field was dotted with similar planes, landing and taking off all day as they ferried personnel and stores southwards towards Egypt and the exercise. Soon after midday a bowser-truck went across to refuel ours, and when it was clear we walked back to the plane to break out the bundle of desert clothes; but we soon spewed out of the cargo bay cursing horrendously, because with its tail-gate closed the aircraft had heated up like an oven, the inside temperature had soared well into three figures – and we decided the job could wait until we were airborne that evening.

It was at lunchtime that we hit a problem. At the far end of the long mess hall Stew spotted someone he'd known pretty well in his parent regiment, the Cheshires. We realised that they must be acting as marshals on the base for the duration of the exercise, and that this created a serious risk that somebody would recognise him and start asking questions – potentially a major disaster, and a prospect which haunted all members of the SAS on covert operations. All Stew could do was slip away as soon as he'd finished his meal and lie low in the room he'd been allocated until it was time to leave.

For the rest of us, the best feature of the sergeants' mess was the supply of fresh oranges. We reckoned they must have come straight off the trees on the island, because they tasted a hundred times sweeter and fresher than any orange we'd had before. A great big basket of them stood at the end of the counter, and after Pat had eaten four, straight down, I said to him, 'Watch it, mate, or you'll have the runs.'

'Last vitamin C for a week,' he retorted as he put away yet another – and we all pouched a couple to eat during the next leg of the journey.

This time our departure ran smoothly, and within a minute or two of take-off we were heading south-east over the Mediterranean. As soon as we were in level flight we sorted out our civilian clothes and changed into them, bundling up our DPMs for return to Cyprus. Our desert gear smelled musty and unfamiliar – Christ alone knew who had worn the stuff last. Whinger yelled that his shirt stank like an Arab's jock-strap, and Stew shouted back, 'It'll stink of you soon enough.' My own shirt wasn't much better, and I shook myself around inside the drab, buff material to get the feel of it. The shirt, a pair of sand-coloured trousers and a thin grey jersey were all I reckoned I'd need.

Our makeshift hammocks had remained in place, so we climbed back into them and lay there in the dim light, ear-defenders in place, each thinking his own thoughts. Mine were of Tim and Tracy – and in particular the boy's paintings I'd found in the desk at home. There was one I remembered in detail: a tank blowing up, with a brilliant, jagged flash of flame all round it and some spiky wrecks of shattered trees in the background. Where could a kid of four have picked up such violent images? Only from the TV, or maybe from listening to me talk about the Gulf. I wished he'd get interested in nature and try drawing the things like squirrels and rabbits that he saw every day. Perhaps when he was older.

And right now? I had a sudden, horrible thought that his captors would be trying to indoctrinate him against me, teaching him foul language and filthy ideas. I remembered how kids his age in Belfast shout 'Fucking pigs!' whenever they see a Brit soldier come past, and hoped to hell that the PIRA wouldn't have time to corrupt Tim's mind in that way.

After a while, unable to relax let alone sleep, I went up on the flight deck, and I was there when we crossed the Egyptian coast. Far off to our left a spread of lights was twinkling hazily in the dusk.

'Alexandria,' said the skipper.

Beneath the nose the odd cluster of lights marked smaller towns along the shore, and the occasional flares we saw were from oil wells burning off gas; but beyond them, inland, the desert stretched away black as night, with nothing to break its monotony. At this point our target lay about eight hundred kilometres away to the east. Pity we can't just fly across and drop a bomb on the bastard, I thought – and I was on the point of saying as much to Pete when I remembered that he knew nothing of our operation, and had been too professional to make the smallest enquiry about what we were up to.

So for the time being I returned to my hammock, but half an hour later Pete called me back to the flight deck to say he'd been in touch with an RAF liaison officer in the control tower at Siwa.

'Your Chinook's ready for you,' he said. 'God knows where it's come from, but it's parked on a pan near the western perimeter of the airfield. As soon as we hit the deck they're going to send out a vehicle to lead us to it.'

'That's excellent. Will there be other Hercs on the field?'

'Absolutely. It's just like Akrotiri. The place is heaving with them – all part of Bright Star.'

'That's what the chopper's been on too,' I said. 'Officially it's gone tits-up and been retired sick from the exercise for a few days.'

Full darkness had fallen by the time we began our descent. The loadies helped us unshackle the quads and get ourselves organised. Without head-sets on it was impossible to hear spoken orders, so Big Alf, who was listening in to the flight deck, resorted to his usual system of hand-signals as we were coming in.

At five minutes to touch-down he gave us five fingers outspread, then three two minutes later. With two minutes to go we started our engines and sat there with the quads ticking over, ski goggles on in case grit flew about when we landed. With all the noise it was hard to tell if the individual engines were still running, so I reached down with my right hand to feel my exhaust. Exhaust fumes began to fill the hold, but before they built up to a serious level we were getting one finger. I realised I needed a piss, but told myself it would have to wait.

The top half of the tail-gate rose slowly, letting in a rush of warm, fresh air, and with it an even fiercer engine scream. Through the rectangular opening we could see lights shining from latticed towers and vehicles moving. Then, with a thump, the plane was on the deck and rolling.

The bottom half of the tail-gate began to go down while we were still taxiing. The Herc made a couple of turns, left and right – I guessed it was following a lead vehicle – and we had barely come to a standstill before Alf was waving us off. First down the ramp was Tony, and the rest of us followed swiftly in single file, Stew and his trailer bringing up the rear.

Outside, the first thing that hit me was the smell of an African settlement, the inevitable stink of heat and drains and dust hanging in the hot night air. The Chinook was within fifty metres of us, tail-gate down, rotors whirling. In seconds all six quads were at the bottom of the ramp, and we leapt off to manhandle the trailer backwards up the slope – first on, last off. Then, one after another, with Stew leading, we reversed into the belly of the chopper and parked in another zig-zag alongside the big, black rubber sausage of an extra fuel tank.

Our new head loadie was sitting in the hatchway of the partition that separates the hold from the flight-deck. He twisted round to get a look at us, and the moment I gave him the thumbs-up he hit the button to raise the ramp. He also passed word to the pilot, who immediately revved up his engines, put on pitch and lifted away.

The transfer couldn't have been accomplished any faster. I didn't believe that anyone could have seen us, but even so for the first few minutes the captain headed due south, to confuse anyone who might be watching, and made sure that he was out of sight before he swung on to an easterly heading. When I waved at the cockpit to indicate that I wanted to make contact, the head loadie pointed to a head-set, which I plugged into a socket on the wall.

I had to think for a moment who our new skipper was. Then I remembered him and his crew coming to Hereford. Of course: it was Steve Tanner, another Geordie, a small, dark fellow with sticking-out ears.

'Evening, Steve,' I went. 'Geordie Sharp here.'

'Hi, Geordie,' came the reassuring voice. 'Good to have you aboard. We've crossed the border already. Welcome to sunny Libya.'

'Great! That was a neat pick-up.'

'Not too bad.'

'What's our flight time?'

'We're estimating one hour fifty. There's no wind to speak of, so you should be on your location just after midnight.'

'That'll do well. Can we just make sure we're all agreed about where we're going?'

We spent a few minutes double-checking not only that night's destination, but also the precise location of ERV Six, the spot in the desert from which the Chinook would recover us once the operation had gone down. There seemed to be no problem: the figures tallied, and I was able to relax for the time being. All the same, I stood for a while, peering out of a porthole. The night was clear, the moonlight bright. I knew that the crew's PNGs must be giving them an excellent view ahead – and they needed it, because they were skimming the desert at 150 m.p.h. and at no more than fifty feet, low enough to stay beneath any radar, and seemed confident that no obstructions lay in our path. Rather them than me.

'As far as we know there's nothing whatever between us and the MSR,' Steve said, 'and that's nearly an hour ahead. A hundred and thirty miles of f-all but sand.'

In the back the guys were sorting out their weapons and ammunition and re-lashing the remainder of their kit. I followed suit, loading one full magazine into my AK-47 and sliding four more into the pouches of my belt-kit. These final preparations didn't take up much time, and there was still an uncomfortably long wait ahead. My mouth felt dry, as it used to before football matches at school, so I ate one of my oranges to slake the thirst.

As we flew, Steve kept up an intermittent commentary over the intercom. 'Got a fire to our left,' he said suddenly. 'Looks like a bedouin encampment on our port front. We'll give that some space, I think.'

The heli took a violent heave to the right and climbed, then, a minute later, another to the left as we straightened back on to our true course. Presently Steve said, 'There's the MSR now. Not much moving on it. One set of lights heading north to starboard, and that's all . . . unless some mad bugger of an A-rab is driving without lights – which is quite possible.'

I felt the Chinook climb again, and imagined the thick red line on the map, which ran across our line of advance almost at right-angles. Then, as Steve banked right, I knew he was swinging north to keep away from three small settlements that lay either side of a kink in the road.

'That those villages on the MSR?' I asked.

'Clearing them now.'

A few minutes later he came on for the last time and in his best railway official's poncified tones announced, 'This is your next station stop. All passengers prepare to alight.' Then he reverted to his normal voice and said, 'When we're on the deck, Geordie, I'll wait for sixty seconds to make sure you're OK. Then, if you don't shout, assume there's no drama and we'll be off.'

'Roger,' I answered. 'That's fine.'

'Good luck, then. See you in a couple of days.'

'Thanks,' I said. 'Nice trip.'

Once more we settled ourselves on our quads. I ran over my equipment mentally, also feeling everything I could: AK-47 slung on my back, spare magazines in belt-kit, Browning in waist-holster, knife in sheath, water bottle on belt kit, ski goggles on forehead, PNGs round neck. I tugged at all the straps on my racks, fore and aft, to make sure they were secure. Looking round, I saw that everyone else was doing the same. Tony, who was behind me, gave a wink and a grin, sticking up his right thumb.

At the two-minute signal we started our engines, wound our shamags round our heads and settled ski goggles over our eyes. I switched my radio to the co-pilot's channel and said, 'OK, Gerry. I'll call if there's any problem. If I don't come on in sixty seconds flat, it'll mean we're OK.'

'Roger,' he answered.

At one minute, the Chinook started settling into a hover with the tail-gate descending. A blast of sand and grit came flying into our faces and there was a bump as the wheels touched; out of the corner of my right eye I saw the tail-gate loadie give me a raised thumb, and a second later I was rolling down the ramp.

Our plan was to fan out in an instant bomb-burst. I aimed forty-five degrees to the left through a storm of dust and sand. Tony did the same to the right, Pat at sixty degrees behind me, Whinger behind Tony, and Stew and Norm straight forward with the trailer to a position in the centre of our circle. In that mass of flying shit it was impossible to tell how far I'd gone, but when I reckoned I was seventy metres out I stopped, brought my rifle to the ready and sat facing outwards with the engine ticking over. Out there, I was clear of the dust-ball, but when I looked back, all I could see was a huge cloud seething and heaving in the moonlight.

If there'd been any sort of drama I'd have called the co-pilot, put a couple of bursts in the direction of the trouble, and driven straight back up the ramp. But after a minute, when no SOS call came, Steve built his revs back to a peak and the aircraft lifted away. In a few seconds the heavy, thudding beat of its rotors had faded into the night, leaving us alone in the desert's tremendous silence.

There was sand beneath me – I could feel it shift under my toes – but it seemed quite firm, as if there was a hard bottom a couple of inches beneath the surface. That augured well for our run in. So did the three-quarter moon, which was on its way down. The air felt warm on my face, and out here, away from civilisation, it smelled completely clean.

My watch was reading eight minutes past midnight. I waited, watching the dust-cloud settle and disperse. Then I switched my radio back to our chatter channel and jabbed the pressel. 'Everyone all right?' I asked. 'Tony?'

'Yeah.'

'Pat?'

'Yep.'

'Whinger?'

'Yep.'

'Norm?'

'Aye.'

'Stew?'

'Fine.'

'OK. Check Magellans.'

I switched mine on and pressed the button for the light that illuminated the little screen. Stuck in its special holder above the handlebar panel the instrument was at easy reading height, but we still had to sit and wait for a satellite to come over the horizon and pass within range. Because the satellites are all in different orbits, they come past at irregular intervals: sometimes you have to wait half an hour, then get three in twenty minutes. We could have moved off right away, and I knew that the guys must be itching to go, but Tony had agreed that it was better to get an accurate fix before we started. With luck, the Chinook should have dropped us right on the spot, but if we were a bit off target we might be all to cock in our navigation.

Five minutes passed. Ten. 'Come on, you sonofabitch,' Tony

muttered over the radio. 'Shift your butt.'

I knew how he felt. We seemed to be very exposed, sitting there in the moonlight with the desert stretching away level all round and not a stitch of cover in sight. I tried to imagine the next satellite, zooming round the earth at 17,500 m.p.h., and smiled at the thought of it shifting its butt in response to Tony's exhortation. Then Whinger came on the net with, 'Oh, for fuck's sake. Let's get going.'

'Chill out,' I told him.

A moment later Tony said, 'There we go. That's number one. It's looking good. We just need two more for a triangle.'

The second and third satellites came up within a couple more minutes. 'OK,' I announced. 'We're on twenty-one East, twenty-four thirty-four. Twenty-eight North, fifty-nine twenty. Everyone agreed?'

Skipper Steve had done us proud. We were within a few yards of the drop-off point chosen in Hereford. Now all we had to do was follow our pre-set course to the location of our lying-up point, about sixty-five kilometres due north – and navigation was dead easy because the displays on our screens showed us if we were on track, or deviating to right or left.

'Right,' I said quietly, 'we've all got the ERVs, if anything happens. Pat, you do lead scout to start with. Go as fast as you can manage comfortably. Probably Stew and the trailer will set the limit at the back. The weight of the stores will make him the slowest – see how it goes. The rest keep in line ahead, at whatever interval we can see at. Try it out. Keep right in each other's tracks if you can. When we get nearer the target, we'll put pickets out.

'On this first leg there shouldn't be anything ahead of us for fifteen ks. Then there'll be a road across our front. After that, nothing till we come in sight of the high-ground feature. Skirt that right-handed, then start looking for the big wadi. Once we're through that it should be only half an hour to the area of the LUP. OK? Let's go.'

Pat led off, with me next and the others following. The combination of moonlight and PNGs gave a good view – I reckoned I could see some detail at nearly three hundred metres – but of course, in those conditions anyone on the move is at a big disadvantage versus anyone stationary. It's always movement that takes the eye, whereas men lying or kneeling on the deck can easily pass for stones . . . until it's too late. Thus we were all well aware that we could ride into an ambush at any moment.

All the same it was great to be moving, the warm air flowing past my face. Riding in second place I had a chance to relax and think while the lead scout carried the biggest load. He had to keep his eyes skinned for dips, hollows and rocks – to say nothing of possible nomad encampments or even Libyan army positions. It was also down to him to hold the right course and keep the speed up. All this put him under heavy stress, and I'd planned in advance to switch the lead every half hour.

Pat looked like a solid black blob bobbing on ahead of me. His wheels raised a small dust-cloud, which a breath of wind from the west was carrying off to our right. At first the going was good: the terrain was flat, with outcrops of rock here and there, and the quads ran easily over the firm sand. I'd taped over all the lights on my handle-bar panel, but the needle of the speedometer was still visible, and from its angle I could see that we were maintaining a steady thirty k.p.h. Every now and then I pushed the light button on the Magellan to check our heading, and kept finding that Pat was spot-on.

We were running through shallow sand, and inevitably leaving tracks. Behind the trailer, which was last in line, we'd rigged up a primitive sweeper-rake – some hessian sacks lashed to a cross-bar – to obliterate our individual wheel-marks so that, even if the Libyans did spot the trail during daylight, they wouldn't be able to tell what sort of vehicles had made it. Even so, it would be easy enough for the pilot of a jet or helicopter to follow the trail and see where we'd gone. I just hoped that a strong wind would blast all our traces into eternity – or else that, in the immensity of the desert, nobody would fly over or come past until we had done our business.

Twenty minutes into our first run, Pat came up on the chatter net. 'Geordie, I'm stopping. There's something ahead of us. I can't make it out.'

'All stations stop,' I replied. 'Switch off and wait out. OK, Pat, I'm coming up to have a look.'

I cruised up beside him and shut down my engine. 'There,' he whispered, pointing ahead and to the right. 'Something black. I thought I saw it move.'

Peering through my PNGs I immediately spotted what he meant: a black shape, possibly two hundred metres off, with an irregular outline, its left side low and its right taller and pointed. It could have been two men close together, one kneeling or sitting, the other standing.

'Can't get it,' I murmured.

'It's the right-hand bit that I thought I saw move.'

I pushed the PNGs up on to my forehead and brought out my binoculars, but the ambient light was so faint that they were no help. With the PNGs back on I watched again. It was quite eerie, sitting there in the great silence of the desert, the gentle puffs of wind coming in over our left shoulders and I felt myself getting jumpy.

'Chill out,' I said under my breath. 'You're doing fine.' I knew from past experience that when you're out at night, almost anything will move in the end – or seem to – if you watch it for long enough. Whether your eyes deceive your mind or vice versa I'm not sure, but if your nerves are on edge even rocks appear to take on a life of their own and start shifting stealthily about.

'Anyone back there make it out?' I asked over the net. 'Two o'clock to our line of advance.'

'Thorns,' said Whinger. 'Couple of thorn bushes.'

'You sure?'

'Reckon so. The right-hand one *is* moving. The top of it's blowing in the wind.'

'OK,' I said. 'I think you're right. We'll carry on. Head left, Pat, and give it some room. I'll cover you until we're past.'

I unslung my AK-47 and sat with it at the ready as Pat set off left-handed. Whinger had been right. The clump of thorns waved in the wind as we passed, and we left it to its own devices in the dark.

After another twenty minutes without incident I decided to bring Pat back. I knew he wouldn't want to give up lead scout – being mustard keen, he'd carry on all night if I let him – but I also knew that he'd inevitably get tired, and that the edge would go off his vigilance.

'Thin out,' I told him over the radio. 'Norm, move up front.'

102

'It's no sweat,' Pat called back. 'I'm fine here. D'you want me to go faster or something?'

'Not at all. You've done a great job. I just want everyone to rotate.'

'OK, then.' As he fell back past me and Norm went forward, I gave them both thumbs up.

Soon the sand seemed to grow deeper; I could feel it dragging at my wheels. The quad started to slew about, the steering grew heavier, and I needed more power to maintain speed. Then Stew, at the back, called to say that he was falling behind; the trailer wheels were digging in, and even on full power he was losing us.

'Ease off, Norm,' I instructed. 'Aim for twenty rather than thirty.'

'Aye, OK,' said Norm. 'I'm throttling back.'

'Good,' I went. 'See if you can hold that, Stew.'

I could feel my adrenalin flowing fast now. At all costs we had to be on target by first light, predicted to be at 0445; by then, we needed to have found a suitable lying-up point and to have built an OP. If we maintained our present speed we'd reach the area of the LUP inside another hour, and we'd be OK. But if we had to start winching our bikes up and down the walls of the wadi our speed of advance could drop from twenty k.p.h. to one, and we could well end up in the shit.

When we'd been running for an hour I called a refuelling halt. I couldn't tell how much petrol we'd used, but it obviously made sense to top up our tanks while nobody was harassing us; also, it took a few kilos off the load on the trailer. Two of the guys assumed defensive positions, twenty-five metres out on either side, while the rest of us tanked up, then two others took over from them while they came in and did the same. Although the desert seemed empty, we couldn't be sure that the Libyans weren't out on night exercises, that a patrol might have heard us coming.

Soon we were rolling again, with Whinger now in the lead, and after only ten minutes we seemed to begin to emerge from the deep-sand belt, the bikes starting to move more easily. But then came a sudden call from the rear.

'Geordie,' said Norm, and from the way he said my name I knew there was something wrong.

'What is it?'

'I've dropped a bollock.'

'How?'

'My fucking Magellan.'

'What's happened to it?'

'I've left it behind.'

'Don't be stupid.'

'I have.'

'Where?'

'At that halt.'

'Bloody hell! All stations stop!' A surge of alarm drove down into my guts. Again and again I'd harped on the importance of not shedding any item of kit, however trivial, in case it betrayed our origins and a Magellan, programmed up with our courses and way-points, was the worst possible object to leave lying in the desert. Norm was usually the most careful member of the whole team. 'What the hell were you doing, taking it off the bike anyway?' I asked.

'I didn't want to risk splashing petrol on it, so I took it out of the holder and put it on the ground while we were gassing up.'

I felt exasperated – but Norm knew he'd screwed up, and I saw no point in mouthing off at him. So I just said, 'You'll have to go back. There's no alternative. We can't risk leaving it. D'you think you can find the place?'

'Dunno. Have to try. How long is it since we restarted?'

'Eight minutes,' said Stew. 'We were rolling for eight minutes exactly.'

'Time yourself back,' I told Norm. 'You should be able to see the marks where we did the refuelling. Whinger, go with him. The rest of us will wait for you here. And take it easy – we're still all right for time.'

So we were, but not by much.

Two of us sat in a hollow, with the other two posted out on either flank. It was reassuring to find that the noise of the quads' engines died away quickly into the night, but tension built up as the minutes ticked by. Feeling restless, I got off my bike and walked away to have a piss.

'Stupid cunt!' Stew muttered as I came back, voicing the anxiety that all of us were feeling.

'Easily done,' I said. 'You might drop the next bollock, Stew. Give him a break.'

Presently in my ear-piece I heard Norm say, 'Back on site.' Then, a moment later, he exclaimed, 'Got the fucker!' and everyone relaxed.

With the party reunited, we rolled forward again to the north until, from in front, Whinger called, 'Stopping, stopping. There's an obstruction ahead.'

'OK,' I answered. 'I'm closing on you. Everyone else, wait out.'

I cruised up beside him.

'See it?' he said quietly. 'Like a wall.'

'It's the road, but it's on an embankment. In the desert they're often built like that, to stop sand drifting over them.'

'Yeah, but there's something this side of it.'

'Wait one.' I reached forward to the top flap of my bergen and undid the straps, feeling for my binoculars. The 10 x 50 lenses, bloomed for light-gathering, instantly revealed the nature of the problem.

'Shit and derision!' I cried. 'It's a fucking pipeline! Two-deck, each pipe about a metre diameter. There's no way we can ride over that.'

'How in hell didn't that figure on the briefing?' said Tony. 'Didn't the CIA guy mention it?'

'Not a dicky-bird.'

'Jesus Christ!'

'Let's blow the shit out of it,' said Whinger. 'Make a passage.'

'Brilliant!' I told him. 'And attract every son of the Prophet in Libya straight on to us. They'd send out all choppers in the country to sweep up and down until they found out what happened. No thanks. There's only one thing for it. Scout right and left. There must be a culvert under it somewhere for herdsmen to walk through. Tony, you and Pat go right. Norm, you and Whinger left. Move up a bit closer to it first, then keep heading along parallel with the road till you find an underpass. Stew and I'll hold here until one of you calls.'

The two pairs went off, disappearing into the dark like black dots. Nearly ten minutes had passed – ten minutes of steadily increasing tension – before Tony came back on the air.

'OK, guys. Head right. We've found a tunnel.'

'Roger,' I answered. 'We're coming. Norm, did you get that?'

'Aye. I'll close on you. No luck this way.'

We found Tony and Pat on their feet, wielding their short-handled shovels like lunatics. They'd discovered a culvert, but sand had drifted into the mouth of it and left only eighteen inches of headroom. At first glance the task of clearing a passage looked colossal; but, as Tony had appreciated, the drift tapered off rapidly inside the tunnel, and we only had to lower the first few feet.

Again we lost ten minutes, at the end of which we were all sweating like pigs. When we moved off again the wind felt icy as it cooled the moisture on our bodies. Now we really were up against the clock. It was 0315, and I reckoned we had ninety minutes at most before dawn broke. In that time we had to cross the wadi, find a site for an LUP, ditto for an OP, build the OP and settle down out of sight. I was needled by the multiple uncertainties ahead. The distance we had to travel was relatively small, probably not more than ten kilometres. What mattered was the nature of the terrain ahead. What would we find in the area of the OP? Would we get a good enough view of the camp? Were the Libyans in the habit of coming out into this part of the desert?

Once more we made good progress, and soon Norm called back to say that he could see the feature hill.

'I have Mont Blanc on my left front, where it should be,' he reported. 'It's quite impressive in the moonlight. Steep sides, crags on top. Reminds me of Stirling Castle.'

For Norm that was an epic, the speech of a lifetime. Boy, I thought, the desert must be really turning him on.

Having given the hill a wide berth we got back on to our northerly heading and pressed ahead, now with Tony in the lead. The ground became more and more stony, until we were jolting around over loose shale. In one way I was pleased – on this surface we would leave no tracks at all – but on another level I began to worry: if the terrain was like this close to the camp, we'd be screwed when it came to building our OP, and we might find ourselves in another Iraq-type fiasco.

The desert started to undulate, with small, dry valleys running north-east to south-west across our line of advance. I guessed they were tributaries of the main wadi ahead – and sure enough, Tony presently called back to say that he could see the valley ahead of him.

There we got our first lucky break. It was obvious that over the centuries winter torrents had cut a deep scar through the desert, and in many places the walls of the trench took the form of rocky cliffs, perhaps twenty feet high. But at the point where we arrived the bank had collapsed into a broad tongue of shingle, and, far from having to resort to ropes and winches, we were able to ride straight down it, leaving no trace. Boulders dotted the floor of the dry watercourse, and we wove our way between them easily enough for maybe one kilometre until another sloping bank took us out the far side.

That simple passage boosted morale and put us nearly back on schedule. By 0330 the moon was low on the horizon to our left, but by then I reckoned we were within five or six kilometres of the location for the LUP as one by one the surrounding features fell into place. First we ran off the shale and back on to sand. Then we saw the ground ahead of us rising in dunes.

I called Tony to a halt and put pickets out to ride level with him, right and left.

Less than a minute later Whinger, who was out on the right, called, 'Eh, Geordie. I'm on a road.'

'A road? You can't be.'

'I fucking am. It's brand-new. Just been bulldozed out.'

'Stand by. I'm coming up.'

Whinger was right, of course. I found him parked on a dark-looking strip of track, with the sand scraped off into ridges on either side. The underlying rock felt pretty rough, but it was easily negotiable by vehicles with reasonable clearance.

'This wasn't on the satellite shots,' I said. 'They must have been working on it in the past few days.'

'It's coming down from the north-east,' said Whinger, checking his compass. 'Remember that track the satellite showed, leading out from the camp towards the range? I reckon this is an extension of it.'

'Looks like it. What a bugger!' I sat still for a moment, considering this new development. It meant that, if things went

107

noisy, the Libyans would in theory be able to drive out behind our temporary positions and cut off our retreat.

'I don't like it,' I told Whinger. 'But we can't stop now.'

By ranging up and down, we found a point where sand gave over to rock and no new banks had been heaped up, and we all crossed the line of the track there, in single file, leaving no trace of our passage. But the mere existence of the road made me uneasy.

On we went, slowly now, into the dune-scape, circling the bases of the hillocks. The sand here was very soft, so that although we were leaving wheel-marks they more or less filled themselves in behind us. Then Norm, who was scouting left, called, 'Watch yourselves, lads. I can smell smoke.'

'Everyone stop,' I went. 'What is it, Norm?'

'It smells oily, like diesel burning. Coming on the wind.'

'Probably some goatherds camping out,' I said. 'They'll be burning old oil in a drum. Can you see anything?'

'Nothing.'

'Pull off, then. Come back this way. Feel your right, everyone. We're going round it.' So we made a detour, and slowly came back on to our heading.

The incident had done nothing to reassure me. I didn't like the idea there were other people besides us out there in the desert.

Soon afterwards Whinger, who was still on the right, went up on to a rise and suddenly called, 'Geordie! Lights ahead.'

I rode over and came up behind him. There was no need for him to point this time. The first thing I noticed, high in the air, was a single bright-red glare, then below it I saw lights burning faintly across our front, some in a line, others in clusters beyond them.

'Got it!' I said. 'That red thing must be the warning light on the comms tower.'

'I reckon so.'

'How far out are we?'

'Hard to tell. Could be one kilometre.'

'We're close enough, anyway. I'd like to put more ground between us and those bastards behind us, whoever they are. But we can't go any nearer the camp than this. Got to find an LUP site around here. That row of lights must be the perimeter fence, with other installations beyond.'

Everyone went lookabout, and within a few minutes Pat called to say he had located a good spot, away to our left. Closing on him, we found him in a gully, with sand underfoot and a vertical rock wall about three metres high along one side. There were fissures in the rock, into which we could drive pegs, and the whole area had a fairly rough texture. I saw straightaway, as he had, that if we parked the bikes nose-to-tail along the wall, and slung cam-nets over them at an angle like a sloping roof, it would make as good a hiding-place as we were likely to find.

The time was 0355, and already I thought I could detect a faint lightening in the eastern sky. We rolled the trailer in backwards, hitched it to Stew's bike again, and manoeuvred the rest of the quads into line ahead of it, ready for a quick take-off. Then we broke out the gear for the OP and prepared to move forward on foot.

'Final check,' I said quietly when I'd gathered the guys round. 'Me and Tony will spend the day in the OP. Depending on what we find, we may decide that the op should go down tomorrow night. If there's any problem, we may have to wait until the night after. Either way, we'll want the support party forward soon after dark tomorrow.'

'Tonight,' Tony interrupted.

'As you were. Tonight. I'm talking about tonight, Tuesday. For Christ's sake – I'm losing track of the days. Cancel all that.'

I pressed the light button on my watch for a check.

'It's now 0400 on Tuesday. If possible, the op will go down tonight. If everything looks OK, we'll call the three of you forward once it's dark.' I jabbed a finger at Pat, Whinger and Norm. 'Stew, you'll be our back-marker. Hold the fort here. OK?'

'Sure.'

'Whinger, get a sitrep back to the Kremlin as soon as you've got an aerial sorted. Tell them we have eyes on the target area and everything's hunky-dory. And *everybody*, go easy on the water. It's going to get hot as hell when the sun rises, and we don't know how long we're going to be here. OK, all?'

Getting no answer except a couple of grunts, I said, 'Right – we're off. Pat and Norm, you help us carry the stuff forward for the OP. Then back here. Let's go.'

109

We settled our bergens and rifles on our backs, slung the other bundles about us, and began to move off.

'Give 'em hell,' said Whinger.

'I'll wait till you're in the front line with us,' I told him. 'Then you personally can stand up on top of a dune and fire the first shot to start the battle.'

SEVEN

On the side of a dune facing the camp we found a hollow fronted by a couple of scrubby thorns. By cutting a few more bushes elsewhere and bringing them across to reinforce the natural thicket, we made a small enclosure. At the same time we deepened the hollow by digging, and used bags filled with sand to make walls inside the thorns.

A rectangular gap left in the front wall gave us a view forward into the camp, and a cam-net stretched across the top, with more thorn branches scattered on it, completed the basis of our hide. The dune gave us natural protection from the rear, its disadvantage being that we couldn't see anyone coming from that direction. We reckoned, though, that the little hill was in direct line-of-sight from the LUP, so that the back-up party could watch our rear for us.

We'd almost finished building when a sudden noise from the direction of the camp made us freeze. The first blast of it – a kind of screeching groan – lasted such a short time and cut off so abruptly, almost like a dog's bark, that we couldn't make out what had caused it.

'Jesus!' exclaimed Pat. 'What the fuck was that?'

Before anyone could answer the sound came again. This time it kept going for several seconds, and Tony let out a gasp, half relief, half amusement.

'Not Jesus,' he said. 'Allah. It's the *muezzin*, giving the first call to prayer.'

We were at least two hundred metres from the perimeter wire, and the sound was coming from somewhere beyond it; yet the volume of the amplified voice was such that it blasted past us like a gale of wind, and we felt sure the guys in the LUP, a kilometre behind us, must be hearing it too. So it proved: they told us later

111

that the grating, metallic, undulating chant of '*Allah akhbar! Allah akhbar!*' carried way past them and on into the desert to the south.

'Sounds like he's underwater, poor bugger,' said Pat.

'That's just their crummy electronics,' Tony told him. 'The old mullah'll be up a tower someplace. We'll see the mosque as soon as it gets light.'

'Come on, guys,' I interrupted. 'Don't piss about. Never mind the mullah. We need to get tidied up here.'

In the eastern sky the dawn glow was coming up fast. It would have been good to carry on working and perfect our camouflage, but time had run out. From previous stints near the equator I knew how quickly the light would strengthen as the sun rose. The Libyans might have eyes on the desert, and I wasn't going to risk any movement after dawn.

'Away you go,' I told Pat and Stew. 'You don't want to be caught with your pants down.'

'Right then. Good luck.'

'Same to you. We'll see you tonight.'

Off they went, walking backwards round the side of the dune and whisking away their tracks with strips of hessian. A few minutes later they called on the radio to say that they were back in the LUP, and that they had eyes on the back of our mound.

Tony and I settled down for a day of observation. For me, breakfast consisted of cold spaghetti in tomato sauce, washed down by a brew of powdered lemonade. Tony had his favourite corned beef hash and pineapple slices, eaten together. We'd been planning to work alternate shifts – two hours on, two off – but found that, despite the fact that we'd had practically no sleep, neither of us felt tired. Our excitement supercharged us, and we both watched eagerly as dawn revealed the secrets of our objective.

The perimeter fence was just as the CIA man had described it: three metres of weldmesh, topped by an outward-sloping overhang of barbed wire. Every hundred metres there was a floodlight atop a slender pole, but several of the bulbs were out of action, and useful pools of darkness lay between the illuminated stretches. The goon-towers – built into the fences several hundred metres apart – might have been run up for a film about some German prison camp in World War Two: primitive wooden boxes on stilts, once painted white but now peeling, with wide-eaved flat roofs to give shade and the sides open to the air. There was one at the corner of the wire, slightly to our left, and another in the middle of the south fence to our right. This second tower stood beside a wide gate, also made of mesh, and the rough track Gus had indicated ran away from it towards the range in the south-east.

The important thing for us was our discovery that the towers weren't manned. Nor was there any patrol on the wire. With our binoculars we scanned every tower for signs of infra-red lamps or microwave dishes or TV cameras, but saw nothing: the whole system looked too primitive for any such high-tech devices.

'As the guy told us,' I said, 'they're not expecting any threat coming out of the sand.'

We'd positioned ourselves opposite the office cum accommodation block, and our binos gave us a brilliant view of it: a scruffy, off-white building, two storeys tall, with patches of discoloration staining its walls, air-conditioning units under every window, and long, dirty, tapering streaks beneath them where condensation had been dripping down over the years. The front entrance was in the middle of the wall facing us, a flight of five or six semi-circular steps leading up to its plain porch.

The door we became more interested in was at the side, to the left as we looked. Soon after six o'clock it opened from the inside, and some kind of *jingli*, or servant, began going in and out. The guy, who was quite old and had frizzy grey hair, wore a khaki shirt and trousers, but no shoes.

'Could be our best entry point,' said Tony quietly. 'Out of sight of most of the camp. Besides, the perimeter light opposite it is down.'

'Just thinking that. The tradesman's entrance.'

The window of the room in which our target was supposed to work was at the top left of the building. When we had arrived on site the room had been dark – but that was hardly surprising, as it was already four o'clock by then.

As the light strengthened the perimeter lights went out, but the single red lamp on the comms tower continued to glow. Then, at about six-thirty, the sun came over the eastern horizon and low rays blazed across the camp from our right. From the scribbled

113

notes and plans I'd made during our brief in London, I soon identified the compound's main features: the approach road coming in from the north, the guardroom, the headquarter block, the tall mast marking the comms centre, the armoury, wired off in its own secure enclosure inside the perimeter, the fuel station, down near the wire to our right, and the mosque, gleaming white, with an onion dome and huge loud-speakers sprouting from the corners of a balcony round its tower. Far off to the right, in a little compound of its own, we could see the comms facility that Gus had given us as a secondary target. The white dish aerial was pointing nearly straight up.

'That damn thing's farther off than he reckoned,' I said.

'What did he tell you?' Tony asked.

'He said two-fifty metres from the wire. It's got to be three-fifty at least. It's still in range, but not by much. Anyway, it's non-essential. We'll see what happens when the time's ripe.'

As the camp came slowly to life, Tony's earlier tour in Abu Dhabi proved invaluable, because he was able to interpret all the small events we witnessed. Apart from the *jingli*, the earliest arrivals on the scene were bread and milk vans, which pulled up by the guardroom on the far side from us and then, after long delays, drove in to various buildings which were obviously messes.

'What's all the fuss on the barrier about?' I asked.

'Typical,' Tony replied. 'The guys on duty have to assert themselves somehow and show they're superior to the ignorant drivers. So they give them a hard time, even though they see them every day. You watch in a minute, when the rank and file arrive. But, Jesus . . . look at this.'

'What is it?'

'See that long building with the green roof? Look right over the top of it.'

'Got it. Rotor blades.'

'Yep. There's a goddamn chopper parked there.'

'Let's hope it's gone u/s. We don't want that bloody thing overhead.'

Soon after seven o'clock, a stream of ordinary cars and land cruisers began rolling down the approach road and on to a big car park outside the wire. By then a man with a mill-board was

114

scuttling about, trying to reserve the spaces nearest the fence, and evidently taking flak from the drivers he chased away.

'See that?' said Tony. 'The bastards are so idle they won't walk a step if they don't have to.'

'Why don't they drive in, though?'

'Against the rules. Bad security. Nobody trusts anybody. I mean, any of these guys might have a bomb in his vehicle and park it next to the headquarter block. One of them might try to top the colonel.'

Within twenty minutes some sort of physical training was taking place. A long straggle of men in shorts and trainers came trotting round the track inside the perimeter, with one instructor leading and another trying in vain to drive on the laggards at the back. The front dozen or so were actually running, but everyone else was walking. A few of the guys were mock-fighting, hitting out and kicking at each other, but most of them were simply chit-chatting as they ambled along.

'What tossers!' I cried. 'What a fucking shower!'

'They are,' Tony agreed. 'But if you quizzed any of them they'd swear they run a marathon every morning.'

At ten past eight, after that virtuoso display, the camp went dead as everyone disappeared indoors for showers and breakfast. By eight-thirty our active night had begun to tell on us. The sun, striking into the OP from our right, was already seriously hot, and, with no action to watch, we both felt tiredness attack.

'Get your head down while there's nothing happening,' I told Tony. 'If any action starts up I'll wake you.'

He shaped to argue but I more or less ordered him to sleep, and in a couple of minutes he was out, lying along our right-hand wall. Looking down at his dark Puerto Rican complexion, I thought that in an emergency he might pass for an Arab, especially at night.

When I squinted up at the sky through our roof of cam-net and thorns, I wished we'd been able to create something more solid in the way of a sun-shade. The best remedy was to tie my sweater horizontally to the underneath of the net, but even in the shade I could feel the sweat going out of me like steam, and I wanted to drink all the time. We'd each brought two belt-bottles full of water, and a gallon can as a back-up, and I knew we were going to need strict discipline to stop us running out.

115

At nine-twenty people started drifting on to the drill square, apparently for some sort of parade. *Jinglis* carried out armchairs and set them in position on a dais under a pointed wooden roof, and various slovenly-looking characters drifted about.

I was just thinking there was no point in waking Tony until the show began, when suddenly I saw something that grabbed my attention. Out of the front door of the accommodation block came four armed men, obviously guards, who formed up, two either side of the entrance. A moment later a big, heavy fellow in white drill shirt and trousers appeared, carrying a peaked cap in his hand. If he'd had the hat on his head I might not have recognised him. As it was, I gave Tony a kick and cried, 'Eh! Eh! Eh! Look at this!'

He was up beside me in a second, binos glued to his eyes. 'Shitface!' he exclaimed.

'Christ!' I felt my heart pounding with a surge of adrenalin. 'If we had the sniper rifle we could drop him here and now without ever going through the wire.'

'Yeah – but the marathon runners would be out after us.'

'I don't think they'd catch us. But if they got the heli airborne, we'd be deep in the shit.'

We watched fascinated as Khadduri smirked to right and left, apparently making small talk to his bodyguards. Then he settled his cap on his head and set off along the front of the building, heading for the parade.

'Doesn't change, does he?' said Tony. 'Great sense of humour. Remember how he used to laugh when he was hitting you on the arm?'

'Will I forget it?'

Soon the parade had formed up, but we never had a clear view of it because a thick heat-haze had begun to shimmer and shudder above the ground. Through the fuzz we saw the officers take their places in the armchairs, with Khadduri in pole position at the right-hand end of the line. In front of them the rank and file sat on the deck in rows, cross-legged; and a tall man in white robes, who could only be the mullah, moved up and down the ranks bellowing into a microphone, his torrent of abuse outrageously magnified by the loudspeakers.

'What's he bollocking them for?' I asked.

116

'Anything he can think of – being late, not saying their prayers enough . . . Look how they're cringing.'

As the priest advanced on each man, shaking his fist and roaring insults, the guy would bow his head in submission until it touched the ground. It was like an amazingly hammy theatre show, and I was loving every minute of it, when a call on the radio jerked me back to the task in hand.

'Watch yourself, Geordie.' It was Pat.

'What's the problem?'

'Camels. There's a bloody great herd coming across behind you from the left. They're going to pass between you and us.'

'Is there anybody with them?'

'Can't tell yet. They're streamed out over hundreds of metres. We can't see the back of them.'

'What are they doing, running?'

'No, no – just grazing on. Stand by till we see the end of the line.'

I looked at Tony. He was pointing at his bergen, asking with his eyebrows if he should stuff everything into it. I shook my head and whispered, 'Not yet. This must be the lot we passed in the dark, when Whinger smelt that fire.'

If we got compromised, all we could do was to leg it back to the LUP, jump on the quads and scoot away into the desert, having called for immediate helicopter evacuation. But that would be a disaster – the end of the operation.

We waited a couple of minutes. I could feel sweat running down my backbone. Then Pat came up with, 'There are two herders, a man and a boy.'

'Have they got a dog?'

'Wait one . . . Yes. There's one dog, like a big grey lurcher.'

'Shit! How close behind us are they going to pass?'

'Maybe two hundred metres.'

'Keep us informed if they start coming any closer.'

'Roger.'

As far as we could tell in our baking hollow, there was no wind at all – not a breath that would carry our scent behind us. Besides, five hours had passed since any of us had crossed the line on which the camels were advancing; I couldn't believe that any dog would pick up any traces from that burning sand.

Presently I heard a shout, then another, from alarmingly close quarters. Over the radio link I asked, 'Pat, for Christ's sake. What are they doing?'

'Chill out,' he replied calmly. 'The lead camels are passing you now. They're just wandering on. Now the leader of all's having the crap of its life. No bother. Sit tight.'

I found I'd unconsciously been holding my breath, so I let it out and inhaled deeply.

'Keeping on,' Pat continued. '*Allah karim*. Half-way across . . . Three-quarters. There must be two hundred altogether. The end of the column's level with you now. Look out, though. The dog's turning in your direction.'

'How far from us?'

'Still the two hundred metres. Stand by . . . No – it's OK. The dog's OK. He's only having a piss on a tuft of dead grass. That's all he's about. Now he's carrying on. Herders the same. One herder pissing . . . Now they're clear. They're squared away.'

'Thanks, Pat.'

'You're welcome. By the way, what's that godawful noise?'

'That's the local vicar clearing his throat, having a gargle.'

'Are his congregation bloody deaf or something?'

'Yeah, I should say they are by now.'

The parade over, everything went dead again, both in the desert and in the camp. The camels vanished into the heat haze, and inside the wire, after their mass bollocking, the inmates dispersed to hangars or classrooms for their morning instruction. I tried to get my head down, but was bothered by the steadily rising temperature. 'What did they predict for us?' I asked fretfully. 'Wasn't it thirty-six? This feels more like fucking forty.'

All the same, I must have dropped off to sleep, because I came to with Tony shaking my elbow and found that two hours had passed.

'Anything doing?'

'The duty officer's been round – a jerk wearing a red sash and carrying a cane under his arm, sticking his nose in everywhere, throwing his weight about. And now they're lining up for the big event of the day, midday prayers.'

From all corners of the camp men were trudging towards the

mosque. The wind had got up, blowing into our faces as we watched, and the heat seemed to have eased a fraction. I reckoned that hot air was rising off the desert floor behind us and drawing slightly cooler air down from the north, ultimately from the sea. At any rate, the breeze had cleared some of the haze, and through our glasses we could see the faithful taking off their boots and socks, which they left neatly set out in a long line before they went in to pray.

'I always wonder how in hell they know whose are which,' said Tony. 'Look at that: three hundred pairs of goddamn boots in a line. Just imagine what a screw-up there'd be if we put a couple of bursts into the tower: they'd be fighting like lunatics to find the right pair.'

But before I could answer another terrible cacophony burst from the loudspeakers as the mullah launched into his chant of 'Allah akhbar! Allah akhbar!', and the prayers were under way.

At 1230 the personnel fanned out from the mosque and disappeared indoors again, presumably for lunch, and the next we saw of them, an hour later, they were ready for the off, queuing at the guardroom for the duty officer to sign their exit chits.

'They all get searched when they go out,' Tony said. 'Nobody trusts anybody.'

'But what could they possibly nick?'

'Weapons, ammunition. Anything liftable.' Tony looked at his watch and added, 'Know what? This is the beginning of their weekend. They're on their way already.'

'What about Shitface? I hope he's not going to thin out as well.'

'He *is*, though. That's him in the white jeep. Don't worry. He'll be back for that special meeting tomorrow.'

The afternoon slowly dragged itself away. The heat hammered in on us, in spite of the wind, and tiny black biting flies hopped around the sand. We squashed dozens of them as they landed on our bare arms and necks, but every nip from the ones we missed left a red mark and started up an itch. We sweated and drank, sweated and drank, but so great was the rate of evaporation that neither of us wanted a piss all day.

During my stag Tony dropped off again with his shamag spread over his face, and I had a struggle to keep alert. Looking down at his peaceful form, I felt glad that he was with me, yet at the same time wondered if I'd boobed in making legal arrangements for him to become Tim's guardian. If both of us got written off now, my affairs would be in chaos.

At 1530 we heard another call to prayer, but this meeting was poorly attended compared with the morning effort, because most of the faithful had departed in that exodus after lunch. Aside from that there was practically no movement inside the camp, nothing to engage my interest. What kept me awake was the succession of disturbing thoughts that chased each other through my mind.

The idea of killing someone in cold blood isn't a pleasant one. It is true that I had a personal grudge against our target, for the way he had treated me and Tony, and for his callous, cynical attitude in general. Yet that alone didn't justify murdering him. To weight the scales against him I mentally threw in the fact that he was financing and supplying the IRA on a massive scale. It was his support – or, at any rate, the support of people like him – that had led indirectly to Kath's death and, now, to the kidnapping of Tim. The flow of money and weapons from overseas was what kept the IRA going.

And in any case, I told myself, this isn't a personal matter. The fact that I happen to have a personal involvement is coincidental. The operation is one that the Regiment has been tasked to carry out, and fate – or luck, or whatever it is – has decreed that I'm the guy in charge. That's all it is: a job to be done.

Trouble was, I had a far more difficult job to do back in the UK. Now we'd got as far as the OP, the topping of Khadduri seemed relatively simple. I felt sure that Tony and I would hack it, no bother. Infinitely more complex was the problem of recovering my family.

As I wrestled with this prospect, my mind kept harking back to the scheme I'd proposed to Pat – that a gang of our lads should take the law into our own hands, spring Farrell from police custody and hand him back to his mates in Belfast. Once again I heard Pat saying, 'You must be fucking *mad!*' and I realised the plan was probably quite unworkable. Nevertheless, I couldn't banish it from my head – and gradually, as the baking afternoon wore on, it evolved into a new version.

What if I kept the basic idea, but instead of trying to do

120

something unilaterally, I brought the Regiment and the police on side, and got their backing? With the co-operation of the police we'd snatch Farrell while he was being moved between gaols, hold him in some safe house, tell the PIRA he was free, and exchange him for Tim and Tracy. But we'd arrange things so he could be immediately recaptured, possibly by putting a bug into his clothes or the heel of one of his shoes, and having a chopper airborne to follow whatever car he got into.

The scheme seemed so brilliant I felt quite lit up, and ceased to worry about the heat or the sand flies. But would the Regiment wear it? Impossible to say. In fact, I supposed, even if the head-shed agreed, authorisation for any such operation would have to come right from the top, from the Home Office, the Home Secretary or the Prime Minister. As in Operation Ostrich, permission would have to be completely unattributable, and deniable. Yet why shouldn't it be? Here I was, stewing deep inside Libya, about to murder a senior army officer with the direct connivance of the British Government. If Whitehall sanctioned the elimination of dangerous foreigners, why should it baulk at a plan that merely ran rings round the IRA?

I was so chuffed with my idea that I wanted to discuss it with someone immediately. But it didn't seem fair to wake Tony, who was sleeping quietly. I could hardly start honking about the plan over the radio to Pat.

So for the time being I had to bottle it up inside me.

I was still on stag when Khadduri reappeared. It was after six, the sun hanging low over the desert, and the heat had at last started to abate. Tony was getting some food down his neck when I saw the clean, white land-cruiser hurrying down the approach road towards the main entrance. Instead of detaining it, as they had every other vehicle, the guards whipped up the barrier and saluted it past.

'Watch this,' I said. 'It looks like the VIP visitor. I thought the bastard was supposed to come tomorrow. Looks like he's a day early – or our intelligence was out.'

The jeep drove straight through the camp to our corner and pulled up outside the front door of the accommodation block. Out stepped Khadduri with one other guy, both went indoors, and the vehicle drove away.

The sight prompted me to a quick decision. 'Listen, Tony,' I said, 'we're going in tonight. There's nothing to be gained by waiting. Quite the reverse. He might clear off before tomorrow evening, after all. D'you agree?'

'Fine by me. Provided the bird stays on the nest.'

'Right, then.' I held in my pressel switch and called, 'You there, Whinger?'

'Roger. How you doing?'

'Fine. Onpass to head-shed that the bird's on the nest and the operation can go down tonight. Get them to clear that, OK? And ask if there's any update from their end.'

'Roger. I'll call you presently.'

I imagined Whinger going through on the Satcom – a direct, one-to-one call to the comms centre in Hereford: 'Zero Alpha, Zero Alpha, this is Delta Four. Over.' At the other end I could see Yorky and Mac, and probably the CO, sitting round in the ops room while the duty signaller kept an eye on the set. 'This is Zero Alpha,' Mac would answer, 'go ahead.' Whereupon Whinger would pass on what I'd said and ask for permission to proceed. There'd be a slight delay after each person had spoken, but the voices would be crystal clear. There was no question of anyone eavesdropping on the exchanges because speech was automatically encrypted; the snag was that a satellite transmission created a much bigger electronic splash than high-frequency radio, and so was easier for a direction-finder to pick up. Exchanges were therefore kept as short as possible.

I also imagined the Prime Minister taking the closest possible interest in the operation. By my calculation the time in London was four o'clock, and probably the PM was in the House of Commons, fielding questions and giving stick to the Opposition. But at the back of his mind, I told myself, I bet he's thinking of us. I bet he's wondering how we're doing.

In the baking, sandy confines of the OP we waited for an answer, and presently Whinger came back on the air. 'OK,' he said, 'I've been through. I told the head-shed that two guys have eyeballed the bird, and that he's definitely on the nest. They just want to be sure you've seen enough and are confident about going in.'

'Tell 'em we're fine. No problem. We've seen everything we need to. We'll aim to go in at midnight, when the rest of the personnel have thinned out. If all goes according to plan, we'll want the chopper on ERV Six by 0200. Check that with them too. And ask if there's any news on the personal front, please.'

'Will do.'

Again we waited, and soon Whinger relayed confirmation through: no personal news, but the operation was on.

'In that case,' I said, 'we need you three guys up here by 2200. That'll give us plenty of time to brief you on details before we move up to the wire. Make sure Norm has his lock-picking kit. Bring both RPGs and the Dragunov. Don't forget – plenty of Semtex, and a can of fuel for a distraction charge.'

We saw them before we heard them: dark figures moving slowly towards us through the moonlight. When they were thirty metres off I said quietly over the radio, 'OK, lads, we have eyes on you. We're right in front.'

We stood up and let the three come to meet us. Then we led them round the front of the dune to give them a view of our objective.

'There's the building,' I began. 'And there's the lighted window. As in the script. The main entrance is the one facing us, but there's a back door round the corner to the left, in the shadow. Look at the fence. See where the first missing floodlight is? Up that side, fourth from the left-hand corner, more or less behind the building. We aim to cut the wire at that point, in that pool of darkness. Once we're through, Norm – you'll accompany me and Tony to the building, to pick the lock on that back door. When we go in, you'll stay in place to cover the door. All right?'

'Aye.' Norm nodded.

'Whinger, you stay on the fence to secure the gap. You'll have the Dragunov as well as your AK-47. If any Libyan threatens our withdrawal, you can drop him from there with the sniper rifle. OK?

'Pat, I want you to range right-handed along the front fence.' I swung a hand across. 'Get down as far as the gate beside the tower there and get ready to crack off a distraction charge. If we can, we'll keep everything quiet. But if things go noisy, set a time-fuse and pull back this way. When the charge goes, put a rocket into the satellite dish where those red lights are showing. From the gate, the range should be about three-fifty metres. Is all that clear?'

'What if it doesn't go noisy?' Pat asked.

'We'll call you as soon as we're back through the wire. Once we're together again, you may still get a go at the dish. Then we'll tab off in orderly fashion to the OP. There we pick up our kit, leg it for the LUP, and away. Any more questions?'

'What if you can't find the target?' asked Whinger.

'We'll find him. We know the bastard's in the building. Ten to one he's sitting in that room right now. But if anything goes wrong we'll have to play it by ear. If he gets out of the building, by any mischance, one or other of you fence guys will probably have to drop him.'

The temptation to go in early built steadily. By 2300 the camp had fallen totally quiet. The light burned on in the target room, but nobody else seemed to be stirring. I imagined Khadduri at his computer terminal, working out details of his strategy for a mass Arab attack on Israel. We'd told the head-shed that zero-hour was going to be midnight, and for a while I reckoned we'd better stick to that.

Then, as we sat in the moonlight on the face of a dune opposite the corner of the wire, Stew came on the air with a question that fairly put the wind up us. 'Aye,' he said, 'Are you guys on the move somewhere?'

'No,' I told him. 'We're sitting tight with eyes on the target building. Why?'

'I've just seen three people moving out to my left as I face you.'

'What were they doing?'

'Walking in single file. Apart from that, I couldn't tell. They were right at the limit of visibility.'

'Any weapons?'

'Not that I could see.'

'Roger. It could be the camel herders. We'll carry on regardless.'

I pretended to be cool, but in fact the sighting changed my mind

124

about waiting. If there were people about in the desert, the less we hung around the better. 'Bollocks to it,' I said. 'Let's go in now. There's no point in farting about any longer.'

I called Stew again. 'Tell the Kremlin we've advanced the deadline: we're going in right away, and we'll keep them informed.'

While the others hung back and covered me, I crawled forward seventy metres to the fence at the darkest point and went to work with bolt-cutters. A thick ground-wire ran along the bottom: it felt as if it was under tension, so I left it alone and made an L-shaped incision in the mesh, with sides two feet long. The wire was fairly soft, and the blades made practically no sound as they bit together through each strand.

Having stowed the cutters in my belt-kit, I pulled up the flap of mesh that I'd made, put my AK-47 through and crawled after it. Tony and Norm followed, and all three of us scuttled for the shadow at the back of the accommodation block.

There we waited, each on one knee, facing outward. Close under the wall the noise of the air-conditioning units was considerable: a steady roar which drowned out all other small sounds. From here I saw that, to anyone inside the camp, the lights on the perimeter fence made the desert beyond seem black as a witch's tit. Even for us, it was impossible to detect that our other guys were out there.

'Right, Norm,' I whispered. 'There's your door.'

Tony and I remained on full alert as he set to with his torch and little bag of tricks, ten metres from us. We were both sweating like pigs, partly from the heat, partly from tension. I saw Tony's forehead gleaming in the faint light and beads of moisture trickling down his cheeks.

Inevitably Norm made a few clicks and scrapes – exactly the sounds I'd heard in my nightmare at the cottage – but nothing to compare with the steady background drone that filled the air, and in an incredibly short time he had the door open.

'Rubbish,' he muttered, indicating the lock. 'Just a Yale-type. Opens from the inside with a turn of the knob.'

'Brilliant! We'll see you soon.'

We slung our rifles over our backs to leave our hands free,

slipped inside and closed the door gently behind us. Inside was a passage, dimly lit by a single fluorescent tube. A smell of spicy food hung in the air – turmeric or cumin – and I guessed we were in the kitchen area. After the heat outside, the air-conditioned atmosphere bit cold. I began to shudder, and felt the sweat congealing in the small of my back.

Two metres to our left the corridor came to a dead end in a closed door; to the right, it turned a corner. I calculated that our target room was almost directly above our heads.

I peeped round the corner. Another passage, longer, with doors on both sides, almost dark. This one lay parallel with the front of the building. I reckoned it must lead to stairs opposite the front door.

The floor was cement painted with some dark-green compound. Our boots made no sound on it as we tip-toed along. In fifteen paces we were at one side of a small entrance-hall or lobby, bare of furniture. The front door was to our right, and stairs with a metal banister rail and the same dark-green paint on the treads rose to our left. Beyond the reception area the passage carried on through the other half of the building.

Tony put a hand on my arm and pointed. Farther down the corridor, on the left, light was showing through the crack of a partially opened door. The room could have been an office – but equally it could have been the bog. Whatever it was, nobody was moving, and I shook my head to show we should ignore it.

I went up the steps first, the Browning cocked, while Tony covered me from below. At the head of the stairs another corridor ran directly above the one on the ground floor. Dim fluorescent tubes glowed in the ceiling.

Standing on the second-top step, I put my head cautiously round the corner of the passage. From under the last door on the left, at the end, light was showing. Without turning back, I waved my left hand to bring Tony up. A moment later I felt him materialise at my shoulder.

There in the heart of the building the noise of the air conditioners was much reduced, and it was quiet enough for me to hear my heart pounding. This was it. This was the spot we'd come 4,000 miles to reach. All we had to do now was creep forward

126

about twelve metres, open the door and drop the target where he sat.

Suddenly we heard a noise below: a chair had been pushed back or the drawer of a filing-cabinet slid shut. Then door-hinges squeaked, and soft footsteps came towards us along the ground-floor corridor.

In a second we were both round the corner, into the upper passage, backs to the wall, in full view of anyone who came out of the target's room but shielded from the stairs. The footsteps started up the first flight. In ten seconds they'd be level with us.

Without a sound Tony pressed his Browning into my left hand and drew his Commando knife from its sheath on his belt. As the newcomer reached the top step Tony struck so fast round the corner that I saw nothing but a flurry of movement. The man made hardly a sound – just one gargling grunt as the blade drove into the side of his neck. If you rip out a guy's jugular and windpipe with one thrust, he doesn't start shouting. Tony caught him by the shoulder as he crumpled, turning the torso away from himself so that the spurting blood flew wide. The limp body slid bumping down the steps and came to rest on the half landing.

I could feel Tony quivering as I handed him back his pistol. Now, I thought: move, *move*.

Before I'd taken a step the passage lights went off. A second later they flickered back on, pinking and clicking, then went off, came on again, and finally died. With them went the air-conditioning, and the background drone sank away into total silence.

Jesus! A power-cut. The extreme tension made me connect the shut-down with the corpse on the stairs. Had we somehow caused the breakdown? Had the fall of that body triggered some switch? Impossible, surely. It must be a coincidence. Whatever the cause, maybe the blackout would work to our advantage. Maybe it would flush Khadduri out and send him straight towards us.

I felt for my torch, down a slim pocket on my left thigh. 'Get ready,' I breathed. 'This'll bring him out.'

For a moment nothing happened. I was stricken by a fleeting panic that Khadduri wasn't in his lair after all. Then we heard movements inside his room, and I tensed myself for the door to open.

Another wait. What the hell was he doing? Maybe he was

127

frantically trying to save whatever he had in his computer. But then, after another few seconds, came back the power: the fluorescent strips clicked and popped back into life; the air-conditioning units started up again.

With the background noise restored I ducked back on to the staircase, jabbed my pressel switch and said softly, 'Pat, what the fuck's happening to the power?'

'Dunno,' came the instant answer. 'The whole system went down for a few seconds. The entire camp was dark. Back on now.'

'OK. Nobody moving?'

'Not a soul.'

I felt my boot slip on the second step down, and realised the stairs were running with blood. Now I'd be leaving footprints. Too bad. Even our boots were Soviet-made.

I gave Tony a nudge and pointed down the corridor, breathing, 'Let's go.' But we'd taken only a couple of steps when the power went down yet again.

We stood still in the pitch-black corridor. I had the Browning in my right hand, torch in the left. Now he'll come out, I told myself. I reached back, hooked the torch round Tony's elbow and drew him forward with me. We crept on, one step, two, three, until I reckoned we were no more than six or seven feet from the target's door.

Noises came from inside the room: somebody stumbling over furniture. We heard the handle turn, then the hinges squeaked as the door came open. Torch on. There in the beam was al-Khadduri – heavier, greyer than I remembered, hair ruffled up on end, but without the slightest doubt the same man – in an open-necked white shirt, carrying a buff file-holder in his right hand.

His eyes had a startled look and he opened his mouth to say something, but before any word came out my 9mm bullet smacked him in the centre of the forehead. The impact knocked him backwards bodily, and he slumped to the floor. On the deck his head turned sideways, and in an instant I was on top of him, putting a second round through his skull just above the ear. At the second shot the body twitched and jerked as if it had had an electric current shot through it, and the feet, which were encased in some kind of soft shoes, went *slap, slap, slap* against the wall as the dead

128

man's knees doubled up and straightened violently, up, down, up, down. I saw now there'd been no need for the second round, because the first bullet had blown off the back of his skull and a mess of brains was hanging out. The papers had cascaded out of his file and scattered along the floor. There was blood on his face, his shirt, the floor, the door.

Subconsciously I knew that even the silenced pistol had made two heavy thuds, enough to have alerted anyone on the upper storey, but our immediate need was to snap some pictures of the dead man so that Western intelligence chiefs got absolute proof he'd been eliminated.

For a couple of seconds I sat on Khadduri's legs to stop that mad thrashing. Then, as the nerve-responses faded, I stood up, and in a pre-arranged move Tony holstered his pistol and grabbed the body under the armpits. The hands and arms were still twitching as he dragged it a couple of steps backwards and propped it against the door. By the time he had it in position I'd got my Instamatic camera lined up, the torch beam giving enough light to aim the lens, and I knew the automatic flash would do the rest.

'For Pete's sake get a move on,' Tony gasped. 'The bastard's bleeding all over me. I hope to hell he hasn't got AIDS.'

'Tip his head back a bit,' I hissed. 'Up! Up! Get him by the hair . . . That's it. Wipe the blood off his nose. There – hold him there. Now turn his head sideways for a profile.'

I fired off six frames, three full-face, three profile, then pouched the camera and turned to go. In a couple of seconds we were at the top of the stairs, but shouts and a rush of feet in the lower corridor halted us on the top landing.

Men were yelling '*Misabeeh! Misabeeh!*'

'Lights,' whispered Tony, 'they're shouting for lights.' Then, voicing my own thoughts, he said, 'They'll find the body on the stairs. That'll stop them. Use the window. It's only a ten or twelve foot drop.'

We ran back to Khadduri's door, stepped over his huddled body, turned the handle and went in. On impulse I reached back, felt for a soft, still warm hand, grabbed it, dragged the body into the room and shut the door behind it.

The room was slightly less dark than the corridor, lit by enough moonlight to make out the pieces of furniture. As Tony picked his way through them to the window I felt for the key and turned it in the lock.

Then he hissed, 'Shit!'

'What's the matter?'

'Can't shift the window. Must be locked.'

I knew from our observation during the day that the casements were made of heavy-duty metal. I came up beside Tony, grabbed the lever-handle and heaved downwards. No movement whatever. Bringing out my Browning, I slammed the butt against the glass – but although the pane buckled it didn't break. Against the moonlight I peered closely and saw that it was reinforced with wire mesh.

I whipped back to the door and opened it slightly to listen. They'd found the body on the stairs and were jabbering like monkeys. There was no way we'd get down past them. We were trapped on the upper storey.

I locked the door again and got on the radio. 'All stations. The bird is down. Repeat, the bird is down. But we've been compromised. We need immediate distractions. Pat, are you hearing me?'

'Loud and clear.'

'Get an RPG into the right-hand end of our building. Upper floor, *your* right-hand end. Now. Then fire your distraction charge soonest. After that, if it's still on, have a crack at the satellite dish.

'Whinger?'

'Hello.'

'Once the rocket's gone, get rounds down into the area of the guardroom. Are there any lights on in the camp? Over.'

'No lights, Geordie. The whole system's gone down.'

'OK. Let me know if anything comes on. We're in the bird's nest itself. We're stuck for the moment. But it's no sweat. When we can, we're coming out through the window that was lit.'

In one of the pouches of my belt-kit I had two small demolition charges, ready made up. It took only a few seconds to mould them on to the window fastening. 'I'll wait for the RPG to hit,' I told Tony. 'Then I'll blow it. Block your ears.'

We both lay flat on the floor at the base of the outer wall, heads away from the window, thumbs over ears. Seconds crawled past. I held the clacker between my knees, willing Pat to let drive. Then, without warning, there came a thunderbolt, an immense roar, and a concussion that shook the entire building. In its aftermath, the boom of our little charge was tiny, but still enough to leave our ears ringing.

Tony and I leapt up. The window had swung open. With my shamag in a bundle I swept the sill back and forth to clear any broken glass and went out feet-first. The barrel of my AK-47 caught on the top of the frame, and I had to wriggle my torso violently to free it. Then I hung down, flexed my knees and let go.

The landing was hard but OK. Just as Tony thumped down beside me, a huge sheet of flame split the night from along by the gate, instantly followed by the *boom* of another explosion. Good on yer, Pat, I thought.

On the radio I called, 'Norm, we're out front and coming round the corner towards you. Are you there?'

'Roger. Ready and waiting.'

We scuttled to the corner of the building, felt rather than saw Norm in front of us, and all three headed fast for the gap in the wire. By then rounds were going down in every direction. Short bursts were coming in from Pat and Whinger, but from several points inside the wire tracer was flying out into the desert, most of it in the direction of the gate, where the explosion had started a small fire.

As we reached the wire I heard the *whoosh* of another rocket coming in. Turning, I saw the streak of it heading for the comms dish. Automatically I began counting: one, two, three . . . By four I knew it had missed. Fractionally later came a *boom* as it self-destructed.

Fuck the dish, I thought. We're not risking our lives for that.

We wriggled through the gap in the wire, ran until we were well clear of the fence, and dropped into a hollow. I was panting and sweating in the hot outside air, but on a high, boosted by a mixture of fear and elation. I felt neither tired nor hungry, not even thirsty – just great. 'Stew,' I called. 'Have you onpassed to the head-shed that the bird is down?'

'Roger. Message passed and acknowledged. The heli's on its way.'

'Brilliant. Let's go.'

We fell in with Whinger easily enough. 'Fucking missed!' he went.

'No sweat,' I told him. 'Where's the launcher?'

'I binned it.'

'OK, let's leave it. We've got problems enough already.'

Little did I know the validity of what I was saying. When we reached the OP — our first ERV — there was no sign of Pat. He should have been there by then.

'Pat,' I called over the radio, 'ERV One, now.'

No answer. I called again, and waited with anxiety mounting fast. Then at last came an answer.

It was Pat all right, but not the jaunty, confident response we were used to hearing. His voice sounded weak and slow. 'Problem,' he slurred, 'I've been hit. Can't move.'

'Jesus!' I cried. 'Where are you?'

'Main gate. Five o'clock, two hundred metres.'

'Hang on there. We're coming.'

We started running in his direction, parallel with the wire, a couple of hundred metres out. Bursts of automatic fire came cracking out over our heads, with the odd red tracer round looping past to show us it wasn't all that high. Whinger kept yelling 'FUCKIN' ARSEHOLES!' like a lunatic. I nearly shouted at him to shut up, but decided he'd pay no attention.

Whether or not the defenders could see us it was impossible to tell, but I guessed not. I reckoned they were just loosing off rounds into the desert to raise their morale. They had plenty to keep them occupied. The blaze started by Pat's distraction charge had died out, but the accommodation block was well alight, with flames spreading along it from the right-hand end. I could see figures running about outside the building, and hear men yelling in high, harsh voices. Vehicles were on the move, headlights sweeping the desert. I tried not to look at the lights or flames because the glare destroyed my night-vision.

The ground was uneven enough to make searching difficult, the hollows containing pools of deeper darkness.

'Spread out,' I called. 'Get a line. It's the only way to find him.'

We fanned out to twenty metres apart in a line end-on to the wire, tripping and falling in the sandy hollows. Whenever headlights swung in our direction, everyone went down and stayed flat until the beams had passed. This made progress erratic, and confused our eyes still more. I was beginning to think we must have gone past Pat when Norm suddenly called, 'Here he is.'

We were round him in a flash. He was lying in a bit of a dip, on his right side, with his left leg curled up but his right leg straight out beneath it. As we huddled round he didn't speak. With my back to the camp I switched on my torch and immediately saw blood gleaming in the sand.

'Right leg,' I said. 'Turn him over.'

He groaned and blasphemed as we got him on his back. With my knife I cut his trousers and slit upwards. One look told me that a bullet had gone right through his leg and caught his femur just above the knee. A splinter of bone was protruding from a bloody opening. I whipped out my shamag and twisted it up into a sausage to make a tourniquet above the wound.

'Get on the radio to Stew,' I ordered. 'Tell him we need the trailer forward, as close behind the OP as he can get it.'

I got the tourniquet in position, broke out two thick wound-dressings from my emergency pack and bound them into place with Norm's shamag, one on either hole. When I shone the torch on Pat's face he looked deathly pale, and his eyes moved slowly. I felt round his neck for the sachet of morphia. It was still in place, so I jerked the cord in half, pulled off the cap and banged the needle into his good thigh.

'He's lost a lot of blood,' I said. 'He needs an IV, fast.'

Suddenly a brighter glare blazed out of the camp, and the beam of a searchlight swept over the desert to our right. 'For fuck's sake!' called Whinger. 'Let's get him into a deeper hole.'

He and Norm took Pat by the arms and began dragging him backwards over the sand, ignoring his protests. I picked up his rifle and went after them. Then I saw the beam of the light swinging fast towards us.

'On the deck!' I snapped. 'Down!'

Down we went, but not quick enough. The light beamed on to

us, swung past, then checked and came back. The operator had seen us. A second later rounds came flying down the line of the beam. The air all round my head was suddenly full of vicious snapping and crackling. It was a machine gun, firing long bursts.

We were pinned down fifty metres short of the dunes and good cover. If we'd all been fit we could maybe have rolled into hollows and got away with it. But Pat couldn't move on his own. To me his body showed up as big as an elephant's, caught in that lethal beam. If anyone had good binos at the other end, they were bound to see it.

There was only one thing to do. I rolled a couple of metres to my left, came up in a firing position and let drive at the light with my AK–47: one, two, three short bursts, raising my point of aim slightly each time. I was aware of someone else firing too, on my right. At my fourth burst the light vanished, but rounds were still snapping close overhead.

'Keep down!' I yelled. 'Give 'em time to lose their point of aim.'

In a few seconds the firing stopped.

'OK,' I called. 'Let's go.'

Whinger got hold of Pat again, but Norm wasn't with him.

'Norm!' I called. 'Where are you? Norm?'

I scuttled four or five steps to where I'd last seen him, and there he was, flat on his front, slumped face-down over his rifle. Feeling desperately exposed, I knelt with my back to the camp and flicked on my torch. Blood was welling from a hole at the base of his neck. A bullet had gone in on the inner end of the collar bone, killing him instantly. The round must have raked through his chest and out through his spine.

I found I was shaking. 'Norm's gone,' I said.

'Want me to carry him?' Tony was lying beside me.

'I'll manage him. You help drag Pat.'

The volume of incoming fire increased again, green tracer now added to the red. There must have been twenty or thirty guys loosing off from various areas of the camp, and now two machine guns were firing. Praise be, the whole lot was going high. Looking back, I saw that the power had been partially restored: a few lights were showing dimly, as though worked by emergency generators. More sinister was the fact that vehicles were lining up one behind the other, facing the centre gate, as if a sortie was about to be launched into the desert.

With the air full of lead, everyone's instinct was to stay on the deck and crawl into shelter. But you can't crawl in soft sand dragging a heavy weight. Scary as it was, the only thing to do was to stand up. With Tony's help I got Norm over my shoulder in a fireman's lift, his arms hanging down my back. Even though Tony had taken his rifle, he seemed a hell of a weight. I started taking very short steps, but my feet slid in the sand and I made practically no progress.

Then out of the air came Stew's reassuring voice: 'On the move with the trailer. Can you give me a steer?'

I was panting so hard I could hardly speak. 'Stew,' I gasped, 'we're in the shit. Norm's been topped. Thirty seconds, someone'll be on the back of a dune. Give you two flashes, repeated.'

I struggled on a few more steps. I could feel Norm's warm blood dripping down the backs of my legs. The other two were dragging Pat on, drawing ahead. Tracer was still sailing high over us. Somehow we had to make the back of the first big dune, in dead ground from the camp.

No breath left. I had to put Norm down. I got hold of his limp left hand and started trying to drag him, but in the deep sand his weight and the pouches of his belt-kit made it almost impossible.

Dimly I realised that Tony and Whinger had got Pat over the lip and into a temporary refuge. A second later Whinger was back beside me. He grabbed Norm's other hand, and the two of us got the body moving. By the time we had it in dead ground Tony had started giving Stew double flashes. With incredible relief I heard the engine of his quad, purring towards us. In a moment he was alongside.

'What happened?'

'Norm got one smack in the chest,' I said. 'Instantaneous. Pat's got a gunshot wound to the right leg. He's lost a lot of blood.'

I knew we ought to put more ground between us and the enemy before I started work on the casualty. On the other hand, I didn't think Pat could last very long.

'Get the body in the trailer,' I said. 'And Pat. I've got to give him an IV right away.'

135

While the others lifted Norm and lowered him into the bottom of the trailer, I broke out the med pack and sorted an IV drip. My hands were shaking so much I had trouble with the packaging.

'Watch that fucking gate for me, Whinger,' I said. 'Tell me if the bastards start out.'

I slit away the sleeve of Pat's shirt and got the needle in his arm, but I had nothing to hang the bag of fluid from, so I handed it to Stew and said, 'Hold that a minute.'

'Watch it, Geordie,' called Whinger, who was observing from up on the mound. 'They're at the gate now.'

'Tell me when they've got it open.'

'Wait out.'

We got a minute or so's respite. Then Whinger called, 'They're coming through. Six, seven, eight vehicles.'

'Head for the LUP, then. Gimme the bag, Stew. I'll ride with him.'

But could we move? When Stew went into gear and revved up, his wheels just spun in the sand. The weight in the trailer was too great. I leaped out, preparing to walk beside Pat, holding the IV above him. But still the trailer wouldn't shift.

I pushed as hard as I could with my free hand. Tony was on the other side, heaving like he was in a rugger scrum. Whinger was still up top, observing the enemy. The temptation was to call him down and get him pushing too, but we needed him where he was.

We made maybe fifty yards at a desperately slow speed, before the quad slewed sideways and slid, dropping into a deep, steep-sided hole, with the trailer jack-knifed round against it. The fall had jerked the needle out of Pat's arm, and I was left with it dangling on the end of the tube. At that very instant Whinger called down, 'Watch it, Geordie, they're turning to come in along the new road ahead of us.'

I took an awful decision: we had to ditch Norm, and Pat we must save at all costs.

'Where's your Semtex?' I asked Tony.

'Some here,' he patted his pouches. 'Most of it's in the trailer. Why?'

'I want you to get rid of Norm's body.'

'Aw, shit!'

'I know. But we've got to do it. Those are our orders. If we keep him with us we'll put everyone at risk.'

By then we were in one hell of a mess. Our only hope of getting the trailer out of the hole was to empty it. But Pat was lying on top of the heap, and before we could get Norm clear we had to shift Pat back on to land, causing him horrendous pain.

I broke out a fresh wound-dressing, wrapped the IV needle in it and laid the whole kit on top of my AK-47. Then I went to work. The body was still warm as in life. Holding it under the arms, I hauled it out and dragged it ten yards clear. Tony came with me, carrying his gear.

'What shall I do?' I asked. 'Put him on his side in a foetal position?'

'I guess. I've never done this before.'

'How much Semtex have you got?'

'Twelve pounds.'

'Put five in his midriff, and we'll wrap him round it. Tie his hands behind his knees.'

'What about the fuse?'

'Wait till we've got the trailer sorted. Then give us fifteen minutes.'

'OK.'

'Can you manage?'

'I guess so.'

'Sorry, Tony.'

I felt round Norm's neck to make sure he wasn't wearing his ID discs on a chain, then scuttled back to the quad. Stew had already unhitched the empty trailer and pulled it up on to level ground. I broke out a rope and called Whinger down to help pull. With Stew driving and us two heaving, the bike scrabbled its way back on to the flat. All the time I was working, my mind was on Tony and his horrible task.

We were all moving fast and silently, shocked by the realisation that Norm, our taciturn but ever-reliable mate, was about to be blown to eternity. We also knew that we were rapidly being surrounded. Still not speaking, we hitched up again, reloaded Pat and the two spare weapons into the trailer, and tried another start. This time the quad went forward without anyone pushing, and I knew we'd made the critical difference to the load.

I got the IV needle back into Pat's arm and told him to hold the bag up above his head with the other hand. 'Keep it up as long as you can,' I told him. 'Then have a rest, and up again.'

Turning to Tony I called, 'How are you doing?'

'Finishing now. What about the fuse?'

'Start it going.'

Whinger had scrambled back to his lookout post. 'Lights moving out,' he said. 'Coming across our line of retreat.'

'Shit!' I muttered. 'Let's go.'

We reached the LUP without further incident. Stew had already ripped down the cam-netting, so we folded it over into a makeshift blanket, to give Pat some padding from the bumps and insulation from the air. In the distance behind us the Libyans were still filling the air with lead.

'Booby trap both spare quads,' I told Tony. 'Pile most of the Semtex on them, and put a jerrican of petrol underneath. Quick as you can.'

I put my head close to the casualty's and said, 'Pat?'

'Yeah.'

'You hear me all right?'

'Sure.'

'Listen. We've got to motor. Keep the bag up for as long as you can, OK?'

'Right.'

I turned to Tony and said, 'Pat's pulled back a bit already. I reckon he's stable now. How are you doing?'

'Matter of seconds. I'm giving this one fifteen minutes of det cord.'

'How long till Norm goes?'

He shot a quick glance at his watch. 'Eight minutes.'

'Let's get moving then.'

'OK. It's burning.' Tony stood back for a second, then crossed to his own quad and jumped aboard.

At last we were properly under way, heading due south, myself in the lead. Already the sand was firmer, the going faster. With every minute that passed, the noise of firing faded behind us. I uttered a silent prayer of thanks for the Magellans. With the coordinates of ERV Six punched in, the needle on my little illuminated dial was giving me our course, and warning me every time I deviated to right or left.

Yet as the seconds ticked away, I felt terrific tension rising inside me. Norm was about to be vaporised. The idea was disgusting, incredible. I thought of the bomb at Warren Point which had killed nineteen Paras. Two of them had literally disappeared into thin air; no trace of them was ever found.

Lights! Lights ahead of us and below, maybe three hundred metres from us.

'Everyone stop,' I called. 'Standby to see how far they're going.'

Like the twats they were, the Libyans were driving slowly along the new road with headlights full on. The vehicles were maybe a couple of hundred yards apart, engines and gearboxes grinding in low gear.

'First explosion imminent,' said Tony's voice in my ear – and then, before I had time to agonise any more, it came. A terrific flash split the sky behind us, and a heavy *boom!* buffeted through the air. Norman was gone. I tried to shut my mind to details about which bit of him might have been blown where; I just hoped there was nothing whatever left. Annihilation.

When I tried to swallow, my throat felt desperately dry, and I was shaking with reaction. Concentrate on the job in hand, I told myself.

I looked at the road and realised something was wrong with the picture I could see.

'Whinger,' I called softly, 'you said you counted eight vehicles through the gate?'

'Correct,' he answered. 'There's only six still moving. Two of the bastards have stopped off somewhere.'

'Wait one.' I pulled up my kite-sight and switched it on. Sure enough, I picked up the two delinquents, one a couple of hundred yards to the left of our line of retreat, the other twice that. 'They're putting out a cordon,' I said. 'The next one will stop in a moment . . . There he goes.'

A third vehicle came to a halt and doused its lights. Scanning the ground with the night-sight, I saw that fortune at last was favouring us. From where we were a shallow gully ran down to the new road;

139

rolling down it we would be invisible, and the sides would contain the sound of our engines.

'We'll slip through between them,' I said. 'How long till the next bang, Tony?'

'Four minutes.'

'We'll use that as a diversion. Give us a count-down. All stations get your eyes shut before the flash. As soon as it goes, we roll. Whinger, stay back to cover the rest of us across. Once we're over, we'll stop and cover you.'

'Roger.'

While we waited, I kept scanning with the sight. As I had expected, Gadaffi's fearless warriors preferred to do their soldiering from the safety of their vehicles. Nobody got out and started to walk about.

'One minute,' Tony announced.

I tucked the sight down the front of my shirt and settled my PNGs back over my eyes. At fifteen seconds I closed my eyes – and it was just as well, because the flash and bang came fractionally before Tony called them.

This second explosion, being much closer, sounded far more dramatic. Anyone looking back towards the camp would have got an eyeful. Before the echoes had rolled away we were bobbing down the gully and across the road. I held my breath and kept going steadily until we were well clear, then stopped everyone and turned to cover the crossing while I called Whinger on.

Now we were on the hard ground and up to full speed. We had a much shorter way to go than on the run-in, because our pick-up point was only a couple of kilometres beyond the south bank of the big wadi.

After twenty minutes of steady travel, I called, 'All stations – comms halt now. Close on me.'

With pickets out ahead and behind, Whinger set up his Satcom and started aligning the little dish-aerial. I thought of the big aerial in the camp, still functioning, and tried to put that minor failure behind me. As Whinger fiddled, I took another look at Pat. When I loosened the tourniquet, blood started to seep through the wound-dressings, so I tightened it again and got another IV going. I stayed with him while Whinger was getting through to Hereford, chatting quietly to encourage him, trying not to think about Norm.

'Fucking great bang,' Pat muttered hazily. 'What was that?'

'Tony put your quad into orbit, to stop anyone else getting their hands on it.'

'Shit hot!'

'Going through,' said Whinger.

I passed the IV bag to Tony and took the handset. 'Zero Alpha, Zero Alpha, this is Delta Four. How do you hear me?'

'Zero Alpha. Loud and clear. Over.' It was Mac's voice, his Glasgow accent unmistakable even via the satellite.

'Delta Four. I confirm the bird is down. We're clear of the target area and heading for the pick-up point. ETA there between figures four zero and figures six zero minutes from now. Repeat from four zero to six zero minutes.'

'Zero Alpha. Roger. Your transport is en route to you. Will confirm your timings to Captain Steve. Over.'

'Delta Four. Roger. We have one casualty. Bravo Seven has a serious leg wound. He's stable, but we need a doctor soonest. Best if we can have one on the Herc. Over.'

'Zero Alpha. Roger. We'll do what we can.'

We found a different way down into the wadi and picked out a path across its boulder-strewn floor without difficulty. After a quick run across the gravel plain, we were on the pick-up location well within the window I'd given. The ground there was flat and hard, with a bit of sand on the surface, but no obstructions, so that the heli would be able to land anywhere. Having chosen the best-looking spot, we spread out in all-round defence and listened for the sound of engines.

The night was utterly quiet, with just a breath of wind from the south-east. Looking back to the north, I could see no lights in the sky, no sign of vehicles moving, and I guessed that after a token watch in the desert the Libyans had retreated into camp. I imagined a fire-crew fighting the blaze in the accommodation block. If the whole building had gone up and Khadduri's body had been incinerated, the home team might never realise that he'd been assassinated.

Scanning through my PNGs, I could make out the other quads

dotted round in a circle. It was difficult to sit still and wait, so hyped-up did I feel. Every minute or two I had a word with Pat, lying in the trailer beside me. During one of the longer silences, the idea of meeting Norm's next-of-kin began to bug me. Because he came from so far away – Glasgow – and spoke so little, I didn't know much about his family. I had the impression that his father was dead and his mum had married again. What was I going to say to her?

I kept trying to work out when our Chinook would have taken off from Siwa and how long it might take to reach us. As we had no solid information, everything was guesswork. From their pre-briefing, the crew knew that ERV Six was twenty kilometres due south of the camp perimeter, and I was confident they were heading for us.

It was Whinger, with his very sharp ears, who heard the sound first. 'Aircraft engines east,' he announced. I switched my radio to the channel I expected the chopper crew to be using and called, 'Hello Steve, hello Steve, this is Geordie. How d'you read me? Over.'

'Hi, Geordie. You're loud and clear. I'm heading two-six-zero. Estimating six minutes to the LZ. Over.'

'Roger. That's great. Keep coming. We can hear you due east of our position. The deck's clear for you to land. We've got a firefly on now.'

'Roger. Do my guys need any particular instructions for loading your casualty?'

'No, thanks. We've got him laid in the trailer, so he can be driven straight in.'

'Roger. Standby.'

'And . . . Steve?'

'Yes?'

'We've only four quads left. Had to bin the others. So the loadies'll only need to count four in.'

'Roger.'

It was a fantastic relief to know that the chopper was on course. Again I gave thanks for the existence of the Magellan and the pinpoint accuracy it offered us. No doubt the crew of the Chinook would have found us in the end by using old-fashioned methods of

142

navigation, but almost certainly the recovery would have taken longer. Most of my anxieties fell away; now the main worry was Pat.

For three or four minutes the engine hum grew steadily louder.

'We're hearing you stronger,' I called. 'Keep coming.'

'Roger,' Steve called, and then, 'OK, OK. I've got you. We were almost spot on. Turning towards you now. OK, the firefly's on the nose. All clear to land beside it?'

'Perfect. We're standing off.'

'Roger. I'll come straight in.'

I went back on to our chatter net and called to Whinger: 'Pull away from his line of approach or you'll get your bloody head cut off. All stations, start up. He'll be here in under a minute. Stew, you'll be first on with the trailer.'

'Roger.'

Pulling the PNGs down on to my chest, I replaced them with ordinary ski goggles, started the quad and turned to face into the circle. For a few moments I could hear the noise of my own engine. Then the thudding of rotor blades and the scream of turbines blotted it out, and all at once a great black monster was looming towards us out of the night, practically at ground level, with a dark sand–cloud seething behind it.

Without wasting an instant, Steve hovered, turned in the air and put his arse down right beside the firefly. In the last few seconds the noise became overwhelming. Sand and dust boiled up furiously, and as I drove into the cloud I found the ramp already down, and there were the loadies, beckoning Stew on. In less than a minute all four quads were safely aboard, and we lifted away.

In the dim light of the hold I could see that Tony's face and hands were smeared with dried blood. Khadduri's. My hands were the same, but the blood was Pat's. The blood all down the backs of my legs was Norm's.

For our lads, the relief of being airborne was overwhelming; we felt we were already half-way home, our troubles behind us. For the crew, though, things were different. From their strained faces I could see they were shitting themselves with the possibility of going down in alien territory. Not until we'd cleared the Egyptian border would they be able to relax. Engine failure, or a SAM from a trigger-happy sentry in some Libyan frontier-post – either would spoil the party in a few seconds. In my mind I ran through the emergency drills we'd talked about in Hereford, what we'd do in the event of a forced landing. We still had enough explosive to destroy the Chinook if need be, but that would be the last resort.

As for Pat, I knew the important thing was to make him keep fighting. On other operations I'd seen guys who'd been wounded hold out well until they thought they were in safe hands, and then suddenly slide downhill as they stopped making a positive effort to survive. When that happens, shock can take over.

I went and looked down over the side of the trailer. Pat's eyes were shut, so I gave him a tap on the arm and shouted, 'Stick at it, mate. There's going to be a doctor on the Herc. Only an hour to go.'

The morphine had put him half-under, but he mustered a bit of a smile and muttered, 'Fuck 'em all!'

I raised a thumb, held my fist above his head for a moment, gave him a tap on the shoulder and moved away.

When I called the head-shed on the secure radio link, I was put straight on to the CO. I told him about Norm and Pat, but there was only one subject he seemed interested in: was I sure that the target was dead?

'As fucking mutton, Boss,' I told him. 'He had two rounds through the head, one from the front, one from the side. His brains are spattered half-way across Libya. We've got photos to prove it.'

'Good work,' he conceded. 'And nobody got a good look at you?'

'Only the target. No one else.'

'Brilliant. We'll see you back here presently.'

EIGHT

When I heard that Tracy had been on the phone the night before my heart leapt, but the surge of hope lasted only a few seconds.

'I'm afraid she made the call under duress,' Foxy Fraser told me. 'The message was very downbeat. Listen for yourself.' He switched on a tape deck, and when Tracy's voice came loud and clear out of the speakers it nearly cracked me up. I had to get hold of myself before I could grasp what she was saying. Apart from the emotional shock of hearing her apparently so near, there was something odd about the rhythm of her speech; it didn't sound natural, and I had to run through the tape twice before I realised she'd been reading out a prepared script.

'Geordie, listen,' she said. 'You *have* to come and get us. You *have* to make the arrangement very soon. We can't wait any longer. If you haven't made the arrangement by midday on the first of June they are going to kill Tim. Tim first, then me. Geordie, I love you. You can't let us die. For God's sake send a message through Sinn Fein in Belfast.'

I clenched my fists under the table, took a deep breath and looked across at Fraser.

He twitched his head quickly to one side, chin out and back, as if to say, 'I'm feeling for you, mate.'

'What do we do?' I asked. 'We've got to move now.'

Fraser cleared his throat. 'We had one false alarm,' he said. 'Not sure what it was – whether the tout was trying to make a quick buck, or what. We got a tip that the hostages were being held in a flat in Earl's Court – not one of the known addresses. We put the place under surveillance immediately. That night three men came out at ten o'clock. Nobody we knew. While they were in the pub a lock-picking specialist slipped in and took a look round.'

'And?'

'Nothing. There was nobody else at home, no sign there ever had been. Our operator left a microphone in the ceiling light, but it's yielded nothing. The men are just Paddies working on building sites. All they talk about is prostitutes and race-horses. It was a bum steer.'

'This call . . .' I gestured at the tape, 'was it a bluff?'

'With the PIRA you can never tell. They're so blasted erratic. Obviously they're trying to crank up the pressure. Somebody in Belfast is probably putting the screws on the London boys. We need to take the threat seriously, whatever.'

'What's this about Sinn Fein?'

'We do sometimes send messages through their office in Belfast.'

'Well, can you do that now?'

'Of course – when we've decided what to say.'

'In that case I'm going to make a move.'

Fraser glanced at me sharply. 'What are you proposing?'

'You know that scheme I told them about the last time?'

'For springing Farrell from a police convoy?'

'Exactly. I'm going ahead with it.'

'Geordie!' Fraser stood up and moved towards me with an anxious expression on his face. 'There are some things you can do, and some you can't. This is –'

'Listen!' I cut him off. 'It's my kid's life that's at stake. I'm not going to sit around and let him get killed. We've got to get off our arses and act.'

'I wouldn't say we're sitting around, exactly. We've got a big operation going on out there.'

'Yes – and what's it producing? Two thirds of three fifths of fuck-all.' Seeing Fraser colour up, I added, 'I didn't mean that personally. I'm not trying to criticise; I know how cunning these bastards are. But they're not getting away with this one.'

I found I was pacing about the room: something I don't usually do. I made myself sit down again and said, 'I've thought it through, and it's perfectly possible.'

'I don't see it,' Fraser replied. 'Apart from anything else, you'll get yourself kicked out of the Regiment.'

'No, no – I haven't explained properly. I changed my mind.

We'll do it *with* the Regiment. Their support will be essential.'

Fraser looked blank. 'I still don't get it. Don't tell me your commanding officer's going to sanction your breaking the law of the land, setting a dangerous criminal free.'

'Maybe he will, maybe he won't. *Everyone's* got to agree, of course.'

'Who's everyone?'

'The Regiment. Yourselves. The prison authorities. The regular police. Then, I suppose, the Home Office and the Home Secretary. Maybe ultimately the Prime Minister.'

'I think you're getting a bit carried away.' Fraser was staring at me as if I'd gone round the twist. 'So what exactly do you propose doing?'

'I'm calling it Plan Zulu. In training or on operations we always start off with Plan A and Plan B – Alpha and Bravo. This is the ultimate plan, the last resort. Therefore it's Plan Z for Zulu.'

I started pacing around again. 'We have a big O-group – collect together all the people I've mentioned, and explain the scheme to them. Then, at an agreed time on an agreed day, the prison authorities move Farrell from Birmingham to somewhere else – it doesn't matter what the destination is supposed to be, as they don't have to tell him. The prisoner'll be in a closed van, and won't know where he's going.'

'He could be going down the road to Long Lartin,' said Fraser.

'Where's that?'

'The nick near Evesham where quite a few IRA prisoners are held.'

I stared at the Special Branch man, amazed that he seemed to be entering into my plan.

'Great!' I went. 'Presumably they don't have any obligation to tell him where he's going.'

'No. When they ship people like that and don't give a destination, it's known as putting them on the ghost train.'

'Got it. So they bring him out. We get guys from the Regiment to drive the police cars and the prison van – the meat wagon, you call it, don't you? – and at a predetermined spot we ambush the convoy, ram the van, force it off the road and stage a realistic battle, with plenty of bangs and rounds going down. We – myself and two or three of the lads — grab Farrell and take him to a safe house. As far as he'll know we're renegades from the army, doing this on our own initiative. I'll tell him I'm so desperate I've taken leave and brought in some civilian friends to help.'

Fraser had his eyebrows raised in a sceptical arch. 'Go on.'

'Then, from the safe house, we'll contact the PIRA and tell them to set a rendezvous for an exchange. But we'll also put a bug into one of Farrell's shoes, or his belt, and make certain that he can be trailed. Then we'll hand him over, do the swap, secure Tim and Tracy, let Farrell think he's got clear, and have the police nab him again.'

'And throw a bridge across the Irish Sea at the same time, just so you can go after him quicker.'

I glared at Fraser. He seemed to have lost heart again. 'Look,' I said, 'you don't appear to realise that all this is shit simple. We're trained to the eyeballs in ambush techniques. We have the cars to do an intercept, we have the weapons to stage a battle, and we can set up a safe house in our sleep. Apart from back-up on the ground, we'll have a helicopter airborne but standing well off out of sight, so that Farrell won't stand a cat in hell's chance of getting away. Nobody else has to do anything except put him in a van and let us drive him a few miles out of Birmingham into the country. All we need is the co-operation of the authorities.'

'And your commanding officer,' Fraser prompted.

'And the CO, of course. I'm due to see him in a minute, for a wash-up on our operation. Once that's over, maybe you and he can get together.'

'You're going to propose Plan Zulu to him, then?'

'Most certainly.'

'Well . . . I wish you luck.'

'Thanks.'

I got up to go, feeling that Fraser was still with me and willing to have a go — but only just. 'By the way, what's become of your assistant? Karen whatever?'

'Oh.' The Commander looked suddenly uncomfortable. 'She's . . . she's gone on a couple of days' leave.'

At the time I didn't challenge his statement, but there was something about Fraser's manner which made me doubt if it was true.

★

148

On the flight back from Cyprus Pat had been given priority and put on board a TriStar, so that within an hour of touch-down at Lyneham he was in the operating theatre of the tri-service hospital at RAF Wroughton, south of Swindon. The rest of us had lumbered back in a Herc, but because our departure was delayed we'd come in so late at night that our debrief had to be postponed until the morning.

Now, in Yorky Rose's office in the Subversive Action Wing, members of the head-shed had gathered to welcome us back.

Apart from Yorky himself there was Mac, the ops officer, the int officer, Gilbert the Filbert from the Firm, and above all the CO, Lieutenant Colonel Bob Brampton – commonly known as 'Wingnut', because of his ears, but liked and respected none the less. A fitness fanatic, he was glowing with good health; he looked like he'd been for a ten-mile run (which he probably had) and then had a big breakfast of vitamins.

The lads in our team were well spruced up, shaved and showered, but it wasn't surprising that we all looked a bit hollow-eyed, and yawns were two a penny.

If it hadn't been for the death of Norm, the atmosphere would have been positively euphoric. As it was, the CO was on a kind of muted high. He shook each of us by the hand, exclaiming 'Well done!', 'Great effort!', 'Tremendous!' and suchlike, but behind his laughing and joking sadness hung like a dark cloud.

He addressed us all. 'The Regiment's going to get a lot more work as a result of this. We're going to be run off our feet by the demand for our services.'

I knew that our success would increase his own credit rating as well – he might even end up with a gong – yet I could tell that he was feeling our loss as much as we were.

When the initial hubbub had subsided, the ruperts took a row of chairs behind Yorky's desk and we sat in a semi-circle facing them. The prize exhibits were the mug-shots I'd taken of Khadduri, full-face and profile. (The film had been whipped off me the moment we reached base and developed in the middle of the night.) The photos weren't a pretty sight, but they were technically spot-on, and proved that Tony and I hadn't been exaggerating. You could even see the tattoo of an eagle on the back of Tony's left hand as he held the dead man's head up by the hair, with the blood-spattered door of the office in the background.

The CO led off his formal spiel by saying a few words about Norm. He confirmed that the families officer was going to contact the next of kin, and said he would let us know the date of the funeral. More cheerful news was that Pat had come through his operation fine, and that the surgeons were pleased by the way things had gone.

Then the CO asked me to run through Operation Ostrich, which I did, with the int officer's gofer taking notes on a laptop. As I went along, the ruperts asked quite a few questions, and we took it in turns to answer. Their main concern was whether the defenders had seen any of us well enough to pick us out at an identity parade. To that the answer was 'Definitely not.' I reassured the int officer in particular that, with the exception of Khadduri, we hadn't met anyone face to face; in fact, I doubted whether the Libyans had actually got eyes on any of us. The fact that Norm and Pat had been hit was purely a fluke: first somebody must have seen the flashes as Pat put bursts into the camp, and sprayed rounds randomly in his direction; then we'd got caught in the searchlight.

At the end of the debriefing the CO told us again that we'd done exceptionally well, were a credit to the Regiment, had performed a service to humanity, and sundry crap of that kind. Then he added, 'You'll be glad to hear that Gadaffi's blaming the Israelis – off the record, of course. No public announcement has been made – Khadduri wasn't supposed to be in Libya at all – but in private Gadaffi's claiming that one of his own senior officers has been killed, and saying he has evidence that Mossad carried out the assassination.'

'Maybe somebody dropped something after all,' I said, giving Whinger an exaggerated look.

'What's that?' The CO turned his long, narrow face in my direction, so that I got his sticking-out ears in profile against the light.

'It was just a joke we had. Before the operation went down, Whinger suggested we should scatter a few Uzis around – or anything with "Israel" written on it – to lay a false scent.'

'But you didn't, I hope?'

'Of course not. As far as I know we didn't leave anything behind except a few shreds of anonymous metal and . . . and whatever remained of poor old Norm.'

'What about the body?' asked the CO.

I gestured at Tony.

'I doubled him up on the ground with five pounds of Semtex in his midriff,' he said. 'There can't have been anything left.'

Nobody spoke for a moment. Then the CO cleared his throat and said, 'OK. That was the right thing to do.'

Again there was a moment's silence. Then the CO adroitly changed the subject. 'You'll be glad to hear you have a fan at Number Ten. I found this fax waiting for me when I came in.'

He handed me a sheet of paper, which had 'FROM THE OFFICE OF THE PRIME MINISTER' embossed at the top, and, in the middle, the brief message:

Delighted with your ornithological success.
Congratulations, and my personal thanks.

'Where's the champagne, then?' I demanded as I handed the note on to Tony. 'I thought the bugger would have sent a few bottles in this direction by now.'

'We'll have a drink in the mess tonight,' said the CO. 'Make up for lost time then.'

The atmosphere was so good that I was tempted to press straight on to the subject of my own predicament. With everyone in such a genial mood this seemed the ideal moment to broach the idea of Plan Zulu. But then I thought, No – not in front of this crowd. I'd rather get the CO on his own. So, as the meeting broke up, I said to him, 'Could I grab five minutes with you, Boss?'

'Sure.' He took a quick look at his watch. 'Ten o'clock?'

'Fine.'

I was outside his office a couple of minutes early, bolstered by the knowledge that, for the moment at any rate, the sun seemed to be shining out of my arse. I wasn't naive enough to suppose that our success on Ostrich would warp the Boss's judgement or make him any more inclined to take rash decisions, but the fact that I'd just done a good job would at least encourage him to give me a fair hearing. Apart from anything else, he had two boys of his own, and could hopefully understand how I felt about Tim. Also he had a good sense of humour, and a reputation for taking the occasional risk when he thought it was justified.

Inside, I perched on one of the bog-standard chairs and looked around the room while he closed down his laptop. His bergen sat in one corner, and in another, curled up on a dark-blue bean-bag, lay his black Labrador, Ben, fast asleep as usual. No doubt he'd been on the ten-mile run as well, and that was him settled for the day.

'God's boots!' the Boss exclaimed when I had outlined my plan. With his elbows on the desk, he put his face between his hands and dug in his thumbs above his ears, as if to squeeze out the craziness of what he'd just heard. 'Pull the other one, Geordie.'

'No, no. I'm dead serious. We're up to our necks in shit, and sinking. We desperately need a new initiative – and I'm convinced Plan Zulu's the one. As I told Fraser – the SB guy – there'd be virtually no risk to anyone. OK, a couple of vehicles would get damaged and the guys in the meat wagon might get rattled around a bit, but that would be all.'

'What about our reputation? Can't you just see it in the tabloids? "SHOCK! TERROR! SAS SINKS TO GANG WARFARE TO FREE IRA CHIEF". You'd drop the whole Regiment in the shit, Geordie.'

'Not if we handled it properly. Nothing need ever get out. It'll be just one more covert operation on the mainland. There's dozens of others going on already, after all. Covert ops are bread and butter to Special Branch, just as they are to us.'

'That's true.' At last the CO looked up, as if seeing some light at the end of a tunnel. 'I have to say, I wouldn't mind if you gave it a go. But how the hell am I going to convince the powers that be? There's the Director, for a start. I can't see *him* sanctioning your scheme. He'll go bananas. Then there's the Home Office and the Home Secretary, if we want the police to be involved at high level. And what about the governor of the gaol? *He'll* throw a major wobbly as well.'

'I don't know,' I said. 'He might be glad to get rid of the bastard. Now that the PIRA know where Farrell is there's a chance that they'll stage a hit on the gaol. The buggers are that mad, you can't tell what they might try.'

'The thing is, they've already got you as a lever.' The CO looked at me steadily before continuing with his list of objections: 'Ultimately, of course, there's the Prime Minister.'

Suddenly I spotted an opening. 'In that case, why not go straight to him?' I suggested. 'It's no business of mine, but we do know he's an old friend of the Regiment. It's not just that we did him a good turn in Libya. He's been on-side for years.' I pointed at a signed, framed photograph hanging on the wall, one of many official portraits presented by Very Important Visitors, among them Prince Charles and Princess Di. 'Remember the time he came down to the Killing House?'

'Of course.' The CO smiled, thinking about the day we'd given the PM and a couple of senior parliamentary colleagues a demonstration of lifting a hostage from a room in the special building used for training the counter-terrorist team. The walls were hung with sheets of thick rubber so that live rounds could be fired inside. As bullets had hammered close past the visitors in the confined space one of the sidekicks had hurled himself to the deck and pissed himself; but the PM had remained super-cool, and came away mightily impressed.

'If *he* OK'd it, that would be all we'd need,' I said. 'What about that fax you've just had, after all?'

I sensed that the CO had become rather taken with my idea, so I continued enthusiastically: 'Word would pass down the chain, and everyone else would have to come on board. With Ostrich having gone down so well he might fancy another unattributable operation.'

'Unattributable!' echoed the CO. 'I should think it bloody well would be. The least attributable operation ever mounted by the Regiment!'

To give himself a moment to think, he started talking about the lack of time. 'According to their last deadline, we've only got until midday on Tuesday,' he said. 'It's Thursday already. Not much room for manoeuvre.'

'Enough,' I said, 'if you can handle the bureaucracy, I guarantee I can manage the logistics.'

I sat back, feeling slightly out of breath, amazed that I was talking

153

to the colonel as if I were of equal rank, planning an operation equally between the two of us. The truth was, we were both caught up in the excitement of the idea.

'Well,' he prevaricated. 'What does Special Branch think of it?'

'The Commander thinks I'm crazy. He doesn't realise how easy it would be, but all the same he's coming round to a position supporting me.'

'Does he reckon the regular police would cooperate?'

'I haven't asked him. I expect the answer's no, but as I said it would be a different matter if word came down from the top.'

'The plan's utterly outrageous, of course. I don't think we've a hope in hell of getting it sanctioned.' The CO looked at his watch. 'I'll play fair with you, though. I'll run the idea through the system. It's now 1035. Give me till lunchtime, OK? Back here at one. Meanwhile, get the bones of your plan on to paper. One of the clerks will do the donkey work for you on a word-processor, but get it all down as briefly as possible in note form. We'll push it up to the Director by secure fax and see what the reaction is.'

I walked out feeling pretty low and extremely tired. I knew the Boss was sympathetic, but he was a realist as well, and it was obvious he didn't think my idea had a chance. I could tell from the look of him that he'd only been humouring me. For a while I walked around outside, trying to clear my head, then I thought, Sod it, I'll get a plan done anyway. I've nothing to lose by that.

In the adjutant's office I grabbed the services of a clerk called Andy, whose grammar and spelling were streaks ahead of mine, and in twenty minutes we'd hammered out the briefing. Back in the incident room I tried to raise my spirits by saying to Fraser, 'Better get your skates on, Commander. It looks like the wagon's going to roll.'

'You're joking.'

'Not entirely. The Boss is taking Plan Zulu seriously. At least, he's making enquiries at high level.'

'Am I supposed to know about it?'

'He knows I told you my idea, but probably it's better not to say anything until I've been back to him. We're meeting again at one o'clock to see if we can take it farther.'

To fill in time I sought out Tony. I'd spun him the outline of my scheme during our day in the OP, so there was little need for further explanation. 'If this goes down,' I told him, 'I'm going to make bloody sure you're on it with me. In fact, I hope we can keep the Ostrich team together. We understand each other as well as we ever will; I know we can muster the necessary skills between us. Listen, it may be premature, but why don't we get a few things planned?'

We settled ourselves at a table in the incident room with a road atlas and a notebook.

'Plotting the revolution, are you?' Fraser quipped as he came past.

'More or less. You don't mind us being here?'

'Not at all. You're welcome to carry on.'

Out of the blue there had come into my mind an image of the new bypass round Ludlow, the market town in Shropshire. The road was a single-carriageway but fast and open, curving gently in a wide semicircle, with several miles from one roundabout to the next and no side-turnings in between. A perfect setting for an intercept. There was a similar ring-road round Evesham, I knew – and in a way that would be a more appropriate location, since it would fit in with rumours that the prisoner was being moved to Long Lartin – but the country through which it ran was too flat and open, with too many houses in sight. Ludlow presented a wilder and therefore more attractive option.

'This is the place,' I told Tony, indicating the northern end of the bypass. 'If the police block out other vehicles for five minutes before the convoy comes through, the entire system will be empty. We can ram the prison van off the road anywhere here. Plenty of room to stage a mock battle, grab Farrell, and away.'

'How do we stop him seeing too much?'

'He won't see anything at all. First, we'll do it at night. Second, when we hit the meat wagon, our opening move is to fill the back of it with CS gas. That'll disable him and the guards as well.'

'How do we get into it?'

'We whack a hole out of the side. Power-saw with a carbon fibre blade.'

155

'OK.' Tony scribbled in his notebook. 'I'm making a list. We're gonna need CS, a saw, breathing kit for ourselves . . . What else?'

'Two cars. We'll draw a couple from the training pool at Llangwern – something pretty fast and beefy. Some kind of a hefty van for the intercept itself.'

'How many guys on the team?'

'Two drivers, and at least three others: two to handle Farrell, one spare in case someone gets hurt.'

'How do you pick the team?'

'As I said, I'd like to stick to the Ostrich crowd – if the head-shed will let us. So it's us two, Whinger and Stew. That'll be the core. We need one more really. Maybe Yorky can spare someone.'

Tony got up and walked around. 'How are we going to control Farrell?'

'Handcuffs. We keep him cuffed to one of us all the time.'

'Two pairs,' said Tony as he wrote. 'Whenever you change his guard, you want him linked to the new guy before the old one lets go. And a chain: when you're hitched to a guy, you need room to manoeuvre.'

'OK,' I agreed. 'Two pairs and a chain. Next thing. He'll be cuffed to a screw in the van before we get to him. So we need bolt shears as well. And a hood to put on him.'

'And what happens when we've got him?'

'We drive him to a safe house and get in touch with the PIRA to set up a rendezvous, where we exchange him for the hostages.'

'What safe house?'

'The Regiment owns several – holiday cottages, mostly. Some of them belong to former members. Tucked-away places where a guy can thin out for a while if he has to disappear.'

'Are there any available right now? I mean, it's holiday season. They could all be full.'

'There'll have to be one. We can probably find something in the Welsh mountains.'

'How about bugging Farrell's clothes?'

'He'll be in prison uniform when we get him. So it'll make sense to have a set of civilian clothes for him to change into. We'll get a belt and some shoes doctored up.'

'In that case we need to get his sizes. I'll make a note of that too.'

We tried to plan timings, but it was practically impossible without knowing how the PIRA would react to the news that their man was out of custody – or rather, out of gaol. I reckoned we should stage the exchange of prisoners as soon as possible after we'd lifted Farrell, to cut down the chance of him escaping or anything else going wrong. The best scenario I could see was that we'd get our hands on Farrell on Friday night, pass word to the PIRA immediately, and set up the exchange for Saturday. But that was only *our* programme. Given the way the terrorists were inclined to piss about, there was no guarantee they would get their act together in time.

'I don't know where they'll propose,' I said. 'They'll assume our lift is going to take place somewhere close to Birmingham. But if they're in London, as we think, they'll probably opt for a handover rendezvous somewhere around the capital.'

'Who are we supposed to be? The other members of the team?' Tony asked.

'Friends of mine. The rest can be former members of the Regiment, but you – well, you're just an American pal, over here on holiday. You'll be a positive help in the deception, because Farrell won't connect an American with the SAS.'

'What's my profession, then?'

'Peanut farmer.'

'Thanks, pal. I'll write that down too.'

Tony grinned before going on. 'Our clothes . . .'

'What about them?'

'Got to be civilian.'

'That's right. And no weapons showing. No covert radios or other specialist gear. Whatever back-up we have has got to be well out of sight.'

After a salad in the sergeants' mess I was back at the CO's office for one o'clock – and from the look of suppressed excitement on his face I could see that we were in business.

'Bit of luck,' he began.

'What's happened?'

'I don't know whether you'd call it lateral thinking or lateral influence or what, but outside events seem to be working to our advantage. This came in from Special Branch this morning.' He picked up a sheet of fax paper and held it off the desk with both hands. At first I thought he was going to give it to me, but it seemed that he preferred to paraphrase its contents. 'Through an intercept, SB have got wind of PIRA plans for a high-level political assassination in London. They believe the target's the Prime Minister himself.'

'Charming!' I muttered. 'They're aiming high.'

'They are. The man SB overheard on the phone was talking about a special weapon they've brought over to do the shoot.'

'Not that rifle they were using in Armagh?'

'The very one. A Barrett Light Fifty – at least, we assume that's what it is. A five-oh, anyway.'

'Jesus! One hell of a weapon. That means they're planning a long-range shoot.'

'Exactly,' the CO agreed. 'That puts the police on the spot. They're organised for close-quarter protection, but they can't occupy every building in line of sight every time the Prime Minister goes somewhere.'

'No.' I thought for a moment, then said, 'What's that got to do with us?'

'Nothing directly.' The CO pushed his chair back. 'Except that SB believes the crowd they overheard are the same lot as the ones holding your people – the West London ASU. The thought is that if Plan Zulu goes ahead, you may get in among them and break up the cell.'

'You mean we can go ahead?' I nearly jumped off my chair.

The Boss gave me a beady look and nodded his head. 'You want to watch yourself. The Director is *not* chuffed with you.'

'What's wrong?'

'He's had to spend the morning at an emergency meeting in the COBR, liaising with Downing Street, the Home Office and Scotland Yard. That meant he couldn't clear other things off his desk, and he reckons you've buggered his weekend.'

I thought of the big fat brigadier, huffing and puffing in the Cabinet Office Briefing Room, the underground sanctum in Central London which is activated to deal with major emergencies . . . but I didn't feel too sorry for him.

'Mind you,' the CO added, 'if you smash the West London ASU I think he'll forgive you. The security forces have been trying to bust the organisation for years, and haven't managed it. They've made a number of arrests, but never got the key players.'

'All right then,' I said thoughtfully. 'What we're going to do is set a fucking great trap, and let the PIRA walk into it.'

When I asked Yorky for someone to replace Norm on the team, he promised to have a quick think; but before he came back to me I had an idea of my own. Living in Hereford having recently retired from the Regiment was a guy called 'Doughnut' Dyson, formerly of D Squadron. He'd had a job BG'ing some Arab sheikh, but at the moment he was out of work. I suddenly realised he would be ideal. For one thing, he was older than the rest of us, and looked it; for another, he really *was* ex-SAS, and if necessary could prove it by talking about his BG work. He'd add credibility to my claim that my team was a private army. Further, Doughnut was a hefty guy, and I foresaw that weight and muscle would come in handy when we were dragging Farrell around.

Doughnut was a larger version of Pat – dark, straight hair, rosy cheeks – powerfully built and into weights, but nippy with it. He was quick-minded too: when I rang him at home to brief him he picked up the situation in a flash. Above all he was cheerful, the sort of guy who fits easily into any team and is a pleasure to have around.

His real name was Eric, but he had once made the mistake of appearing for a rugby trial in a cream-coloured jersey with a red blob in the middle. He never wore the damn thing again, but from that moment he was Doughnut.

He possessed one other minor advantage: whereas the rest of us has short, scrubby haircuts, his was fairly long and had a less military appearance.

A full O-group was called for 1700 that evening. But before the forces of law and order could assemble we had a pile of things to do. My first reaction was to collect the lads and put it to them straight.

As Plan Zulu was my benefit number, none of them was obliged to take part; they were officially on leave after Ostrich, and could

159

duck out if they wanted. The fact that nobody did gave me a big boost. Far from trying to slide off, they all came on-side with so much enthusiasm and emotion that it nearly choked me.

By the time we'd cleared the air on that one, we had three hours left before the O-group. A safe house had been found – Laurel Cottage, near Ruardean in the Forest of Dean, less than half an hour to the south-east of Hereford – so we despatched Whinger to suss the place out. Stew and Doughnut shot off down to the Llangwern Army Training Area over the Welsh border to collect a couple of the intercept cars, while Tony and I hammered away to Ludlow to recce the bypass and pick a spot for our interception.

In the MT Section in camp a dark-blue Ford Transit van, bought second-hand for cash an hour before, was being prepared for use as the ramming vehicle. Half a ton of concrete blocks were wired and bolted to the floor in the back, a heavy bar was welded to the front bumper, and an anti-roll cage fitted inside the cab.

Other people pressed ahead with the logistics of the operation, sorting out food and drink for the cottage, finding out Farrell's sizes from the prison authorities and buying civilian clothes for him, and bugging a couple of pairs of shoes.

Before Tony and I set out, I needed to send a message to the PIRA, to gear them up for action. 'How do we do this?' I asked Fraser. 'If anything goes through your channels, they'll smell a rat and realise I'm working with you.'

'That's right. It's got to be a direct call. Make it from your own number, and if they bother to trace it back they'll be happy. Dial 192 and get the Sinn Fein number in Belfast from Directory Enquiries.'

With Fraser's guidance I composed a cryptic message – but when I got through I was disconcerted to find myself connected to an answerphone. I put my hand over the receiver and whispered as much to Fraser, who indicated that I should talk anyway. So off I went:

'This is Geordie Sharp speaking from Keeper's Cottage, Hereford, at 1400 hours on Thursday the twenty-seventh of May. I have a breakthrough as regards your man. He should be with me by midnight tomorrow, Friday the twenty-eighth of May. If he reaches me safely, I'll contact you again immediately to arrange a mutually convenient rendezvous, location to be proposed by you. Leave a number for quick contact. Message ends.'

It took us only forty minutes to whip up through Leominster and on along the A49 towards Shrewsbury. The weather had turned thundery with heavy cloud cover, and on that gloomy afternoon there was little traffic moving. As we passed a sign for Kimbolton to our right Tony said, 'Hey, I know that name! It was a USAF base during World War Two. I'm sure it was . . .' but he couldn't remember which squadrons had been stationed there.

Heading north, we came on to the Ludlow bypass from the wrong direction, so to speak, and drove straight to the northern end of it before slowing to check things in detail.

'OK,' I said as we hit the northern roundabout. 'The ring-road starts here. Call this Point Alpha.'

Once again Tony was taking notes and making sketches. 'What d'you call this damn thing? A circle?'

'Roundabout. Don't you have them in the States?'

'We may have, but I don't think I ever saw one.'

'Point Alpha, anyway. I'm going round it again. That other road leading off is the A4113 to Knighton. Get that? OK . . . let's time ourselves from here to the next roundabout. I'll take it steady, simulate the prison convoy.'

I headed back south at 40 m.p.h. We went over the old main road on a bridge, then under a smaller one, and reached the second roundabout in two minutes and twenty seconds. 'Point Bravo,' I told Tony. 'Signed Ludlow to the east, the A4117 to the west. I reckon this next link will be the one for us.'

I continued driving slowly, and after a minute or so we came to a stretch where there was a wide verge on the left with a big, gently sloping grass bank behind it.

'Look at this!' I exclaimed. 'Could have been made for it. One minute twenty after Point B. Got that?'

'Sure.'

Through a cutting in the grass bank on our left, a farm or forestry track ran down a shallow ramp to join the road. Clearly it had been built as a concession to the landowner when the new road went through, to give him access to the highway. Changing down

161

into second, I swung left off the tarmac and eased the Cavalier up the track, gravel scrunching under the tyres. 'Hear that?' I said. 'They went so far as to put down hardcore for our benefit. Even if it's raining, the van'll get up here no bother.'

At the back of the bank, out of sight of the road, we found a small turning-area, with a wooden-rail fence and gate bordering a plantation of young oaks: an ideal LUP for the rammer van.

'All we need do now is measure the distance to the centre of the highway,' I said. 'What is it? Sixty metres?'

'Seventy,' Tony suggested. 'I'll step it out.'

'OK. Stand on the edge of the tarmac, and when there's nobody coming, wave me down for a trial run.'

As he strode off down the ramp, taking deliberately long paces, I turned the car and lined it up five metres back from the lip of the bank. Then, at his signal, I started forward, gently at first, to simulate a laden van, then accelerating, before I braked hard and slewed to a halt on the shoulder of the road.

'Seven seconds,' I reported. 'They'll need to practise with the van itself, but that'll be it, near enough.'

'Sixty-eight metres,' Tony announced as he climbed back aboard. 'What do we call this place?'

'Impact Ramp. It's a nice site for a shoot-out, too. A few bursts into the banks won't hurt anybody.' I pulled off on to the grass again for a moment.

On the other side of the main road the ground fell away into a shallow drainage ditch. 'If we can hit the prison wagon into that it'll be perfect,' I said. 'The van'll probably roll over and we can go in through the roof.'

Driving on again, we took three and a half minutes to reach the third roundabout – Point Charlie – south of Ludlow, where the old main road headed back into the town. Between Bravo and Charlie lay a three-mile stretch of road with no side turnings. That gave us bags of space: even if something went wrong on Impact Ramp, we'd have several minutes clear in which to sort ourselves out.

'We're OK,' I told Tony. 'We've hacked it. Let's head for home.'

The O–Group took place in the main lecture hall, a big room with rows of seats set out in semicircular tiers. There was a full turn-out from the Regimental head-shed, and the outsiders included Gilbert the Filbert from the Firm, a senior representative from Special Branch in London, a leading light from Winson Green prison, and police chiefs from Warwickshire, Shropshire and Herefordshire.

The CO set the pace by announcing that, although Plan Zulu was certainly unorthodox, it had been ordered in the national interest by the highest authority. The immediate aim was to recover the hostages, but the wider strategy was to flush out as many players as possible in the West London ASU, and to break the power of an organisation which was posing a serious threat to the government. He therefore hoped everyone would give of their best in making the plan work.

In fact, most people seemed only too willing to co-operate. The only big-wig who caused any trouble was the guy from the gaol, a frowning superscrew with a pock-marked face, who started in whingeing about his responsibility for the prisoner's health and safety. 'You don't seem to realise that the man is still recovering from gunshot wounds,' he said, when asked for his comments. 'If he gets thrown about in a crash it may lead to serious complications.'

'He'll have to take his chance,' said the CO firmly. 'Your responsibility for him will cease when he leaves Winson Green, so his continuing health won't be your concern.'

That ended the complaints, and by cracking on in such positive fashion the CO got everything squared away within the hour, so that the meeting broke up soon after six.

The arrangement was that the intercept would go down the following night: Friday 28 May. The police would close all three roundabouts on the Ludlow bypass at 2215 and divert traffic, on the grounds that the road had been blocked by an accident. The convoy, consisting of a van with unmarked police cars fore and aft, would reach Point Alpha as close to 2225 as the drivers could manage.

By then our intercept cars would be parked nose-to-nose at an angle across the road half a mile south of Point Bravo, their panic lights flashing as if they'd had a crash. Our rammer van would be waiting in the turning space above the road. When the convoy

163

approached, the lead driver would slow down as he saw the stranded cars ahead and report a blockage over his radio. At that moment our van would start its run down the ramp, aiming to hit the front of the meat wagon . . .

By 1830 I was feeling pretty knackered. It was five nights since I'd had a proper sleep and I was keen to get my head down for more than two or three hours at a stretch. All the same, Whinger and I were determined to call on Pat in hospital, because we knew he'd be fretting about his chances of regaining full fitness, and we reckoned he could do with a bit of moral support. Besides, once Plan Zulu went down, it might be days before we got another chance to see him.

After a quick bite to eat I phoned Pat's wife, Jenny, to see if there was anything she'd like us to take along, but it turned out she wasn't feeling very sympathetic. 'Take him a bottle of arsenic pills,' she said. 'That'll sort him.'

'OK, I get the message.'

I turned to Whinger and said, 'Cow,' then I called the hospital to make sure they'd let us in. There was the usual palaver about 'no visitors', but I bluffed our way with the sister in charge by telling her that we were special mates of Pat's, and got her to agree that we could spend a few minutes with him.

On the M4, Whinger gave me details of the safe house, which sounded pretty good. Laurel Cottage, he said, was made of brick and solidly built. It was small, with three rooms (including the bathroom) downstairs and three above, but it had been modernised recently and had a new kitchen and a Calor-gas hot water and heating system. The windows were adequate if not great – lockable, but not double-glazed. Whinger had been through all the drawers in the kitchen and removed a couple of receipted bills which gave the names of local tradesmen. He'd also checked the immediate area for estate agents' signs with giveaway phone numbers on them. The house was in a secure position, isolated as it was up a lane on the side of a hill, and there was a tumbledown wooden garage about thirty metres from the door. The place wasn't overlooked, and there were no other buildings in sight.

The only slight worry was one other house, which stood beside the lane where it joined the main road; anyone there would be in a good position to monitor comings and goings. But enquiries had revealed that this second building was also let intermittently, and at present unoccupied.

Comms wise, the cottage was well placed – not in a hole where radios and mobile phones wouldn't function. Whinger had taken along with him a technician from Box, who'd installed a special phone containing an encrypting device and a chip that prevented anyone tracing a call back. Tests had shown that all forms of communication functioned well.

As we drove, I tried to imagine myself in Pat's position. When I got my arm smashed in the Gulf War I'd been in a fairly bad state myself, but I never thought that the wound was serious enough to threaten my career and basic fitness. A shattered femur was something else, and I knew how daunting it must be. At least he was in good hands. I knew that Army and RAF surgeons train to deal with bullet wounds by operating on pigs anaesthetised and shot at the secret defence establishment at Porton Down.

I'd made several visits to Wroughton before, to have my arm checked while the bones were re-knitting, and as we drove up the long approach road to the old airfield on top of the downs I thought once again how strange it was that a service hospital should have so little security. There was no fence, no barrier, no guardroom; anybody could proceed straight to the front entrance. Mind you, you needed to be fit to find the person you were looking for, because the building was about half a mile long, with wards leading off central corridors on its two floors, and it was a fearsome hike from one end to the other.

Hospitals bug me. The gleaming surfaces, the smell of disinfectant, the bright lights, the impersonal passages and doors . . . the whole environment seems alien, exactly the sort of world you spend your life trying to avoid.

After a marathon tab, we eventually came on Pat in one of the high-dependency units – a small side-ward with an RAF police corporal sitting guard outside the door. I'd had the sense to conceal my flask-shaped half-bottle of Johnny Walker against my stomach inside my loose shirt, so we got past the guard and the sister without hassle.

It was a shock to see such a physical guy as Pat laid low, flat on his back, amid a tangle of drips and drains. His left leg was in plaster, with a cage of stainless steel pins coming out through the case above the knee, and drain-tubes leading out of it. The sight of all the gear took me straight back to the hospital in Baghdad, and the Iraqi surgeon who'd threatened to blind me with an anaesthetic syringe before he operated. Of course, I also thought of Bully-boy Khadduri coming to the gaol and hammering on my plaster cast with his swagger stick. At least *he* wouldn't torment any more patients.

As we went in, Pat turned his head and gave a big grin. But although his brain was working fine, his responses were slow, and I could see that he was quite heavily sedated.

'They haven't killed you yet,' I said.

'They keep trying.'

'Lot of pain?'

'Nothing. It's fantastic.' He pointed at a little domed rubber pump, taped to his left arm just above the wrist. 'Whenever I get the gyp I give myself a shot with this thing.'

'What is it?'

'Morphine, I reckon. Got a bag of it up there somewhere. Want to try it?'

'Thanks a lot,' said Whinger. 'Time for a shot.'

'Look.' I brought out the Scotch. 'This is for when you're on the mend.' I laid the bottle at the back of the cupboard in the cabinet beside his bed and put a box of Kleenex in front of it.

'Brilliant!' Pat said. 'Thanks, Geordie.'

We began to chat about his journey home and things at Hereford, then suddenly he remembered my own problem and said, 'Aye – what about the family?'

'Bit of a breakthrough. The PIRA sent a taped message from Tracy advancing the deadline for us to hand their man over, and we're preparing a response. We may get some action quite soon.' I'd already decided not to pass on details about Plan Zulu, just in case Pat started muttering in his sleep.

As I was talking I saw him get a twinge of pain, and he primed his morphine pump a couple of times. By the time I'd told him a bit about the wash-up after Ostrich I could see him losing concentration; so I was surprised when he suddenly said, quite loud, 'I hope you told them about the priest clearing his throat up his fucking tower.'

'The mullah! I did, Pat. Don't worry. I told them about your diversionary explosion by the gate too, and the RPG blowing shit out of the building – the lot.'

He gave a faint smile, but his eyes were closed, and he drifted off into a doze. I adjusted the position of the Kleenex box slightly, and we slipped out of the room.

In the corridor I saw a doctor whom I recognised from my own visits. It turned out that he had helped with Pat's operation, and he welcomed the pair of us with a friendly mock-salute. I knew word had been put about that Pat's wound had been caused by an accident on the ranges, so I didn't refer to its origin; but the doctor raised one eyebrow and said, 'You fellows are getting a bit trigger-happy, aren't you?'

'Well . . .' I spread my hands. 'These things happen.'

I could see he knew more than he was letting on, so I changed the subject. 'What's the long-term prognosis?'

'Pretty good, we reckon. He's a strong lad. The leg should knit up OK, provided we can keep infection out.'

My mind flashed to Farrell and his septicaemia – but all I said was, 'Back to full mobility?'

'We can't be sure, but there's every chance.'

'He'll be all right,' said Whinger loftily. 'Hot cross bun. This one will run and run.'

NINE

It turned out to be a filthy night of rain and wind – but that made no difference to our plans. By 2145 we were rolling along the bypass towards Impact Ramp, and five minutes later all three vehicles were parked in the turning area. Our main getaway car was a souped-up Audi Quattro that had seen service in Northern Ireland. It had been brought back to the mainland because it had been compromised: after a couple of successful operations the IRA knew it too well, so it had come home for a respray and the issue of new plates.

From the outside it looked the same as any other silver Audi; but lurking beneath its skin it carried potent extra assets. One was the engine, which had been given racing specification during a visit to the workshops at the Donington Park circuit in Leicestershire. The tweaked unit fired the car with fearsome acceleration and a top speed of 150 m.p.h. There were also slices of Kevlar armour in the doors and down the backs of the front seats – and to cope with the extra power and weight, both brakes and suspension had been uprated. The result of all this was that the driver could throw it about the road like a racing-car – which was just what Whinger fancied.

Our other vehicle was an old black Granada – less brutal, but solid, dependable and fast enough for most contingencies. I'd nominated Stew as driver, with Doughnut Dyson as his co-pilot. The rammer van was being driven by two other guys from the Regiment.

Someone had pointed out that, as the police were not going to give chase after the intercept, there was no need for us to use such a high-performance beast as the Audi. I countered with the possibility that other people might get caught up in the operation

– accidentally or on purpose – and we might in the end be glad of a genuine getaway car. In any case, it was important that, once we had Farrell on board, we should cover a few miles at seriously high speed, as though the law were truly on our tail.

In our jeans and trainers we looked like any old layabouts, but covert radios and pistols in shoulder holsters under our sweatshirts gave us the teeth we needed. In the boot of the Granada were three MP5s, a box of loaded magazines, and a case of flash–bang stun grenades.

On our vantage point at the top of the Impact Ramp we sat in the dark and waited, the raindrops pearling on the windscreens. The Audi was first in line, with the Granada behind it, and the rammer van last.

The traffic on the bypass below us was spasmodic. For several seconds at a stretch the road would be empty, then a car or truck would come past, its lights glistening on the wet tarmac. The first sign of activity – or rather, lack of it – should come soon after 2215, when the police were due to seal off all approaches to the ring road.

'Does he know what's happening?' asked Tony quietly.

'Who?'

'Farrell.'

'Can't tell. It's possible word's got back to him, but I doubt it. He hasn't seen any outsiders since the ban on visitors was imposed.'

'Where does he think he's going, then?'

'I don't suppose he's got a clue; they don't have to tell prisoners where they're taking them. That's why it's called the ghost train. He may think he's going down to the IRA nick at Evesham. Or there's another one called the Dana at Shrewsbury. That's not far off, either.'

Time dragged. I stared out of the window at the dismal conditions, thankful that at least all the guys on the team knew what our target looked like. Mug-shots of Farrell, full face and profile, taken in the nick, had gone up on the board in the incident room. Seeing them, I had realised that even after months of pursuit I had never had a really good look at him. The night I'd seen him at the barn outside Belfast he'd been thirty or more metres off, standing in poor, flickering light; it was my colleague in the OP, a guy from the Det, who'd recognised him. And when I had chased him into the edge of the Amazon jungle it was in half-darkness, and in any case I'd been nearly blind with rage. The pictures taken in Winson Green showed him looking pretty rough, with hollow cheeks and dark shadows under the eyes.

Something else was niggling at my mind as we waited: a sheet of a telephone transcript which I'd glimpsed on Fraser's desk in the incident room. It was a record of a conversation with the PIRA which had obviously taken place while we were in Libya. Somebody had rung in, demanding to speak to Geordie Sharp, and 'KT' – Karen Terraine – had taken the call. For a while she'd stalled the man with stock answers, but when he had insisted on talking to me, she'd said: 'Well, you can't. He's not in the country. He's gone abroad for a few days.' Beside these words somebody had made a couple of big red crosses with a felt tip, as if to draw attention to a major breach of security. Why, for Christ's sake, had the woman said that I was overseas? Was it just carelessness, or was it spite – revenge for my giving her the brush-off in that bout of midnight fisticuffs? Either way, I got the impression that Fraser had moved her smartly out of the team working on my problem. He told me she'd gone on leave, but I reckoned she'd been fired. Whatever had happened to her, one potentially dangerous fact was now in enemy hands. To some extent Operation Ostrich had been compromised.

I looked at my watch again and said, 'Now. It's quarter past. The road blocks should be in position.'

For a while we saw no change; the occasional vehicle continued to come past. Then, after one last lorry from the south, the flow from that direction ceased. A couple of minutes later the same thing happened from the north – a single car came down and disappeared southwards trailing a cloud of spray – and then everything went quiet.

'Standby,' I said over our chatter net. 'Engines running.'

Whinger turned the ignition key, and the Audi burbled into life with a deep, throaty grumble. I switched to the police channel, and a moment later heard a voice I recognised as that of Ross Tucker, driver of the lead vehicle in the convoy: 'Point Alpha now.'

Back on our own net I called, 'OK. Take up position.'

Whinger switched on his headlights, which blazed out across the bypass, and rolled the heavy car down the slope. He headed a few yards to the left, so as to leave the rammer van a clear run, and brought the Audi to rest at an angle across the carriageway, its nose pointing south. In a couple of seconds Stew had eased the Granada round ahead of us and backed it up so that its rear-bumper was touching our front mudguard. By the time he'd switched on the alarm flashers and raised the lid of the boot, the two vehicles presented the very picture of an unfortunate shunt.

I nipped to the boot of the Granada, grabbed the power-saw, switched on and gave a couple of pulls on the starter cord to make sure it would run. At the second tug the engine burst into life, and after belching out a cloud of white smoke, revved up smoothly. I switched off and returned the saw to its place. The rest of the team stationed themselves on the south side of the barricade, away from the impact area.

'Standby!' called Tony. 'Lights to the north.'

On the chatter net I called the driver of our rammer van. 'All set, Joe?'

'Turning and burning,' he replied calmly.

'Fine. Listen out for my count-down.'

The lights bore down towards us, at first only one big glare through the drizzling rain, then three distinct pairs of headlamps, with blue police lamps flashing fore and aft. They were less than a quarter of a mile off when Tony's voice suddenly broke into the chatter net. 'Geordie,' he called. 'The cops are saying a rogue vehicle's bust through the cordon. There's a fourth car coming down the road.'

Jesus! I thought. Somehow the PIRA have rumbled us. They've overheard one of our planning conversations. They're coming to join the party.

I had about five seconds in which to make a decision. Abort or carry on? Pointless to abort. If this *was* the PIRA, we were fairly well equipped to take them on here and now. If it was someone else pissing about we could stuff them with the greatest of ease. I said, 'Carry on as planned. Whinger, watch for a fourth fucking vehicle.'

In the distance, beyond the convoy lights, another faint glow was already visible. But I had no more time to worry about it. Ross, driving the lead police car, had seen our obstruction and began to brake. The middle vehicle closed on him a bit, then slowed, increasing its distance again. The little group cruised on towards us at a diminishing pace. I kept mentally calculating the distance they had to run.

'Stand by to roll,' I told Joe. 'Five, four, three, two, one . . . GO!'

We stripped off our covert radios and dumped them in the boot of the Granada. Tony and I pulled on pairs of lightweight goggles. My eyes were glued to the approaching convoy, but my ears were listening for the engine of our van. There it was, running at high revs in second gear.

I flailed my right hand at the oncoming lights, urgently waving them down. The lead car had barely coasted to a halt when the van, its engine screaming, hurtled down on to the carriageway at right-angles and caught the meat wagon broadside. With a huge, crunching crash of metal and a screech of tyres the wagon was hurled sideways. As the wheels caught on the tarmac, the impetus toppled the van on to its right side and sent it powering on, sparks flying from the side that scraped over the road. From close quarters the violence of the impact was shocking. With a sudden stab of alarm I thought that the van was going to catch fire. If Farrell got roasted alive, that would be the end of everything.

It came to rest with the roof vertical, on the edge of the shallow ditch. Then things happened very fast. I dived for the power saw, grabbed it, ran to the ditch, started up and applied the carbon blade to the metal. Tony stood beside me, directing a torch on to the roof. Above the scream of my saw I heard rounds going down in bursts, then the *boom* of flash-bangs.

The saw bit through the thin metal sheeting of the roof as if it were cardboard, and in a few seconds I'd made two big cuts running downwards and outwards from a central point at the top. A hail of fiery red sparks flew in all directions, and I thanked my stars that the fuel I could smell spilling out over the verge was diesel, not petrol. Out of the corner of my eye I saw somebody struggling out through the left-hand door of the cab, which was uppermost. Knowing it was one of our own guys I didn't worry; he'd keep out of the way, or maybe just lie down.

One more cut across the bottom of my triangle and the job was done. As the piece came away, Tony stuck his head in through the hole, swept his torch beam and fired off with a canister of pepper spray in the direction of the tail. Then he scrambled in through the opening and I followed.

The vehicle's lights had gone down in the crash, so the torches were our only illumination. In the beams I saw two figures piled into one back corner, struggling on top of each other, gasping and cursing and rubbing at their eyes. Tony reached them first and lifted the upper man bodily into the air, only to find he was attached to the second by a handcuff and a short chain. Which was which? The top man had fair hair, the bottom one was dark; the minder was uppermost, Farrell on the deck.

Bolt shears out. Snap through the links. Blood shining on the floor of the van – or rather on the wall. Grab Farrell.

He yelled a string of obscenities as I slammed him face-down, wrenched his arms behind him and got a pair of plasticuffs pulled up tight on his wrists. 'Take it easy, Seamus!' he managed between coughs and splutters. 'That fucking gas! It's you, Seamus, is it not? Jaysus, man, get off me! Get me out of this!'

That was all he could manage. He couldn't open his eyes. Blood was frothing out of his mouth, and as the pepper got to him properly he relapsed into incoherent roars. The spray was getting to me as well. My eyes were OK inside the goggles, but my nose, mouth and throat were burning, and I tried not to inhale.

I saw Tony had Farrell under control, so I dived back through the hole into the open and gasped in a few breaths of fresh air. Outside it sounded as though a full-scale battle was in progress: bangs, flashes, rounds clattering down, police sirens screaming. The moment Farrell's head appeared in the opening I grabbed him by the hair and pulled him bodily out. He collapsed on to the ground, bellowing and choking. A second later Tony dived out as well. Between us we hoisted the prisoner to his feet and gave him the bum's rush in the direction of the Audi. To right and left I noticed bodies lying on the ground.

It had originally been my intention to get Farrell in the back seat between Tony and myself. But on impulse I opened the boot, dumped him bodily inside and slammed the lid.

'Let's go,' I yelled.

Whinger loomed up in front of me, thrusting his MP5 in my direction as he went for the driving seat. I grabbed the weapon, pointed it up in the air and squeezed the trigger, purely to make sure it was unloaded. To my amazement, five or six rounds hammered off into the night before the magazine was empty.

'For fuck's sake, Whinger!' I shouted.

'Get in! Get in!' he yelled. 'Stop pissing about.'

He already had the engine running. I leapt into the passenger seat, Tony into the back and with a squeal of tyres and the engine howling, the Audi shot away down the bypass.

'Those guys on the deck,' I panted. 'What happened to them?'

'Nothing.' Whinger sounded perfectly cool. 'They just lay down when we started firing.'

'What about the extra car?'

'A pale blue Lexus. It went past.'

'How?'

'Scraped round the front of the Granada, on the verge.'

'What was it doing?'

'Not a clue. But it was going like shit off a shovel.'

'*Phworrh!*' I was still choking and spluttering. 'Your fucking pepper, Tony.'

'I know. But it did the trick. I don't reckon our guy saw anything at all.'

In seconds we were nudging 120 m.p.h. Having tried an experimental ride in the boot earlier that day, I knew that Farrell couldn't possibly hear us talking: the noise inside the tin can was diabolical. 'Take it easy,' I told Whinger. 'At this rate Stew'll never keep up.' On the radio I called, 'Zulu One to Zulu Two, what's the score? Over.'

'Zulu Two,' came Stew's voice. 'Mobile towards you. We have you visual.'

Looking back, I saw the Granada's lights in the distance. 'Zulu One to all Papa stations,' I went. 'Clear Point Charlie now. Anticipating Point Charlie figures six–zero seconds, repeat six–zero seconds.'

'Papa Nine,' came the answer. 'Roger.'

Whinger had throttled back to ninety and the lights of the Granada had closed a little. But then ahead of us our own lights picked up the shape of another car parked beside the road.

'Fuckin' 'ell!' cried Whinger. 'It's that bastard Lexus.' He put his foot down again and the Audi surged forward.

'Zulu One to Zulu Two,' I called. 'Watch yourselves. The intruder vehicle's parked up ahead.'

As we hurtled down towards it I had to remind myself that this was Shropshire, England, not some godforsaken bog outside Belfast. I was so hyped up by the intercept that our best option seemed to be to spray the Lexus with a few busts from the MP5s as we went past . . . Take it easy, I told myself. You can't do that here. The guys in that car may easily be PIRA. Farrell hoped I was Seamus. Was he *expecting* an intercept? But equally, the Lexus crew could be drunks trying to evade the breathalyser, or joy-riders baiting the police.

By the time we reached the Lexus it was already rolling, gathering speed. I caught a glimpse of three young faces, two in front and one behind. Just after we'd roared past, its lights came on.

'Hey!' I yelled. 'These bastards are after us. Sort them, Whinger. Don't kill 'em, for fuck's sake, but put them out of contention.'

Over the radio I called, 'Zulu One, the intruder's now between us.'

We were rounding a gentle curve. A moment later our speed had carried us out of sight of our tail. From our recce I remembered that there was a picnic site coming up on our left, a pull-up with rustic chairs and tables, screened from the road by conifers.

'There!' I exclaimed. 'Dive in there!'

Whinger had seen the entrance too. He hit the brakes with such a thump that the Audi slewed left and right. With a juddering rush we banged down off the tarmac on to the gravel of the pull-up. Whinger doused his lights and simultaneously switched off the ignition so that the brake-lamps wouldn't light up.

'Slow down, slow down!' I called to Stew. 'Keep back. We've bombed into a lay-by. We're going to hang in here, then take them out.'

In about five seconds the Lexus overshot. Maybe the driver had been confused by the disappearance of his target – at any rate, he seemed to be moving more slowly than before. Whinger watched the lights go past outside the screen of firs, then started the engine again and came out after him.

Like a greyhound after a hare, the Audi surged up behind its prey, showing no lights at first, then with everything blazing. Before the other driver had time to react Whinger was up beside him, still accelerating hard. Then, just as our tail was about to clear the Lexus's front, he braked fiercely and jerked the steering wheel to the left.

The hit was perfectly timed. There was no way the other driver could have avoided us. In a split second he found his car whacked sideways and sent out of control. As Whinger straightened and accelerated away, I saw the Lexus spin through 360 degrees, go half round again, and finally roll over on to its side.

'Brilliant!' I went. On the net I said, 'Zulu One. Problem solved. Continue as per schedule.'

'Roger,' Stew answered.

'That's as far as they'll get tonight,' said Whinger. 'Whoever they were.'

'Dickers, for sure,' I told him.

'You're joking. I reckon they were joy-riders, I bet the car'd been nicked.'

'Maybe.'

'I got to see their faces quite well,' said Tony. 'I shone my torch on them as we came past. All youngish – twenties, I guess.'

'Irish?'

'Coulda been. I don't know. How do you tell?'

'You can't,' I said. 'SB'll show us some mug-shots when we get back. See if you recognise any of them.'

'Ah, come on!' said Whinger. 'You're getting PIRA on the brain. We shook 'em up, anyway.'

After all that things quietened down a bit, and I had a moment to wonder how Farrell had fared during the violent manoeuvring. At Charlie Three, the southern roundabout, there were no police cars in sight. I guessed that some were about, but standing well back, as arranged. We went across unopposed, and sped on southwards past Leominster to a spot where a side-road carried up through some woods. There, on the brow of a hill, we were due to switch from the Audi into a minivan – another precaution laid on

176

to bluff Farrell, who would certainly have the wit to realise that in any real chase the police would radio details of the getaway car ahead, leaving it liable to arrest.

Just before we reached the rendezvous I said quietly to the other two, 'Don't forget – from now on we've all got to *act*.'

They knew what I meant: until then we'd been on our own, but for the next few hours or maybe days we were going to be at close quarters with our man. Everything we did or said in his presence must confirm our claim to be renegades, acting on our own for my personal benefit. No hint must be given that we had the full backing of the Regiment and the security services.

The white van was standing on the designated spot beside a bus-shelter on the outskirts of a village. Although there was nobody in sight, I knew that some guys from the Regiment had the place staked out; they'd be somewhere in the background, eyes on the vehicle. They would pick up the Audi as soon as we were clear, and drive it back to base.

As Whinger pulled in and parked alongside the van, I jumped out and went round to open the boot. My torch beam revealed Farrell lying on his right side, hands cuffed behind him, his knees drawn up to chest.

'Out!' I snapped. 'Get out!'

'Get out yerself, yer fucking twat!' he exploded. 'What in God's name d'you think yer doing, giving me shite treatment like this?'

'Out!' I repeated.

I noticed that his voice had sounded thick and peculiar, but I grabbed him by the upper shoulder and dragged him into a sitting position. 'On your feet.'

'Is Seamus with you?' he spluttered. 'Or is he not?'

'He's not.'

'Who are you, then?'

'You'll find out. Come on.'

His voice definitely sounded odd – thick and lisping. It was something I didn't remember from before. Slowly, painfully, his wrists still tied behind him, Farrell knelt up on the floor of the boot, then lifted one knee over the back of the car so as to lower his foot to the ground. 'Get these fucking cuffs off me,' he gasped. 'They're after killing my hands.'

177

I ignored the complaint, heaved him upright, dragged a balaclava hood down over his head with the eye-holes at the rear, and propelled him in the direction of the van. He walked unsteadily, and I remembered that the man had a chronic limp, apparently the legacy of a car accident.

'OK,' I told him. 'You're beside the other vehicle now. Get in, to your left, and sit in the middle of the back seat.'

With Tony to his left on the bench seat, me to his right and Whinger back at the wheel, we set off again, heading south. The arrangement was that the Granada, which had stood off while we switched vehicles, would proceed to the cottage independently.

We went by a roundabout route – although, with his eyes full of pepper spray, the hammering in the boot of the Audi and now the hood, I didn't think Farrell had a clue where he was or whether he was facing east, west, north or south. It gave me an odd feeling to be shoulder-to-shoulder with this murdering, torturing pride of the Belfast Brigade. Because of his plasticuffs he had to sit forward awkwardly, and I could see he was in some pain, but I just thought, Ah, stuff the bastard.

Occasionally he asked some question about where we were and where we were going, his voice muffled by the hood, but when none of us answered he gave up. The silence left me time to think. I was trying to work out what he knew and what he didn't. The fact that he thought he'd been lifted by his own guys showed – surely – that he was totally in the dark: maybe the PIRA had been trying to set up a lift, but obviously he hadn't got wind of Plan Zulu, and it dawned on me that he might not even know that Tim and Tracy were being held hostage. After all, we'd captured him in Colombia before they were lifted, and, including the first two days in Bogotá, he'd been in the nick ever since.

Looking back over the interception, I couldn't remember anything we'd done that would give our game away. I started to wonder: did Farrell even know who *I* was? He'd shown no sign of recognising me. Then I remembered that on the only occasion he'd seen me, when we had fought in the Amazon jungle, I'd had my face blacked up for the night operation.

Whinger drove brilliantly, never missing a turn, even when he came to the steep, winding lanes of the Forest of Dean. Admittedly he'd recced the approach to Laurel Cottage the day before, but his route-finding was impressive. Not knowing that part of the country myself, I found the roads thoroughly confusing. On the final stretch I reminded myself *not* to make some stupid remark like 'Is this it?' which would betray the fact that our destination was new to me. In fact, I decided I was going to say as little to Farrell as possible. My aim was to move him on as fast as we could. He surely knew by now that we weren't his own people, and I hoped he'd be in shock for a few hours after the lift, and that the prospect of a quick escape would stop him trying to analyse the situation too deeply.

Eventually we climbed a steep gravel track through a wood, passed a battered white gate that stood open, and pulled up outside a house which was already lit up; Stew and Doughnut, in the Granada, had got there ahead of us. While Whinger went on in, Tony and I got Farrell out of the van and hustled him through the front door into a small hallway and on into the kitchen. Only then did I bring out a pair of regular steel handcuffs. Having locked Farrell's right hand to Tony's left, I cut the plasticuffs away with my Leatherman pliers. And none too soon; because the prisoner had been tugging away at them, the cuffs had ratcheted themselves up tighter and tighter and his hands had started turning blue.

Removal of his hood gave me a shock. He looked a right mess: face pale, eyes red-rimmed and bloodshot from the pepper, dried blood crusted over one cheek, and his upper lip all puffed out with a split down it to the right of centre – I guessed from being thrown against the wall of the meat wagon in the crash. There was blood on his blue and white striped prison shirt as well, and on his regulation-issue brown trousers.

'Better wash your face,' I told him. 'Use the sink there.' It wasn't that I felt sorry for him, just that I didn't fancy looking at such a wreck.

While Tony led him across to the sink and stood beside him as he scrubbed off his face, I took a quick look round the house with Whinger: lounge, bathroom and separate bog on the ground floor, three bedrooms upstairs. Everything was painted white, with terrible, twee little pictures of animals on the walls. A woman laid on by the Regiment had been in to make up the beds and put out towels and suchlike. The place was so small that the idea of spending days there gave me instant claustrophobia.

'Get a brew on, Whinger, for fuck's sake,' I said quietly. 'We've got some talking to do.'

I found Tony and Farrell side by side on the settee in the lounge.

'He's bitten his tongue,' Tony told me. 'He's got his teeth smacked together in the crash. That's why he's speaking kinda funny.'

'Does it need stitches or anything?'

'No, no. The bleeding's stopped. It'll be fine. He just can't talk any sense.'

The telephone stood on a glass-topped coffee table near Farrell's left hand, so I pushed it towards him and said, 'Right. You'd better get talking.'

The dark-blue eyes glared at me from out of their inflamed rims. 'Talking?' he spat. 'What about?'

I stared back at him. Was he trying to wind me up, or had he really no inkling of what was happening?

'D'you know who I am?' I asked.

'Not a clue.'

'In that case, I'll start from the beginning. My name's Geordie Sharp. I'm in the SAS. Some of your people in the PIRA have lifted my four-year-old, Tim, and his guardian, Tracy. They're holding them hostage, to get you released.'

I watched the information sink in. Farrell's eyes were wary, as if he didn't believe what he was hearing. He said, 'SAS? Like fuck you are. How would the SAS be after attacking a police convoy?' With his split upper lip and swollen tongue, Farrell couldn't get his mouth round the consonants and he was lisping.

'They wouldn't,' I said. 'That wasn't the SAS. That was myself and a few pals – my private army.'

'But you're in the regular army. You just said so.'

'I'm on leave. I've taken time off specially, to sort this out.'

'Who are these other turds, then?'

I gestured towards Tony. 'He's a friend over from the States. He's doing some BG work here.'

'BG? What's that?'

'Bodyguarding. Close protection.'

'All right. And these others?'

180

'Also friends. Former members of the Regiment, in civvy street now.'

Farrell looked out through the doorway, towards the rest of the guys in the kitchen. Again, he seemed to be weighing up what he was hearing. 'So . . . what's the game?'

'The game's dead simple,' I told him. 'Your people have told me that if we get you out, they'll release my two. We've got you out. As soon as the kid and the woman are in my hands, you can go.'

At that moment Whinger came in with a couple of mugs of tea. 'Will I do one for him as well?' he asked.

I was about to say no, but I changed my mind and told him, 'All right, then. Give him a cup.'

'You can keep yer fucking tea,' Farrell snapped. 'Whisky if you have it, but not fucking tea.'

Ah, sling yourself, I thought, but all I said was: 'Just get on the phone – right? And set up a rendezvous for an exchange.'

He shot me a look of hatred and said, 'Look, I've not been in Belfast for over a month. I don't know where any of the lads are.'

'You'd better find someone, and quickly. Otherwise you may not make it until daylight.'

Farrell reached for the phone, but stopped and withdrew his hand. 'Hey! Sharp! You're the little prat that was after shooting me at Ballyconvil.'

'What if I am?'

'You made a fair cock of that operation, didn't you?'

'Dial!' I told him. 'And get something set up for first thing in the morning.'

At last he moved. Holding the receiver in his left hand, he had to draw Tony's left hand across with his right in order to pick out the buttons. I knew the call would be monitored and recorded, so I didn't bother trying to memorise the numbers, although I did notice the dialling code for Belfast, and guessed he was calling one of those sleazy bars on the Falls Road where IRA players drift in to drink at all hours of the day and night.

The first man he got was evidently pissed out of his mind.

'What are you at?' Farrell snapped after a moment. 'Answer my question, will you?'

'Bollocks!' came the answer, so loud I could hear it across the table.

'Bollocks yourself!' Farrell shouted. 'Pull yourself together, man.'

A bellow of laughter came down the line. Farrell held the receiver away from his ear and I heard a voice say, 'By the powers, we have a right prick on here!'

'Get off the line, twat!' yelled Farrell. 'I'll speak to someone sober . . . Hello?'

The man had gone. Another came on, apparently in little better shape.

'Is Eamonn there?' Farrell demanded.

'What's that?'

'Eamonn! It's Eamonn I want.'

'Eamonn who?'

Getting nowhere, Farrell banged down the receiver and dialled again. This time he found a contact who was making more sense, a man he knew called Charlie.

'Now, Charlie,' he said. 'It's Declan here . . . Yes . . . More or less . . . I don't know – some charming friends . . . What? Of course it's me. It's me fucking tongue, that's all – I bit it in a car smash . . . Yes . . . Certainly not. Not at all . . . Where *am* I? Wait one.' He put a hand over the mouthpiece and looked at me enquiringly. I spread my hands out and down. 'No idea,' he went on. 'About two hours from Birmingham, but God knows where . . . Yes. These fellers are looking to swap me for the woman and kid . . . That's right. Are they with you? . . . Oh, I see . . .'

Talking to this guy, whoever he was, Farrell was fairly polite. Eventually he was given another number and hung up. While he dialled again, although I knew the SB monitors would pick it up, I watched the first four digits and saw that they were 0802 – a mobile.

The moment the call was answered, Farrell's manner changed. He became arrogant and hectoring, just as he had been on the night at the barn outside Belfast. He wasted no time on explanations, just yelled, 'You'll get me out of this shit-hole first thing in the morning. You know that?'

Whatever the other guy said only seemed to enrage him further. 'When I say tomorrow, I mean *tomorrow*!' he shouted. 'Upgrade your fucking ideas, man, or I'll see you regret it! I'll give you

182

quarter of an hour to sort something. Then I'll be back.'

I noticed Farrell was trembling as he hung up. 'Jaysus,' he said, 'the fever is on me again. I thought I had the better of it too . . .'

I put the back of my hand on his forehead, which felt burning hot. 'Your wounds, is it?' I said.

'It is.'

'What happened?'

'Some fucker shot me.'

'Really! Where was that?'

'South America.'

'You get around.'

Farrell's face contorted, as if in sudden pain. 'Listen,' he said. 'I need the bog.'

'Go on, then. Tony'll take you.'

'I'm not going with him. I need some privacy. Take these cuffs off.'

'No way. Tony's watched plenty of guys taking a dump. You can shit in company or not at all.'

Farrell gave in grumbling, and while the two were in the bathroom I said quietly to Whinger, 'Have you got those tablets the Med Centre packed?'

'Sure.'

'Fetch a couple out, then, and a glass of water. We need to get something down the bastard. We can't have him dying on us.' Special Branch had found out from the prison hospital what antibiotics Farrell had been getting, and the Med Centre had made up some of the stuff into plain white pills that looked like Paracetamol. When Farrell reappeared, I gave him two.

His response was predictable. 'What – are you after poisoning me?'

'Don't be daft. Alive you're worth a lot to us; dead, you'd be worth fuck-all. These are just aspirin. Can't do you any harm. And listen – when you get back on to your man in a moment, I want to speak to him myself. That's the only way to get ourselves straight with details of the meeting.'

Farrell took the tablets and drank the water. A few minutes later he put the call through, and while he was talking I quietly asked Tony, '*Did* he want to shit?'

183

'Sure did!' He held his nose and scrunched up his eyes. 'Boy, has he got the runs.'

'Got to watch him,' I went. 'We don't want him getting too sick to travel.'

After a few exchanges Farrell handed me the phone. I put my palm over the mouthpiece and asked, 'Who is it?'

'Feller called Malcolm.'

'Hi, Malcolm,' I said. 'What's the score?'

'The M25, northbound,' went the Belfast voice. 'Between junctions fourteen and fifteen. One mile north of fourteen there's an emergency phone on a pillar. Be there on the hard shoulder at eight forty-five in the morning – eight forty-five on the dot. Our people will pull up fifty yards behind you. The hostages will walk forward towards you. You'll bring our man back. The exchange will take place when the parties meet in the middle.'

I repeated the details carefully, then had to check something: 'Farrell was saying tomorrow but it's today, Saturday, we're talking about?'

'It is. And no more than two of you in the car.'

'Your man plus two.'

'All right. And no surveillance, either.'

'You're joking!'

'Just so you know.'

'What vehicle will you be in? . . . Hello? . . . Hello?'

The man had gone.

'No point in asking,' said Farrell. 'They probably haven't got the wagon yet. They'll nick some old banger in the morning, and come in that.'

TEN

The night wasn't exactly a rest cure. First I'd had to put fresh
dressings on Farrell's wounds. A furrow through the flesh on the
inside of his upper arm was healing well, but the twin punctures,
fore and aft, at the edge of his abdomen just below the bottom rib,
didn't look so good. I could see that somebody had made an
exploratory incision – presumably to clear out debris drawn in by
the bullet – but there was an angry flush round both ends of the
wound, and some suppuration coming out through the stitches.
Even though medical training had killed the last of my
squeamishness, I didn't enjoy patching up this particular patient; I'd
rather have stuck a knife through his ribs and be done with it.

For the rest of the night we chained him to one of the iron
bedsteads in the double room, wrist and ankle. To make doubly
sure he didn't do a Houdini on us, Tony volunteered to sleep in the
other bed.

With Farrell safely shackled upstairs I took a walk down the
drive with my mobile phone, and called the incident room from
the middle of the wood. Ever since the intercept I'd been shitting
myself with worry that we might have hurt or even killed
somebody, so when I got through to Fraser, my first question was,
'Was everyone OK on the bypass?'

'Fine, fine,' he answered. 'No problems at all.'

'What about the guys in the van? Both vans.'

'A few bruises. A couple of vehicles bent. Otherwise, nothing.'

'That's great. Who were those guys in the Lexus?'

'We don't know yet. They cleared off on foot into the
hinterland. By the time the cops got there they'd gone. The car'd
been stolen in Shrewsbury.'

'So we don't know if they were players or joy-riders?'

'The last, we reckon.'

'Well – hell. They gave us a fright and a half. And did you monitor those three calls?'

'We did. We got some numbers to work on. What about your lot?'

'We're all in good shape.'

'Your guest behaving?'

'More or less. But listen, we've set up the exchange for the morning . . .' I confirmed details of the arrangement and asked for back-up, both from SB and from the Regiment.

'Crafty bastards!' Fraser said. 'Typical, to call the RV on a motorway. Especially *there*. At that point the M25's four lanes in each direction, and at that time of the morning it'll be heaving with traffic, even though it's the weekend. Hell of a place to put on surveillance.'

'I know. But for Christ's sake don't do anything obvious. Don't have a car on the hard shoulder anywhere, not even on the opposite side. The slightest thing could put them off.'

'Leave it to us,' said Foxy. 'We'll be watching you. And once you've done the swap, we'll be going for a quick intercept of the PIRA vehicle.'

'OK. Can I speak to Yorky, please?'

Yorky came on, and when I had gone through things with him he echoed Fraser's disgust about the choice of location. 'Bah gum, it's bang under the flight-path out of Heathrow.' He paused. 'We'll have a chopper airborne, but it'll have to stand right off. There's no way it can come overhead around that area.'

'I know,' I said. 'For Christ's sake keep everyone out of sight.'

'Fear not, Geordie. I've been in this business longer than you have.'

'I know. I'm getting jumpy, that's all. Any media leaks anywhere?'

'A reporter from a local paper got on to the police in Ludlow, and they told him there'd been a minor accident, that was all. That choked him off.'

I didn't get to sleep until nearly three o'clock. And all too soon the alarm went and Doughnut came in with a brew. Farrell, he told me, claimed he hadn't slept a wink, but Tony knew this was garbage because he'd heard the man snoring. I was glad to hear that Farrell had made no fuss about putting on the clothes we'd bought for him: black jeans, a white T-shirt and a dark-blue sweat top. Of course, he hadn't much option but to wear them: he couldn't carry on in his prison kit of striped shirt and brown trousers, and his own clothes, such as they were, had been left in a bag inside the police meat wagon. Having discovered from the screws at Winson Green that he had a thirty-six-inch waist, we'd deliberately gone for the next size up so he'd have to winch the trousers in with the belt that had been doctored to contain a tracking chip. When we got him he'd only been wearing a pair of cloth slippers on his feet, and so he also went happily for the new trainers we'd supplied. They looked like brand-new Reeboks, but they'd had a little expert attention around the heels.

By the time I got up, Doughnut already had some porridge on the go, and Farrell surprised me by consenting to get a bowl of it down his neck. His face and tongue had swollen more during the night and he had problems swallowing (he also looked fairly grotesque), but at least his fever seemed to have eased.

Nobody spoke much at breakfast. I think we were all feeling shattered. After a quick nosh we hooded our prisoner again, to make sure he didn't pick up any idea of where the safe house was, and set forth.

We pulled out in the minivan at 0500, Whinger again at the wheel, myself beside him, and Farrell cuffed to Tony in the back. To give each of them slightly more freedom we'd put them on two pairs of cuffs with a short chain linking them. We'd left Doughnut and Stew to look after the cottage, confident that the Regiment would have put plenty of other guys out to OP the rendezvous.

The rain had moved away, leaving the sky clear, but mist still hung in the hollows and made driving tricky until the light was strong.

We headed down through the Forest of Dean to the M4, and by the time we hit the motorway my spirits had really picked up. The thought of seeing Tim and Tracy again in a couple of hours gave me a tremendous lift. The dawn mist had burned off, and the glorious day that was developing exactly matched my mood. The early sun shone in our faces as we headed east, but I welcomed every ray of it.

To help while away the time, I tried to work out how many days had passed since I'd got back from Bogotá. It was twenty-eight or twenty-nine, but with Libya thrown into the middle the time seemed longer. No doubt it was the same for the hostages. With no word from me or anyone on our side, the four weeks must have stretched out like eternity. I worried that Tracy would be blaming me for not making more effort to find her. Well, I thought, it shouldn't be long now.

All went well until we were on our way past Reading. The traffic had been steadily building up, but all three lanes were still moving fast and everything seemed normal. Then, maybe three miles short of Exit 10, where we wanted to turn south for Bracknell and the M3, Whinger let out a curse as he saw brake-lights coming on in front of us. There was no chance of sliding up some slip road; all he could do was stick to the outside lane and wind down to a halt in company with everyone else.

'Shunt,' he said. 'Must be. What do we do?'

'Sit it out,' I told him. 'We've time yet.'

We sat and waited. Five minutes, ten, fifteen . . . and no movement. Twenty minutes, and we couldn't even see any flashing lights in the distance ahead. The block had tailed back for miles behind us.

The irony of the situation was not lost on me. If we'd have been responding to a real emergency we'd have ignored the rules and gone like shit off a shovel up the hard shoulder, prepared to front it out if the police turned snarky. But now, the last thing we could afford was any entanglement with the law. I knew SB would have warned off the force operating in the area of our rendezvous, telling them to keep their hands off a white Renault van with our plates on it, but down here in Berkshire it might be a different story. If coppers caught us with a hooded, cuffed prisoner in the back, our entire deception would be up the spout, Farrell would realise that he was being conned, and the only chance of recovering my family would be gone.

At last the lines of massed cars began to creep forward, only to stop again after a few yards. Whinger kept cursing and muttering under his breath, and presently his impatience started seeping into me. I shifted around in my seat, wondering what we could do.

'What the hell are all these people doing, heading into town on a Saturday?' I said irritably.

Nobody answered. Our covert radios were on board, but bundled up inside a bag. Because, we couldn't afford to let Farrell see or hear us using them. What we *could* use, though, was the mobile phone.

I turned round and said to Farrell, 'Here – we're in the shit with this traffic. You'd better call your contact in London on my mobile. Say we've got held up and may be late.'

'Jaysus,' he mumbled through his hood. 'I don't have the number. I left it in the house.'

'Call Belfast then, get the number again.'

'Get this fucking hood off of me first.'

'Not likely, mate. You can keep it on and talk through it. What's the number over there?'

Before Farrell could give it there was a sudden movement in the traffic ahead, and we began making ground again, reaching a reasonable speed. 'Cancel that,' I said. 'Hold on a minute. Looks like we're going now. I don't think you need call after all.'

Then, inevitably, everything slowed down. This time, before we came to a halt, I spotted a break in the central barrier. A section of the heavy rail had been removed, maybe for repair, and the gap was blocked only by plastic cones. The traffic coming the other way was light.

To alter the RV time would be the final resort. Anything rather than that . . .

'Through there, Whinger!' I said on impulse, pointing at the cones. 'Whip through and turn round. We'll go some other way.'

Whinger wasn't the sort to query a decision like that. He watched for a gap in the oncoming traffic, made the U-turn in a second and joined the stream flowing west. Some officious turd hooted in protest, but as I looked back in the wing-mirror I saw one or two other cars following our example.

'If any self-righteous bastard reports us, I'll murder him,' I said. 'Now for a bit of map-reading.'

Heading west, we came off the motorway at the next exit, and immediately entered a nightmare of suburbanised villages and towns: Spencer's Wood, Swallowfield, Finchampstead, Crowthorne, Bagshot, all crawling with pottering weekenders. As I called the turns, Whinger went as fast as the van, the road and its competing users would let him, and eventually we battled our way through to Junction 3 of the M3. From there I calculated it was sixteen miles to our RV: sixteen minutes if we kept to sixty m.p.h. and met no more hang-ups. Since we had four minutes in hand, I told Whinger to pull into the forecourt of a garage, keeping well away from the pumps and the office.

'Where are we?' Farrell wanted to know.

'In some godforsaken arsehole of a lay-by,' I told him. 'We're going on in a minute.'

'I need a piss,' he said.

'You're not getting one here, with that hood on or without it. There are too many people passing. The cops have probably put out mug-shots of you all over the country. They've probably had pictures on the TV news. It only needs one person to see you and that's it.'

Four minutes later we slipped on to the M3 and stuck with the inside lane, which was moving at just about sixty. I felt my adrenalin coming up. Our target area was practically in sight, yet still there were umpteen things that could go wrong. I kept thinking of Tim, seeing the boy so clearly that I was pretty much talking to him. Tracy, too: I was getting the feel and smell of her again.

We reached the junction with the M25 in eight minutes – exactly what I'd reckoned. Eight more minutes to go. On our side of the big ring-road a solid river of traffic was flowing northwards, four lanes abreast. Again we kept in the slow lane, reaching Junction 13 in four minutes. As Yorky had predicted, the traffic there was yet more dense, all four lanes jam-packed with vehicles, nose to tail.

Three minutes to Exit 14, then a minute more. I looked at my watch, at Tony, at the hooded figure of Farrell. Jesus, I thought, the trouble this guy's caused me.

'Fourteen,' announced Whinger coolly, pointing up as we passed under the blue and white board. 'Sixty seconds to run. There's the phone, up ahead now.'

'Just pull in gently, as if we've got engine problems. There — go over now.'

Whinger put on his left indicator and cruised in. All we need now, I thought, is an AA or RAC van on patrol, coming to rescue us without being asked.

I checked my watch. We were thirty seconds early. As yet the RV was empty.

As Whinger came to a halt and switched on his panic lights, I said to Farrell, 'OK. We're on site. Stand by to transfer. The drill is going to be this: they'll park fifty metres behind us, one guy will walk towards us with the hostages, Tony will go back with you. In the middle of the gap, once my people are past him, he'll release you. Are you with me?'

'I am.'

'And don't fuck about. Don't start pulling or trying to run before he unlocks you, OK?'

Farrell nodded. Through the hood I could hear him breathing fast. I knew he was hot — we all were — but was sure this panting was caused by adrenalin.

'Pull the bonnet catch,' I told Whinger. As soon as I heard the click, I jumped out of the passenger door and whipped round the front of the van. There in the open the traffic roar was horrendous, and a wide-bodied jet, labouring up off the runway at Heathrow, added its scream to the general clamour. When I dialled the incident room on my mobile, I could hardly hear the voice on the other end.

'*Zulu One on RV now!*' I yelled, and I just made out a man's voice say, 'Roger.'

At least I'd confirmed that we were in position, and word would fly out over the radio to the guys deployed around us. The head-shed's intention was to go for a hard arrest on the PIRA wagon as soon after the exchange as possible. As I looked round I wondered where the hell anyone could have established an OP in this urban jungle. All about me were asphalt, brickwork, concrete walls, the blank ends of buildings, electric wires, pylons, roaring lines of traffic. Yet doubtless the guys were deployed in there somewhere, watching me.

I raised the bonnet of the van and propped it with the stay, pretending to tinker with the engine. A British Airways 747 came roaring over, drowning out even the traffic. I wondered where it was heading. America, maybe. I thought of the passengers settling themselves for a long flight, the stewardesses putting on their aprons to start serving breakfast.

My watch said 0847. Already the opposition were late. Typical PIRA. I felt sure that at any moment some of their dickers would pass in some vehicle of their own – maybe two separate lots of them – and send word back over their CB radio links: 'Yeah, yeah, they're there. It looks OK. It's clear. It's on.' I tried not to stare at the drivers as they whipped past, for fear of putting the wind up one of the scouts.

Back round the passenger side of the van, I stuck my head in through the window. The noise was less deafening inside.

'Late!' I yelled at Farrell. 'We made it on time. Your bloody people are late.'

'Don't worry,' he shouted. 'They'll be here.'

Yet his composure was only skin-deep. When another minute had gone by with no sign of action, he began to fidget and curse. I stood by the passenger door, gazing back at the unending flood of vehicles pouring up from the south. Another jet screamed out of the airport. It looked like the control tower was launching a plane every two minutes.

At five minutes past H-hour, Farrell started effing and blinding, abusing the underlings in the PIRA for their incompetence. 'They're swine,' he went. 'They get pissed out of their minds at night, and can't get up in the morning for wallowing in their own shite.'

His tirade was getting on my nerves. 'Swine yourself!' I shouted. 'It was you who got us into this mess in the first place.'

At that instant Tony snapped, 'Look out! What's this?'

Through the small rear windows he'd seen another vehicle pulling up behind us. The first sight of it made my heart jump. It was an old banger of an estate car, beige-coloured, scruffy, decrepit, lop-sided, with patches of rust showing along the bottoms of the doors; exactly what I'd expect the PIRA to be driving. But a second later I realised there was something wrong. The arrangement was that the PIRA would pull up fifty yards short of us, not five. Besides, this wagon was going down fast. Steam and smoke were pouring out through the radiator grille and from the sides of the bonnet.

The smouldering wreck wobbled to a halt about four feet from our rear bumper. The driver's door opened, and a stout, middle-aged Indian, a Sikh with a grey beard and white turban, eased himself out on to the hard shoulder. He took one despairing look at the smoke and steam, then waddled towards me.

Shit, shit, shit! I thought. Of all the world's disasters, this is the worst that can befall us. With that thing there, nothing on earth will make the PIRA stop.

The Sikh came lurching up. 'Sir, I am apologising most profoundly,' he began. 'Car is overheating. You help me with rope? Yes?'

It flashed through my mind to say, 'Do the fucking rope trick yourself, mate, car and all,' but it wasn't the moment for jokes, and I didn't want to be rude. What could I tell the poor bugger? Even if I'd drawn my pistol and ordered him to get his jalopy away from me it would have been impossible for him to obey.

All I said was, 'Sorry, no rope.' I spread my hands, and fervently hoped that was it. But the brute had spied the mobile sprouting from my pocket.

'Make call, please,' he went, pointing at it.

'Sorry, it's not working. No batteries.'

'Sir – you are very kind gentleman. You are giving me lift to garage.'

I felt frantic. I glanced at my watch. Six minutes past the deadline. Through the open window of our van I could hear Tony relaying events to Farrell.

'Sorry,' I said. 'I'm broken down as well.' I pointed at the raised bonnet. 'That's why I stopped by this phone.' Then I had a brainwave. 'There's a service station a couple of miles ahead,' I said, inventing the place on the spur of the moment. 'If you go on slowly, you'll make it.'

It was a shameless lie; I knew there was no service station for miles.

As I stood looking at the stranded Indian, my face twisted into a grimace of totally false goodwill, some sixth sense made me glance out into the passing traffic – and there, right beside me, was a small, grey van, old and dirty. The vehicle had slowed down, causing others to concertina behind it. Somebody clapped a hand on his horn, and others responded. For a second I had direct eye contact with the driver and front-seat passenger. Both were staring sideways at me, two pale young faces concentrating in a way that could mean only one thing: this was the PIRA wagon.

By the time I'd made the connection it was past. For a few yards it wavered in and out, as if the driver was about to pull on to the hard shoulder, but he never did. A few seconds later the van straightened and carried on to the north.

I stared after it, suddenly out of breath. Jesus, I thought: Tim was in that thing. Tracy was in it. My family had gone by within inches of me. I felt a terrific pull, as if that vehicle had been a powerful magnet.

Ignoring the Indian, I leapt back in front of our own wagon. Using the raised bonnet as a shield to make sure Farrell couldn't hear, I redialled the incident room. When I heard a voice answer, I said loudly, 'Zulu One. The PIRA wagon's gone past the RV. Heading north. Didn't stop. It's a grey Morris Thousand van with some black logo on the side.'

Again I heard, 'Roger,' and that was about all.

I slammed the bonnet shut. The Indian was still hovering, a hurt look on his face. I brushed past him, jumped aboard, closed the door and said to Whinger, 'Let's go!'

Whinger started the engine and we eased back into the slow lane.

'See 'em?' I asked.

'Yep.' Whinger nodded. 'The grey van.'

'That's the one. Get after it! Oh, Jesus!'

'What happened?' Farrell snarled from behind us.

I told him in words of one syllable: 'Why the hell did they not stop?'

'How could they, with another fucking vehicle up your arse? It might have been full of coppers or anything.'

'It was full of big, fat Indian women in headscarves,' I told him. 'They could have seen that. What the fuck did they think they were doing? And what'll they do now? Will they wait up ahead or come back on another run?'

'Not a chance,' said Farrell. 'That's it for the day. One run, and that's it. They'll never try again at the same place.'

'In that case, we won't either.'

Using hand–signs I indicated that Whinger was to ignore the M4 west, our natural route for base, which was coming up fast, and carry on clockwise towards the M40.

As he drove I was struggling to make a mental readjustment. The let-down was colossal. In spite of my attempts not to, I'd been counting chickens prematurely. I'd assumed that in about five minutes the whole drama was going to be over, that we'd be rid of Farrell and I'd have my loved ones back, that we'd all be able to go home in peace and get on with our normal lives.

Now everything had ended in fiasco, and we were faced with the task of setting up another meeting somewhere else. The prospect was so appalling that for a few minutes my mind went blank. All I could focus on was the fact that Farrell knew the precise location of the RV. Therefore he knew we were on the M25. Therefore we needed to confuse him about the route we were taking home. My own priority was to confer with the incident room, and with Stew and Doughnut back at the cottage – but to do that I had to get out of Farrell's earshot.

First of all we needed a pit-stop so that everyone could relieve themselves; Farrell wasn't the only one bursting for a piss. A service station would be out of the question – we couldn't march a manacled prisoner into the bog without attracting attention – so the only alternative was open country. We took the M40 west and came off at Junction 2. From there we headed south until we were in some dense woods. At last, when he'd made sure there were no giveaway signs in sight, Whinger pulled off on to a cart-track, and we all thinned out into bushes to do our business. Once again the guy who had the worst of it was Tony, chained as he was to Farrell.

While they were busy I got in another call to the incident room, to say that we were returning to base. I told Fraser what had happened, and asked him to pass word to the cottage. His only news was that the grey van had been found abandoned within two miles of where I'd reported it. The PIRA must have had another vehicle coming along behind, and transferred personnel only a couple of minutes after the van had passed the RV. Sure enough, Fraser told me it had been stolen earlier that morning in North London. There were some old cushions on the floor in the back, and forensic examination might reveal whether or not the hostages had been on board, but for the time being there was no indication. Our guys had established an OP in a factory overlooking the motorway, and although they'd watched the RV for a further hour, no other vehicle had stopped there.

As we set off for base my mind was reeling with disappointment. But at the same time I couldn't stop thinking about the wretched Indian, who was probably still where we'd abandoned him. The incident must have convinced him that all Englishmen are heartless bastards, racist to the roots of their hair, and treacherous to boot.

ELEVEN

'Get on the phone,' I told Farrell the moment we were back in the cottage, 'find out what the hell happened, and fix another RV for this evening. But keep it short: we don't want anyone tracing calls to this number.'

With ill grace he started dialling his contacts in Belfast. I'd already discovered from Fraser that one of the numbers was the Rock Bar, a drinking den on the Falls Road, which stayed open twenty-four hours a day and was frequented by most of the leading players in the Belfast Brigade. The RUC naturally had eyes on the place, and filmed all the comings and goings, but the PIRA men were so arrogant and sure of themselves that they patronised it regardless. The Falls Road was their territory, and they weren't going to stand for any interruption of their favourite routines.

On our way back Farrell had thrown me by identifying a piece of classical music that had blasted out of the radio as Whinger was jumping stations. We only got a few seconds of it, but our prisoner suddenly woke up and cried, 'Beethoven! *Leonora* number three.' The music sounded pretty dire to me, and the rest of us looked at each other with expressions of alarm, but I could see that on Farrell's part it was a spontaneous reaction, not designed to impress us. Once again I thought it very strange that a man with his record of crime and thuggery could also have genuine cultural interests.

Back at base, the only two guys on our team still functioning properly were Doughnut and Stew, who'd got their heads down while we were on the road, managing to catch up on a bit of lost sleep. The rest of us were edgy with hunger and exhaustion – and I knew that sheer tiredness could lead to somebody making a fatal mistake. Farrell himself seemed almost comatose, but still we were aware that one careless remark from any of us might arouse his suspicion. I had therefore asked Doughnut to take over as warder-nanny so as to give Tony a break, and I stood over them as they swapped the handcuffs.

Stew had had the brilliant idea of putting some potatoes to bake in the oven, and the cottage was full of the smell of them, good and crusty. I told the others to get on and eat – breakfast or lunch or whatever it was – and said I'd join them as soon as we'd set up another meeting.

Farrell finished his call to Belfast, then dialled the mobile number, which SB had traced to West London.

'Mother of Mary!' he exclaimed after talking for a minute. 'Whyever didn't they stop?' He listened for a few more seconds then said, 'That's no way to carry on. He'll have to be reported . . . What? . . . Of course I was. Bursting for a run-out as well.'

I grabbed the receiver from him and said, 'Hello. This is Geordie Sharp. Stop pissing about and fix a rendezvous tonight.'

'It was yous fellers that fucked it up,' retorted the voice.

'Bollocks, mate. We were there ahead of schedule.'

'But you never had our man with you.'

'What d'you mean? He was there in the back of the van. He just told you.'

'Why wouldn't you let us see him, then?'

'You would have seen him if you'd stopped.'

'And a second vehicle up your arse-end as well.'

'That was nothing to do with us. The guy's engine had overheated, that was all. He arrived at the last minute. If you'd bloody well been on time he wouldn't have been there.'

There was a sick laugh at the other end of the line, and the man said, 'You fucking wee bastards! That's all you are if you expected anyone to stop with that circus parked there.'

'Listen,' I said, struggling to keep my temper, 'insults aren't going to get your man back. Like I said, name another time and place for an exchange. We'll call you again in fifteen minutes.' With that I slammed the receiver down.

'Come on,' I told Farrell. 'We've got to get something down our necks.'

At about 11.30 we had a peculiar brunch of fried cod steaks and baked spuds with plenty of butter in them, and tea to drink. It bugged me to have Farrell slurping and spluttering alongside the rest of us in the kitchen – I would have liked to see the bastard starve – but I knew it was in my interest to keep him in reasonable health. Again he surprised me, this time with the way he ate. Considering that one hand was cuffed, his table manners were immaculate. We didn't give him a knife, but he held his fork properly, and when he'd finished he laid it down neatly on his plate. He didn't stuff his mouth full of food and swill tea down through it; he ate first and drank afterwards. It was only his swollen tongue and lip that made him clumsy. At least, while he was eating, he didn't try to make conversation.

With food inside me, my mind came back to life. I urgently needed to confer with the head-shed, but reckoned I'd do best to wait until we had the second RV lined up.

'This time,' I told Farrell, 'I'm talking to your man myself.'

'Please yourself. You've got the number.'

When I dialled, the phone was answered instantly, as if the guy had been waiting for the call.

'All right,' I began. 'Where's it to be?'

'No exchange,' went the voice.

'No exchange? Why not?'

'We're not satisfied with the identity of your hostage.'

'What the hell d'you mean? You know bloody well who he is.'

'We know who you *say* he is. But we've no proof that it's him.'

'Jesus!' I took a deep breath and put my hand over the mouthpiece. 'They don't believe it's you,' I told Farrell. He flipped his left hand up and back in a gesture of disgust, and I talked into the phone again. 'He's spoken to people he knows in Belfast. They must have recognised his voice.'

'That's the point, exactly. They said it didn't sound like him at all.'

'He's got a split tongue and lip, that's why. He hit his face when we rammed the prison van and got his teeth smacked together. He can't use his tongue properly. That's why he sounds peculiar.'

'We need to get a proper look at him. We need to see it's himself.'

'Ah, bollocks! Like I said, you *would* have seen him if you'd been on time this morning.'

'We need to see him, or there's no deal.'

The way the man kept repeating himself, like a zombie, really got to me. I put my hand over the mouthpiece again and exclaimed. 'This is shite!' Opening up again, I said, 'Wait one.'

With my hand back in position I asked Farrell, 'D'you know this guy?'

'Not at all.'

'Well, speak to him anyway. He doesn't believe you're you.'

'Holy fucking Jaysus!' Farrell grabbed the phone and blasted off, bollocking the fellow to kingdom come. But for all his obscenities he made little progress; the man at the other end was like a brick wall. In the end Farrell yelled, 'All right, then! I'm going to call one or two of my friends in West Belfast and get them to put a fucking bomb under you.' He would have rung off if I hadn't signalled him urgently to give me back the phone.

'So what are you proposing?' I asked.

'Come to the Great Western marshalling yard at Swindon at eleven tonight.'

'Wait one, I need to write this down.'

I looked round for a pen and paper, but it took a hell of a search before we dug out a pencil from a drawer. The only thing we could find to write on was the opened-out packet which had held the cod steaks. At last I was ready. 'Carry on,' I said.

'Go down Brunel Road to the bottom, past the station . . .'

'Brunel,' I repeated, 'OK.'

'At the bottom, don't turn left where the main road swings round, but carry straight on through a gateway. There's wire mesh gates across it. They may be closed, but even if they are they aren't locked, you can push them open. Are you with me?'

'I am.'

'There's two brick pillars at the entrance, holding the gates. Pass between them and you're in the old yard.'

'Got it. Eleven o'clock, you said?'

'Eleven, so it is. Farrell and two. No more.'

'Three,' I said. 'One to drive and two to look after your man.'

'All right. Three. In that case there'll be three of us as well.'

The line went dead.

Farrell's face was dark with anger. 'What a shower of cunts!' he

200

snapped. 'They've got some bloody cheek, demanding to see me. Wait now while I get the bastards sorted.' He started to dial Belfast numbers again, but things quickly went yet further downhill. One after another, his cronies gave him the brush-off. Either they refused to speak to him and let their side-kicks take the call, or they told him to get stuffed and stick to the plan already made. With every call I could see him growing more rattled; it was clear that he couldn't understand why the players in Belfast were behaving as they were. It didn't make sense to him. Something had changed.

Gradually his bluster abated, and by the end of his calls he was looking really scared.

'What's the problem?' I asked. 'They don't sound very happy.'

'Fucked if I know.' He shook his head in a mixture of disbelief and alarm, muttering, 'They've all gone round the twist.'

I tried to draw him out, but he wouldn't say any more – and as I knew the telephone conversation had been recorded I didn't press very hard. We could check it out later.

As if to change the subject, Farrell suddenly said, 'I need a shower.'

Since he was smelling like the ferrets my Uncle Phil used to keep at the bottom of the garden I said, 'Good idea,' and suggested that after he'd had a clean-up we should all get our heads down.

We'd taken the precaution of screwing the bathroom window shut, so that it presented no security risk, and I reckoned it was safe to unshackle Farrell while he washed, provided there were two of us present when he came out again.

'You can let him go,' I told Doughnut. 'But he's to get undressed in the passage and leave his clothes outside.'

The ablutions went according to plan. When Farrell stripped off, I saw that he was indeed well built, with powerful shoulders, but running to fat around the midriff. When he went into the shower I stepped outside and walked round the back of the cottage to keep an eye on the bathroom window, just in case he tried anything funny. For a few minutes I stood there, enjoying the sunshine, listening to the birds, and fervently wishing that we could bring this horrible nightmare to an end, so that life could return to normal.

We'd bought Farrell shaving kit, toothbrush and so on before the intercept, and when he emerged ten minutes later, he was looking a lot more spruce. The wound dressings had got wet, so I peeled them off and put new ones on. The inflammation seemed to have gone down a bit, but as a precaution I made Farrell take a couple more of the white tablets. As soon as we had him shackled to the bed again, wrist and ankle, everyone felt more relaxed.

I was all for getting my head down as well, but first I had to take another walk into the wood. Half-way down the hill a grey squirrel ran across the track in front of me and raced up the beech tree I was proposing to stand under. For a moment it sat on a horizontal branch with its tail fluffed up behind it, but when it saw me coming in close to the trunk, it whipped up into the greenery above. Saucy little bastard, I thought. It's all right for you. You don't have much to worry about.

'We're OK so far,' I told Yorky over the mobile. 'Did you pick all that up – the details of our rendezvous for tonight?' I confirmed the arrangements, such as they were, and asked him to get surveillance on the site as soon as possible. 'The PIRA are bound to send in dickers,' I said. 'But probably they won't turn up until evening. It would be great if we could get eyes in there first.'

'No problem,' Yorky replied. 'There's two guys on their way already. I sent them off as soon as I heard the plan. The other thing we need to do is stick a tracking device on the PIRA car. This should give us a great chance. As soon as we've got an idea of the topography, we'll work something out – the optimum placing of your vehicle and all.'

'Thanks, Yorky. We're going to need some back-up, too. It's possible the PIRA will try to lift Farrell. We could do with a QRF somewhere close.'

'That's no problem either. Again, we'll suss out the site and make arrangements. Geordie, you sound tired.'

'I am. I'm fucking knackered. We've been on the go since five this morning. Didn't get much sleep, either.'

'Why not get your head down, then?'

'I'm going to. There's not a lot we can do between now and then. Er . . . Yorky?'

'What's that?'

'Any more news about PIRA safe houses? Any news at all?'

'Yes. They're concentrating on two flats in Acton. Our Red Team's moved up to Hounslow Barracks. They're on standby there. Twenty guys, all their vehicles and kit. The police have a team from SO19 standing by as well. In fact, the commander of SO19 has just been here, going through various options with the head-shed.'

'So there is some movement?'

'Definitely.'

'Thanks, Yorky. That sounds great.'

'Don't worry, lad. Everything's in hand at this end. Listen – your prisoner doesn't sound a very nice guy.'

'What d'you mean?'

'The RUC faxed us his dossier. The things he's been suspected of but never got for: three murders, GBH, arson, extortion.'

'Didn't I tell you?'

'You did,' Yorky admitted. 'But when you see it written down . . . Keep a good grip on him, anyway.'

'Will do. But the bastard doesn't seem very happy. Something in those last calls pissed him off.'

'I know,' Yorky suddenly sounded quite chuffed. 'I've been listening to the tapes. His people seem to have turned against him, for whatever reason. They were giving him two fingers. One of them was talking about putting a CAT team on to investigate him.'

'No wonder he's shitting himself, then. I don't know what he's done, but obviously he's dropped a bollock somewhere. Since those last conversations he's really gone down.'

'That's right.'

'The sooner the miserable sod's off my hands, the better,' I said. 'Listen, Yorky, I'll call in again at four o'clock to check the form. OK?'

Now I understood why Farrell had become so agitated. The Civil Administration Teams are the PIRA's notorious means of enforcing discipline within the ranks. If someone gets a call saying, 'We need to come round and have a talk,' he knows he's for it – at the very least a few cold baths and some beatings to make him produce information, at worst a kneecapping or even an execution.

For three and a half hours I was dead to the world, and I awoke with the unpleasant but familiar sensation of not knowing where I

203

was. Staggering up, I found Tony in the kitchen, heating up some soup.

'Get to sleep?' he asked.

'Yeah. How about you?'

'Sure did. Couple of hours. I feel a whole heap better. Like some soup?'

'Great. In a minute, though. I'm just going to put in a call.'

Again I slipped out, down the track and into the wood.

'Yer daft bat,' said Yorky straight away. 'Where've you been?'

'Kipping it deadly,' I told him.

'Well done, lad. I was hoping you'd come on. We have two guys in an old railway wagon right alongside the RV site – Andy Peake and Terry Mason, from the SP team.'

'Fabulous,' I said. 'What wagon is it?'

'It's a closed freight car with the serial number zero nine two painted in big white numbers on the side. The sides are fairly intact, but part of the floor's gone, so they've got easy access to the track. They've a good view of the yard, and they're pretty sure no PIRA have shown yet.'

'All right. So what do we do?'

'You'll need to decoy the PIRA car as close to that wagon as you can. Then, while the players are concentrating on you and Farrell, somebody will slip out from between the wheels with a little goodwill package . . .' Yorky explained that the yard was a couple of hundred metres long but only fifty wide. Our best tactic, he said, would be to drive in along the left-hand side, close to the rails, and then at the end do a U turn, so that we came to rest facing back towards the entrance gate, with our left-hand doors close to the high wall that bounded the yard on the road side. Parked there we'd be opposite the occupied railway wagon, and the logical place for the PIRA to pull up would be right beside it, across the yard from us.

'Sounds good,' I said. 'What about back-up?'

'There'll be two cars, each with four, in the road above. There's a pub up there, the Railway Arms, so there should be enough people coming and going to create a bit of a distraction. But our guys won't do anything or show themselves unless the PIRA start messing about. They'll only intervene if there's an attempt at a snatch.'

'Fair enough. Will you brief the police to stand off?'

'Of course. What vehicle will you be in?'

'The Granada. And I'm not taking any chances on this one. We're going to be there early.'

We set out in good time, with Farrell blindfolded once again. To give Whinger and Tony a break I had left them to house-sit, taking Stew to drive and Doughnut to act as principal minder. Another belt of wet weather had moved up from the south-west, and a soft rain was falling – no bad thing, as it would reduce visibility at the RV site. In another conversation with Yorky and Fraser I'd learned that, sure enough, two young fellows with every appearance of being PIRA dickers had appeared outside the Railway Arms at about half-past four and walked along the road that ran above the marshalling yard. They'd made one pass out and another back, and were presumably based in a car parked up there on the high ground. Without doubt they'd report our arrival to colleagues over a mobile phone or CB radio.

Whether or not Farrell had any inkling about where the safe house was, I couldn't be sure. On our way out to the rendezvous in the morning we'd made one diversionary detour off the M4 and driven through a few of the roundabouts on the outskirts of Swindon, purely to confuse him and give the impression that we weren't doing a sustained motorway run. Next, back on the M4, we'd come on the block at Reading and had to turn round, which providentially added to his disorientation. Then on the way home we'd come via the M40 and Oxford, so that once again there hadn't been any long stretch at high speed. All in all, it seemed to me that he'd have to be a bloody genius to work out the location of the cottage.

This time, as a further variation, we went north-about through Gloucester and across country to Cirencester, so that we came into Swindon from the north-west. By the time we hit the outskirts it was almost fully dark, and under the sodium lamps the streets were glistening with rain.

It may be that some other town in Britain has more roundabouts per square kilometre, but if it does I don't know where it is. We went through dozens of the bastards, some single, some double, and many of them practically touching each other.

'The town planners went fucking mad here,' I said as we missed a turn and had to circle yet again to pick up the right road.

'Too right,' Doughnut agreed.

We found Brunel Road with fifteen minutes in hand, so we decided on a drive-past.

'There's the entrance,' I said as we came towards the left-hand bend. The big mesh gates were shut, as predicted, and we only caught glimpses of the yard beyond.

'Pretty damn dark in there,' said Stew.

'Yep,' I agreed. 'But that's to our advantage.'

Again we were caught up in an insane network of roundabouts and one-way streets, with the result that it was nearly 2255 by the time we made our second run. This time I jumped out, slid back a bar-catch and pushed the right-hand gate open. Its base scraped over a rough surface – earth or cinders – but I forced it back, left it wide open and nipped into the car again.

'Now,' I said. 'Just take a swing round and park. Anywhere will do.'

Stew knew that my last remarks were cover. I'd briefed him on the exact procedure that Yorky and I had worked out.

There were the old railway wagons, on a line right beside the yard. They looked very tall, because there was no raised platform at that point and we were down on the same level as the tracks. Farrell was still hooded, so as we came level with number 092 I pointed at it silently, and Stew nodded. He drove past, then swung right-handed into a U-turn, brought the Granada to rest about three feet from the high wall, switched off the engine and doused the lights.

'OK.' I turned to Farrell. 'We're there. Now it's up to them.'

He only grunted in reply. I think he felt as nervous as we did, and I don't blame him. If anyone did attempt a snatch a fire-fight would erupt within seconds, and he'd be in the middle of it.

The only light in the yard was a feeble spill-over from street-lamps along the road above. Under the wall, we were in deep shadow. The floor was uneven and pock-marked with holes. I presumed it must once have been covered with railway tracks, and now pools of water glistened in the depressions left behind where the sleepers had been ripped out. The whole place looked black as coal, and whenever a train went by on the main line, only a few yards away, the noise sent my mind back to the steam engine which used to pull a few tourist carriages up and down a branch line near where I was brought up, in the north.

I wished to hell we could use our covert radios. I was a good friend of Andy Peake, one of the guys hidden in 092, and I longed to chat him up. Had he seen the dickers any more? Had they come down and sussed out the yard? Had any other car made an approach? Were our own guys in position up top? Andy would be listening in on the net, and would know the score exactly. All *we* could do was hope that the lads had everything under control.

Once again the deadline came and went. To cover my anxiety, I began mentally rehearsing possible moves.

'When they arrive,' I told Farrell, 'you're going to stay put. You're not getting out. If they want a good look at you, they'll have to come up close and take a shufti through the window.'

'We'll see,' he said. 'I can't vouch for what cunts like that may do.'

Suddenly I found myself thinking of the hot, clear nights in the Libyan desert, a world away from this soft English rain. I thought of the moment when Norm had found he'd left his Magellan behind, and the crazy, blaring crackle of the *muezzin*'s first call to prayer as dawn was about to break. Once again I saw our target in his death throes, and heard his slippered feet going *slap, slap, slap* against the wall.

'Watch yourselves!' Stew's voice jerked me back to the present. 'There's a car trying to turn in at the gate.'

The driver had his right-hand indicator on, waiting for a couple of oncoming vehicles to pass. But when the road cleared, all he did was drive into the yard, swing straight round and out again.

'Lost,' said Stew. 'Can't blame him. There must be hundreds like him in this bloody maze.'

Five more minutes crawled past. Already the PIRA were ten minutes late.

None of us had anything to say. With the windows of the Granada open, we could hear sounds of revelry from the distant pub: drunken shouts and outbursts of song. I began to think the opposition had succumbed to temptation and gone in there. I'd known it happen in Ulster. Bombers or shooters, on their way to a hit, would stop off for a quick pint to steady their nerves, and end up drinking six or seven, so that they'd be out of their minds and the operation would have to be aborted. But this was only a harmless meeting, without danger, so, surely . . .

'Here we are!' said Stew.

This time a pair of lights swept through the gate without hesitation and blazed in our faces. In retaliation Stew snapped his headlights on to full beam and lit up an elderly-looking red Peugeot, cruising gingerly over the potholes. I held my breath, willing the driver to keep straight on along the line of the tracks.

Our psychological reading of the site must have been spot-on, because he did just that, and came to rest within a few inches of where we wanted him. Then he doused his lights and sat waiting.

I let half a minute tick by before declaring, 'If they're not coming, I'm going.'

I got out and walked round the front of the Granada. By then I'd un-zipped my jacket so that I had quick access to my shoulder holster, but as I strolled across I deliberately kept my hands well away from my hips. Out there in mid-yard I felt cold and exposed. I knew Andy was in the wagon straight ahead of me, beyond the Peugeot, and I was confident that I had more support behind me, up above, but if one of the players lost his nerve and opened fire, I'd be the first to get it.

A yard from the driver's window I stopped. The face inside the rain-spattered glass was still a blur. The flash of a torch in the fellow's eyes might be taken as a provocation, so I waited till he wound the window down by hand.

'Come to see someone?' I went.

'Where is he?'

'In the car.' I jerked my head backwards.

'Bring him over, then.'

'Not a chance. You can come and look.'

'Not fucking likely. You bring him here.'

In line of sight over the roof of the car, not ten feet away, I detected movement down among the wheels of truck 092. Jesus! I thought. Andy's not waiting. He's crawling out with his tracking device. Whatever might happen later, I had to keep the PIRA fully occupied for the next few seconds.

'Listen,' I said. 'Are you the guys who came up the M25 this morning?' As I spoke I leant forward and rested my hands on the edge of the roof, deliberately making the car rock in the hope that the movement would help cover any slight disturbance that Andy might create.

'Get yer hands off!' snapped the driver.

'I was only asking.'

'Get off anyway!'

'Was it you, then?' I stood up, letting the Peugeot rock back.

'What difference does it make?'

'You fucked up, that's all.'

Now I thought, I'm getting him well stropped up. I'll switch on the torch anyway.

The effect was excellent. The driver twisted in his seat, rocking the car again. 'Get that thing off!' he hissed.

But I'd already recognised him. He'd been the passenger in the grey minivan that morning, the guy with whom I'd had that flash of eye-contact. His companion in the passenger seat was an older man with stiff grey hair cut short, definitely not the driver on the M25. He was the one, I guessed: the player who'd come to make the identification.

I flashed my torch round the inside of the car, partly to make sure there was nobody else on board, partly to dazzle the occupants. Both of them twisted about in their seats, shielding their faces from the beam.

'I said, get that thing off,' said the driver.

'You told me there'd be three of you.'

'No, only two.'

'What happened to your mate?'

'He couldn't make it in time.'

'All right, then.' As if climbing down, I switched off the torch and said, 'Well, I'll make a compromise. We'll bring him half-way across. But that's all.'

Another main-line train trundled past, shaking the ground and filling the yard with the scream of big diesel engines as it picked up speed out of the station. Once again I caught a hint of movement under the railway wagon, and reckoned what I saw was Andy's heels going back into cover, his job done. He'd certainly had time to place a magnetic device on the petrol tank and crawl away to shelter. Stepping back ostentatiously, I turned round and walked towards the Granada.

'Get him out after all,' I told Doughnut. 'We'll take him half-way over.'

I opened the door and stood back, expecting Farrell to start creating. But he said nothing as Doughnut wriggled out crab-wise, and he followed him into the open without fuss. When the pair were on their feet I took off Farrell's blindfold and said, 'Right. We'll go twenty steps and stop.'

We walked forward three abreast to the middle of the yard, Doughnut on the right, Farrell in the middle, myself on the left. I was stepping on the tips of my toes. If any attempt at a snatch was going to be made, this was when it would come. And no snatch *would* take place, because if they tried anything, Doughnut and I would drop the pair of them.

For a few seconds there was no movement from the Peugeot. Then the passenger door opened, on the side away from us, and I knew it must be the grey-haired guy getting out.

As he advanced towards us I muttered to my two, 'Keep still. Your arms particularly.'

Behind us I heard a click, and I knew that Stew was opening the boot of the Granada so that he had immediate access to the loaded MP5s. I could just make out that the PIRA man was carrying some light-coloured object in his left hand, but it looked harmless, like a big envelope. He stopped a yard from us, and I spotted his right hand coming up. In a split second I had my torch beam on him, and saw that he too was holding a flashlight, which he switched on and shone into our faces, first mine, then Doughnut's, then Farrell's. There the beam stopped.

'So it *is* you, yer fuckin' wee cuntie,' he muttered in a quiet, menacing voice. 'Even better looking than usual, with that pout on yer.'

If Farrell had been free, I'm sure he'd have hit the guy. As it was, he just said, 'Holy Mary! It's Marty Malone.'

There was a moment's silence, as if both men were getting over the shock of seeing each other. Then Farrell said, 'Jaysus, but I never thought I'd see you this side of the water.'

'Maybe you didn't. But you've seen me now. Which of these turds is Geordie Sharp?'

'I am,' I said, 'and watch yourself.'

'I'm watching, and I don't like what I'm seeing. So it's the mighty assassin I have before me, is it? Here.' He held out the manila envelope. 'Take this. It contains your orders.'

'Orders for what?'

'You'll see. If you go murdering our allies overseas, it's only fair you do something for us in return.'

A shiver of alarm ran up my back, but I had the presence of mind to come straight out with, 'I'm not with you. What are you on about?'

'Come on! We know you've been abroad.'

'What d'you mean? I've been nowhere.'

'Oh no? Not even to north Africa.'

I shook my head.

'Libya?' queried the man in a horrible, taunting voice. 'Ajdabiya camp?'

'Sorry, mate. Your wires are crossed somewhere. Those names mean nothing to me.'

The temptation to drop the guy was fearsome. From Farrell's reaction I knew he must be some big player. We could smack him and his driver in about five seconds. But if we did, that would be the end of Tim and Tracy.

The man shone his torch in my face again and said, 'You wouldn't be lying to me, would you, Sergeant?'

'Listen, I told you. I've never heard those names. I don't know what the hell you're on about.'

'General al-Khadduri was very important to us. We didn't like losing him.'

'General who?'

'The man you shot.'

'Look,' I said, 'piss off, and stop all this rubbish. Now that you've seen your man, you'd better get going before the law arrives to break up the party.' I made a half-turn to the right and said to my lot, 'OK. Let's go.'

As we walked away, the PIRA guy stood looking after us until we were nearly at the car. Then he too turned and went back to his vehicle.

'Let them thin out first,' I told Stew. Internally, I was seething. Jesus Christ! an inner voice was shouting. How in God's name did they find out about Libya? Or *do* they really know about it? Are they just guessing that the SAS was involved? Then suddenly I realised: it was Karen, that bitch of a policewoman, telling them I was abroad when they called. *That's* what they'd cottoned on to. They can't have any proof, I told myself, they've simply put two and two together . . . and made about ten.

The worst thing was that I couldn't utter a syllable of these violent thoughts, or Farrell would have been on to it in a flash. I just sat there in the dark with my mind racing as we waited for the opposition to clear. After a minute it became clear that they were doing just the same, and I said to Stew, 'Ah, fuck it, let's go. Fast, as well.'

Our back tyres spun on the cinders as he put in a scorching take-off. In a second we were through the gate and burning up the hill. Behind us I saw lights come on as the Peugeot also got going. From its speed down the yard, I reckoned the party was going to try and tail us.

'Take the first left you can!' I snapped. 'They're going to play funny buggers.'

Though not quite in the Whinger class, Stew was no slouch as a driver. Before the Peugeot had even gained the top of the hill and come into sight, he'd dived left-handed into a residential street, pulled into the kerb between two parked cars and doused his lights. Looking out through the rear window, we saw the Peugeot hurtle past along the main drag.

'Great!' I said. 'Now we can take it easy. Give it a minute, and we'll slide out the way we came.' Then, as though it were a casual afterthought, I added, 'What the hell was that guy on about – Libya and all that?'

'Ask me another,' said Stew.

'Any idea, Doughnut?'

'Not a clue.'

'Nor me. Sounds as if they lost a key player or something. Some

212

Arab, by the name . . . whatever it was. Tell you what, I could do with something to eat.'

'Me too,' said Stew. 'There's a good few takeaways about. I was eye-balling them on the way in.'

My mind was very much on the contents of the buff envelope, but instinct told me to play that down as well. So for the time being I left the package on the floor behind my feet. Five minutes later, with no further manifestation of the red Peugeot, we drove back on to the highway, and at the fifty-seventh roundabout (or thereabouts) we found a Chinese takeaway still open. Chicken and chips all round put us back in good heart; we ate sitting in a lay-by, and didn't hood Farrell up until we were ready to set off for home.

Then, as Stew pulled out on to the Cirencester road, I picked up the envelope and switched on the map-reading light to examine its contents. The first thing I saw was an Ordnance Survey map, a sheet of the 1:25,000 series, two and a half inches to the mile, covering part of the Chiltern Hills. Next I came on a page of what looked like instructions, typed in short, numbered paragraphs. Only when I unfolded it and looked at the head of the page did I realise that it was addressed to me. And when I read it, my breath seemed to lock up in my chest.

With the motion of the car and the feeble light, I couldn't take in every word. But the gist of the document was all too clear. Because I had been personally responsible for the murder of a leading financial supporter, it said, I was now ordered to carry out an operation for the IRA. To secure the release of my family, I not only had to hand Farrell over, I was also required to shoot the Prime Minister on the terrace of Chequers, his official country house in Buckinghamshire, on the morning of Thursday 2 June – two days' time. If I failed, the hostages would be killed and their weighted bodies would be dropped into the Thames.

I think we were nearly in Cirencester, a dozen miles down the road, before I fully took in what I was reading. The idea was so outrageous that at first I thought it was some grisly joke. Assassinate the Prime Minister? They couldn't be serious. Then I saw the notes that somebody had made after a recce of the park at Chequers, with bearings and distances, and details of the security arrangements protecting the house, and I realised that the plan was in deadly earnest.

Stew must have seen that I was shaken, because he glanced sideways at me and said, 'Everything OK, Geordie?'

'Yeah, yeah.' I switched off the map light and tried to sound flippant. 'Just the usual bloody nonsense. We'll sort it out when we get back.' But everything was far from OK. I felt the whole world was coming down on top of me.

TWELVE

During the journey back nobody spoke much: Doughnut kept the music going on the radio, and when Farrell asked me some question I pretended to have dozed off. I knew Andy would have reported direct from the railway wagon, so that the SB guys in the incident room would already know that our meeting had taken place. All the same, they'd be panting to hear our version of the story; but with Farrell in the car I wasn't going to start honking off about it while we were on the road.

It was after one when we reached the cottage. Whinger and Tony had sat up waiting for us, and they got a brew on as soon as we arrived. Of course they wanted to know how things had gone, so I described the meeting a bit and said that everything had been OK. I told them that Farrell's identity had definitely been confirmed, but I didn't mention the PIRA orders. When Farrell started asking about them, I said they were a load of shit and we'd deal with them in the morning. Then, after we'd all had a cup of tea, I asked Tony to put the man to bed.

'It's like looking after a goddamn baby!' he protested. 'The next thing I'll have to do is wipe his butt for him.'

'I know. But someone's got to do the job. And anyway, our baby's special. When this is all over, I'll see you're issued with a diploma, so that you can get a job as a nanny.'

As for me – I couldn't imagine going to sleep. I needed to call the incident room, but first I wanted to talk things through with the other lads. So, with Farrell safely shackled to the bed and out of carshot upstairs, we settled into a Chinese parliament in the living room.

At first the others were as incredulous about the orders as I'd been. The scheme was so monstrous they couldn't believe it. But

215

as we went through the PIRA reports, we could see how thorough the terrorists had been in their reconnaissance and research. The documents were semi-literate in places, but neatly laid out by a word processor, and full of information.

'Listen to this,' I said, and I read out a paragraph labelled 'Political Background':

A conference for Commonwealth Heads of State will take place at Chequers on 2 and 3 June. The first of the foreign dignitaries is due to arrive there at 1100 hours on 2 June. The first full session of the meeting will start at 1430 that day.

The Prime Minister will travel down from London by car the night before, 1 June. When in the country during the summer months it is his habit to walk out into the garden before breakfast, and before any guests are up. He is a very early bird. Often out by 0630. Being a rose freak, he likes particularly to go round the rose garden on the south terrace. There is every chance that on the morning of 2 June he will be attacking the greenfly by 0700 am at the latest. This will present a sniper at Point D with an ideal opportunity . . .

I picked up another sheet of paper and said, 'There's no doubt they've been and cased the joint.' I read them some more:

The range from Point D to the retaining wall at the front of the south terrace is 580 yards. The security screen round the house extends no more than 200 yards. Therefore Point D lies well beyond the reach of cameras and other security devices.

'Sounds as though their intelligence is shit-hot,' I added. 'They must have people all over the place. I mean, we know they've got men in London, but it looks like they've got Swindon sewn up, they've spent a lot of time at Chequers . . . They can put guys in wherever they need them. The question is, how the hell do we respond?'

'We can't handle this on our own,' said Whinger. 'Got to tell the incident room and the head-shed.'

'We'll call them in a minute,' I agreed. 'Fraser's going to do his

216

nut. He's been wittering on about a shoot in London – but wait till he hears this.'

Tony, practical as ever, asked, 'What weapon are they proposing for the shoot?'

'There's something here . . .' I flipped back a couple of pages and read out: ' "The sniper weapon will be collected from a transit hide, details later." '

'Gotta be some weapon, to be effective at the range they're talking about.'

'Wait a minute,' said Whinger. 'It's not that fucking great five-oh they had in Ulster, is it?'

'Could be,' I told him. 'Could easily be. SB had wind that some big cannon was being brought over, or maybe *had* been brought over already.'

'A five-oh!' Tony whistled. 'That's something else.'

'We're jumping to conclusions,' I said. 'But that's what it sounds like.'

Everyone in the Regiment who'd served in Ulster knew about the fearsome rifle with which members of the security forces had been taken out in the late eighties and early nineties. It was so accurate that it could hit a man at a thousand yards, so powerful that a round would go straight through a flak-jacket and blow the wearer away. The guy using the weapon had become such a menace that the SAS had twice tried to get him. They'd set up special patrols that appeared to be from the green army, in the hope of luring the sniper to take a shot and give his position away, but by a combination of luck and guile he'd always evaded them and had never been accounted for.

'If they're talking about a range of six hundred yards,' said Tony, 'that's peanuts for a weapon of that calibre.'

'All right,' I said. Somehow, thinking about the big rifle had suddenly cleared my mind. A flash of intuition had shown me the way ahead. But all I said for now was, 'What are we going to suggest?'

'Suggest?' Whinger looked baffled. 'Who to?'

'The head-shed and Special Branch.'

'Isn't it up to *them* to suggest something?'

'I mean, are we going to have a crack at this or not?'

'At what? Sorry, Geordie, I'm not with you.'

'The shoot. Why don't we go through with it? Keep the charade going. Tell the PIRA we're on-side with them for the big hit.'

The others leant back in their seats with expressions of amazement on their faces. Stew said, 'You have to be joking.'

'The bastards have me over a barrel. The only thing we can do is play for time, right up to the last second. We know the search for the hostages is closing in, but we're not at the end of it yet. It's the only option I have. It's the zero option.'

'Take it easy, Geordie,' said Tony. 'Don't tell me you're going through with this?'

'Of course I'm not. But I might as well pretend I'm on, just to play the PIRA along.'

This time nobody spoke. They all stared at me in silence as if I'd flipped completely.

'Listen,' I continued, 'everything's gone brilliantly so far. The whole idea of the intercept was outrageous, but we hacked it. Nobody got hurt. No security leak. Nobody any the wiser. One van wrecked, but so what? We've had fantastic back-up from the Regiment and the police. And from the politicians, come to that. *And* the Prime Minister. If we just stay cool, we can carry the process one stage farther.'

Whinger shook his head. 'I still don't get it. Unless you *do* drop the guy, how are you going to make the PIRA hand your family over?'

'It's all a question of timing. We buy more time by shaping to go through with the shoot. In the two days between now and the second of June, SB may crack the puzzle.'

'Time . . .' Doughnut said suddenly. 'Did Andy get a device on the PIRA car, I wonder? If he did, Special Branch may have a breakthrough already. The car may have led them to the hostage location.'

'Possible,' I agreed. 'Look. I'm going down to camp.'

'Now?' said Whinger. 'It's two o'clock on Sunday morning.'

'The incident room will be manned. They need to know about this soonest. After all, this is a national emergency – or about to become one. And the head-shed need to know that Ostrich is blown.'

'Ostrich!' exclaimed Whinger. 'What a fuck-up!'

'You didn't leave the Libyans a little present after all?' I went. 'Like a copy of the head-shed's secret telephone directory?'

'Piss off, mate.'

For a few seconds silence prevailed. Then Stew said, 'The powers that be will never sanction a phoney shoot. It's too dicey. They'll tell you to screw the nut on that one.'

'Why?' I challenged him. 'Hitting a guy at six hundred yards *does* take a bit of doing. But missing him – that's a piece of cake. If I'm holding that rifle, I can tell you, the man'll be as safe as houses.'

'Sorry, Geordie.' Whinger shook his head. 'I still don't see how this is going to work.'

I cleared my throat and started again. 'We show Farrell these orders, right? We tell him we're prepared to go ahead. But he has to come with us on the shoot, so he can see for himself what's happening. You with me?'

'More or less.'

'Also we tell him that, immediately after the shot, things have got to happen fucking quick, or we'll be nicked in the park at Chequers. That means that he's got to give the word for the release of the hostages the moment the shoot goes down.'

'So?' Whinger still looked highly sceptical.

'The head-shed briefs the Prime Minister. On the morning he's to take a wander out on to his terrace, as per normal. By then we're in an OP, watching the house. We fire a single shot, close past him. At the crack, he drops and lies still. As soon as Farrell sees he's down, he gives the order for the hostages to be handed over at a prearranged RV.'

'How's he supposed to communicate?'

'Over my mobile.'

'And how does he think he's going to get his own arse away out of the park?'

'We'll tell him to have his guys lay on a chopper. They can hire one to come in and pick us up. We'll fly out together. Then, later, we ditch him. I need to think that bit through . . .'

Whinger shook his head again. 'They'll never buy it.'

'Who won't?'

'The police, for one. Can you imagine them letting a leading

IRA player creep up on the Prime Minister with a bloody great five-oh rifle? The very idea'll send them fucking ballistic.' He broke off and screwed up his face in his efforts to imitate a plod on the beat: ' "Hexcuse me, sah. Before you pull that triggah, may I hinspect your firearms certificate, please?" For fuck's sake!'

'Farrell won't have the rifle,' I insisted. 'I'll have it. That's the point. There'll be two of us with him, one to mind him, one to shoot.

'In general, if we seem to be co-operating with the PIRA, we'll keep the lid on the whole thing. There'll be no risk to anyone. On the contrary, by agreeing to go through with the shoot, we'll bring a serious threat under control. We'll take possession of a dangerous weapon, and with any luck we'll bust the London ASU in the process.'

I looked round the tired faces, and thought I saw a couple wavering. 'What if we *refuse* to co-operate?' I persisted. 'Number one: I don't get the hostages back; the PIRA will kill them and dump them in the river. Number two: we're stuck with Farrell. Number three: the PIRA still have the rifle; the shoot will go down anyway, probably at some later date. The security forces will be left with the same problem. The threat may be deferred, but it'll still exist. The London ASU will remain intact, and they may easily get the Prime Minister in the end.'

'Well, whatever,' Tony began cautiously, 'you better move pretty damn fast. There's less than two days to get organised. If we pick up the weapon at all, we've got to test-fire it someplace. Farrell will insist on that. Otherwise, how in hell are we supposed to know where it's shooting?'

'Good point. That's why I'm heading for camp right now.'

'Want me to come with you?' asked Whinger.

'Thanks, Whinge, but I'll be OK. You might be needed here. I'll probably get my head down in the sergeants' mess for a couple of hours, then come back first thing in the morning.'

'What if Farrell starts asking where you are?' Stew asked.

'Tell him I'm asleep,' I said. 'Or just don't tell him anything.'

For a quiet take-off, I rolled the Granada down the hill and started the engine by letting out the clutch in third gear when I reached the gate at the bottom of the drive. Then, as soon as I was under way, I called the incident room on the mobile and got a duty officer strange to me.

'Geordie Sharp,' I said. 'I'm coming in. There's been a big development. I'll need to speak to Commander Fraser. Can you get hold of him?'

'Not to worry,' came the answer. 'He's here already. I'll put him on.'

'Geordie?' came Fraser's voice. 'Where are you?'

'Heading your way. I'll be there in half an hour.'

'What's new?'

'Can't tell you from here. Any luck with that car?'

'Yes and no. Tell you when I see you.'

'OK . . . and listen.'

'Yes?'

'I need an urgent meeting with the ops officer. Yorky Rose as well. Can you alert them?'

'Right away?'

'Afraid so.'

Rolling into camp at three in the morning made me feel I was back at the start of the whole drama, back to the night we had got in from Bogotá and I found my family gone. That now seemed as though it had been light-years ago. The last two days and nights alone had been so full that I felt I hadn't seen Stirling Lines in months.

By the time I ran up the stairs to the incident room a full reception committee was there to meet me: not only the SB team, but Mac Macpherson, Yorky, and the CO. The only man anywhere near correctly dressed was Fraser, in a shirt, tie and pullover; the others had track suits or sweat tops over what looked suspiciously like pyjamas. As always, there was a brew on the go.

We had no banter or pissing about, but went straight into an informal O-group – and you could have heard a mouse fart in the next county while I explained what had happened.

When I started to outline the programme for the Chequers shoot I was seriously worried Yorky might explode; he turned red in the face and his eyeballs rotated at high revs. In fact, such a proportion of what I said was so utterly outrageous that all of them, one after the other, soon looked close to apoplexy. I don't know who was most agitated – Fraser, when he heard that we'd met Marty Malone in the railway yard, or the CO when I told him that Operation Ostrich had been blown.

Fraser muttered, 'Marty Malone!' in a voice he might have used if he'd won a million on the pools. 'This is the guy who's been masterminding the bombing campaign on the mainland. But so far he's always operated out of West Belfast, never dared cross the water. I'll bet my trousers it was him who brought the big rifle across.'

He took a deep breath and added, 'If all this resulted in our nicking Marty Malone – boy, would that be something! He's one of the most evil pigs in the whole organisation.'

Remembering the lean, drawn look of the older man's face in the marshalling yard, I said, 'Maybe it was him who was down to do the shoot.'

'Possible,' Fraser agreed. 'In fact, more than possible. The fact he's here at all means there's something really big in the offing.'

The Boss cried, 'God's boots!' Then, turning to Mac, he said, 'You haven't had wind of any leak on Libya?'

'Nothing at all.'

'Get on to the Firm immediately,' said the CO. 'See if they've heard anything.'

As Mac went next door to make the call, the Boss muttered, 'I don't believe there *has* been a leak. I believe the buggers are guessing, trying to bluff their way.'

'I tell you what,' I said to Fraser. 'It was that miserable girl of yours. It was her that dropped us in the shit on this one.'

'Well,' he went, 'it may have been. But I tend to agree with your commanding officer. All the PIRA heard was that you'd gone abroad for a few days. You could have been anywhere in the world.'

'That's right,' said Yorky. 'They can make what they like out of what the woman said, but I'll lay a hundred pounds to a penny they haven't got a scrap of evidence to back it.'

'These PIRA orders,' said the CO. 'Where are they?'

'Here.' I opened the manila envelope and began to pull out the documents.

222

'Wait!' Fraser snapped. 'Prints.'

'I've handled the papers already.'

'Never mind. Forensic can try. Give them to Sergeant Alden. He'll photocopy them while we're talking.'

I handed the package over, and the tall duty sergeant took it out of the room. On the way he passed Mac, who came back in shaking his head. 'Nothing known to the Firm on Ostrich. Not the slightest suggestion of a leak. The Libyans are still blaming Mossad, and Egypt's denying all knowledge of the operation. But I've asked Gilbert to call first thing in the morning.'

'All right,' said the CO. 'We'd better ring round to make sure everybody's ready with their denials – the FO for one.'

'I reckon you're right about the PIRA trying to bluff us, Boss,' I said. 'But even if you are, it doesn't make much difference. No matter how much or how little they know about Libya, they still have me over a barrel. So what I propose is this . . .'

I launched into my spiel again – and the reception was much the same as in the cottage: a mixture of alarm and incredulity. At first the ruperts couldn't believe I was being serious. Yorky really thought I'd gone round the bend. He walked up and down at one hell of a pace, exclaiming, 'Eh, lad, you're in it now,' throwing up a pencil and, as often as not, missing it when it fell. His movements became so distracting that the CO told him for Christ's sake to sit down.

'As for Chequers,' I went on, 'the PIRA have really done their homework. You remember that fuss a few years back about getting a footpath diverted, so that it wouldn't pass so close to the front of the house? Well, that got done. But still the path is only five or six hundred metres from the terrace, and the PIRA have it all sussed out for a shoot from there. Everything's in those papers – distances, elevations, bearings, routes in and out, prevailing winds, security arrangements . . .'

As the logic of what I was saying got through to them, they all began to calm down a bit. The CO was the first to crack. 'In purely operational terms it's feasible,' he admitted. 'I can see that. I'd trust you to handle the shoot, Geordie. But we're going to have the devil's own problem selling it to Whitehall.'

'The point is, the situation hasn't changed from when we

started,' I said. 'Except that now the person directly threatened is the Prime Minister himself. That makes it all the more important to go straight to the top. He's the one at risk. It's him who'll benefit if we get these bastards sorted. If we take on the shoot ourselves, it'll increase our chances of busting the ASU.' I started going through the benefits of proceeding, as I had with the lads in the safe house: that we would hijack the PIRA's plan for the shoot, get the weapon, and so on.

'Geordie!' The CO scratched his head. 'I have to give it to you. You make everything sound dead simple.'

Now it was he who got up and went walkabout. 'What you're going to have to do is present an appreciation, in the normal way.'

'No time, Boss. If we're going to pick up the rifle, we've got to do it tomorrow night – tonight, I mean.'

'OK. That leaves the morning. I vote we all get our heads down for a couple of hours. Sleep on the problem, then have another brief. How about that, Commander?'

'Fine by me,' said Fraser. 'Just bear in mind that none of this caper may be necessary. There's a chance that we'll get to the hostages first. That car your fellows bugged has narrowed the field a bit.'

'Oh, great!' I said. 'Where did it go?'

'We followed it to Earl's Court. It's there now, parked in a stack off Oldbury Road. We've put round-the-clock surveillance on it. Unfortunately we couldn't keep tabs on the occupants, but as soon as they come back we'll get a tail on them.'

'You mean you lost them?' Suddenly I saw red. 'For fuck's sake! How did you manage that?'

'Take it easy, Geordie. It wasn't that simple.'

'Bloody hell, though! After we'd been to all that trouble to get a device on the car . . .'

'I know. But listen: the guy in the passenger seat got out and jumped straight on to a bus a couple of blocks short of the park. Then, at the barrier on the entrance to the stack, the driver swapped places with someone else, who put the car away.'

'Couldn't your guys keep on him, though?'

'He was gone like a rat down a bloody drain.'

'Ah, hell!'

I saw Fraser giving me a wary look and half getting up from his chair, as if he expected me to throw another track and start smashing the place up again.

'Chill out, Geordie,' Yorky said. 'Everyone's doing their best.'

As I felt the rush of anger draining away, I let out a deep breath and said, 'Sorry I shouted. All this is getting to me.'

'No sweat,' Fraser replied evenly. 'They're cunning bastards, they really are. All the hints we've been picking up from intercepts have suggested an assassination attempt was being planned for July, and in London – when Clinton's due to visit. Now it looks as though all that was cover, a blind.'

'Typical,' I said. 'At least we know what the real plan is. But we've got to budget for the worst. These telephone calls Farrell's making – aren't they leading anywhere?'

'We tried following up the last mobile number, but it's gone off the air. They're using quite a few different phones.'

The sergeant reappeared with a sheaf of photostats, and the ruperts started passing them round. The detail in the papers made them gripe and groan, and had the effect of reinforcing my presentation.

'Curses!' went the CO. 'I see what you mean. You'd better leave the originals with the Commander, for the forensic boys.'

'That's fine. Copies will do for Farrell. He doesn't even know what the envelope contained. What about the map, though?'

'We'll get another in the morning.'

The meeting was about to break up when Fraser said, 'This Farrell – what's he like?'

'A pain in the arse. We're keeping him cuffed to one or other of us all the time. It's like having a bloody bear or something in the house.'

'Has he tried to do a runner?'

'No. Physically, he's in fairly poor shape. The bullet wound in his flank hasn't healed properly. He's on antibiotics, and that's dragging him down a bit. The brush-off he got from his pals in Belfast knocked him back a bit too. But we're not taking any chances.'

'Quite right,' said Fraser. 'We picked up some good stuff in an intercept yesterday. The boyos are after him for laundering funds from Colombia. They think he's filtered out seven or eight million dollars.'

'Ah – so *that's* what it is.' Suddenly those peculiar reactions made sense. If Farrell had been creaming off cocaine money, and had been rumbled, no wonder he was getting nervous. 'Maybe, in the end, they won't want him back,' I said.

'On the contrary,' said Fraser. 'They'll want him all the more, so they can give him a going-over. Also to stop him spilling any secrets.'

'Perhaps he won't want to go, then . . . On the other hand, he's arrogant enough to think he can talk himself out of it.'

'It can't be very comfortable, being cooped up with him,' suggested the CO.

'Could be worse. I'm having as little to do with him as I can. I don't want to get drawn into conversation, in case I give anything away. I tell you one thing, though.'

'What's that?'

'He's into classical music. Beethoven.'

'How d'you know?'

I told them about the episode with the music on the car radio, and when I said the piece was something called *Leonora* number three the Boss got it immediately.

'I know,' he said. 'Beethoven wrote three different overtures for his opera *Fidelio*. Couldn't decide which to use. There's one called *Leonora* number three. Great stuff. Come on, now. If the guy's into that, he can't be all bad.'

'He is,' I insisted. 'He's shit from head to toe.'

It's surprising what three hours' sleep can do for you, especially if you're running on adrenalin. When I finally got my head down in my room in the sergeants' mess it was nearly four o'clock, and once again I felt I was back at the beginning of the nightmare, on the first night after the kidnap.

But come seven o'clock, and a good breakfast, I felt a new man.

By 0745 the cast from the night before had reassembled in the incident room. The CO kicked off with, 'Right then, Geordie, what have you got for us?'

I'd already jotted down a few headings in my notebook, in the hope of making things reasonably clear, but I was glad to find that one of the int office's gofers was present with his laptop to make a proper written record.

'Mission,' I began. 'The mission is obviously to recover the hostages held by the Provisional IRA. To give Special Branch and the other security forces more time, we propose to simulate our willingness to carry out a shoot on the Prime Minister at Chequers . . .'

I ran through place, date and time as if this were a normal operation, and then listed the steps that I expected to take:

1. Contact PIRA, agree to carry out shoot.
2. Receive instructions for collecting weapon.
3. Collect weapon.
4. Move up to Forward Mounting Base in vicinity of target location.
5. Test-fire and zero weapon.
6. Negotiate with PIRA to set final RV site for exchange of Farrell and hostages. Deal will be that Farrell will authorise release of hostages by mobile phone soon as he sees the target is down.
7. Make Farrell arrange escape from RV site: helicopter to be hired by PIRA.
8. Carry out early-morning shoot as detailed, in Farrell's presence.
9. Fly out of target area. Land at intermediate RV, switch to vehicle, drive to final RV.
10. Exchange prisoners.
11. Security forces follow up tracking devices, recapture Farrell and accomplices.

The CO was at his sharpest, challenging each point as I brought it up, probing for weaknesses in the plan and scouting for problems.

'What have you got in mind for an FMB?' he demanded.

'We need another holiday cottage. The one we're in now has been perfect for down here, but it's going to be too far from the job. We need something on the edge of the Chilterns, within a few miles of Chequers. Not too close.'

'Not so easy up there,' he said. 'We don't have any tame house-owners in that area.'

After a pause he asked, 'What's the point of zeroing the rifle, if you're not trying to hit the target anyway?'

'Farrell will insist on it. He'll want to come with us when we do it – he's that sort of guy, very practical.'

'Where will you do it, then?'

'Depends where our safe house is. When we know where we've landed, we can pick an out-of-the-way spot in the country and go out there with a target at first light. I've been looking at the map: there are plenty of big, deserted valleys up there.'

The CO had adopted his favourite thinking attitude, forehead in hands, ears sticking out well to either side, and elbows on the desk. 'The PIRA will know when the shoot's going to take place,' he said. 'On the morning, they may send dickers to stake out the park.'

'I thought of that. We're going to need back-up on site. There's a farm just behind Point D. Here.' I twisted the map round so that the Boss could see it right way up. 'Brockwell Farm. It would be ideal if we could get some of the lads in there under cover of darkness the night before. Then, if Farrell did try to do a runner, or if anyone tried to lift him, we'd still be covered . . .'

Mac, the ops officer, was his usual sarcastic self. 'Of course, all this may be so much moonshine,' he said. 'If SB find the hostages first you can forget all this fancy caper.'

'Christ!' I exclaimed. 'If that happened, nobody would be happier than me. I'd be over the bloody moon. If I never saw Farrell again – if I didn't have to go back and meet the bastard again now – I'd be chuffed to bollocks.'

So it went on. The CO was pretty sceptical at first, but, as usual, he fancied having a go at something outrageous. When I left camp at 0830, I had his permission to carry on planning for the time being, and the promise that once again he would take things to the highest level in Whitehall.

Back at the cottage, I gave Farrell short shrift. When he asked where I'd been I told him to mind his own business. Then I brought out the PIRA orders. While I read out the main points, he listened with a variety of expressions passing across his face. Sometimes he looked amused, sometimes contemptuous, sometimes interested – but he never seemed particularly surprised.

'Last night you told me this was all shit,' he said.

'At first I thought it was.'

'But now you'll go along with it?'

'Have to,' I replied. 'I don't see I've any alternative. I've drawn the zero option.'

'The boyos have changed their minds, then.'

'What about?'

'The plan for the shoot. They were going to have it in London. This looks more like business. Better than trying to drop a mortar into the garden of Number Ten Downing Street, anyway.'

'What have you fellows got against the Prime Minister?' I demanded. 'He seems a harmless enough guy to me.'

'Harmless!' Farrell nearly shouted. 'Harmless, begod! He's the head of the British Government, is he not? It's him who's the architect of repression in Northern Ireland. The number of murders that fucker's got on his hands – Holy Mary, they can never be avenged. A bullet's too good for him!'

'If we hack this,' I said, 'and the shoot goes down, I don't want your people crowing about how they got an SAS man to do their dirty work for them. You get me?'

Farrell nodded.

'The Regiment would deny it anyway,' I told him. 'They'd rubbish any story that came out. But publicity's the last thing I want.'

'Don't kid yourself,' said Farrell scornfully. 'If the job gets done, the PIRA will claim a major success. They're not going to give the credit to some prat in the Brit forces.'

'All right, then. Find out our RV for collecting the weapon. We need to go for that tonight.'

Using my mobile, he went through to Belfast and started one of his usual hectoring exchanges. The prospect of action seemed to have put new life into him; he was half-way back to his former aggressive self, as though he were taking charge of the whole operation. The upshot of the conversation was that we would get our instructions for the pick-up through an intermediary in Ulster.

We were not to call the PIRA on the mainland any more – we were only to ring Belfast.

'They're getting jumpy,' I said to Whinger when we were alone in the kitchen.

'Don't blame them,' he answered. 'I am too.'

'This fucker Farrell,' I said. 'He's starting to give me the shits. I've got a horrible feeling that he's invincible, and that somehow he'll get the better of us in the end.'

'Come on, Geordie,' said Whinger. 'Pigs might fly.'

From exposure to countless previous Whingerisms I knew that meant 'Never say die', so I just said, 'Good on yer, mate,' and put an extra spoonful of sugar into my tea.

As I sipped the piping-hot drink, I couldn't stop thinking about an account I'd read in a magazine of the murder of Grigory Rasputin, the peasant monk who bewitched the Russian royal family in the years before revolution. Rasputin had an amazing hold over the Empress, Alexandra. Some people said he was secretly screwing her, others that he was the only person who could comfort her son Alexei, who was mortally ill. Anyway, when the army officers tried to murder the monk they found they couldn't do it. First they gave him enough potassium cyanide to kill an elephant, and it had practically no effect. Then they shot him through the heart with a revolver from point-blank range, and still the bastard wouldn't die. One moment he was stretched out on the flag-stones of the palace like a corpse, the next he was up, roaring, and attacking them with his hands, so violently that he tore an epaulette off one of their tunics. When he staggered to his feet and ran out through the courtyard towards the street, they couldn't believe it. Again they gunned him down, and finally they dumped his trussed body into the river through a hole in the ice. But the performance had left them shattered. They thought their victim was the devil incarnate, and they were terrified he'd return to haunt them.

Stupid as it sounds, I was beginning to feel that Farrell was another Rasputin, an evil and indestructible force. The magazine article had carried pictures of the peasant, with his wild black beard and staring eyes. I started to think I could see likenesses in Farrell's swarthy features, and I felt I was in the grip of some malign

230

influence, which was driving events forward in a way I couldn't control. It was easy to believe that, whatever I did, I would never get the better of him . . .

Deep down, of course, I knew I was suffering from cumulative lack of sleep and letting my imagination run away with me. And the best way to control my anxieties was to concentrate on the practical details of the task ahead.

When we went back through to Belfast I took over the call myself, so that I could make sure I understood everything properly. With a man dictating and myself checking back, I wrote down a grid reference for the transit hide somewhere in Oxfordshire, and a series of detailed instructions: a road junction, a lane, woods, fields, paths, a clearing on the edge of the forest, an old well with a cast-iron water pump. On paper, the notes meant practically nothing, and I could only hope they'd relate accurately to features on the ground.

At the end the contact said, 'That's all. The weapon is there, and can be collected any time after dark tonight.'

THIRTEEN

Tony and I set out at two o'clock, leaving the rest of the team to guard Farrell, close down the cottage and move up-country to whatever FMB the head-shed managed to arrange. As we drove off in the Granada, I felt a terrific relief at being away from the grotty presence of our prisoner. The man had wanted to come with us to collect the weapon, sure enough, but I told him we could manage the pick-up on our own.

As we headed east, my mind spun with conflicting possibilities, and in an attempt to clear my head I bounced some of them off Tony.

'I'm trying to puzzle out what the PIRA's state of mind is,' I began. 'They're so bloody devious, you can never be sure what they're up to.

'One thing we do know is that they want the Prime Minister dead. That's obvious. Also obvious: they want us to do their dirty work for them. But what do they reckon *my* intentions are? I suppose they think I'm so shit-scared of losing Tim that I'm simply going to do the shoot on their behalf. But what do they imagine I'll do after it's gone down? Bugger off? Disappear? Perhaps they think I'll just be able to keep my head down and nobody will find out who did it.'

'Maybe you should tell Farrell you've got a passage booked back to Colombia,' Tony suggested. 'Let him know you've fixed yourself up with a slot there, and give the impression you're going to quit Britain immediately, taking the family with you.'

'Thanks a lot! It's still possible the PIRA have no intention of handing over the hostages, whatever we do. Maybe they don't intend I should get away at all. If they stake out Point D at Chequers, they could drop us immediately after the shoot.'

'Possible,' Tony agreed. 'But unlikely. They've been to the place. They've seen it. They know it's heaving with security. You let one round off there and the park will be like an anthill. They'd never make it out. The thought should keep them away.'

'Yeah – but if they lay on the chopper, like we've suggested . . .'

I drove in silence for a few minutes, then said, 'They must trust me to some extent. After all, they're letting us get our hands on one of their most valuable weapons.'

'We haven't got the damn thing yet. They could be staking out the pick-up site right now, planning to hit us when we show up.'

'I know.' I turned and grinned at him. 'That's why we've got the MP5s.'

I drove on, heading up the M4 for Reading. The site of the transit hide had been described as the side of a wood, up in the hill country near the village of Nettlebed, maybe fifteen miles overland from Chequers. The PIRA guy had described the cache as an old well on the site of a former cottage. I was tempted to do a daylight drive-past, get a feel for the area – but I ruled it out on the grounds that if any dickers were about a passing car would be bound to alert them.

In Reading our first port of call was a general bookshop, where we bought a copy of the local 1: 25,000 map. That showed some detail, but what we really needed was the relevant sheet of the six-inches-to-the-mile Ordnance Survey, and we ran one to ground in a specialist map shop in London Road. Thus armed, we stoked up with some good spaghetti in an Italian restaurant, and pored over the maps while we drank our coffee.

'Roman coin hoard found here, 1953,' Tony read out, twisting the map at an angle.

'Is that right? Near where we're heading?'

'Not far off.'

'They'll have to add another line to the next edition,' I said. 'Barrett Fifty sniper rifle found here, 2002.'

The site of the transit hide was easy enough to identify within a hundred yards or so, even though we couldn't pinpoint it. The PIRA guy had said the old well was on the southern edge of a small, triangular wood called Kate's Copse, which had its apex pointing north and its base running east and west. We found the wood all right, but we couldn't tell how far along the half-mile base the well would be.

The route given us by the PIRA would bring us in along a lane which ran one field away from the northern point of the wood. If we took that road we could park within a couple of hundred yards of our objective. I checked the route through, turn by turn, against the map, and saw that the description was painstakingly accurate: go south off the main drag on unsigned side road, three cottages on corner; 500 yards, farm on right; 500 yards, sewage works on right, ninety-degree turn left; 700 yards straight, then deciduous wood on right; 200 yards on, grass ride on right. Leave car here . . .

The more I looked at it, the less I fancied it. If dickers were out that was where they'd be: watching that lane, anywhere between the main road and the site. With the motivation of the PIRA so uncertain, my instinct was to keep well clear.

'Look at this,' I said. 'Kate's Copse is on the brow of the hill. But there's another track here, to the south of it, along the bottom of this valley. We can park down here and walk up over. Then, if anyone's watching the top lane, they'll miss us.'

'I'm with you,' Tony agreed. 'It's not much farther. Better all round.'

Back in the car, I called Whinger's mobile. The first time it didn't connect, and I assumed that he was on the move in some low-lying area. When I tried again five minutes later he came on, patchily, but clear enough to say that they were on their way to a new safe house 'with ten miles of target', with an ETA of 2000 hours. I didn't want to ask the place's precise location because I knew Farrell would be listening to the conversation, so I told Whinger I'd call again when they'd arrived.

The evening was dim and murky. No rain was falling but there was heavy cloud cover, and I could see that darkness was going to fall early. All the same, we had an hour in hand, and I'd been planning to stop in a quiet lane so that we could get in a few minutes' kip. But by the time we cleared the northern outskirts of Reading the old adrenalin was running again, and I felt too hepped up to be sleepy.

'Tell you what,' I said, 'I don't want to count any chickens, but we've got time to recce a site for the test-shoot tomorrow. Let's take another look.'

I pulled off the road on to a patch of earth under some big beeches, and we'd hardly started scrutinising the map again when Tony pointed with his forefinger and said, 'Hey! Whaddaya know? A genuine rifle range, all ready for us.'

Sure enough, in a remote, wooded valley a few miles east of our site, the 1:25,000 map showed a narrow rectangular opening in the forest, nearly half a mile long, marked white among the green, and bearing the legend 'Rifle Range'.

'I don't believe it,' I said. 'If it's like the map shows, it's got everything: six or seven hundred yard sight-line and a remote location, no houses for miles. Let's go for it. You drive, though. Those little roads could be private tracks; if we get stopped, you do the talking. We'll be American tourists, lost in the great British jungle.'

'What do I do?' said Tony in mock alarm. 'Act dumb?'

'Act yourself,' I told him, 'and that'll fool anybody.'

He gave me a look as we changed places.

Twenty minutes later, we left the main road and dived down a spectacularly steep lane. At the bottom the ground flattened out, but soon the road swung left-handed into the beginning of the secluded valley. We passed a pair of cottages on our right, then a farm on our left. Beyond the farm the surface suddenly deteriorated from tarmac into pitted gravel, and a hand-painted notice, black on white, proclaimed it a PRIVATE ROAD.

'Thought so,' I said. 'Keep going.'

We crawled on, lurching through potholes, with steep grass fields lifting away on either hand. A few minutes later we passed the remains of some ancient building on our left, walls smothered with ivy, standing back from the road.

'Jesus!' Tony exclaimed. 'It's the ruins of a church. This place is getting spooky.'

Soon we were into the woods, which turned out to be dense beech, with branches hanging over the lane and turning it into a tunnel. In there the light was already so dim that I instinctively glanced at my watch to make sure we weren't running out of time. In fact we were fine, and I could see from the map that we were almost at our objective.

235

'Round this next corner, it'll be on our right,' I said. 'I'll believe it when we see it.'

But see it we did. Tony swung left, and after a couple of hundred yards we came upon an opening in the trees on our right, with a red and white barrier pole across it. We pulled off the track, got out of the car, dodged under the pole and walked through the gap, to find ourselves, sure enough, on a rifle range. A long, narrow strip of rough-mown grass sliced through the forest along the contours at the foot of the hill, and ended in a natural butt away to our right. There was a firing point every hundred yards, and although the place had an amateurish, partially-kept air about it, the range was clearly in use. Tyre-marks in the mud showed that quite a few vehicles came and went, the grass had been cut lately, and a couple of poles for flying danger flags had recently been repainted white.

'Incredible!' I said quietly. 'It must be the TA who use it. There's not even a range hut. They must bring everything with them when they do a shoot. But what a place! We've even got the distances marked out for us: no need to step them out.' We'd come out at the 200-yard mark, and away to our left we could see five more firing-points stretching away, giving 700 yards in all.

'That big rifle's going to make one hell of a noise down in here,' said Tony, looking up at the sides of the valley all round. 'It'll sound like a cannon.'

'Won't matter. We'll just take a couple of shots and slip away. I don't fancy driving in along this bottom track, though. We could easily get trapped. There must be some way we can come in on foot.'

Recourse to the map showed another track running steeply uphill to the north, past the far end of the range, towards a main road on the next ridge. We took it, but soon saw we'd made a mistake: rainwater had carved deep channels out of the mud, and even a four-wheel-drive vehicle would have had problems negotiating the track. Seeing that the Granada wasn't going to make it, Tony eased off and backed carefully down.

'That's our way in for tomorrow, all the same,' I said. 'Park at the top, walk down, shoot, and away on foot. If anyone turns up we can disappear into the trees. Let's get round there now for a shufti – back the way we came, out along the valley, then up and over. All

236

we need is to find a place where we can park in the morning.'

As I'd forecast, night came early while we were driving towards the transit hide. Full darkness had fallen by the time we reached the lane I'd earmarked. Again we parked under trees, and we hadn't gone fifty metres from the Granada before the car had vanished from sight. Our walk-in to the site was relatively short – about a mile – and as we were in no hurry, I took it at a snail's pace. For camouflage purposes we'd pulled on DPM smocks over our civilian gear; we both had pistols in shoulder holsters, and each of us carried an MP 5 with spare magazines. From camp, I'd also brought a night-sight of the kind we'd used in Iraq – an image intensifier that gives really good vision in the dark. I had it slung round my neck on para-cord so that I could bring it up with a single movement. And for the first time since the intercept at Ludlow, we were wearing our covert radios.

Tony and I kept about ten metres apart as we walked uphill over a grass field beside an overgrown hedge, myself leading. Even with my eyes accustomed to the dark I could see very little – but memorised details of our route were printed in my mind.

There was practically no wind, and what there was – a breath from the west – was coming from our left, through the hedge.

After four hundred metres, another hedge led off across the hill to the right at ninety degrees to the one we were following. Luckily cattle had pushed their way through it, creating gaps, so that we were able to slip through with scarcely a sound. Another five minutes brought us to the point on the brow of the hill where our guiding row of bushes came to an end. A barbed wire fence ran across our line of advance, just visible on the horizon against the cloudy sky. I beckoned Tony forward and held the top strand down taut while he went over it, to prevent the wire twanging. Then he did the same for me, and we crept on silently over the big field beyond, the last before our target wood.

Still the breeze was steady on my left cheek. I stopped. Ahead and to our left, something pale was showing. The night sight revealed it as a sheep, outlier of a large flock. Hearing Tony move up close behind me, I whispered, 'Sheep. We'll detour right so we don't panic them.'

237

On we went. Frequent checks with the sight showed that the sheep were aware of our presence – they had their heads up and were looking in our direction – but by skirting round them we persuaded them that we weren't a threat, and they stayed where they were.

Now the southern face of the wood loomed ahead of us like a black wall. We were coming in towards its right-hand corner. About a hundred yards out I stopped and went down on one knee for a thorough scan. The sight revealed fence posts and tree-trunks, but nothing sinister. Thinking back, I remembered the PIRA's instructions about a clearing and a disused chalk-pit. The old well, they said, was just inside the wood, close to the fence, but the clearing and the pit were behind it. Therefore, I reckoned, I should see some sort of opening in the trees.

'Got it,' I breathed. 'I can see an open space. OK. We're on course.'

Heading slightly left, we approached the straight boundary of the wood at an angle. Our feet were making no sound on the sheep-mown grass, and the night was so dark that anyone without special equipment would be practically blind. Nevertheless, something made me stop twenty yards out from the trees.

When I went down flat, Tony did the same a few feet behind me. For a minute we lay listening. Nothing. Then on the wind I caught a very faint whiff: cigarette smoke. A shiver went up my back as I thought of the moment in the Libyan desert when Whinger had smelt smoke, just as we were about to establish our LUP.

Reaching round, I snapped finger and thumb quietly, and I heard faint rustling as Tony wormed up beside me.

'Cigarette smoke,' I whispered. 'There's someone out to our left.' I raised the night sight and scanned again. 'There he is,' I said quietly. 'A man, on the corner of the wood.'

'What's he doing?'

'Standing there. He's got binoculars. Looking round.'

'He'll never pick us out – too dark.'

'No, but let's get into cover.'

We crawled forward, belly to the ground, and in a few seconds were under the bottom strand of another barbed wire fence. Inside it, out of sheep-reach, longer grass and shrubs were growing.

Leaning outwards, I took one more look at the corner. The man hadn't moved. 'You stay here,' I breathed. 'Get your arse backed into the undergrowth while I go and look for the hide. Take the sight and keep an eye on our friend. If he heads this way, warn me, and we'll lie low till he's gone past.' I lifted the cord over my head and handed the sight over.

'OK,' Tony whispered. 'Good hunting.'

In the cover of the woodland edge, it was safe to stand up, so I got to my feet and shuffled carefully forward. My mind was moving far faster than my body. The guy on the corner could be a gamekeeper, on the look-out for poachers, but at this time of the year that seemed unlikely. More probably it was a dicker – and if it was, what was his brief? What the hell was he doing here? Was he supposed to intercept us as we came to the hide? Or pretend he'd caught us stealing the weapon, and drop us in possession of it? Did he have a colleague on the hide itself?

My sixth sense told me that the answer to the last question was no. Already I was on the edge of the clearing and very close to the hide, yet I had no feeling that anybody was near me.

I moved on, pushing each foot gently through the long grass. At the south-western edge of the clearing – according to my brief – there should be an old iron hand-pump mounted on a brick base . . . I nearly bumped into it before I saw it, standing shoulder-high in front of me. This was the means by which people living in the cottage had once brought their water up out of the ground. I reached out and touched the rounded top of the pump. From the rough feel, I could tell that the cast iron was pitted with the rust of ages.

The opening of the well had been described as six feet out from the base of the pump. I dropped on to hands and knees. The temptation to use a torch was strong, but I resisted it – better to operate by feel. I was looking, or groping, for a circular wooden cover covered by sods of turf. Pulling my Commando knife from its sheath, I began jabbing the blade vertically into the ground, and after four or five soft touches I suddenly hit something hard, which gave out a quite different sound. I reached out farther and jabbed again. This time I got a definite hollow thump.

A moment later I had located the two wooden handles. Steady, I told myself. This could be booby-trapped to blow when someone moves it.

Feeling carefully about in the surrounding mulch, I picked out the perimeter of the cover and ran my fingers round it. When I came on no wires or catches, I reckoned all was well, and lifted the cover clear.

For a moment I sat back on my heels and held down the pressel switch of my radio. 'Tony,' I said quietly. 'I'm on site. Found the hide. What's our guy doing?'

'Hasn't moved.'

'Nobody at the other corner?'

'Nope.'

'OK, then. I'll get the weapon up.'

Below ground level it was safe to use the torch, so I reached down into the cavity and switched on. The beam lit up a blue nylon rope, anchored at the top to an iron ring set into the neck of the well, and dropping ten feet into the old, brick-lined cistern. On the dry mud floor at the bottom lay a fat grey cylinder about five feet long.

Quickly I switched off, pocketed the torch and began hauling the rope up. The tube was a fair old weight – thirty pounds, I guessed – but it came up hanging at an angle, so that I was able to bring it through the neck of the well without it touching the sides.

Just as I laid it in the grass Tony's voice suddenly came in my ear. 'Watch it, Geordie. The guy on the corner's heading this way. Fifty yards . . . forty . . . thirty. Ah, Jesus!'

I wriggled the MP 5 off my back and knelt silently with the weapon at the ready, watching, waiting. I kept thinking, if this were Northern Ireland we'd simply grab the guy, hand him over to the police and have him whipped away.

When nothing happened I asked, very low, 'What's he doing?'

No answer. That could only mean the man was extremely close. 'Is he within ten yards?' I went.

Back came one brief *psssch*, as Tony gave his pressel a single nudge. That meant yes.

'Is he within five yards?'

Psssch.

240

Bloody hell! I concentrated intently on keeping still, and counted seconds to give myself an idea of how much time was passing. I'd gone past 180 – three minutes which seemed like thirty – when at last I got another beep in the earpiece.

'Moving off?' I asked.

Psssch, pssssch.

'Great. Tell me when he's clear.'

I waited another whole minute. Then Tony came up with, 'OK. He's down at the other corner.'

'I'm coming out then.'

Hurrying now, I brought out my knife again, cut the cradle of rope round the container, dropped the severed ends down the well, replaced the circular lid, swept the grass back and forth a couple of times to mask the edge of the cover, picked up the pipe by the webbing cradle round it, and nipped back to the fence.

Seconds later Tony and I were away across the middle of the field at a fast walk; but only when we got back to our marker hedge, out of sight and hearing of the wood, did he burst out with, 'Boy, was that a close one! The bastard was standing with his heels three feet from my head!'

We ran the other lads to ground at the new safe house not far from Great Missenden. Whinger guided us in on the phone, calling the turns, until finally we pulled round the back of a farmyard to find a hideous modern bungalow built alongside the biggest heap of shit in Buckinghamshire – or so it seemed: there was a mountain of old straw and manure piled up right in front of the turn-around, and the air was full of the stink of cows.

'What have they done to us?' I yelled as I walked in. 'What a shower!'

'Close the door, for fuck's sake,' said Whinger. 'The only hope is to keep the smell outside.'

Cowshit apart, the place was nothing like as good for us as the cottage in the Dean. For one thing it was too close to the main road and to the farmyard; for another, it had big plate-glass windows, so that anyone passing could see in. A third defect was that the internal walls were paper-thin, so people could hear what was going on in the room next-door. And to make matters worse the

241

telephone was insecure; there hadn't been time to instal a new one.

'Oh, well,' I said. 'At least it's in the right area, and we're not going to be here long. Nothing new from Fraser, I suppose?'

Whinger shook his head. 'All quiet on the western front, I'm afraid.'

'All right, then. Let's suss out this damned rifle.'

In the past I'd done quite a bit of sniper work, and at one stage I'd worked as commander of the sniper detachment on the Regiment's SP team. Stew, also, had been on the team. But for that work we'd used 7.62 calibre PM rifles – far smaller, lighter weapons. The only one of us with experience of a .50 was Tony, who'd trained on it in the States.

The carrying case for this one was home-made but practical: a tube of rigid grey polythene, like a length of outsized drainpipe, with a cap on each end carefully sealed with parcel tape. Inside, we found the rifle cocooned in a jacket of bubble-wrap. As I drew it out on to the kitchen table, everyone crowded round, including Farrell, who was now cuffed to Stew.

'Are those curtains good enough?' I gestured at the window behind me. 'They look bloody thin to me.'

'No, no. They're OK,' said Whinger. 'I've checked from outside and you can't see through.'

Afterwards, I wished I'd been watching Farrell's face when the wrappings came off the weapon. As it was, I kept my eyes on the job in hand, but when the angular grey metal frame appeared, he gave a low whistle.

'What the hell is it?' I said. 'Not a Barrett at all. No woodwork.'

'No,' said Farrell. 'It's a Haskins. I know that feller.'

'You mean you know this actual rifle?'

'Ah . . . I mean, no. It's the type. I've seen the *type* before.'

Even in the excitement of unveiling the fearsome beast I had noticed that odd hesitation, but I carried on peeling off the layers of bubble film until the weapon lay revealed. The rifle comprised a long, thick barrel with a sound-deflector at the muzzle, a skeletal action, a bipod hinged under the fore-end, a high-grade telescopic sight on top, and, strangest of all, a short metal stock joined to the action by twin hydraulic shock-absorbers, clearly designed to soak up some of the recoil. The rifle had seen service – its metalwork

242

was scratched here and there – but it looked beautifully clean, and when I drew the heavy bolt back it moved sweetly in its oiled bed. I noticed that there was no magazine: single shots only.

Also in the pack were two short belts of rounds, twelve in each, every cartridge six or seven inches long, as big and menacing as an anti-tank shell.

'Bloody hell!' said Whinger. 'That thing would kill a fucking elephant.'

'So it would,' said Farrell. 'And leave a big hole in the bastard, too.'

I picked the rifle up – it weighed at least twenty pounds – and flicked down the legs of the bipod to set the weapon up on the floor. Then I lay down behind it, brought the stock into my shoulder and shuffled myself into an easy position. Of course I couldn't see much through the sight, because it was out of focus, pointing straight at a wall about five feet away, but I liked the look of the reticle: crossed bars, thick at the edges, thin in the middle. I imagined it centred on the distant figure of a man, probably wearing a loose, woolly jumper. Altogether the rifle felt comfortable and solid. I opened and closed the bolt to cock the mechanism and applied the first pressure on the trigger. At the second pressure it went off crisp and clean, giving a loud click, with a pull I estimated to be four pounds.

When Tony also got down for a trial, I told him, 'Don't touch the sight. It's suppose to be set at six hundred yards, which is just right. We'll try it in the morning.'

'No sweat,' he grunted. He too took a couple of dry pulls on the trigger and said, 'Yeah – it feels quite nice. I could hit something with that.'

I lifted the rifle back on to the table, and over a brew we all got talking about long-range shoots, not least the effect of wind on the bullet.

'The thing is,' said Tony, 'even if there's no wind at the firing point, there can be some farther out. You need to watch for that – anything like leaves or grass moving near the target.'

'Yes,' Farrell said, 'and you have to look out for mirage, too.'

'Mirage?' said Whinger. 'What the hell's that?'

'You know when you get a heat-haze, and see the air kind of

boiling? If there's no wind the air will be rising vertically, and you get what's known as a boiling mirage. Lateral movement – what you might call drift – looks like a stream of clear water rippling over a bed of pebbles. That can affect the bullet quite badly, so you've to learn how to judge it.'

'OK,' I said, 'but we're not going to get that in the early morning, are we?'

'Probably not,' Farrell agreed. 'But then temperature's going to be a factor. A high temperature will increase your muzzle velocity and throw your bullet high.'

'Yeah. But again, early morning's likely to be cool.'

'Sure, so you may need to aim fractionally high. Humidity's another thing. If you get a mist, that means the air's more dense. Your bullet meets greater resistance and drops – so again, you need to give it more elevation.'

'Light,' said Tony. 'That's important. If it's dull and cloudy like today, you're liable to shoot high. Dunno why, but that's how it seems to work.'

'It probably will be like that at seven in the morning,' I said. 'Anyway, we can try it tomorrow.'

'Have you got somewhere lined up for a practice shoot?' Whinger asked.

'Yep. We found a place.' Because Farrell was with us I didn't describe the little range in the woods. I turned to him. 'It's amazing how your people find the sites for hides. I mean, the one where we collected the rifle – it was miles from anywhere. How the hell would they know about a place like that?'

'Easy,' Farrell replied. 'Some Paddy gets a job working on the farm. Maybe he does a bit of pigeon-shooting or something. Gets to know the woods, finds the old well. Next thing he's in the pub, blathering about it, and there's a man listening. Or maybe the Paddy falls out with the farmer. Maybe he gets the sack and thinks, I'll fuck this fellow up a bit. Use his property without him knowing.'

'Is that how guys get drawn into the organisation? As simple as that?'

'Sometimes, yes.'

I stared at our prisoner, with his heavy but still handsome face and his thick, wiry black hair. The swelling on his lip had gone down, and his eyes were back to normal, so that he looked quite presentable again.

'Don't you ever feel guilty about some of the things you do?' I asked.

'Guilty?' He gave a kind of snort. 'What about? It was those stupid fuckers of ancient Greeks who invented the idea of guilt. They thought there were creatures called the Furies who came after you if you did something bad. They called them the Eumenides, the Kindly Ones, to try and make them seem less frightening. It was all a load of bollocks, of course – but people have been foolish enough to go on believing it ever since.'

'Some people call it conscience,' Tony said drily.

It was on the tip of my tongue to ask why the dickers had been out, watching the approaches to the hide, but instead I said, 'How does someone like you get into the PIRA? I mean, you went to university. You're an educated guy. You could have a good job and a settled life. If you'd gone straight you could be making a good living by now.'

'Making a living!' Again Farrell gave that derisive snort. 'What d'you think *you'd* be like if *you'd* been brought up in Belfast? You'd be the worst fucking killer of the lot. I know. That's all you army fellers are, anyway – trained killers. Are you not? A tribe of murdering bastards.'

As Farrell glared at me and I glared back at him, I suddenly realised that we'd all started chatting over the weapon and listening to his advice as if he were one of us. The way he'd been talking, he could have been a sniper instructor. Obviously he was hot on the subject; but not only that – it had sounded as if he'd had training from Americans. Some of the phrases he'd used were out of American text books.

In a flash it occurred to me that maybe it was he who had done all that damage in Ulster. Maybe he was the mysterious long-range assassin who'd harassed the security forces so badly. To my disgust I realised I'd been drawn into discussion with him in a way I'd vowed I would avoid. It was bad enough that for a few minutes I'd been treating him as an ordinary human being; far worse was the fact that I'd talked things over as though speaking with an acknowledged expert.

245

Once again I felt that he was casting some sort of spell over me. To break it I stood up and said, 'There's one thing certain. Once this is over, if I ever come across you again, make no mistake, you'll be going down.'

'The same yourself,' Farrell spat back. 'If you ever set eyes on me again you'll need to start saying your prayers.'

I took a deep breath and moved away. 'Let's spruce up the barrel,' I said. 'We need a target, too.'

The PIRA had included a cleaning kit within the tube: a springy steel rod with a jag on the end, and a roll of white flannel four inches wide, marked off by red lines every two inches. For smaller calibres, like 7.62mm or 9mm, a single piece of four-by-two is enough to make a tight fit in the barrel; but for this cannon I cut a double piece, a four-by-four, and wrapped it round the jag. Even that lump went through the barrel without too much friction, and when it came out at the other end it was perfectly clean. With the bolt out, I held the rifle up and looked straight through the barrel towards a lamp. The swirl of the rifling gleamed in the light, and I could see that the PIRA had taken good care of their prized weapon. I also had a close look at the telescopic sight, a high-quality optic with magnification variable up to the power of nine.

While I worked, watched by Farrell, Doughnut and Tony sorted out a target. The best option was a shallow cardboard box, eighteen inches wide and three feet long, in which some groceries had come up from the cottage. The bottom of the box was unmarked, and in the middle of it they stuck a piece of white paper six inches square, using paste made out of flour and water as glue. The result was a good aiming-mark in the middle of a target about the width of a man's torso. For zeroing purposes we could have done with a broader background. Although above and below the bull there was at least a foot to spare, if the first shot went more than nine or ten inches wide of centre we'd probably never see its point of impact.

Once again we were in for a short night. It was close to one in the morning before we stopped fiddling about, and I'd already set reveille for 0500.

'What about you?' I said to Farrell as Tony was about to chain him to his bed. 'You coming with us in the morning?'

'Sure I am. I need to know the rifle's in order. I wouldn't want to rely on what you fellers might tell me.'

'OK, then. Five o'clock it is.'

I'd known the answer to those questions before I asked them. Tony's prediction about Farrell wanting to witness the practice shoot was spot-on. Even though we seemed to have conned the bastard properly about our intentions, he wanted proof that we'd be able to hit the target.

'He's fired this thing himself,' I said quietly to Tony when we were alone again. 'This actual rifle. I'm sure he has.'

FOURTEEN

In the morning we used our covert radios openly for the first time. I told Farrell we'd been out and bought them specially, as they'd be the only means of co-ordinating our operations efficiently during the Chequers shoot. 'Bloody ruinous they were, too,' I added.

'How much?' he asked.

'I wouldn't like to say.'

Rather than take the Granada, which somebody might have spotted the night before, we drove the dark-blue Opel Rekord in which the lads had come up-country. As far as our prisoner knew it belonged to Stew, but in fact it had come from the pool at Llangwern. We'd given Farrell a DPM smock to wear over his sweatshirt, and because the grass would be soaked with dew we all wore rubber boots. The Haskins was in the boot, cradled in bubble-wrap alongside our makeshift target, and I'd brought one belt of twelve rounds.

We pulled out of the stinking farmyard soon after five-thirty, and by six, after a twisting, up-and-down drive across the hills, we were on the ridge above the range. It was another dull, murky morning and the light was late in coming, but my intention was that we'd get our rounds off the moment we could see properly, and clear out before any locals came looking to find out what was causing the disturbance.

I planned to walk in down the muddy track which had defeated the Granada the afternoon before, and on the map we'd pinpointed the spot at which the path came up to join the road. As we arrived I did a drive-past, to make sure nobody was hanging about.

Half a mile down the road we found a single, enormous old beech tree standing out from the upper edge of the forest, and the moment I saw it I said, 'OK, if anything happens, that's our ERV.'

With that established, I went back and parked the car out of sight of the road, in the neck of the muddy lane.

The Haskins was an awkward bastard to carry. The easiest way seemed to be to grasp it near the muzzle and hold it with the barrel slung back over my shoulder and the rest of the weapon hanging behind me. So we set off down the steep hill, Tony cuffed to Farrell and holding the target in his spare hand.

Down among the trees in the valley the light was even worse than I'd expected, but it improved marginally as we came out on to the 700-yard firing point. As I looked up the long corridor of grass with my binoculars, I saw some small brown animal standing out in the open.

'What's that?' I asked, handing Tony the glasses.

He watched for a moment and said, 'Some kind of deer. Now there are two of them.'

'Can't be deer, surely.' I took the binos back. 'They're too small. Wait a minute, though. You're right. They're muntjac. Barking deer.'

Tony began asking what in hell a barking deer was when suddenly Farrell exclaimed, 'Shoot one of the fuckers!'

'Why?'

'It's a perfect target! Four hundred yards. If you can hit that it'll show the rifle's bang on. Get down, man! Shoot!'

I almost agreed. Then my mind skipped back to an episode on an exercise in Africa, when one of our lads had shot some small animal and the local Bushmen had gone ballistic, saying he'd angered the spirits of the mountain. Next day an SAS guy fell off the rocks while climbing and was killed, and the whole troop got so badly spooked that we couldn't get our arses out of that place fast enough.

No, I thought. I'm not going to run a risk by killing something needlessly. In any case, if we shot one of the deer we'd have a body to dispose of. Luckily, before I could argue, both animals moved off into cover and the chance was gone.

Farrell didn't hide his disappointment. 'You'd a great chance there,' he griped. 'You were too slow by far.'

Ignoring him, I asked Tony to take the target down-range. 'In fact,' I added, peering at the butt in the far distance, 'in this light,

249

our spotter scope's not going to be a lot of use. See if you can tuck yourselves into a niche that's safe, somewhere close to the target. Then call the shots back to me on the radio.'

'Sure,' Tony agreed, then turned to Farrell. 'Come on, Danny Boy.'

As the two figures moved away side by side, I followed in their wake as far as the next firing-point. At the edge of the sloped bank a little white-painted marker post had '600' cut into it.

I made myself comfortable. As I'd expected, the grass was wet, but I paid no attention as I settled the angular stock of the Haskins into my shoulder and looked through the sight. The heavy rifle sat rock-steady on its bipod, and the light-gathering capacity of the scope was excellent. Through the lens the prospect looked far brighter, and with the magnification set on six the men came up a good size in the scope. Wait though, I told myself, they're still only half-way to the target area. I moved the sight off Farrell's back and tried the trigger with a dry pull. *Click!* went the action, and once again it felt good.

Through my binos I watched the pair move up towards the target bank. In the trees around me the wood pigeons were cooing – a soft, heavy sound that suited the dull morning. Not a breath of breeze stirred the forest, so wind was not a factor. Poor light tends to make you shoot high, I remembered; on the other hand, moisture in the air tends to make the bullet drop. So today, I guessed, one circumstance should cancel the other out, and I decided to fire right at the centre of the aiming mark.

Now the men were on the bank. I saw Tony looking round for something to steady the box. He must have found a flint or a clod of earth, because in a moment he had the target standing upright.

His voice in my earpiece asked, 'See that OK, Geordie?'

'Fine, thanks.'

'OK. There's a kind of a cave cut into the side of the hill about thirty yards back. We'll get a great view from there. I'll tell you when we're in.'

'That's good. I'm ready when you are.'

The whole point of long-range shooting is to be relaxed. The worst thing, for a sniper, is to have to react suddenly to a command like 'Standby, standby . . . GO!' Far better if he can take his own time and think himself into the right frame of mind. Now, with nothing to pressure me, I concentrated on lying tight, elbows and wrists tucked in, and settling my breathing down into a steady rhythm. My technique has always been to take the shot so gently that, when it goes off, it comes almost as a surprise.

When Tony called that he was in place, I acknowledged briefly. Then I loaded one massive round into the breech, breathed down again, took up the first pressure on the trigger, and at the end of an out-breath squeezed the shot off.

BOOM!

The noise was colossal, and the report thundered away into the wooded valley; but the recoil was less than I'd expected. Although the heavy weapon pumped back into my shoulder all right, the twin shock-absorber arms had taken the meat out of the jolt.

All at once the sky above the range was full of pigeons – black shapes going like the clappers in every direction. My ears were still ringing from the explosion, but I could tell that the chorus of cooing had come to an abrupt end.

'Great shot!' Tony was reporting. 'It's dead central, twelve o'clock, two inches above the top of the white.'

'OK,' I said, 'I'll try another. Same point of aim.'

I loaded a second round and went through the same sequence: tuck in, breathe down into a rhythm, try not to blink or flinch . . . take up first trigger pressure . . . breathe out . . .

BOOM!

'Same again,' came Tony's voice. 'Dead centre, two inches above your first shot. Perfect grouping.'

'I'm aiming at the centre of the white. So the MPI's six inches high. Is that right?'

'Exactly.'

'OK, then. I'm going to put the sight down three clicks and fire again. Standby.'

It took me a couple of minutes to make the adjustment with the little turret on top of the scope. Then I told Tony I was ready, settled again and touched off a third round.

'Dead on,' he called. 'Now you're in the white, an inch below the top edge. You're not going to do better than that.'

I was on the point of saying we'd call it a day when Tony came

251

back on the air with, 'Watch it, Geordie. Some goddamn vehicle's pulled up by that barrier. It's a Land Rover. Two guys.'

Instinctively I collapsed the legs of the rifle to lower its profile, and wriggled backwards down the slope of the firing point. Then I realised that two empty cartridge cases were lying there in the grass. Leaving the weapon, I wormed forward again to grab them just in time to see two figures appear at the entrance we'd come to the previous day. They popped into view as if they'd been running, and looked wildly up and down the range. Then, spotting the target, they ran towards that.

'Tony,' I said, 'I'm going to fire a diversionary shot. Then I'm heading for the vehicle. Get out of there when you see a chance. Make your own way up and RV at the tree as soon as you can.'

'Roger,' he called.

I got my binos and the empty cases into the pockets of my smock, loaded a fourth round, moved into the bushes at the side of the grass, took a good grip of the rifle and fired it into the ground from a standing position. This time the recoil nearly blew me over backwards, but I kept on my feet, pushed through the cover to regain the path and started up the earth track.

For the first hundred yards or so I ran. Then lack of breath forced me down to a fast walk. Over the past few days I hadn't been able to do any training, and now the effects were coming through. What with the gradient and the weight of the rifle, I was soon gasping like a pair of bellows. All the same, I kept going fast to the crest of the hill, and when I reached the edge of the wood I paused to get my breath back.

As soon as I'd recovered I tried to call Tony, but got no answer. From the angle of the hill, I knew he must be out of my line-of-sight, and probably wouldn't come back on the net until he too had climbed out of the valley.

The Rekord was where we'd left it, with nobody in sight. In a couple of seconds I had the rifle rolled back into its protective wrapping and laid under an old blanket in the boot. I also pulled off my DPM smock and threw that in. Already I was thinking, Shit! I can't stay here now. Those guys in the Land Rover might power up to the ridge at any moment.

Rather than risk a confrontation, I started the engine and drove

252

away northwards, back towards base. As long as nobody associated the car with the shots, it wouldn't attract attention. My plan was to turn round after a couple of minutes, make a reverse run past the big tree, and keep talking until Tony came back on the air.

But I'd only been going about thirty seconds when a police car appeared, travelling fast in the opposite direction. Even though the two guys in it hardly looked at me as they hurtled past, I didn't like the speed at which they were moving. It looked as though they were responding to a call-out.

I drove on slowly, trying to read the local map as I went. Finding I couldn't see it properly, I pulled into a lay-by and took a steady look. That reassured me.

A car following the main road, as the police were, would have to go six or seven miles on a roundabout route before it could reach the rifle range. That would give Tony and Farrell at least ten minutes to get clear. 'Chill out,' I told myself. 'They'll make it, no bother.'

I got out of the car and raised the bonnet as if I had engine problems. An old banger of a white pick-up truck came from the south and went by without slowing. As the minutes passed I began to sweat. Calls on the radio produced no answer. What the hell could the other two be doing? The worst scenario was that they'd got captured. The idea was horrendous. If Farrell fell into the hands of the police at this stage, our entire plan would be scuppered. I tried to put that possibility out of my head.

More likely, I told myself, they were stuck in the thicket above the range. During our recce the night before I'd noticed that there were few big trees on that side of the hill. It looked as though a fire or a storm had taken out the main crop, and all that was left was hawthorn, brambles and other scrub which had grown up in the vacuum. One man, crawling on hands and knees, could probably push his way along tunnels made by deer; but for two, cuffed to each other, progress would be a nightmare. I thought of the wait-a-while thorns which had torn us to pieces in the Colombian jungle, and of Farrell collapsing at the edge of the forest.

Ten minutes after seeing the police car, I turned round and made a run past the big tree, calling all the way on the radio. Nothing. Driving on, I found the road twisted downhill through another big wood, then emerged into open farmland as it dropped into a valley. I followed it right down to a T-junction at the bottom, and there turned to come back.

Another drive-past, more calls. Still nothing.

Back at my lay-by, I pulled in again and called Whinger on the mobile.

'Bit of a fuck-up,' I went.

'Been compromised?'

'Yes and no.'

I told him what had happened. 'Anything doing your end?'

'All quiet in the shit-house, but things are moving outside.'

'How?'

'I don't know exactly. You'll have to ask Fraser. But apparently the PIRA are getting nervous. I don't know what they've seen, but they're starting to feel pressure coming on them. There's been some talk about moving the hostages.'

'Oh, God! I'll call the incident room. And listen . . . Whinger?'

'Yes?'

'I'll be back there just as soon as Tony and Farrell emerge from this fucking jungle.'

'OK, mate. We'll be waiting for you.'

I restarted, turned and headed south again. 'Hello, Tony, hello, Tony, are you reading me? Over.'

Still nothing.

At the bottom of the hill I stopped and called the incident room. Fraser was off duty, but Yorky was there. 'Yes,' he confirmed. 'SB have got it down to three locations. One's a semi in Sudbury, next to Wembley. One's a block of flats in Greenford, and the third's a house in Ealing. They're all under round-the-clock surveillance, but we desperately need confirmation.'

'Can't we hit all three at once?'

'It's not on, Geordie. We're not certain of any of them. Until we *are* sure, it's not worth the risk. If it turned out we were wrong and the hostages were somewhere else, they'd certainly get topped.'

'What's this about the PIRA moving them?'

'It's only talk so far. Nothing's happened yet.'

'Where's our team now?'

'Still on standby in Hounslow Barracks. They couldn't be better placed – only a few minutes from all three locations.'

I took a deep breath and asked, 'What's the position on approval for the shoot?'

'Nothing confirmed yet.'

'Ah, shit!'

'How are you doing, Geordie?' Yorky sounded quite concerned, like some old uncle.

'Slight local difficulty. But basically, we've got the weapon and done the practice shoot. Once we're out of here, we're going ahead with the recce of the park itself.'

'You'd better carry on, then. As soon as we hear anything, we'll pass it to your safe house.'

'Roger, Yorky . . . and thanks.'

I was about to switch off when I heard him say, 'Hello?'

'Yes?'

'The Commander's just come back in. I'll put him on.'

I waited a moment, then heard Fraser's cheerful voice. 'Geordie? How's it going?'

'So so.' I filled him in on what I'd told Yorky, and got back the same stuff about the three locations. But then Fraser added, 'From what we're hearing, the PIRA aren't very happy with your man.'

'Don't they want him back, then?'

'Oh yes, they want him all right. But now their aim is to top him.'

'Delightful!'

'It is,' Fraser agreed. 'Does he realise that?'

'He knows he's in the shit. But he's that arrogant, he probably thinks he can talk his way out of it. At least, that's how we read him.'

I switched off feeling very low. This thing seemed never-ending. It had dragged on so long already that I couldn't imagine it coming to any definite conclusion. I tried to galvanise myself with the thought that it was going to *have* to come to a conclusion within twenty-four hours – by this time tomorrow. Either the shoot would go down as the Prime Minister walked out into his rose garden before breakfast, or the PIRA's patience would run out.

Yet again I turned, drove up the hill and past the big tree. No answer on the radio. It could still be that the curve of the hill was blocking us, even if Tony had climbed clear of the range and was struggling up through the scrub. He, if anyone, would get Farrell out of the mess safely. I trusted Tony at least as much as I trusted any of my British mates, not only for his physical strength and capability, but for his level-headedness.

Back at the lay-by, I pulled in for the third time and sat looking at the map. I'd just tried the radio yet again when I looked in the mirror and saw a car coming up from behind.

Police. Pulling in behind me, too. Jesus! I sat tight, watching, while the two men got out and advanced on the Rekord. I just had time to scramble the earpiece and throat-mike out of sight before they drew level.

I wound down the window and said, 'Good morning.'

They returned the greeting civilly enough, but immediately began to ask questions. The boss figure was a sergeant – beefy, red-faced, with a big belly, like a rugger player gone to seed.

'Can I ask what you're doing here?'

'On my way up to Great Missenden. Had a bit of time in hand.'

'You came the other way just now.'

'That's right. I was delivering a parcel.'

'Where to?'

'An address in Stonor.'

'Do much delivering, do you?'

I was uncomfortably aware that the second copper was walking round behind the car, giving it the close eyeball. Probably they thought I was a poacher, and had a deer in the back. Probably they were scanning for traces of blood.

'Look,' I said. 'What's the matter?'

'Nothing,' went the sergeant. 'May I have a look in the boot of your car?'

I got out and faced the guy, to find that he was a couple of inches taller than me. 'You'd much better not,' I said.

'What's in there, then?'

'Nothing to do with you.'

'We haven't been poaching, have we?'

'Certainly not.'

'So why all the secrecy?'

'I can't explain.'

256

The radio in the sergeant's breast pocket began honking off, and he was distracted for a moment as he dealt with the call. What could I do? It was possible that the police in the Chequers area had already been squared away and told to stand off, but the guys down here would know nothing about our operation. If I did a runner I'd be chased, and the car would be traced, and Tony would be stranded. If I refused to open up, I might be arrested for obstructing the police.

Before I could take a decision the sergeant said, 'I'm afraid I require you to open the boot.'

'Listen . . .' I stood between him and the back of the car. 'I'm a member of special forces, on a classified operation. Will you please get on the phone to my control room?'

Without answering, the sergeant lumbered forward and jabbed his thumb on the boot catch. Short of knocking him out of the way, there was nothing I could do to stop him. Up came the lid. With the movement of the car through the bends, the rifle had rolled over once, partially unwrapping itself, and the barrel lay there plain to see.

'What the hell . . .?' began the sergeant. His beefy face suddenly turned even redder as a surge of adrenalin flushed up through him until I thought he was on for vertical take-off. Reaching down, he pulled away the bubble-wrap and exposed the main body of the weapon. 'What the devil is this?'

'It's a Haskins five-oh sniper rifle,' I told him in the most casual voice I could muster.

A second later I saw him reaching for his radio in a kind of automatic twitch.

'NO!' I said sharply. 'Don't put through any report. Not until you've spoken to my control. Here.'

I pulled out my mobile, dialled the incident room, and providentially got straight through to Fraser. 'John,' I said. 'Geordie. I have a problem. I'm with a police sergeant. He's seen I've got a big rifle in my possession, and I need you to explain what we're at.'

'All right.' Fraser sounded imperturbable as ever. 'Where are you?'

'Out in the Chilterns, above the range I told you about.'

'Has he caught you with the weapon?'

'Yes.'

'OK, I'll speak to him.'

I handed the phone over and stood back, watching the sergeant's face go through every conceivable expression: shock, incredulity, alarm, bewilderment. It took several minutes, but I could tell Fraser was winning the battle, because after a while the sergeant began giving details of his own head of station, along with the telephone number. In the end he said, 'Very good, sir,' and handed the phone back to me.

'Is he going to speak to your boss?' I asked.

'That's right.'

'Great. I'm sure they'll sort it out between them.'

The sergeant looked shattered. 'Never heard anything like it,' he went. 'Never seen a weapon like that out here. Buggered if I have.'

'You live and learn.'

I didn't know what Fraser had told him, and I wasn't going to ask; but now that our practice shoot was partially blown, I reckoned I might as well resuscitate my covert radio.

'I got separated from a colleague,' I explained. 'I'll just see if I can raise him.'

This time the first call produced an answer.

'We're on the RV,' Tony confirmed.

'Has anyone seen or followed you?'

'No.'

'Standby, then. I'll collect you in a few minutes.'

A moment later the sergeant's radio came to life again, and he got a stream of instructions to thin out. From the way he kept repeating, 'Yes sir, no sir, very good sir,' I knew it must be his boss. At the end he said to me, 'Well, that's it. I'm to leave you alone.'

'Thanks,' I said. 'And you won't talk about this, either?'

I made it sound like a question, but it was more or less an order – and when he said, 'no' he almost added 'sir' again.

'Cheers, then.' Without more ado I closed the boot, got back in the car, swung round and set off for the ERV.

Not knowing quite what the plods had heard, I didn't want them to see Tony come out of the undergrowth with Farrell cuffed to him, so I went back down the road at a fair bat and scorched to a halt under the big tree. Almost at once Tony emerged from the bushes behind it. Even though I was expecting him, he gave me quite a shock, because his face was covered in blood, with sweat-streaks coming down through it. Farrell's was the same.

'Get in, get in!' I snapped, holding a back door open. Then, when we were rolling, I asked, 'What happened?'

'Goddamn thorns!' Tony exclaimed. 'We're ripped to bits by the bastards. We got bushed in that thicket. Jesus Christ – I never knew you had jungle like that over here.'

Back at the shit-house, it took us a good hour to sort ourselves out and get some breakfast down our necks. After they'd had showers, Tony and Farrell didn't look too bad. Their faces were scratched, but only superficially, as if they'd been caught on the job by their girlfriends. As I'd anticipated, they'd had a miserable time forcing their way uphill along animal tunnels under hawthorn bushes and through brambles, while the gamekeepers, decoyed by my distraction shot, charged around in the valley below.

As if to confirm my earlier suspicions, Tony told me that Farrell had gone over the moon about the rifle. When he had seen the bullet holes opening up in the white he nearly pissed himself with delight. 'I'll tell you one thing,' Tony added. 'Boy, do those rounds make a racket! It's a supersonic crack like nothing on earth. If the Prime Minister gets one of them go close past him he's going to jump a mile.'

'No he isn't,' I said. 'He's going to drop down like a sack of potatoes.'

As soon as I'd got myself together, I called the incident room again.

'I hear you've been advertising your presence throughout the Home Counties,' said Yorky.

'Bollocks,' I told him. 'We couldn't help it. We did land up in a tight corner, though.'

'Not to worry. The Commander's got it sorted. And you've got your permission.'

'What? For the shoot?'

'Yes. A secure fax from Number Ten came in a few minutes ago.'

'Jesus!'

'The Prime Minister has OK'd it. In fact, he's definitely in favour.'

'He must have balls, then.'

'He has. But he's been listening to what Special Branch had to say. They advised him that he's in a dangerously vulnerable position. The threat from the PIRA has intensified, and they can't guarantee to contain it. In other words, they were saying there's a good chance he's going to get bloody shot sooner or later. This operation you've hatched is seen as the best means of defusing the situation.'

'Got it.'

'By gum, you'd better get yourself sorted,' Yorky went on. 'If this goes wrong, it could bring the government down.'

The PM's reaction was what I'd been expecting – what I'd been wanting, really: anything to get me out of this mess. But when the go-ahead finally came through it was a shock all the same.

Yorky hadn't finished. 'So – you're on. But you still may be saved the trouble. The SP team are going ahead with plans to assault the hostage location, just as soon as we've got it pinpointed.'

'What's the latest on that?'

'I'll hand you over to the Commander. He'll fill you in.'

'Geordie?' It was Fraser.

'Hello.'

'I got your local copper straightened out.'

'Thanks. Sorry to come at you out of the blue like that.'

'Don't worry. You shouldn't get any more hassle from the law. Now, listen. As for the hostages: we're concentrating on our second alternative. The flat. It's number fifty-seven Cumberland House, on the fifth floor of a block in Ellerton Road, Greenford.'

'Oh, God! You think they're there?'

'There's a good chance. It's a two-bedroomed flat. Quite an old block, built in the sixties. Your guys are going to do an outside recce, and meanwhile we're trying to trace the owners of the apartment. Also, we need to get the original architect's plans, so that we know the exact internal layout. The trouble is, the flats aren't standardised – quite a lot of variation from one to another. One minute . . .'

He paused, as if he was looking through his notes, and then

260

continued: 'Various owners have carried out alterations, as well. The firm that designed the block has been taken over, but we're hoping to find the plans with their successors. Also, we're hoping to occupy number fifty-eight next door, to do a bit of through-the-wall surveillance.'

All at once I felt choked, and couldn't speak. The fact that so many people, all highly skilled, were working away on my behalf, doing their utmost to save Tim and Tracy . . . Suddenly it seemed too much.

'Geordie? Are you there?'

I got hold of myself and said, 'Yep.'

'Take it easy, lad. You'll be all right. Call again when you're back.'

'Will do.'

'Here's Yorky again.'

'OK.'

'What are your plans now, Geordie?'

'Tony and I are off to recce the park. I don't trust the PIRA measurements and details. I need to see for myself.'

'Fair enough. But as soon as you get back, we need a detailed breakdown of your projected movements and timings. OK?'

'Sure.'

Farrell had predictably tried to muscle in on the recce, but I told him there was no way Tony and I would take him with us. 'Walk around the park of the Prime Minister's official country residence with you cuffed to one of us?' I had said. 'Pull the other one. You'd be back in the nick within minutes – and we'd be there with you. You're not walking round on your own, either.'

A few minutes' drive northward through the lanes had brought us within reach of Chequers. It was now 2.30 pm. The day had heated up a good deal but the sky remained overcast, and the air was muggy. I was still high on adrenalin, feeling tense and brittle, both exhausted and hyper-alert at the same time. I'd deliberately left behind the PIRA notes and instructions, but I carried them word-for-word in my mind.

Once again, in an attempt to clear my head, I was bouncing theories off Tony. 'If Fraser's squared things away properly with the

261

local cops, I presume he's done the same with the security force at the house,' I said. 'So we shouldn't get any aggro, either today or tomorrow morning.'

'I guess not,' Tony agreed. 'But presumably normal security will be operating. If the home troops see anybody acting suspiciously, they'll challenge them. I mean, they may see us walking round, but they won't know who we are.'

'That's right. We could be a couple of PIRA dickers. But we've got to get a good look at the place. Good enough to be able to convince Farrell that we've done a proper recce.'

'Sure. Take it easy now. Only a mile to go.'

We were driving northwards along the bottom of a broad valley, farmland rising on either slope, and woods high above us to right and left. I slowed down, and a moment later Tony pointed right, saying, 'Dirtywood Farm. Hell of a name for a house. In a minute we'll see the lodge and the park gates of Chequers right in front of us.'

There it was. The lodge turned out to be a substantial building made of brick, with pillars supporting wrought iron gates. Beyond the formal entrance the drive ran straight along an avenue of trees towards the main house, which was visible in the distance. Here the main road swung hard right, and we followed it round to the east. Three or four hundred yards on we came to another sharp bend, a left-hander this time, with a rough parking-place on the outside of it. A couple of cars were already standing there, at the point where a long-distance footpath crossed the road. Obviously it was a favourite take-off point for walkers setting out on a hike.

I pulled in on to the sandy verge. 'This'll do,' I said. 'We can tab it from here.'

We'd dressed as casually as possible, in check shirts and jeans, to make ourselves look like run-of-the-mill hikers. Our binos could be just a sign of our interest in birds.

There were already a couple of other people ahead of us on the footpath, so we set off after them, through an iron kissing-gate and across a big open field of young corn. Now we were heading west, back towards the drive and the entrance lodge, with the house sitting in its shallow valley away to our right. Immediately features began to chime in with the PIRA descriptions I'd committed to memory: the back drive coming in to the house at right angles from our right, the clumps of trees, the memorial obelisk high on a hill in the distance.

Soon we came to the avenue and the main drive.

'One camera here,' said Tony quietly.

'Got it.'

A closed-circuit camera, flanked by an infra-red light, was mounted on a pole so that it could scan the outer stretch of the approach road which lay in dead ground from the house. Without looking at it overtly, we gave it a quick inspection as we went past. Then, carrying on across the drive and up the gentle slope beyond, we followed the footpath to the corner of Maple Wood.

'Point D,' we both said simultaneously.

Whoever the PIRA scout had been, he was obviously right. This was the place from which to take the shot. By now we had gained a bit of height, so that we were looking down across a wide-open field towards the south front of the house. At our back was a dense beech wood – immediate cover if we needed to disappear. Our binos could pick up any amount of detail around the house itself: a brick wall across the front of the terrace; a little brick summerhouse with a pointed roof at each corner; low, neatly-clipped box hedges, rose beds, a big, ugly conservatory to the left, and behind it all the tall, stately building of soft red brick, with mullioned windows, high chimneys, and numerous sharply-peaked gables.

But it wasn't the architecture that grabbed our attention.

'There's a camera on a post just to the left of those two little trees,' said Tony.

'Got it. And another alongside the wall, mounted on a pole. Go further left, and you'll see three more.'

'I have them. There's also an electronic device of some kind on the third pillar along from the summerhouse. It could be a microwave, covering the walls.'

'That summerhouse,' I said. 'Go to the bottom left-hand corner of the window. There's some other device there. That looks like a microwave as well. I bet it's pushing out across this field to pick up any movement. Jesus! They've got the place really sewn up. You couldn't get much closer than this without being detected.'

'They must have a massive array of TV monitors somewhere,' Tony said. 'Banks of them in a control room, and a large number of guys keeping an eye on them. Watch yourself, Geordie. There's someone in an upstairs window.'

'Where?'

'See the main door? Go up to the top floor and right. There – the curtains moved again.'

'OK. Probably a cleaner.'

I looked to my left and saw a young couple walking towards us along the footpath. I wanted to stay where we were for a bit longer, so I sat down on the grass, took off my right boot, and pretended to feel inside it for an offending nail until the hikers had passed.

As I retied the laces, I said, 'Even first thing in the morning there are liable to be people coming past here. We can't hang around in the open waiting to do the shoot.'

'Lie up in back there, maybe,' said Tony, pointing into the wood.

'Yep. That's the answer. Then come down into the open at the last moment.'

Under the old beeches the forest floor was fairly clear. There were straggling elder and hazel bushes and patches of bramble, but plenty of open spaces between them.

'We'd have better elevation from up one of the trees,' I said.

'Yeah, but with that rifle you need the bipod on the ground. If there was the slightest movement in the branches you'd be all over the place. What's the range?'

'What they told us – six hundred. I'd say that's spot on . . . I've just noticed something else as well.'

'Oh yeah?'

'Those evergreen shrubs – the clipped ones on the terrace. What I'll do is put the bullet into one of them. If we hit one of the walls, shit and corruption would fly in all directions. But that bush of box – or whatever it is – will conceal the strike. From this range, nobody will be able to see the real point of impact.'

'Good thinking. And here's something else.' Tony pointed at some muddy, well-rolled wheel-marks which passed close in front of us, following the edge of the wood and parallel to the footpath. 'There's a regular vehicle patrol along here. Another reason to keep back in cover.'

As we walked on, Tony said, 'Know what? *Any*body who can shoot a rifle could take out the Prime Minister from here. People talk about the special skills you'd need, blah, blah, blah – it's all baloney. Just lie down and fire one careful shot.'

'OK,' I agreed. 'But number one: you'd need a special weapon. Number two: you'd need to know when the target's going to be around. Number three: you'd need a means of getting out – unless it's a kamikaze mission. And number four: you've got to be fanatical enough, or crazy enough, to want to do it in the first place. It's just unfortunate the PIRA's organised in all departments.'

Our next focal point was at grid reference 834055, the spot at which the PIRA had told the incoming helicopter to land for the pick-up. Again we confirmed it as a good choice because it was in a different field, behind another wood, out of sight of the house, and could be approached by a chopper coming low out of dead ground to the west, where the land fell away in a succession of steep valleys.

Back on the main path we carried on our clockwise circuit, swinging right-handed through a belt of trees and across the track beaten down by the vehicle patrol. On either side of the official footpath were frequent notices, white on green, saying PRIVATE – KEEP OUT, shutting off side-tracks and blocks of woodland. For a while we respected them, but when we saw the mast of what was obviously a small re-broadcasting station on the bare summit of a hill, we let curiosity get the better of us. Our instinct, in any case, was to check out all the high ground near the house in the hope we could find a better vantage-point for the shoot – but a rebro station: that definitely needed investigation.

Having climbed a barbed-wire fence, we scrambled up some steep, sheep-mown turf alongside a stand of box and emerged on to a rounded summit, to find that the relay station was dug well into the ground. A flight of concrete steps led down to a steel door in a brick surround, and the short mast was anchored by guy-wires.

'This must be part of the security set-up,' I said. 'It'll be a booster station, giving radios a wider coverage.'

Closer to the house, maybe a hundred yards away, was another small summit on which young trees had been planted within a ring of fence.

We'd just come up to it, and found that the view of the terrace was blocked from that angle, when Tony snapped, 'Keep down!'

I ducked instinctively. 'What is it?'

'A Land Rover Discovery heading this way on that track outside the wood, where we've just come from. Looks like the cops. Let's get out of here.'

We quickly backed off the skyline and slithered down the steep turf. We were half-way down the edge of the box thicket when the Land Rover came back into sight, heading straight for us. Without a word we both plunged backwards into the tightly-packed stems. Luckily for us, box has no thorns, but the intense dark-green smell of the leaves made me think of churchyards and tombstones. A couple of yards inside the thicket we were completely hidden, and we heard the vehicle come grinding uphill in low gear. Assuming the guys on board had seen us from a distance and had come out to chase us off, we lay low where we were for ten minutes or so. Then, from above us, came noises of men at work: hammering, and an electric drill screaming, as if some kind of maintenance was in progress.

We wriggled our way back into the open and slipped downhill to rejoin the footpath. 'Better stop messing about,' I said. 'There's nothing for us round this side. Point D's the place.'

Our next task was to recce the drop-off point that we'd already selected on the map, and to walk the route in that we'd use in the morning. That meant back-tracking round our circuit and returning to the car. On the way, we could see the Discovery still at the rebro station, and the figures of a couple of workmen on the skyline.

As we passed Point D, we lingered once again to get the feel of the position. I brought out my compass and took a quick bearing on the centre of the house: 11 mils.

'What if the worst occurs and there's pea-soup fog?' I said.

'Might not be the worst,' Tony replied. 'Might be the best. You'd have a cast-iron excuse for not carrying out the shoot, and your own guys would have that much more time to find the PIRA hide-out and hit it.'

'Yes, but the bastards might go ahead with their threat.'

Tony looked steadily at me, as if to say, 'They won't.' Then he studied the map again and said, 'Know what? Right now, we'd do better to hike from here to the drop-off point and then walk back in, rather than go round by car.'

'All right. We'd better keep inside the wood, though. We don't want to walk up the field and get spotted by any more damned gamekeepers.'

Instead of heading back eastwards across the park and the main drive, we cut away to the west, along the southern edge of Maple Wood. Outside the trees, on our left, a long, narrow field ran up between the blocks of forest, and towards the far side of it stood Brockwell Farm.

'That's where our QRF wants to be, or part of it,' I said as we passed the huddle of buildings. 'We'll confirm that when we get back.'

At the head of the field we came across a well-used bridleway running through the wood across our front, and we turned left along it, heading gently down a shoulder. Just after we'd joined the path two fair-haired teenage girls came cantering uphill on glossy ponies, and the leader shouted 'Thanks!' as we stood out of the way to let them pass. How happy they looked, I thought, how healthy, how normal, how carefree. What a difference between them – an ordinary, harmless part of the country scene – and ourselves, creeping furtively about with our minds full of death and deception.

The sight of them nearly choked me again, and I knew my mental reserves were running down. When Tony said, 'Nice piece of ass, that first one,' all I could do was give him a sickly grin.

Fifteen minutes' steady tab brought us to the point where the track ran out on to a metalled lane, and there we found a muddy lay-by, big enough for a car to pull off the road, the spot conveniently marked by a sign of a rider on horseback.

'This is it, then,' I said. 'We drive in to here. Quick drop off, Doughnut carries on northwards. We walk in. No problem.'

Our return journey took almost exactly the same time: fifteen and a half minutes to Point D. Given that in the morning one of us would be carrying the Haskins and the other would have Farrell hitched to him, I reckoned we should allow twenty minutes to get ourselves into position.

Back on the corner of Maple Wood, we took one more scan with the binos across the park to the house. Now there were a couple of men working in the terrace garden. Although the top of the retaining wall obscured their legs from the knees down, the upper parts of their bodies were in full view. With the brilliant green of the young corn, the trees in full leaf and the mellow brickwork of the old building, the scene looked as peaceful as could be.

'It just shows how much tourists miss,' I said with a touch of bitterness. 'Thousands of them must walk along this path every year. They come and gawp at the place and think how beautiful it all is. But they only see the surface, and they haven't the first fucking clue about what's going on underneath.'

At 1700 I walked out of the shit-house and round the back of the farm to call Fraser on the mobile.

His first words were, 'We've taken possession of number fifty-eight Cumberland House.'

'Oh – great! Any luck?'

'Yes. We've got echo-phones on the walls, and we can hear next door fairly well. They've got the telly on a lot of the time, probably to mask voices, but we're listening. SO19 will be there any minute now with a drill. We're going to bore through the party wall and see if we can get a fibre-optic probe in place.'

He paused, then said, 'That's the good news. The bad is that the PIRA have put in another death threat. The final one, they call it.'

I said nothing, waiting in dread for him to go on.

'If the shoot on the Prime Minister doesn't go through, or if the Prime Minister escapes, they say they'll kill the hostages at nine tomorrow morning.'

'Oh, Jesus! Can't you hit them before that?'

'We're trying to, of course. But as things stand, we're not hopeful of going in before ten, at the earliest.'

'In that case, it's just as well we've got this mock shoot lined up. Can you put me on to Yorky, please?'

'With pleasure.'

A moment later Yorky came on, and I said, 'Listen, this is what I've fixed with Farrell.'

268

'Fire away.'

'Our sniper party will be dropped off at 0530. The drop-off point's at 838045, where the bridleway leaves the lane. We'll proceed on foot to the PIRA's Point D, 839052. I estimate the walk in will take twenty minutes. So we'll be in position before 0600. We'll conceal ourselves in the wood and wait for the PM to appear, presumably any time after six-thirty.'

'Roger,' said Yorky. He was obviously looking at the 1:25,000 map, because he said, 'Which side of that narrow field will you go down?'

'North side,' I told him.

'OK. Part of our QRF will be in that farm – Brockwell Farm. They'll probably see you go by. Just so they know what to expect, how many of you will there be?'

'Four. Myself with the rifle, Tony with Farrell, and Whinger for back-up. Doughnut's going to drive the Granada, and Stew will bring the Rekord in later.'

'OK. And what about after the shoot?'

'If the target goes down, Farrell will use my mobile to phone through the authorisation for the hostages to be released. He guarantees they'll be driven to our final RV point, on the M25 between Junctions fourteen and fifteen.'

'That was where you had the aborted RV the other day, wasn't it?'

'Yep, but that was northbound. This one's heading south. The first emergency phone past Junction fifteen.'

'Trust those bastards to hold it somewhere we can't have a chopper overhead.'

'I know. But we'll make sure Farrell's wearing his magic shoes. Also, as soon as the handover's been done I can put the make and number of the PIRA vehicle out over the radio.'

'OK. Go back a bit, though. How do you get out of the park at Chequers?'

'The chopper's laid on to be standing by from 0630. The idea is that the pilot will put down somewhere out of sight a mile or so to the west. The moment Farrell calls him, he'll come straight in to pick us up from 834055. That's in a field west of Whorley Wood.'

'Got it. Looks as if it's out of sight of the house.'

'It is.'

'Then what?'

'We fly south for two or three minutes, then west, and put down in a field, just east of Junction Six on the M40. Doughnut will be waiting there with the Granada. We pile into that, and away towards London. Off at the next exit, number five, where Stew's waiting with the Rekord. Switch into that, and on to the M25.'

'Right, right. Got all that. I'll go back through it with you.' Yorky ticked off the points, one by one, then said, 'What if there are more PIRA on board the aircraft? What if they try something funny?'

'They can't. A Jet-Ranger can only take four passengers. There'll be me, Farrell, Tony and Whinger. That's it. Anyway, we'll all have pistols and knives.'

'All right.' Yorky paused. 'Now – d'you want to hear my side of it?'

'Of course.'

'So. We've established a forward control room in Chequers itself. I'm heading up there myself in half an hour, to direct operations from now on.'

'Great!' I said. 'That's really good.'

'We're putting a comms centre into the house as well. Did you see the rebro station on the hill to the west of the house?'

'Yeah, we went up and had a look at it.'

'Our signallers stuck up an auxiliary mast this afternoon. That'll give us secure comms over the whole area.'

'Wait a minute!' Suddenly I had twigged the identity of the vehicle which gave us such a fright. 'Was that them in a police Land Rover? About four o'clock?'

'Sounds like it.'

'Christ! They scared the shit out of us. We were up there when they started heading for the site.'

'That was your bloody fault, for pissing about. The net's up and running, anyway. The signallers have stayed put, and we're bringing up a team of medics. The QRF will consist of three four-man teams: one in the farm, one in a vehicle, standing back, and the third in a chopper, ditto. Their call-signs will be Black One, Black Two and Black Three – in that order. Got that?'

'Sure.'

'You'll be Green One, the Granada Green Two, the Rekord Green Three. Our local head-shed will be Zero Charlie. Got all that?'

'Yeah, yeah. I'm making notes. It sounds as if half the Regiment's getting seconded to this operation.'

'It is. And of course we're liaising with the Prime Minister's own close protection squad. So you'd better not drop a bollock, Geordie.'

'No way. I'm going to play it straight down the line. I take it the Prime Minister's been briefed on the shoot itself?'

'Absolutely.'

'You'd better warn him about the noise. According to Tony, the sound of a five-oh round going past is like the crack of fucking doom.'

'OK. I'll see he's told that. Now . . . what's the time? I should be up there for half-eleven. D'you want to call me again then for an update?'

'Sure. What's the number?'

Yorky gave it, and I rang off feeling relieved that at least the situation in the country would be well contained. As for London – I could only hope. I kept saying to myself, 'Find them! Find them!'

The whole evening seemed to consist of briefing sessions. No sooner had I finished with Yorky than I had to run through everything again with Farrell. Of course, many of the points were the same – our drop-off, walk in, and selection of firing position – and I had to be careful not to say anything that would betray the fact I'd just been in touch with the security forces.

'Let's get things straight,' I said. 'If the shoot goes down, you'll use my phone to give the codeword for releasing the hostages. Right?'

'I will.'

'What *is* the codeword?'

'You'll hear soon enough.'

'So we make for the helicopter pick-up point.'

'We do.'

'And the chopper lands us here, by junction six on the M40.'

'Agreed,' said Farrell. 'He's going to fly south first and disappear through the valleys, to confuse anyone who might see us take off. Then he'll turn east and head for the motorway.'

'Fair enough. Then, at the pick-up point, Doughnut's waiting with the Granada. By the way, you'll need to put your spare kit into the car before we start in the morning: dry socks and shoes and so on. Wear wellies for the shoot. The grass'll be full of dew. Keep the trainers for later . . . As I say, Doughnut collects us and drives us to the next exit. Stew's there with the Rekord. We switch cars and carry on to the final RV on the M25.'

'Correct.'

'What about the rifle?' I asked. 'What d'you want done with that?'

'Jaysus, man. That's coming with me. I wouldn't be leaving such an asset behind, would I?'

'OK. You take it. And the spare ammunition. Next, how do we correlate timings? I mean, where will your lot be coming from?'

'They've a shorter distance to travel than we have,' said Farrell cryptically. 'Once we're on the road, we'll call them to set a time.'

'Well . . .' I pretended to measure distances on the map, although I'd thought them through already. 'They'll have to shift, because it won't take us long. From our pick-up point to the motorway interchange is only twenty miles. Say twenty minutes if we take it easy, twenty-five including the switch from one car to the other. But when we hit the M25 it may be a different matter.'

'What d'you mean?'

'It's going to be the rush-hour. Any time between about seven and nine-thirty the motorway can seize solid along that section.'

'It's no problem. We'll be in touch with the boyos on the mobiles. If we get late, we'll tell them to hold back a bit.'

'All right,' I said, 'but this time I don't want any fuck-up at the RV.'

'And neither do I. I'm wanting out, I tell you. I've had enough of being chained to some stinking turd of a Brit or a Yank day and night.'

'It's OK for you.' I glared at him, deliberately not rising to the insult. 'If anything goes wrong, the worst that can happen to you is that you land back in the nick. For me, it's a matter of life and death.'

'Come on, now. Nobody's threatening you.'

'Not me, but they're threatening my family. What's going to happen if we can't carry out the shoot for any reason? What if the Prime Minister doesn't appear?'

'He'll appear,' said Farrell heavily. 'He's always at his filthy roses.'

'He might not come out tomorrow. He might feel under the weather or something. He might just be late. How long do we wait, for God's sake? If it gets to mid-morning and we haven't seen him . . .'

'So what?' said Farrell calmly.

'There'll be people about by then. Hikers all over the place, coming along that footpath. We saw quite a few today.'

'They'll not bother us. We'll keep back inside the wood until the right moment, so we will.'

'And the chopper. What about him? He can't sit around half the day in somebody's field.'

'I can always call him up and tell him to pull off until I give him a new deadline. Ach, don't bother yourself. We'll be away and gone by seven o'clock, I'm certain of it.'

Farrell sounded confident enough, but I could sense that under his veneer of calm he was nearly as tense as I was. Thank God, he seemed to have no inkling that a huge net was being spread to capture him and the leading lights of the London ASU.

At least, so I thought, until he started talking again.

'And yourself, now. What are you going to do if you get your people back?'

'Collapse with relief, I should think.'

'Yes, but on the ground – in the flesh, I mean.'

'Drive home, I suppose. I've hardly dared think about it yet.'

'Yes, but your unit . . .'

'The Regiment? What about them?'

'How will you account for the hostages being let go?'

'I won't know anything about the reason. I'll only know there's been a phone call telling me to get to the RV.'

'How will the Regiment contact you to pass on the details?'

'They've got my mobile number.'

273

'Where do they think you are now?'

'They don't know. I could be anywhere. I'm on leave – they haven't been in touch for days.'

Farrell gave a non-committal grunt. 'And afterwards?'

'As long as your chopper pilot performs properly, we'll make a clean getaway. The murder will be put down to the PIRA, and that'll be that. There'll be nothing to connect it with me. After all, I don't happen to own a five-oh rifle.'

'This house, though . . . and the other one.'

'We took them in false names, and paid cash.'

'The cars?'

'We changed the plates for the duration of the exercise.'

'All right, so you've done well.'

For the first time in my life I saw Farrell smile. But when he put in a final check-call to one of his mobile numbers, the temperature fell sharply once more.

'They're suspicious,' he said, holding his palm over the receiver. 'They think you're acting in concert with the security forces, and with the military.'

'Ah, bollocks!' I went. 'If the Regiment knew what I'm doing, they'd kill me. I've told you, these guys are just friends. Let me speak to him.'

I reached for the phone, but Farrell lifted it back to his ear. 'Sharp wants to talk to you . . . No? Fair enough.' He covered the mouthpiece again and said, 'He'll speak to another one. Not yourself.'

'All right, then. Tony. You talk to him.'

'Not Tony,' Farrell snapped. 'They know about the Yank.'

'Doughnut, then,' I said. 'For fuck's sake, tell him what you do.'

Doughnut was brilliant, very cool and laconic. He'd been waiting for this. 'Yeah, yeah,' he went. 'BGing . . . Yeah. Body-guarding . . . An Arab sheikh . . . No, I'm not allowed to say which . . . Only when he's in London . . . Now? He's in South Africa, on holiday. That lets me out . . . He comes here on business, but that's in quotes. It's really to procure women. Bloody amazing they are, too: Zanzibar, Morocco – you name it, he has them . . .' On he went, mainly about the colossal amounts of money the Arabs threw around. When he said that the sheikh had twenty-four cars –

including three Rollers and a pre-war Lagonda – in his London garage, the guy on the other end capitulated.

'There you are,' I said to Farrell. 'What did I tell you? Now, for God's sake, let's all go to bed.'

FIFTEEN

When Doughnut shook my shoulder and brought me a mug of tea at 0500, I couldn't believe I'd ever been asleep. I seemed to have been twisting back and forth all night in spasms of anxiety about things that might go wrong. The worst was that the PIRA would take fright and murder the hostages prematurely; the next worst, that the Prime Minister would get killed by mistake; the third worst – but still unfaceable – was that we'd go through the whole charade, and then for some reason the RV would fail once more.

I had learned that at 58 Cumberland House specialist technicians from SO19 had completed one penetration of the party wall and successfully introduced a fibre-optic probe into the flat next door. They'd gone through the wall low down – so that there would be less risk of plaster-crumbs making a noise tumbling to the floor when the tip of the drill emerged – and by sheer bad luck it had come out behind a piece of furniture, a sideboard or a free-standing cupboard, moved there since the owner of the apartment had gone abroad. The result was that we still had no positive identification. So the technicians had begun drilling all over again.

This I'd been told by Yorky, when I had last spoken to him just after midnight. By then he was established in the new control centre, designated Zero Charlie, inside Chequers itself, and sounding well in command of the situation.

After that, with Farrell out of the way in the end bedroom, we'd held one last briefing session in the kitchen, squaring away final details: we'd run through everybody's roles, verified map references and timings, cleaned our pistols, checked magazines and made sure that our radios and mobile phones had fully-charged batteries. 'During the shoot,' I told the lads, 'the overriding factor we've got to bear in mind is this: *we* know we're going to be acting out a

276

charade, but to Farrell every detail has got to seem credible.'

Eventually, at half-one, we'd gone to get our heads down – but I, for one, couldn't drop off. Every minute that had gone by I was hoping for a call from Yorky to say that the assault on the flat had gone in, the hostages had been safely recovered, and we could stand down our whole crazy plan. The Greenford operation, I knew, had been named 'Fruit Salad', and the codeword for a successful recovery was 'Bananas'. That would mean both Tim and Tracy were safe.

For hour after hour – or so it seemed – I had lain there thinking of a man patiently drilling through the wall of a room using an old-fashioned bit-and-brace, giving it just half a turn at a time, to make certain no sound would be heard in the flat next door. The process I had envisaged was agonisingly slow – half a turn . . . wait . . . half a turn . . . wait – the wire-thin bit going in a millimetre or two at a time, the microphones listening all the time for reaction on the far side . . .

All night I had lain hoping that the three magic syllables – ba-na-nas – would bring our manoeuvring to an abrupt end. If that happened, we'd drive Farrell straight to the back door of Chequers, hand him over to the resident security force, and call Doughnut and Stew back to base. The only faint amusement I had got was from the thought of the PIRA helicopter pilot, sitting in some farmer's field at 0600, waiting endlessly for instructions that would never come. Farrell had let on that the operator of the Jet-Ranger they'd hired had charged them £5,000 in cash, paid in advance, for the morning's run. It was clear that the man had realised they were up to no good, because the price was exorbitant. But since the money probably came from Libya in the first place, I couldn't care less.

Now we had a bare half-hour in which to prepare for take-off. I had a wash, got a bowl of raw porridge and milk down my neck, drank a second cup of tea and sorted my kit. Stew was in charge of Farrell at that stage, and when the brute began effing and blinding about being hassled I yelled at him to get hold of himself. 'Ah, sling yourself!' I snapped. 'You can cut that out now. Once we're in the open I don't want to hear a fucking sound out of you. Otherwise you'll screw up the whole bloody operation.' I could see he was suffering from nerves, like the rest of us, but that didn't make me feel any more charitable towards him.

277

Outside, my spirits lifted a fraction when I saw that at last the weather had changed. The clouds had gone, leaving the sky brilliantly clear, and high over our heads a jet had spewed out a slim, white trail that reached far to the north. When I moved out of range of the dung-heap the air smelt fresh and clean, and there wasn't a breath of wind. If a fine day was to be taken as a sign of hope, we'd got one.

Our short drive to the drop-off point went without incident. We saw no other vehicle, and after just ten minutes all four of us were standing in the dark lay-by watching the tail-lights of the Granada disappear up the lane and into the distance.

After waiting for my eyes to acclimatise to the half light I set off along the bridleway carrying the Haskins over my shoulder. Behind me came Tony and Farrell, cuffed together by a short length of chain, and Whinger bringing up the rear. Though the sky was already bright, inside the wood the darkness hung on. Just like our morning at the range, the trees seemed to be full of wood pigeons, cooing all round us. I knew the noise should have been soothing, but somehow it annoyed me, and whenever a bird flew out from above us, disturbed by alien creatures passing underneath, its wings made a terrific, give-away clatter.

When we reached the top of the long, narrow field, I told the others to hold on while I did a quick recce to make sure the coast was clear. 'Stay here while I check the field,' I whispered. 'I'll be back in a moment.'

'OK,' said Tony. 'Take it easy.'

With exaggerated stealth I crept out into the open and went on fifty metres or so until I knew I was out of earshot. With Farrell left at a safe distance, I held down the pressel switch of my covert radio and said, 'Hello Zero Charlie, this is Green One.'

'Green One, send,' came the immediate answer. Yorky's voice.

'On course and on schedule,' I told him.

'Zero Charlie. Roger.'

If there had been any dramatic news from London, Yorky would have told me. His brief, professional response meant simply that we had to carry on.

I retraced my steps to the others and whispered, 'Can't see anything. But we'll keep right in to the side of the wood, in the lee of the trees.'

So we went steadily on, the light growing all the time but remnants of gloomy darkness lurking along the fringes of the wood. As we passed Brockwell Farm I thought of the QRF, skulking about the barns or haylofts, and bet myself they had eyes on us. Sure enough, up into my earpiece came a Welsh voice saying, 'Black One. Geordie and his team are passing us now,' followed by Yorky's quick, 'Zero Charlie. Roger.'

At the corner of the wood, fifty metres short of Point D, an extraordinary sight confronted us. Away in the distance the house was dark, but the lower half of the field between it and us was covered by mist lying in a dense white blanket. The effect was ghostly and unreal, as if Chequers had been constructed on the far shore of a milky lake.

'If that lot rises up a few feet we're buggered,' I whispered.

'It won't,' Farrell replied. 'It'll fall away and disperse as the air warms up. This often happens on a fine morning.'

'You'd better be right.'

'Watch it!' said Tony. 'There's something moving out in the middle.'

We stepped back into the trees to watch. Binos revealed the dark object as the head of a deer, which had popped up out of the fog. I realised the animal must have been grazing with its head down, and that the top of the fog-blanket was just over the level of its back. As we stood looking, another head came up beyond the first, and the two began moving to our left.

'You hang on here,' I whispered to Whinger. 'Stay back in the wood, but keep eyes on the lodge and the drive. If you see any movement, let us know.'

'Roger,' he said softly, and we left him there.

At Point D we moved into the recess among the bushes which we'd identified during the recce. When we raised our heads we could see out over the field to our front, but if we kept down the screen of shrubs shielded us from the footpath. My plan was to stay in cover until our target appeared on the terrace, then to nip forward on to the mossy bank at the very edge of the trees and take the shot from there.

The drawback of our lying up place was that it had no view

along the footpath to right or left, and it was possible that somebody could approach without our seeing him. I therefore decided to leave the other two where they were, with the weapon, and position myself farther forward.

I pulled down the legs of the Haskins's bipod and set it on the deck, keeping the belt of ammunition in the right-hand pocket of my smock.

'What effect will the mist have on the flight of the bullet?' I asked quietly.

'Negligible,' Tony said. 'No wind, either. No lateral allowance needed. The only thing is, in half an hour the light will be pretty bright. That could cause you to shoot a touch high.'

'Agree with that?' I looked at Farrell, who nodded.

'OK. I'll bear it in mind. Sit tight here while I take a look up the footpath.'

I went back to the edge and took a scan with the binos. The two deer were clear of the mist and walking up towards the wood on my left. A light had come on in one of the first-floor windows of the house. Maybe the guy's up even earlier than usual, I thought. Taking advantage of a lovely morning. I looked at my watch: 0610.

I walked slowly along the edge of the wood, in the shadow of the trees, until I was seventy or eighty metres from the others. Away to the east, my right, the sun was still below the ridge, but only just, and the sky was glowing. Even as I watched I saw the fog blanket beginning to thin and break up into patches.

I was fizzing with tension, electrified. I'd already taken one dump, back at the farmhouse, but excitement brought on another, and I withdrew into the trees to deal with it. When I came out again the deer had gone, and most of the mist had vanished. Only a few wraiths still trailed across the young corn.

Suddenly Yorky's voice was in my ear again: 'Zero Charlie for Green One. Fruit Salad going down at figures zero six three zero.'

'Roger,' I answered automatically. Then the meaning of the message struck me. Jesus! It meant the guys in the Greenford operation had definitely found the hostages. It meant they were going in – and in less than fifteen minutes' time! A hit on a single-floor flat couldn't last more than one or two minutes. In less than half an hour from now, the whole thing should be over.

I felt my heartbeat speed up still faster with the news. I wanted to run out into the field yelling with elation. Thank God I kept my head, because I became aware of a noise to my left, and saw a jogger in a harlequin track suit pounding along the footpath towards me. Easing deeper into the trees as he went by, I passed a quick call along to Tony and Whinger, warning them to keep their heads down.

Now time really crawled, second by slow-moving second. Behind me the pigeons cooed relentlessly. The sun hauled itself over the eastern ridge and sent rays flashing low and long across the park. The last traces of mist vanished.

Then Whinger called, 'Discovery coming up from the right,' and the peace of the morning was spoiled by the grinding diesel engine as a routine security patrol went past. There were two coppers in the front seats, but – no doubt following orders – they were looking away from us and towards the house, rather than into the wood.

At 0626, with the Fruit Salad assault deadline four minutes off, I finally persuaded myself that we weren't going to have to fire a shot. For a moment I allowed myself the luxury of imagining the look on Farrell's face when I told him the score, and the language he would let fly. Then my little day-dream was shattered.

'Zero Charlie for Green One,' said Yorky again. 'Fruit Salad postponed. Technical problem.'

Cumberland House is a seven-storey block of flats on the south side of Ellerton Road, in the West London suburb of Greenford. There are nine flats on every floor, with each of their front doors giving on to a corridor that runs the length of the building. The rooms on that side of the block – kitchens and bathrooms – are dark and gloomy because their windows give on to those internal passages.

Access to the block is by two doors, one at either end; there are two lifts, also one at either end, and two staircases, east and west, as well as an external metal fire-escape on each end wall. The numbers of the apartments start from one in the east and rise to nine in the west, and incorporate the floor number as the first digit, so no. 57 is the seventh flat from the eastern end on the fifth floor.

Behind the building, on the south side, lies a scruffy, narrow

281

open space which passes for a garden. This is bounded on its long side by a six-foot brick wall, separating it from the next street to the south, Longfield Drive, and at the eastern end an alleyway that provides a short-cut between Ellerton Road and Longfield.

(Although I wasn't present during the raid, I got the following details from Fraser and from the guys who took part. Because I'd been on similar operations as a member of the SP team, I could piece together the sequence of events in what I hope is an accurate reconstruction.)

By the afternoon of Wednesday 2 June, while Tony and I were doing our recce at Chequers, SB sources had assembled a fat file of information on the suspect flat. The freehold belonged to an oil engineer, Ernest Wilson, but he'd gone off to work in Venezuela the previous October, letting the apartment fully furnished for a year to a man called Bingham. Suspicion about the tenants had hardened when a Special Branch investigator discovered that the monthly rent of £400 was being paid into the local branch of Lloyds Bank in cash, and in irregular amounts (in November £1,200 had arrived – the first payment in more than two months).

Because of the layout of the building it was impossible to maintain a continuous close-in watch on individual apartments. Surveillance had to be maintained mostly from outside, from vans or other buildings, because any stranger lurking about the corridors or on the stairs would immediately have attracted attention. One known IRA player, thirty-year-old Danny Aherne, described as a travelling salesman, had been seen to enter the building several times during the last days of May. He always went in through the eastern entrance, took the lift to the seventh floor, and disappeared into no. 72, where he had an apparently legitimate arrangement renting a bed-sit from the family that lived there. Yet the mere fact that he was resident in Cumberland House focused the police attention sharply on the block.

When the DF vans had begun tracing PIRA mobile phone calls to the area, the janitor, Stan, had unfortunately fallen ill with a viral infection and was replaced by an SB stand-in called Tom. By dallying with his mop and bucket on the top floor corridor, the new man discovered that Aherne often left no. 72 a few minutes after arriving home from a shopping trip still carrying his supermarket bag, nipped down the stairs to the fifth floor, and slipped into no. 57.

In the early evening of 1 June, with the PIRA deadline approaching, SB decided that it was essential to evacuate the occupants of no. 58 and take the flat over for their own purposes. Fortunately the only person at home was Edith Treadgold, an elderly spinster addicted to detective novels, of which she had hundreds arranged in glass-fronted bookcases. Normally she lived there with a companion, but that day the friend had gone to stay with relations. When Miss Treadgold suddenly found herself called on by a woman detective sergeant she was at first horrified, but then openly thrilled to be caught up in a real-life drama. She needed little persuasion to pack a few things into an overnight bag, surrender her keys, go down in the lift and take the waiting taxi, which bore her off to a comfortable hotel room for the night.

One by one, a team of specialists filtered into the block, using both entrances and taking the lifts to different floors before working their way up or down to no. 58. They were surprised to find that Miss Treadgold had another addiction besides Dorothy Sayers and Agatha Christie: when they pulled back a sofa into the middle of the room to get at the party wall, they exposed a sizeable collection of magazines dedicated to bondage and flagellation.

By chasing up the owner of the flat through Interpol contacts, the SB had established a clear picture of the layout of no. 57. Inside the front door was a central lobby, with the kitchen off it to the left, and the bathroom and a separate toilet to the right. Beyond the bathroom, having a common wall with no. 58, was the main bedroom, which had a window on the south face of the block. Next to it was a smaller bedroom, also with a south-facing window, and next to that the sitting room and dining area, which abutted the kitchen at its inner end.

The windows were old-fashioned and made of wood, and the doors of the bedrooms opened inwards, away from the central lobby. Monitoring of the water and electricity supplies had suggested that at least four people were living in the flat, even though none had been seen to come out, and the only known visitor was Aherne. The regular telephone line remained unused; during the past week not a single call had gone in or out.

At first the listening devices were frustrated by television sound, but at one point the eavesdroppers picked up the noise of a child crying and a woman shouting at him or her to be quiet. The sounds caught by the microphones strongly suggested that the hostages were being held in the main bedroom, so it was into that wall that the drill had started to bite.

Meanwhile two six-man teams, Red and Blue, from the Regiment's counter-terrorist unit, were standing by in their holding base at Hounslow Barracks, a few minutes' drive to the south. As always in emergencies of this kind, control remained in the hands of the police, and would do so until the final moment before an assault went in. But during the evening the CO and the ops officer flew up from Hereford by chopper to take overall command of the military element of the operation, installing themselves in a control room established in Police Headquarters at Hendon.

Further up the chain, an open-ended meeting was in progress at COBR, the Cabinet Office Briefing Room underground in Whitehall, where the director of the SAS, a brigadier, was liaising with senior representatives of the Metropolitan Police, the Home Office and the Prime Minister's personal staff.

In no. 58 drilling continued all night. As Yorky reported to me, the first probe, which went through at 2315, proved ineffective because its view was blocked by furniture. The second, higher up, penetrated the wall of the main bedroom by 0320, near the corner with the outer wall, but by then the room was dark and for the time being nothing could be seen. It was only at 0405, when one of the occupants got up to go to the lavatory, that a light was switched on.

For the top brass, listening in to commentary from the front line, events suddenly became gripping.

'There's a bumping noise,' said the Scots voice of the fibre-optic operator. 'They're moving the furniture around. There's a bed across the door – they have to move it to get out . . .'

The pitch of the voice rose sharply as the man said, 'The light's on. The kid is there! It's definitely him. He's in a camp bed. He's woken up. He's sat up and looking round. Seems to have a black eye. Right eye swollen.

'The woman's gone to the bathroom. Wearing white pyjamas . . . now she's coming back. Two women. One's small, stocky and

284

fair. The other's tall and slim. Not a redhead, though. Wait till I get a look at her face. Yes, it's Tracy all right. But her hair's very dark. Black. Could by dyed. Could be a wig . . . No – she wouldn't wear a wig at night. Her hair's been dyed. Pass that to the teams. Don't be looking for a redhead. We don't want any identities mistaken. The guard isn't much over five foot. You can't confuse the two.'

The news precipitated immediate action. In the control room at Hendon the assault plan was finally ratified. Details were confirmed over the secure net to the Red and Blue teams, and to the assault commander, Captain Terry Morris, who, along with Staff Sergeant Bill Brassey, had set up a forward command post in another commandeered flat, across the street from the north front of Cumberland House. It was from there that the main surveillance had been conducted for the past three days; now closed-circuit television cameras were watching both entrances.

By 0515 both teams had been bussed to the site. One by one they infiltrated via the garden passage. The six guys in Red crept up the fire escape, taking care not to let their MP 5s, axes or other equipment clank against the steel guide-rails. Out on the roof, among the dish aerials and ventilation shafts, they sought anchor-points for their ropes, so that they could abseil down and come in through the windows of no. 57. Simultaneously the six guys in Blue went quietly up the eastern staircase to the sixth floor, moved along the corridor and back down to level five, where they slipped silently into no. 58.

Farther out, two snipers crawled on to the roof of a warehouse which commanded a view of Cumberland House's south front. Their primary role was to report any movement in the hostage flat's windows, which had been numbered One (the main bedroom), Two (the second bedroom) and Three (the sitting room). A secondary task was to watch the windows of no. 72 for any change. When the raid went down, the snipers would also act as cover and take out any terrorist who tried to escape from that side of the building. Also waiting nearby, hidden in the drive of a private house, was the hostage reception van, with another six guys from the Regiment on board. Their job would be to scorch in and whisk everyone away from the scene – hostages and soldiers alike – the moment the assault was complete.

From all these sources quick reports flowed in over the secure net. 'Sierra One,' called the lead sniper. 'We're on. In position. All curtains drawn. No lights showing.'

'Zero Bravo. Wait out,' Local Control replied.

The Blue Team had few preparations to make, and soon the leader reported, 'Blue One in position and ready to go.'

Again Control answered, 'Roger. Wait out.'

It was the Red Team who needed most time to prepare. There were no easy anchor-points for their ropes, and as the light came up the guys felt very exposed on the bare, flat roof. 'Red One,' called Fred Daniels, their leader. 'We need to get a shift on or we're going to get compromised up here. There's people on the move in the streets already.'

'Zero Bravo. Roger,' responded Terry Morris. 'Wait out.'

As the minutes ticked past tension mounted. Danger lay in the fact that the security forces were not certain how many terrorists the flat contained. The aim, in situations of that kind, is to work out the position of every X-ray in advance, so that the teams can be certain precisely where their targets will be before they go in. But in this case it had proven impossible. Thanks to the fibre-optic probe it was known for sure that Tracy, Tim and one PIRA woman were in the main bedroom. The pattern of mobile telephone calls had suggested that there were also two men in the flat – but whether both were sleeping in the second bedroom, or one there and one in the sitting room, nobody knew. The only option was to hit the apartment from both sides simultaneously – Red through the windows, Blue through the door.

The intention all along had been that the assault should go in before 0630, to forestall any need for the shoot at Chequers. But permission had to come down from COBR, and then at the forward control room Terry had to sign an order from the senior police officer present, taking over command of the incident.

While these formalities were being prepared, the Red Team lay flat on the roof beside their coiled ropes, to keep out of sight of passers-by or people in other buildings. By 0625 everything was in place, and Terry was about to sign the hand-over order when a man appeared, walking fast along Ellerton Road with a plastic shopping bag in his right hand. One of the cameras picked him up as he went into the eastern entrance of Cumberland House, and he was immediately identified as Danny Aherne, the tenant of no. 72.

Where had he come from? What was he doing, heading back to his lodgings at that time of the morning? What was he carrying in the bag?

'Zero Bravo for Tango One,' said Terry, calling the reserve team into action. 'A suspect X-ray has entered the building. Move to seal both entrances immediately.'

'Tango One. Moving now,' came the answer, and then from Terry: 'All other stations, this is Zero Bravo. Hold, hold, hold.'

Crouching at the edge of the wood I felt like I'd had a kick in the crotch, and it took me a couple of minutes to recover. I felt physically sick at the thought that something had gone wrong. At that stage I didn't know what had happened. I'd only heard Yorky's message, but surely the security guys couldn't have mistaken the identity of the people in no. 57. Surely they'd got the right flat . . .

Fighting down the disappointment, I made my way back through the trees to rejoin the others. From the way Tony looked at me I could tell that he knew how I was feeling. Through his covert earpiece he too had heard Yorky give me the bad news, and he was suffering along with me. I was grateful for that.

But all he said was, 'It's such a hell of a morning, the target may come out early. Hadn't we better get ready?'

'We *are* ready,' I replied. 'We just have to whip forward and fire.' All the same, I withdrew the bolt from the Haskins and looked through the barrel to make sure it was clear. Then I gave the lenses of the telescopic sight their hundredth polish. I was half-way through getting up from behind the rifle when Tony, who was watching the house through binoculars, said, 'Look out! A door's been opened.'

I had my own binos up in a flash. Yes, there was movement at the back of the terrace. A man in a white shirt and black trousers had come out and was shaking something pale – maybe a rug or a tablecloth.

'It's a butler or some similar jerk,' I breathed. 'At least it shows the household's on the move.'

All three of us were kneeling in a line, Tony on the right, then

Farrell, then myself. I glanced sideways at Farrell and saw that his eyes were gleaming, his lips drawn slightly back from his teeth. Watch yourself, twat, I silently told him, you're in for a nasty surprise in a moment.

The butler figure disappeared inside again and the door closed. Now waiting became even harder. The hands on my watch barely seemed to move. By the time they had crawled to 0635 it felt like midday at least.

Temporary relief came with a short, sharp, sudden rushing noise. There, right in front of us, a buzzard was pulling out of a steep dive just above the ground. Whether the bird had swooped at a rat or mouse and missed, I couldn't tell. After a moment he soared up again, talons still extended, his wings working furiously, and the roar of air through his pinions took me straight back to parachuting and free-falling.

All at once I was thinking of the first two training jumps I made, at Weston-on-the-Green. I remembered how somebody went past me, falling after my chute had broken out, with a load, hoarse roar, like that buzzard, only bigger . . .

More movement on the terrace jerked me back to the present. Jesus, I thought. This is it.

The same door had opened again but a different man had come out. The binos clearly picked out the familiar figure: smooth grey hair, slightly long; pale face, spectacles glinting. He wore a big, sloppy, light-coloured sweater nearly down to his knees, and he was carrying something in his right hand – a small canister, no doubt to blitz the bugs on the roses.

'Begod! It's himself!' Farrell exclaimed.

'Come on then!' I snatched a glance at my watch: 0645. No hope of a reprieve from London now.

I snatched up the rifle and started forward, asking quietly over the radio, 'All clear your end, Whinge?'

'All clear,' came the answer.

I reached the bank and set the Haskins down. The target was moving slowly out into the terrace garden, turning back and forth as he peered at the rosebeds. I looked through the sight and saw that, although the scope was good, it wasn't like a pair of binoculars: it gave a clear general picture but not close details.

'Now!' I stood up and faced Farrell. 'There's a slight change of plan. It's you to shoot, not me.'

'What the fuck!' His face turned deathly white. Then a red flush of anger came up from the neck. 'What's this?' he croaked incredulously. 'What the fuck is this?'

'Get down and shoot,' I told him, 'or the chance will be gone.'

'Treacherous cunt!' he said out loud, and then, almost shouting: 'Fucking treacherous *bastard*!'

If his right wrist hadn't been cuffed to Tony's left I'm sure he'd have taken a swing at me. Then he saw the Sig levelled at his chest and stumbled backwards, heaving for breath.

'You're the shooter here,' he gasped. 'That's the deal.'

'You have the choice,' I said. 'Shoot or die. Simple as that. There'll be few enough questions asked afterwards.'

'I can't shoot that thing.' He flicked his right foot in the direction of the rifle. 'Holy Mary, I never saw a weapon like that in my life. I couldn't hit the house, let alone the target.'

'Bollocks! It was you who shot the British soldier with it at Crossmaglen last August. It was you who killed the man long-range on the border in February. It was this very rifle, and yourself firing it. I don't know how many murders you've got on your slate, but one more's not going to make much difference.'

From the way Farrell flinched I knew I was right. 'Get down and shoot,' I repeated.

'Never,' he said. 'If you're wanting your family released it's you to shoot, and that's all.'

'I'll give you ten seconds,' I said.

He took a step towards me and made a sudden movement with his free left hand, but Tony jerked him backwards so violently that he fell over and landed on his arse. 'Unless I give the codeword they'll never be let go,' he warned. 'They'll be dead by noon.'

'I'll take a chance on that,' I said. 'I'm counting now. Ten, nine, eight . . .'

At six he made a gesture with his right hand, which I took to be one of capitulation.

'Christ Almighty!' he cried. 'How will I shoot trussed up like this?'

'You'll manage. Tony'll get down alongside you. Now shift yourself, or the target'll be gone.'

Through all this Tony had waited impassively, poised for action. I'd told him beforehand what I was planning, and he'd agreed not to intervene unless he had to.

The rifle was already in a perfect position, its bipod sunk into the moss on top of the little bank. Farrell was shaking violently as he positioned himself behind it, and the ferret stink wafted all around us. Tony went down beside him, extending his left arm to give the rifleman freedom of movement at the end of the short chain.

Farrell gave one more curse – a long-drawn-out groan of 'Ah, you bastards!' – then gathered his concentration, settled his elbows into the leaf-mould on the forest floor, aimed through the scope, opened and closed the bolt, and clicked off one dry shot. The practised ease of his movements made it plain he knew the weapon well.

The target was still meandering about the terrace, but by now he'd moved nearly to the front of it, close to the right-hand summerhouse. In the clear early light his pale sweater showed up a treat.

'Let's have a bullet, then,' Farrell snapped.

I leant over between the two men and laid one of the six-inch rounds in the breech. As Farrell slammed the bolt forward I gave three consecutive double jabs on my pressel switch to warn Yorky that the shot was imminent.

Farrell had the rifle up and aligned, but the target was moving, walking slowly across to our right.

'Wait, man, wait!' I hissed. 'Let him stop. Now! No! Wait again.'

Once more the target had ambled on. But at last he came to a standstill with his back to us, right in front of one of the trimmed box bushes.

'There!' I said. 'Take him now!'

I put my hands flat over my ears and held my breath.

BOOM!

I saw the big bullet go. At least, I saw the grey streak of disturbance in the air along its path. I was aware of movement at my feet as the recoil jolted Farrell backwards, but I tried to keep my binos on the target. For what seemed an age he remained

290

standing. Then suddenly his arms flew half up, away from his sides, as if his hands had been lifted on strings, and he pitched forward away from us in a flat dead-man's dive. Once down, he was out of sight behind the box hedges, and we could see no further movement.

'Fantastic!' I yelled.

'Bejaysus, I got the fucker!' cried Farrell. 'I nailed him! I fucking dropped him!' In his excitement he forgot he was linked to Tony, and tried to jump up, only to be dragged down again.

'That's his lot,' I said. 'The bullet lifted him right off his feet. Now – send that fucking codeword and we'll get out of here. Quick, they're on the move.' As Farrell stood up I handed him the mobile phone.

The shot had sent pigeons clattering out over the field; dozens of them flashed blue-grey and white in the low rays of the sun as they fled from the clap of thunder. Away in the distance, figures were pouring out of the house. People were running back and forth, and clustering round the spot where the target had gone down. More doors opened, windows too. From somewhere to the right a police siren began to wail.

'I'll call the chopper first,' said Farrell. He punched numbers into the phone, listened and said, 'Yes. Come in now. Pick-up immediately.' As he was doing that I called Whinger to close on us. Then Farrell ended the first call and dialled again. This time his face creased into a frown. He muttered something, switched off, switched on again and punched once more. When he moved the receiver away from his ear I could hear the metallic, electronic voice saying, 'I'm sorry. It has not been possible to connect your call. Please try later.'

'What the fuck are they doing?' he cried. 'The bastards have switched off. Holy Jaysus! They know the timing. They should be on the ball and waiting.'

'Come on!' I shouted. 'We can't wait. Run!'

In Greenford a breathless wait ensued as Aherne disappeared into the building. In less than a minute the reserve team had secured both entrances and fire-escapes, but there was no sign of the player. By then SP technicians had replaced the fish-eye peephole in Miss

Treadgold's front door with another fibre-optic lens, which gave them a wide view down the corridor, and enabled them to keep watch on the entrance to no. 57. Everyone expected Aherne to show up there, but minutes passed without anyone getting eyes on him. Had he gone up to his own flat? Was he skulking on the staircase or in the lift? If he was at large somewhere, there was a chance he might appear just as the Blue guys were taping their charge to the front door to blow it in.

'Zero Bravo for Sierra One,' called Control. 'Any change in the windows on the top floor?'

'Negative,' came the answer. 'All the same.'

At last the suspect came back into view. 'Blue One,' the Blue leader reported. 'He's walking along our corridor, west to east . . . He's left a shopping bag against the wall outside the door of fifty-seven. Now he's gone on to the far end.'

Again he vanished. In forward control, Terry was left with a difficult decision. The bag might conceivably contain a bomb. More likely it held supplies for the people in the flat. Should he ignore it? Should he get Blue to remove it? Should he wait or go?

At 0644 the sniper leader called, 'Sierra One, movement in window figures two. The curtains have been opened.'

'Zero Bravo,' Control answered. 'What about the others?'

'No change.'

'Roger. Wait out.'

'Red One,' came a call from the leader on the roof. 'We've definitely been compromised. There's a crowd gathering in the street out the back. They've got us marked down.'

'Zero Bravo. Roger. All stations remain on listening watch.' Then a minute later came, 'All right. Ignore the bag. We're going in. I'm being handed control. All stations into position.'

The Blue leader slid out into the passage and silently taped a length of det cord down the line of the hinges on the front door of no. 57. At the same time all six members of the Red team came down the south wall on their ropes, squeezing the handles of their pretzels to descend, and then letting go so that the devices locked up when their feet were just above the fifth-floor windows. Down in the street the crowd was swelling rapidly, but it was too late for anybody there to intervene.

Both leaders reported themselves ready. Then Terry called, 'All stations, wait out . . . I have control . . . Standby, standby . . . GO! GO! GO!'

The Blue leader, hanging back in the open entrance to no. 58, closed the clacker in his left hand. *BOOM!* The door of no. 57 burst inwards and disintegrated. Smoke and dust filled the corridor. The Blue team piled through the opening.

In the same couple of seconds the Red team dropped the final few feet, smashed all three windows with fire axes and piled into the rooms. The two into the main bedroom, Geoff Hope and John Ryle, instantly identified Tracy in a single bed against the left-hand wall, and Tim in the camp bed at its foot. Another bed had been pulled across the door, blocking it. As the female terrorist sat up in it, reaching for a cabinet beside her, a quick double-tap in the head put her flat on her back. Blood flew out over the pillows and ran down the pale wall.

While Geoff went down on one knee to give cover, John dragged the bed away so that the door would open. 'Get down! Get down!' he yelled at Tracy.

Geoff yanked her roughly out of bed, forced her on to the carpet and knelt with a knee in her back. 'Don't look over there!' he yelled. 'Look that way!' With his other hand he grabbed Tim and flattened him on the floor as well.

Before the door was open, two more double-taps cracked off in the other bedroom. When John burst into the hall he found it full of smoke, with his two black-clad mates from Red team down on one knee, covering the guys from Blue. Two terrorists lay dead in the small bedroom, one on the floor, one sprawled across a bed. It took just seconds more for the lads to rip open the cupboards, turn over the beds and sofa and case the bathroom and kitchen to make sure there were no more PIRA in residence.

'Zero Bravo for all stations,' called Control. 'Secure?'

'Blue One,' replied the Blue leader. 'We have three dead X-rays on the location. Two men, one woman. The flat is now secure.'

'Red One,' said Fred Daniels. 'Confirm flat secure.'

'Tango One,' said the boss of the reserve team. 'One suspected X-ray detained in hard arrest. He tried to do a runner when he heard the explosion. We got him on the stairs.'

'Zero Alpha. Roger,' replied the main Control, cutting in. 'All stations, evacuate the building.'

John set Tim on his feet, seized a blanket, rolled him in it and picked him up in his arms. 'Come on, love,' he said to Tracy. 'We've got to go.'

Later he told me she'd gone into shock at this point and didn't seem able to move. When Geoff had lifted her to her feet she nearly fell straight back over, so rigid had she become. Then she appeared to wake up; still without making a sound, she snatched up a dressing gown, stepped into a pair of slippers and ran out on to the landing, with John and Tim following close behind her.

Already the corridor was full of people from the other flats, some excited, most angry, demanding to know what in God's name was going on. The assault had been so swift that no policeman had yet reached the fifth floor.

One of the Blue team had grabbed the lift and was holding the door open. While John, Tim and Tracy rode down, the rest took the stairs at a run. At ground level the hostage reception wagon was already outside the door. Within seconds, rescued and rescuers were packed into it with all their equipment, and heading clear of the scene.

Running with the Haskins was no joke. The rifle was not only heavy, but awkward too. Farrell was in no shape to run far, either – and being cuffed to Tony didn't help him. Whinger caught up with us after a hundred yards and offered to take the rifle, but I panted that I was OK. Nevertheless, the temptation to head out on to the edge of the open field was strong – the going would be far better along the footpath. But it would strike an obvious false note with Farrell if we revealed ourselves prematurely, and to keep our RV and complete the exchange we positively needed to get away.

We struggled on as best we could, dodging between trees, scrambling over fallen trunks, ripping through brambles, until at last we reached the northern point of the wood. Now we had no option but to break cover; we were on the edge of the field in which the chopper was due to put down. As we paused to recover our breath I could hear the thudding beat of its rotor in the distance.

By now several sirens were wailing from the direction of the house, and my earpiece was full of rapid exchanges, most of them calls for the police to seal off the surrounding roads.

I pushed out through the screen of leaves and scanned up the sloping grass field that rose gently to our left. The ground was clear. The chopper was still out of sight behind the nearest hill, but the sound of its engine was growing rapidly.

'You two carry on,' I said to Tony. 'We'll cover you till the chopper's in. Go for it!'

I launched the pair with a flick of the hand and watched them run out awkwardly, Farrell dipping on his lame left leg. I'd intended that Whinger and I should follow them after a few seconds, but at the moment I scrambled to my feet I realised that I was getting something different in my earpiece.

'Zero Charlie for Green One,' Yorky was saying. 'Bananas. I say again – bananas.'

Of course it was what I'd been dying to hear. But I'd been so engrossed in our own scenario that my mind was entirely at Chequers.

The message made me stop dead. I hit my pressel and said, 'Green One. Confirm that.'

'Zero Charlie,' Yorky repeated. 'Bananas. All good.'

I let out an almighty yell – no words, just a continuous noise so loud that it made Whinger jump. Tony heard it, too. He looked round for an instant and stumbled.

Before I could get myself back together I heard the abrupt reports of small-arms fire. Jesus Christ! Rounds were going down across the field in front of me. The helicopter was in sight now, a blue-and-white Jet-Ranger, lifting over the skyline and heading our way. But also in sight a little posse of men had appeared suddenly out of a dip, and were running towards our pair. I saw by their irregular DPM overalls and lack of headgear that they were PIRA. The one in the lead was carrying a pistol; the other two had sub-machine guns and were firing from the hip as they ran. They were already within thirty or forty yards of their target.

Instantly I hit my pressel and called, 'Green One. Three armed X-rays on helicopter pick-up point. Request immediate back-up.'

As I spoke, Tony and Farrell suddenly went down. They didn't just fall over, they were hammered to the ground, and one of them let out an almighty roar. Jesus! Had Tony been shot? I yelled out, but it was not enough to distract the leading PIRA guy, who bore down on the struggling heap, obviously intent on finishing off the man he'd wounded.

There wasn't time to get the cumbersome Haskins loaded and aligned. As an instant deterrent I whipped out my Sig and began spraying rounds at the leader. But the action was taking place more than a hundred yards off, and at that distance the shots were all over the place. In any case I had to keep high, for fear of hitting one of my own men. The leader ducked but continued towards the two on the deck, using them as cover. Whinger was firing now, but the guy kept advancing. By the time my magazine ran out he was within a few feet of the fallen couple. He stopped and deliberately extended his right arm, the pistol canted downwards at point-blank range.

By then I'd thrown myself down on the turf outside the wood and got a fresh round into the breech of the Haskins. Feverishly I flicked the bipod into position. The range was barely a hundred metres. Aim low, aim low! I told myself. But before I could bring the sight to bear I heard two shots from the PIRA man's pistol crack out, and with a surge of dismay I thought I'd lost my closest, staunchest friend.

The PIRA gunman was still rooted a couple of yards from the fallen pair. Holding my breath, I brought the cross-hairs of the sight on to his torso and, without waiting another instant, fired. I didn't even notice the recoil.

But – Jesus! I'd missed. Then instantly I remembered: I'd fiddled the sight to make certain Farrell couldn't hit the Prime Minister.

Amazingly, the PIRA guy was standing on the same spot, now looking my way. In a second I had another round up the spout and aimed one body's width to his left. This time the five-oh bullet blew the man away. The impact lifted him backwards off his feet and threw his body on to the ground as if it were made of rags and cardboard.

His mates checked and looked around for a moment, uncertain where the shots had come from. Then the threat of that fearsome firepower evidently became too much for them, and they turned tail and began running back across the field. I loaded a third round, swivelled to my left and touched off another shot at the higher of the two. A burst of chalk and flint chips exploded from the ground above his right shoulder. A second later, before I could load again, he'd vanished into dead ground over a ridge.

The Jet-Ranger had been in a hover – the pilot evidently not fancying what was going on below him – and when he saw the contact erupt he had started to climb. By the time I'd fired my last shot he'd banked hard and was pulling off to a safe distance. I was getting so carried away that I almost loaded another round and let drive at him too. I was sure the Haskins was capable of bringing the chopper down. But within seconds another helicopter was on the scene – a Puma, drab military olive in colour, which swept over the wood from our left, swung round to the far side of the hilly field, hovering just beyond the skyline, and disgorged a shower of black-clad guys who fast-roped down out of our sight. The ensuing crackle of small-arms fire told me they'd caught the two fleeing PIRA operatives in the open. Moments later a voice came on the net saying, 'Black Three. Two X-rays dead in vicinity of pick-up point. Area secure.'

By now I'd loaded a full magazine into my pistol. I left the Haskins on the edge of the wood and sprinted forward to the tangle of bodies in the middle of the field. Both were lying face down. Expecting the worst, I pulled Tony over first. He gave a groan. He was very much alive.

It was Farrell who'd got a double-tap through the temple. As I rolled him on to his back I saw that the whole left-hand side of his skull had been opened up. The mess of blood and brains took me straight back to the corridor in Libya.

Farrell – dead! I could hardly take it in.

Tony was pale and in severe pain. It was he who'd gone down first, with a bullet through the left upper arm. Once both of them were on the deck, Farrell, struggling to break free of his shackle, had yanked the wounded limb all over the place. There was a lot of blood sprayed about the grass. My first action was to get a tourniquet on to Tony's arm above the wound.

Then I called over the radio for urgent casevac. 'Green One. We have two more dead X-rays on the same field, with me. No live

X-rays seen. One of our guys is wounded. Get that Puma here soonest. We're only about four hundred metres east of where the QRF landed.'

'Let's have these fucking cuffs off you,' I said to Tony. 'Where's the key?'

Without speaking he patted the breast pocket of his smock with his right hand. I felt inside, brought the key out, unlocked the cuffs and gently took them off his wrist. I knew I shouldn't move Farrell's body before the scene of crimes officer arrived to make his assessment, but I couldn't help straightening out the cuffed arm.

'Better,' Tony muttered, with an attempt at a smile.

'What happened? Did the guy try to top you and hit Farrell by mistake?'

'No way. He went straight for Farrell like a lunatic. Put the muzzle of the pistol right on him.'

'What a bunch of arseholes!' I said. 'Only death can stop them feuding. OK, Tony. Hang on. That chopper will be here any second. Stay with him, Whinger.'

I stood up unsteadily and moved a couple of steps to look at the other dead terrorist. Immediately I recognised the short, grizzled grey hair. 'Christ! It's that bugger from the railway yard. Marty Malone. Old Foxy'll be chuffed to bollocks. This was the one he wanted most.'

The man was wearing a DPM smock. The huge round had gone straight through his right arm and on through his torso, and his pistol had fallen to the ground. Instinctively I bent to pick it up, but then thought, No, the SOCO will want it left where it fell. Looking at the far side of the body I saw that the exit wound was as big as a saucer. The left back ribs gaped open, and blood, scraps of lung and pieces of bone had been sprayed ten metres on to the grass beyond.

In my earpiece Yorky was saying, 'Zero Charlie for Green One. Geordie, the med team's on its way to you. Who's hurt?'

'It's Tony. Bullet through the upper arm. I've contained the bleeding. He could be worse.'

'OK. The guys will be with you in seconds. What's happened to Farrell? Is he still with you?'

'Affirmative. But he's dead.'

I looked down at Tony and said, 'Hear that? The chopper's on its way.'

His eyes were shut, but he nodded.

I knelt beside him, feeling stunned now that the situation was over. When I turned my head sideways I realised that the sun was shining on my cheek. The warmth seemed to bring me back to reality.

'Yorky,' I called. 'Is the Prime Minister OK?'

'The Prime Minister's in roaring form. He's ordered champagne for breakfast, and he's invited you to join him.'

'Don't be stupid.'

'He has. I mean it.'

'Christ, I can't. I've got to see Tim.'

'I know. We've said as much, and he understands. I'm sure he'll ask you again.'

'He put on a bloody good act, anyway.'

'Come on, lad!' Yorky sounded delighted. 'You didn't think that was him, did you?'

'Who was it, then?'

'Scrubber Jenkins, wearing a poncy wig and two flak jackets, one on top of the other. He was shitting himself too.'

'Why?'

'You might have hit him by mistake.'

'It wasn't me on the rifle, Yorky. It was Farrell.'

'Farrell! Jesus! How the heck did that come about?'

'I told him he had to do the shoot or I'd top him.'

'God almighty! Yer daft bat! He might have killed the PM.'

'Not a chance. I twisted the sight off twenty clicks to the right during the night.'

'Jesus, Geordie . . . I didn't hear that. Never mention it again or you'll be up to your neck in shit.' And with that Yorky went off the air.

The seconds ticked slowly past. My mind was full of puzzles, and after another minute I called in again.

'It was another PIRA guy who topped Farrell,' I said. 'What the hell were they up to?'

'Drug money, as we thought,' Yorky replied. 'I heard Fraser talking about a bank account the Firm discovered in the Cayman islands. Farrell had eight million dollars in it.'

'Eight million!'

'Yeah. He'd been creaming off coke deals for years. If he'd escaped today he'd have done a runner.'

'Where to?'

'Three guesses.'

'Colombia?'

'You got it. He was planning to cut out and make a fresh start there.'

'So the PIRA never really wanted him back?'

'Only to top him.'

'In that case, I've been a pawn to their game all the way through.'

'More or less.'

'Fucking hell! The devious, twisting bastards.'

'Never mind, Geordie. If you're talking chess, it's checkmate to you. You've cleared the bloody board. King, queen, bishops – the lot.'

SIXTEEN

After a hit like that, all the lads are supposed to head straight back to camp. There, they sit down and calm down, and with a solicitor each one goes through every event that's occurred, every move made, every shot fired. The point of this routine is to prevent anybody talking to the police while they're still fired up with adrenalin and might say something out of place. As soon as the police get a chance they quiz you like there's been a murder, and you need to be careful.

So usually the first evening is spent having a monster piss-up, and everyone gets mongolised; and then, next morning, there is a proper debrief.

But in my case all that went out of the window. Because of the special circumstances an exception was made, and I was given permission to see my family straight away.

'Take the chopper,' Yorky told me. 'Go with the casualty. They're taking him straight to Hendon Hospital, and that's where the hostages are anyway.'

'What's happened to them?' I was so hyped up that I immediately became suspicious. 'Did they get injured in the recovery?'

'No, no. Relax. It's just that Tracy's exhausted. She's had more than enough for the time being.'

'OK, Yorky. Thanks. Have you called Doughnut and Stew back in?'

'Done that. They're on their way.'

'Great. I'll leave Whinger here on the ground to deal with the SOCO.'

'Fair enough. One more thing. You can't walk into the hospital in your DPMs – too high profile. There's a pair of plain police overalls on board the chopper. Slip them over the top during the flight.'

'Will do.'

I was still kneeling in the middle of the field, trying to chill out, unable yet to believe the nightmare was over.

'The Haskins is still on the edge of the wood, Whinge. You'll need to collect it and take it with you.'

'No bother. I'll get it now.'

Away he went. As I looked for the last time at Farrell's body, my mind took off on a fast re-run of all the aggravation he'd caused me: Kath's death, the night he'd appeared at the farm outside Belfast, my own attempts to top him, the firefight in the Colombian jungle – and now all this. My loathing for him still burned, but for the hundredth time I wondered how people like him and Marty Malone could let their whole lives be shaped – and cut short – by an irrational hatred of people they don't know, people they haven't even seen. How could anyone be so twisted by religion and history?

Tony gave a grunt, trying to sit up, but I made him lie down again, saying, 'You lost a lot of blood. Just wait for the chopper.'

'Geordie?' he murmured.

'I'm here.'

'Have you got Tim back?'

'Not yet. But he's safe.'

'Tracy?'

'Safe as well.'

'Thank God!'

Unable to speak, I gave him a gentle thump on his good shoulder. Luckily Whinger chose that moment to return with the Haskins and launch one of his rhyming summations. 'Bacon and eggs,' he said.

'Where?'

'The dregs.' He pointed at the bodies. Despite the gore around us, the mention of food had suddenly made me feel starving.

'Talking of eggs, I could eat four easily,' I said. 'Maybe six.'

'Me too. And a few slices of ham with them. And a few pints of Stella along with it.'

The PIRA helicopter had vanished, but I could still hear an

aircraft engine, and a minute later the QRF Puma lifted over the horizon, heading for us. As it came in to land a few yards away I crouched down beside Tony to shield him from the blast of the down-draught. I could see several of our guys in the cabin, and they stayed put, giving thumbs-up signs, while two medics whipped out with a stretcher. The nature of Tony's wound was pretty obvious, from the tourniquet and the blood on his DPMs, so I didn't try to tell them what to do, and in a few moments they had him expertly trussed, ready to be loaded. As soon as the stretcher was safely in I gave Whinger a wave and followed aboard.

The flight lasted only fifteen minutes. I slipped into the overalls somebody handed me, and looked down at the sunlit scene below. The time as still barely 0730, and on the motorways the morning rush hour was building up. As we skimmed over thousands of houses and roads jammed with crawling cars, I thanked my stars that I wasn't in the Granada, with Farrell very much alive and kicking, on our way to a doubtful rendezvous under the flightpath out of Heathrow. One more near-miss on the M25 and I'd have gone round the twist.

The Puma was too big to land on the hospital's helipad, so it put down on a playing field, where an ambulance was waiting. I rode in the back with Tony the few yards to the casualty entrance, and suddenly there we were, back in the world of stainless steel, green gowns, starched white caps and smells of disinfectant. I found myself thinking of Pat, with all the pins sticking through his thigh. I realised I hadn't given him a thought in days, and now I resolved to check he was doing all right. Almost certainly Tony would end up alongside him in Wroughton.

They took Tony straight into theatre, and for a minute I was left alone in a waiting room. Then a nurse, a pretty blonde woman, appeared and said, 'Sergeant Sharp?'

'That's me. Where are they?'

'I'll take you up.'

She led the way up a short flight of steps and along a corridor. I followed, uncomfortably aware that in those ultra-hygienic surroundings I cut a peculiar figure. My boots were smeared with mud, and it was three days since I'd shaved. Thank God they couldn't see the Sig in its holster under my arm.

The nurse walked so fast that I almost had to run to keep up with her. 'Are they all right?' I asked.

'Well, they've had a pretty bad time.'

I didn't like the sound of that, but I asked no more questions.

We went through some swing-doors into what looked like a private ward, with single rooms leading off it to either side. A uniformed copper was hovering, and out of an office came a woman in a smart, dark-blue uniform. Dimly I realised that this was the matron – but one hell of a matron: young, chic, and with a dazzling smile.

'Your wife's there, in number one,' she said, pointing at the nearest door.

I ignored the mistake and said, 'Is she OK?'

Before the matron could answer, a terrible noise burst through the door – half a scream, half a hoarse roar, inarticulate, but unmistakably Tracy's voice.

I was through the door like a rocket. A doctor in a white coat was standing in the middle of the room with his back to me. Facing him, perched on the edge of the bed in white pyjamas and robe, was Tracy. Her appearance gave me a terrible jolt. Her hair had gone black – of course, no one had warned me of that – and her face was as white as her pyjamas, and screwed up with tension. She looked ten years older, the ghost of the girl I knew.

I came to a halt, rooted by shock. Then she saw me. With another awful cry she sprang off the bed, knocked the doctor spinning, rushed at me and flung her arms round my neck. When I hugged her to me she felt like a sackful of bones.

Hardly had we come together when she went slack in my arms and started sinking to the floor.

'She's fainted again,' said the doctor calmly. 'She's done that twice already. Put her on the bed.'

I did as he said and stood back, breathless with dismay, and with a dreadful fear that the ordeal had sent her mad.

'What's the matter with her?' I gasped.

'Delayed shock. She'll be all right, but she's having a rough ride for the moment.'

I glanced at the doctor and saw he was only about my age, ruddy and fit-looking. He gave me a sympathetic look and explained,

304

'When she arrived she was on a terrific high. But it only lasted about quarter of an hour. She was laughing and joking all over the place, then suddenly she went right down. And this is the result.'

'What's the answer?'

'The best thing is to sedate her for twenty-four hours.'

'Can't I take her home?'

'Not really – it could be dangerous. She might become violent or do something crazy. She ought to remain under observation. Besides, Special Branch want to interview her as soon as she's stable.'

'You don't think her mind's impaired?'

'Oh, no. Give her time and she'll be fine.'

'Where's Tim?'

'A doctor's looking at his eye. He got a blow on it some days ago.'

'Is he as bad as this – mentally, I mean?'

'Not as bad. Of course, I don't know what he's like normally, but he seems very withdrawn. There – she's coming round now.'

Tracy stirred and opened her eyes. I dragged a chair up to the side of the bed and sat down, holding her hand, my face close to hers.

'It's OK, Trace,' I said gently. 'It's me, Geordie.'

She turned her head and looked at me, but not with any affection. On the contrary, she gave me a hard stare, then turned away again, as if she equated me with the enemy and wanted nothing to do with me. She closed her eyes tight and began to gasp and shake. A shudder coursed down her body, head to toe, so that her whole body frame began quivering on the bed. I realised that the devils were coming out of her, but the violence of it was dreadful to see. Then out burst another terrifying hoarse roar, a noise so ugly I couldn't believe she was making it.

I held on to her hand tighter, feeling my own tears coming, until gradually she quietened. I heard the door close behind me and turned and blinked at it. The doctor had gone. I held on, letting time pass.

The doctor was right. This wasn't something that I could handle. At least Tracy's fingers were clutching mine. Perhaps some contact was getting through.

Presently her shakes subsided completely. I stroked her gaunt cheek with the back of my hand and whispered, 'Stop worrying, Trace. You're safe now. It's all over.'

At last she turned to look at me properly and said, 'Where were you, Geordie? Why did you take so long to come?'

'Sweetheart, I was trying. I was nearly killing myself trying to find you. You can't imagine what's been happening. As soon as you've had a rest, I'll tell you.'

She kept on looking at me, and in her eyes I caught a glimpse of the person I loved.

'Listen,' I said. 'Are you all right? I mean, did they . . . they didn't . . . molest you?'

She shook her head slowly.

'Is the baby OK?'

For a terrible moment she stared at me silently, her eyes like stones. Then, very low, she muttered, 'No. I lost it.'

'Oh Jesus!' I grabbed her hand, but not quickly enough. Again she was off into those dreadful animal roars, doubling her knees up to her chest and writhing all over the bed. To stop her falling off and hurting herself I got her by the shoulders and held her down until the shudders died away and she fell back exhausted, the tears pouring down her cheeks.

When I leant forward and kissed her on the temple, she gave a wan smile and said, 'You need a shave.'

Somebody knocked on the door. The fair-haired nurse came in carrying a plastic beaker in one hand, a shallow dish in the other.

'Take these, dear,' she said. 'They'll make you feel better.'

Tracy looked at me in a questioning way, so I nodded, and watched her swallow the two white tablets. Then I said, 'Back in a minute,' and followed the nurse into the corridor. I was meaning to ask the matron how long Tracy would have to stay in when I saw another nurse coming towards me, holding the hand of a small, fair-haired boy.

'Tim!' I let his name out louder than I had meant to, and my voice echoed down the passage. As the pair approached I rushed forward, bent down and scooped him up in my arms. But at the very moment I touched him, I felt his body go rigid inside the grey track suit, and when I went to kiss him on the cheek he twisted his head away.

Then he said, loud and clear, in a passable Belfast accent, 'Yer fucking wee murderer, yer.'

The nurse took a step backwards. Her mouth fell open, and her face coloured to the roots of her hair. As for me, I was so amazed I didn't know what to feel. I didn't know whether to laugh, cry, curse, smack Tim or what. All I could do was hold him tight and take a deep breath.

'It's those filthy people who've been keeping him,' I said, by way of excuse and explanation. 'They've had a month to brainwash him.'

'That's right,' the nurse replied, recovering her composure. 'It'll wear off soon enough.'

'What about his eye?' Even with Tim's head twisted away I could see that his right eye was swollen and discoloured.

'It'll go down in a day or two,' the nurse replied. 'It seems he got a belt from the woman in charge of him. But Dr Best has had a look at it and apparently there's no damage to the eye itself.'

'Hear that, Tim?' I hefted him up and down. 'You're all right. Come on, now. You've got to help me look after Tracy.'

Still he wouldn't face me, and in desperation I suddenly remembered Billy, his teddy bear. 'Tell you what,' I said. 'We've got to go and find Billy. He's at home, and he's really been missing you.'

Even that produced no reaction. I turned back to the nurse and said, 'Thanks. I'll take him now,' and I carried him back into Tracy's room, stiff as a board. When I put him down on the floor, he stood like a zombie, not moving.

At least Tracy seemed more relaxed. The sedative was taking immediate effect, and some of the strain had gone out of her face. But as I thumped down on the bedside chair I reflected bitterly on how different this was from the homecoming I'd imagined. Over the past four weeks, whenever I had allowed my hopes to rise a degree or two, I'd seen us all back at the cottage, in high summer, out in the garden, a happy family, doing our own things.

Now, in this bleak hospital room, I felt incredibly exhausted. I looked at the frozen boy and the horizontal woman, and thought, 'It isn't one life that I've got to rebuild. It's three.'